JAWS OF THE TIGER

A fast-paced, action-packed international thriller

ANDRÉ K. BABY

Thierry Dulac Thrillers Book 3

Revised edition 2022
Joffe Books, London
www.joffebooks.com

First published in Great Britain by BWL Publishing in 2018

This paperback edition was first published
in Great Britain in 2022

Cover art by Jarmila Takač

ISBN: 978-1-80405-493-2

To my dear wife and first editor Louise,
who convinced me to stick to my original story.

PROLOGUE

Climbing through the window was easier than he'd expected. His senses on high alert, he crouched down onto his left knee, feeling the cold dampness of the hangar's cement floor through his track suit, his right hand wrapped tightly around the canvas handles of his duffel bag. The place reeked of a musty mix of saltwater, diesel fuel and engine oil. He waited, watching, listening for any signs of life. None. He looked at his watch: 2.31 a.m. At 2.50 a.m. the night watchman would do his rounds again. His eyes adjusting to the semi-darkness, he could make out the shapes of the lifeboats resting on their cradles, some with electric cords dangling from their decks, others with masking paper taped to their fiberglass hulls, ready for painting.

He got up, slung the heavy duffel bag over his left shoulder and started walking among the lifeboats, looking for his target, carefully avoiding the pieces of wood, coils of rope and extension cords lying haphazardly on the ground. *Where is it? Hassan said it would be easy to find.* Amid the two dozen or so lifeboats, none fitted the description given by Hassan. *There will be a ladder on the side.* He glanced at his watch again: 2.37 a.m. Running out of time. He fought the sense of panic mounting from his gut.

1

Then he spotted it: *Caravan Star* 9, the red lifeboat with the wooden ladder resting against its hull, leading up to the lifeboat's open hatchway. He took in a breath of relief.

He re-slung the duffel bag over his shoulder again, climbed up the ladder and into the lifeboat. Inside, he turned on his headlight, grabbed the bag and went forward. Overhead, life-vests hung above two opposite rows of seats. He put down the duffel bag on the seat to his right, knelt and lifted one of the floorboards, then placed it on the seat beside the duffel bag. He unzipped the bag and took out the six Micro-Uzi submachine guns, five Glock pistols and clips of ammunition, each wrapped in a transparent, watertight bag. He tucked them underneath the floor, carefully wedging them between the hull's fiberglass ribs. His task finished, he got up, looked at the bilge and smiled. Nothing showed. He replaced the floorboard, slung the empty duffel bag over his shoulder and descended quickly down the ladder.

2.43 a.m. *It'll be close.* He reached down, took the Sig Sauer 9mm from his leg holster and removed the safety. He walked across the hangar to the far wall and leaned carefully out of the open window. The yard was deserted. He threw the empty duffel bag out onto the ground. Replacing the Sig Sauer into his leg holster he climbed out, closed the window carefully, grabbed the duffel bag and walked, not too fast, not too slow, to the exit road, to the rented Opel. Reaching the car, he opened the driver's door, threw the duffel bag onto the passenger seat and sat down. He threw a glance at the rear-view mirror and caught sight of the night watchman, walking slowly, sweeping the front of the hangar with his flashlight. The watchman stopped and checked the locks. Satisfied, he started again and disappeared around the side of the building.

Saquil turned the ignition key and put the Opel in gear. *Tariq will be pleased.*

CHAPTER 1

Southampton, October 13, 7.35 a.m.

Inside P & W Cruise Lines' one bedroom apartment on Stratford Street, Capt. Goran Peterson went to the closet, took out two of his white suits, folded them neatly and put them in his suitcase atop the bed. Next, he went to the small dresser, opened the top drawer and pulled out four shirts he'd picked up from the dry cleaners the day before. He deposited them carefully on top of the suits, mindful not to squash their lightly starched collars. Satisfied, he closed the suitcase's lid and zipped it shut. He looked at his watch: 7.35 a.m. He still had time for a quick breakfast and a phone call to his wife Nelly and daughter Frida in Stockholm. He went to the kitchen, poured himself a cup of coffee and heated it in the microwave oven. Next, he went to the fridge, took out a loaf of sliced rye bread and a jar of pickled herring. He pried out three pieces of herring and spread them neatly onto the bread, careful not to spill the fish oil onto the table. The pungent, salty smell always reminded him of the fishermen's wharf of Smogen, his native town, and the wooden racks of drying fish lining the road from the harbor to the center of town. Nothing like a good Swedish breakfast, he thought.

Moments later, Peterson got up, put the dishes into the sink, walked to the minuscule desk in the living room next to the TV and turned his on computer. Although P & W Cruise Lines would be sending a full weather report to his cabin on board ship prior to departure, he always liked to get a head start, so he scrolled down to the maritime weather channel to the radar section and typed in "Area 3, mid Atlantic. Animation". Seconds later a large, dark green patch appeared, moving slowly from West to East indicating a major depression heading from Newfoundland and stretching from Bermuda to the southern tip of Greenland. Peterson felt a burgeoning dose of anxiety. If the track of the storm headed southeast, he'd have to make a major course alteration to take his ship out of harm's way. Schedules would have to be altered. Lost time would have to be made up.

Next, he typed into the National Oceanographic Atmospheric Administration tracking website, and immediately felt a modicum of relief: the storm's anticipated trajectory was well north of the *Caravan Star*'s planned route, and NOAA was by far the most reliable of the weather tracking sites for the mid-Atlantic region.

He clicked to his emails, and opened the one sent by James Archer, the company's passenger coordinator. The text read:

> *Caravan Star repositioning: Southampton to Miami via Gibraltar and Cancun.*
> *To all concerned,*
> *This is to advise you of the manifest of passengers and crew as of GMT 1800 hrs. 2017 October 12.*
> *Passengers: 353*
> *Crew: 154*
> *Please see attachment for details.*
> *Yours truly,*
> *James Archer,*
> *Chief Passenger Coordinator, P & W lines.*

Peterson smiled. Barely a sixth of the ship's passenger capacity had registered for the repositioning trip. Fewer passengers meant fewer problems, less daily obligations to be charming and show the ship to all and sundry. With any luck at all, he'd have a chance to catch up on his reading between quarters.

He flicked onto the Skype logo and dialed his wife Nelly's number. After three rings, her face, slightly distorted by the camera's wide-angle, appeared on the screen. He couldn't help noticing the black pouches under her eyes and deep lines on her forehead.

"Hi darling," she said.

"Hi Nelly. Just a quick hello before I leave. How are you?"

"A little tired, but I'm ok. Frida—"

"How's she doing?"

"She had a bit of fever last night, but it went down this morning."

"How much?"

"From 37.4 down to 36.8, but she's still coughing. Sort of a dry cough."

"Did you see Luks?"

"He's out of town. I have an appointment tomorrow morning with Dr. Magnuson at the clinic. That's the earliest I could get."

"Shouldn't you go to emergency?"

"And wait three hours like last time? No. Besides, the nurse at the clinic said to go to emergency only if her temperature went up."

Peterson didn't have to be reminded how fragile Frida's health was. Only nine years old and she'd already had pneumonia twice. Now even the slightest cold was cause for alarm.

"Keep me posted," he said, trying to mask his worry.

"I will. Have a good trip, darling," said Nelly.

"Love you," said Peterson, then clicked off.

He looked at the picture on the desk of his wife and young daughter, blonde hair in pigtails, her sunshine smile showing a missing front tooth. Nelly's arms were wrapped around her daughter's small waist in a maternal embrace. He felt a sudden warmness in his heart as he carefully replaced the picture onto the desk.

CHAPTER 2

Dulac's flight from Paris to London had been delayed half an hour at takeoff due to heavy fog, so he'd missed his earlier connection and taken the next train to Southampton. An hour and a half later, sitting in his plush first-class window seat, Dulac looked distractedly outside at the drab gray buildings of the city's outskirts as the London to Southampton Express began decelerating. Moments later, the train reached the entrance to the station and came slowly to a stop.

Dulac got up, grabbed his suitcase and computer from the overhead bin, and made his way through the doorway and off the train. He walked briskly down the quay, winding and jostling past slower passengers through the station's main hall and onto the street, where he joined the taxi queue of waiting passengers. After what seemed like an interminable amount of time, Dulac was finally hustled brusquely into a black Skoda by the turban-wearing dispatcher.

"Where to, guv?" said the cabbie, sporting a rust-colored handlebar mustache.

"To dock four. The Queen Elizabeth II Terminal and make it fast. I'm late."

"Right, guv."

The taxi drove off, winding its way through narrow streets. Ten minutes later, Dulac caught his first glimpse of the dozens of cruise ships berthed along the quays of England's busiest port. All along the shore, white behemoths were lining the docks, waiting to on-load their cargo of vacationers. He winced at the thought of soon joining the multitudes being carted off to sea on thousands of tons of less-than-seaworthy steel.

As the taxi slowed amid thickening traffic, Dulac's mind drifted back to Karen Dawson, his American 37-year-old on-and-off girlfriend he'd met four years earlier during his investigation of the archbishops' murders, as the case was known in Interpol. Three months earlier, they'd had a particularly acrimonious falling out so he'd been somewhat surprised when three weeks ago she'd phoned and tried to convince him to join her for a cruise aboard the *Caravan Star*, on a repositioning trip to the Caribbean. She'd won two tickets at the faculty lottery at *La Sorbonne*, where she taught animal mythology.

"Come on, it'll be fun," she said. "All the more so because it's free. All expenses paid by P & W Lines. You can't get a better deal than that."

He'd been torn between his intrinsic though slightly prejudicial distrust of cruise ships (since he had to admit he's never actually been on one) and trying to patch things up with Karen.

His initial reaction had been "Yes, but what does one do all day on one of these ships?"

"Well, for one, you can relax."

Her point had hit home. Two years without a vacation were beginning to take their toll: bouts of insomnia, quickness of temper with his secretary and Interpol's junior agents, digestion problems, occasional melancholy even. All the signs were there. He'd known for months he was stressed out and needed a rest, but he kept pushing away, pushing back the very idea of a break. There was always another case to be solved.

Now, the timing was perfect. He had nothing pressing on his agenda for the next two weeks. His professional conscience at ease, Dulac had concluded he really had no reason not to accept Karen's invitation. And besides, Dulac was certainly willing to give the relationship one last shot. Being away from Karen had made him realize he cared for her much more than he was willing to admit. He hadn't even begun to forget the easygoing, forthright Karen, her unvarnished, healthy beauty, her high degree of intelligence, that air of the exotic American women so frequently held for Frenchmen, and the greatest sex he'd had in decades. Besides, he really did need a break. As Deputy Director of Crimes against Persons at Interpol, Dulac had completely revamped a function his predecessor had let drift into a morass of disorganization and neglect. Now, the 16-hour days he'd spent doing so were taking their toll. He felt mentally and physically drained. Unwittingly, Karen's timing had been perfect.

Maybe a cruise-ship vacation won't be so bad after all.

Dulac rolled down the window and took in a lungful of fresh salt air. In the distance to the right, he spotted what looked like a small marina, the morning sun bouncing off masts of sailboats piercing the blue horizon, instantly triggering memories of his youth in Sables D'Olonne off the coast of France. Sailing on *Esmeralda*, the family's 41 ft. sloop off France's Bay of Biscay, had been among the happiest times of his life. That is, until the accident. That day was forever etched in his mind. A clear, crisp autumn day in late September, Esmeralda, a bone in her teeth, running before the wind in a brisk Northeaster, his father at the helm.

Then the sudden gust. The boom gybed over violently.

His father shouted to his mother. "Look out!" Too late. Dulac could still hear the sickening crack of the boom on her skull. It had caught her squarely on the left temple, knocking her overboard. For a second, he saw his mother wallowing in the turbulent waves, blood on the side of her head, her eyes half-dazed in confusion and fear while he stood, helplessly frozen in shock, unable to move. By the time they'd brought the boat about and attempted to rescue her, she'd disappeared beneath the waves. He was fourteen then, and for years thereafter, he'd felt pangs of guilt for not jumping in to try and save her. Most of the time Dulac's recollection of that tragic day lay dormant, but the sight of sailboats invariably triggered mixed feelings. Happiness, guilt and pain were interlaced and twisted together like the boughs of a grapevine.

The cabbie honked his horn at a slow car ahead, jolting Dulac out of his thoughts.

He looked at his watch again: 10.50 a.m. He took out the booking slip from his satchel and read it. "Boarding Time: 8.30 am to 11.00 a.m."

That's when he felt his taxi come to a complete stop. He leaned forward and peered through the front window at the lineup of jammed traffic that extended well beyond the next traffic light, a quarter mile away.

Dulac pulled out his phone and dialed Karen's cell. After three rings, an automated recording kicked in. "I'm unable to take your call right now but—" He pressed the redial button and got the same reply. He pressed off, took out his booking slip and dialed P & W lines' help-desk number. "You are a valued customer. We appreciate your patience," said a mellifluous voice. "Please hold until a representative is free. The approximate wait time is . . . seven minutes."

Dulac continued to press the phone to his ear, and his taxi started to move slowly again.

Moments later, a sign to the left of the road read "QE2 Terminal, Next Right." Dulac looked right and spotted a lone white cruise ship of modest size docked alongside one of the many quays. He counted only six deck levels and felt better already. The cabbie turned right, then stopped before the QE2 Departure Station.

"Here you are, guv. That'll be seven quid."

"What?" said Dulac.

"Seven quid. Seven pounds if you prefer."

Dulac paid the cabbie, grabbed his bags and rushed out of the taxi to the entrance of the Departure Station.

He looked about and spotted Karen standing next to the check-in counter. She started waving frantically as she recognized him. She was wearing a light blue two-piece pantsuit, which accentuated her long legs, and a dark pink scarf slung lazily around her neck. Her thick, auburn hair was drawn back and tied into a ponytail.

Ravishing. Still holding his bags, he rushed up and kissed her.

She broke away hurriedly and grabbed his arm.

"Quick, they're about to close the gate, and we still have to go through security." She pointed at the doors leading to the dock.

"Well, yes, my trip was fine. Glad you asked."

"Sorry, but cruise ships don't wait for late passengers."

"What about you?"

"I've already checked in."

He deposited his bags next to the counter where a young woman with jet black hair and thick horn-rimmed glasses was waiting, twiddling her pencil and looking down at a document on her desk.

"Passport and ticket please." She looked up and smiled at Dulac.

Past the security check and twenty minutes later, Dulac and Karen had deposited their luggage in their cabin, then joined the throngs of passengers along the metal railing of Deck Five, peering down at a group of waving well-wishers below. The boarding gangway had been withdrawn and large eddies were forming in the water below them, as the ship's bow and stern thrusters slowly pushed her away from the concrete dock.

Dulac turned to Karen. "That's cutting it a bit close."

"Anyway, you made it. I'm so glad you did." She smiled and hooked her left arm around his waist and brought him in closer.

"Me too."

CHAPTER 3

15 October, aboard the Caravan Star

After two days onboard ship and with Karen's help, Dulac had to admit he was actually having fun. He'd managed to unplug himself from his files, leave his computer and the satellite phone his secretary had convinced him to take "just in case" in his satchel, and enjoy life aboard. The previous evening, Karen had talked him into the nightly karaoke contest, and Dulac had won first prize amongst twenty-two participants with his imitation of Elvis Presley's You Ain't Nothing but a Hound Dog. After an exhausting romp of lovemaking earlier that morning, they'd taken a late breakfast, then spent the remainder of the day lounging around the deck area, sipping Pina Coladas and Mojitos between occasional laps in the pool. Still, the underlying subject of their breakup hung in the air, neither of them wanting to bring it up and break the exotic albeit artificial atmosphere of the vacation. Three months earlier Karen had walked in on him unannounced at his apartment late on a Thursday evening and found him half-naked in the company of a nude, bosomy blonde. They hadn't spoken again until her invitation to go on a cruise.

Maybe it was time to clear the air, thought Dulac, but he hesitated, wondering if he shouldn't let sleeping dogs lie. What the hell, here goes.

"It was just a one-nighter," he said. "I'll never see her again."

She turned slightly toward him. "Thierry, you don't have to justify yourself. We don't have any commitment of exclusivity and besides . . ."

"Still, I felt I owed you an explanation. I was tired, had too much to drink at the bar that night and . . ."

"Let's just drop the matter, shall we?"

"I just want you to know that it's not my style."

"Fine."

"Sure?"

"You wouldn't be here if I thought it was."

"Got it."

Dulac reached down and took a sip of his Pina Colada, and Karen looked at her watch. "Gosh, it's already 6.00 p.m. I'd almost forgotten we have an invitation to the captain's table tonight." She got up and offered her hand. "Come on, lazy bones. A good supper will do us good."

Dulac stood up and looked into her eyes.

"We okay?"

"We're okay," she said. "Just don't make it a habit."

Back in their cabin, Karen picked out a light blue dress from the closet, laid it on the bed and started selecting matching accessories. Dulac showered quickly, dried himself and returned to the bedroom. Donning his boxer shorts, he stood in front of the closet.

"What's the dress code for one of these gigs?" said Dulac.

"The Captain's steward said casual chic but I got the distinct impression the accent was on the chic."

"Meaning?"

"Anything nonchalant and dressy."

"You're a great help." Dulac took his dark-blue blazer, beige pants and white shirt off the hangers and turned back towards Karen. "This had better do, because it's the dressiest I've got."

"I'm sure the captain won't refuse you at the dinner table wearing that."

Dulac deposited the blazer and shirt on the bed, sat down and started to don his pants. He couldn't help noticing the fit was significantly tighter than the last time he'd worn them at his neighbor's cocktail party two months ago.

"Any idea who else will be at the Captain's table?" said Dulac.

"None. We were lucky enough to get the last two seats."

Karen looked at her watch. 6.32 p.m. "Let's go. Don't want to be late."

They left the cabin and walked along the richly carpeted corridor, past the two safety lockers housing fire hoses and axes and stopped before the elevator.

"Let's take the stairs," said Karen. "I need the exercise."

"Sure. Where do we—?" Dulac looked right, then left down the corridor.

"That way." Karen pointed left to the arrow sign with a pictogram of stairs. Moments later, they reached the end of the corridor, opened the door and walked along the platform leading to the staircase.

They paused for a moment as Dulac stood silent, over-whelmed by the flamboyance and glitziness of what lay before them. A monstrous crystal chandelier with multilayered circles of pink lights hung from the ceiling and illuminated the staircase and hall below, looking like a huge, upside-down Christmas tree. Underneath, the wide staircase descended in a slow swirl towards the main floor in castle-like opulence, its white marble stairs bordered by railings of wrought iron carrying small, winged cherubs in various poses of alleged cuteness. Dulac couldn't help thinking the décor was more suitable to a casino than to the inside of a ship.

Dulac took in a quick breath and shot a side glance at Karen, who seemed to sense his discomfort.

"A bit much," she said.

"A bit? Welcome to Vegas-on-the-Sea."

"Oh come on, it's not that bad."

"Gaudy comes to mind."

They took the stairs and upon reaching the bottom level, turned left towards the main dining area. The room was far from full and a number of passengers were busy chatting away, seemingly waiting for their first course. Overhead, clusters of gilded chandeliers with candle-shaped bulbs lit the room with their soft, yellow glow.

In the center of the room, a dozen guests were sitting at an oval table, and a man in officer's whites, seated at the head of the table, was busy talking to a gray-haired elderly woman dressed in a fuchsia-colored dress.

Dulac and Karen were standing at the entrance of the dining room when Dulac thought he recognized one the guests sitting at the large table in the center, next to what appeared to be the captain. Just then, a steward carrying a note pad approached them. "Your names, please?" He flashed an obsequious smile at Karen.

"Karen Dawson and Thierry Dulac," she said. "We're at the Captain's table."

"Ah yes, of course. Right this way. Please follow me," he said, pointing at the table with his right hand.

As they approached the table, Dulac's intuition about the man he thought he recognized was confirmed. The man with light brown, short cut hair, a low forehead and slightly arched eyebrows that gave him the appearance of being in a constant state of sadness was none other than Governor George Dickinson of Florida, the front-runner Republican candidate for the upcoming American presidential elections.

They reached the table and the steward introduced them.

"Captain Goran Peterson, this is Karen Dawson and Thurley . . ."

"Thierry Dulac."

"Yes, of course, terribly sorry Mr. Dewloc." The embarrassed steward retreated slightly, turned and eclipsed himself.

Peterson smiled and stood. "Welcome aboard Ms. Dawson, Mr. Dulac. Please," he said, pointing to the remaining two seats. Dulac and Karen sat down, and Peterson continued.

"This is Governor George Dickinson and his wife Mary, and to their right are Senator Durward Easton and his wife Sandra," said Peterson, eyeing the couples to his immediate right. "I'm not very good at remembering names, so I ask that everyone introduce himself or herself to Ms. Dawson and Mr. Dulac."

Dickinson looked much older than his 65 years, thought Dulac. Amazing what a TV makeup artist can do.

"Hi, I'm John Panetti," said the man with a strip of hair over his bald pate. He stretched over the table and offered his hand to Dulac. "And this is my wife, Gina. I'm in the meat business in Pasadena."

Dulac shook his hand and smiled perfunctorily. To Dulac's right, a tall man, good looking, mid-fifties with a definite Mediterranean complexion was busy talking in Italian to a pulpous-lipped, botoxed blonde fifteen years his junior. Her deep cleavage showed propped-up, tanned breasts. He summarily acknowledged Dulac and Karen with a quick smile, then returned to his conversation with the blonde.

From across the table, another man reached over and proffered his hand to Dulac.

"Sam Watson from Minneapolis. Since we're talking shop, I'm in the garbage disposal business. We make bins for the whole of North America. Even sell into Canada. You could say I pick up where Panetti left off." He laughed uproariously. "We stash your trash." Another guttural laugh from the man in a pink open shirt, wearing a huge opal stone mounted on a gold ring ostentatiously occupying his right annular. He turned slightly and eyed Panetti.

"Maybe you and I can do business, Mr. Panetti. You know—"

"Whatever."

Watson reached into his jacket pocket and pulled out a business card.

"Here, take this. Now we can say we did business. That way I can say that this was a business trip." He gave Panetti a conspiratorial wink.

"And what do you do, Mr. Dulac?" said Watson, his expression patronizing and haughty.

Dulac decided to wipe that supercilious smile off Watson's face.

"Actually Mr. Watson, I sometimes work with the IRS."

The conversation at the table suddenly screeched to a stop. All heads turned towards Dulac. Dulac locked his deadliest gaze onto Watson and continued. "What did you say the name of your company was?"

The passengers looked at Dulac with a mixture of incredulity and awe, then all eyes fixed on Watson, whose face had turned white.

"I, I didn't mean . . . I meant only to . . ."

"Of course you did. Let me be more specific, Mr. Watson. I'm an investigator with Interpol, and I often work with Revenue departments of various countries in cases of tax fraud. But don't worry. Cases have to be on a more sizable level to interest the likes of Interpol."

A look of relief came upon Watson's face as he slowly regained his composure. The Mediterranean Golden boy turned away and resumed sweet-talking the blonde.

"Mr. Dulac," said Senator Easton, "your name sounds familiar. Weren't you involved in the archbishops' murders case a while back? Monsignors Conti and—"

"— Salvador. Yes, I was."

"So actually, you were involved with the Vatican scandal surrounding the—"

"Sorry, but I can't get into specifics of any case, even if concluded." Dulac shot a side glance at Peterson.

Peterson nodded back in understanding. "Ladies and gentlemen," said Peterson in a warm, conciliatory tone, "this is hardly the place and time to be talking about such serious matters. Let's enjoy this trip and as we say at P & W, leave your troubles ashore." Peterson lifted his glass of red wine.

"On behalf of the crew and everybody at P & W, we wish you all a most relaxing and enjoyable trip."

"Here, here," said Easton, lifting his glass.

An hour and a half later, after a dinner filled with idle chatter about the advantages of cruise ships over hotels, such as never having to repack and unpack, and sleeping in the same bed for the length of the cruise, Dulac signaled Karen he'd had enough banalities for one evening and they headed back to their cabin.

"Strange, isn't it?" Karen said as they walked down the corridor.

"What's strange?"

"They never ask what the women do for a living."

CHAPTER 4

Later that evening from the comfort of the 300 count Egyptian cotton sheets of their first-class cabin, Dickinson lay awake beside his sleeping wife, wrestling with his conscience. The thought of being unfaithful to Mary again brought back pangs of guilt, which he thought he'd atoned for and absorbed long, long ago. In their thirty years of a relatively happy marriage, Dickinson had cheated on his wife twice, or five times, depending on how one counted. The first occurrence was twenty years ago, at the International Conference of Trial Lawyers in Kuala Lumpur, where he'd been corralled by a group of American colleagues into a visit to The King's Choice, a high-end brothel. There, four euro-Asian beauties had introduced him to sexual delights and positions beyond his wildest imagination. He'd rationalized that what Mary didn't know couldn't hurt her, but just the same, upon his return home, he'd assuaged the remaining traces of guilt at the confessional of St. Edward's, in Palm Beach.

The second transgression had occurred seventeen years ago at the Republican Florida Primary Convention in Miami, where Dickinson met Sandra Williams, a tall, stunning brunette and ex-model, presidential candidate Timothy

Meakins' assistant campaign manager. After a three-day stint of scorching lovemaking, Dickinson had come to his senses and told Williams he'd made a big mistake, loved his wife very much, and was ashamed of himself. Predictably she'd initially thrown a fit of rage, but eventually resigned herself and moved on to greener, less complicated pastures.

Dickinson had shoved the affair into the deepest recesses of his memory and all but forgotten about Williams, or at least he had until the evening he and Mary had gone out to dinner at Washington's posh Lafayette's and bumped into Senator Durward Easton of Florida, a long-time friend and mentor, and his dinner partner—Sandra Williams.

Dickinson had nearly had a stroke when Easton introduced Williams, at least twenty-five years his junior, as his fiancée. Shortly thereafter, Dickinson contacted Williams and met her at a bar, to find out her intentions. An uncomfortable exchange of accusations made it clear that a mutual pact of silence was the best solution. He wouldn't tell Durward, and she wouldn't tell Mary. Reassured, Dickinson had left it at that, but Easton had taken advantage of their chance meeting at Lafayette's to re-solidify his friendship with the Dickinsons. During the past years, Easton and Sandra had invited the Dickinsons to dinner in their house in Palm Beach at more than one occasion, and Mary had reciprocated.

Mary had grown fond of Sandra, and found they had a common interest, golf. They'd arranged to take a week's lessons together at Mary's prestigious club, The Breakers.

The idea of the Eastons joining the Dickinsons on the cruise to help celebrate their 35th wedding anniversary had been Mary's, to which Dickinson had initially offered resistance. Upon his wife's insistence, he'd finally agreed.

Everything had gone well until that first evening during dinner, when Sandra had dropped her napkin and while retrieving it, squeezed Dickinson's left thigh. At first, Dickinson thought nothing of it, passing it off as a momentary friendly gesture. But during the rest of the dinner, Sandra had insistently rubbed her leg slowly and sensuously against Dickinson's, making her intentions unequivocally clear.

Initially, he had retracted his leg slightly, but after her continuing advances, he'd stopped resisting and was enjoying the experience, fully aroused by her boldness and the clandestine nature of the situation. After dinner and nightcaps at one of the ship's bars, the Eastons and Dickinsons had retired for the evening.

At 2 am, while Mary snored peacefully beside him, Dickinson still lay awake wrestling with his demons, alternately praying and thinking of fondling Sandra's full breasts.

. . . and lead us not into temptation but deliver us from evil.

CHAPTER 5

The following morning, Dulac was awakened by a streak of sunlight streaming in a slit between the curtains of the cabin's window. Beside him in a fetal position, Karen lay sleeping, oblivious to the sun's warm rays. He felt that somehow, something on board ship had changed since the previous night but couldn't quite put his finger on it.

Then it hit him. The ship had stopped.

He got up, went to the window and, careful not to part the curtains too wide lest he disturb Karen, he peeked outside. The sight was breathtaking. Before him, its white limestone slope illuminated by the morning sun, the imposing mass of Gibraltar stood imperially, a small puff of cloud crowning its summit. At the foot of the mountain, the city of Gibraltar's densely packed buildings filled the lower slopes, temporarily tolerated by the sleeping giant.

Dulac looked directly below. The dock was a beehive of activity, stevedores rushing to and fro on their pallet carts, carrying provisions from the food trucks onto the ramps leading to the inside of the ship. To his right, the Port of Gibraltar extended from the edge of the peninsula to the coast of Spain, its calm waters harboring a few dozen ships at anchor, waiting their turn to dock.

Dulac looked at his watch. 8.15 a.m. At that moment, Karen awoke and turned towards him. She smiled mischievously, stretching her arms open in a sensual invitation.

An hour later, Dulac and Karen had breakfasted, left the ship and were on their way to visit The Rock. They had missed the ship's organized tour, so equipped with a map and a booklet on Gibraltar, they decided to take the cable car to the top of the mountain. They walked along the narrow path of Main Street towards the base of the cable car, enjoying the scents of freshly brewed coffee and baked croissants emanating from the city's quaint cafés. Twenty minutes later, they boarded the télébenne, already half-full of eager tourists speaking a variety of languages, and Dulac smiled as he read the small sign on the widow. "When near the apes, do not leave loose items dangling. You may never see them again." The door closed and the cable car started up slowly at first, then accelerated. Dulac and Karen looked in amazement as the grandiose view expanded before them. To their right, the sun shimmered off the waves of the Atlantic. Directly across, Morocco and its rugged, mountainous shores, harboring the cities of Ceuta and Tangiers. To the east, a string of cargo ships, small dots on the dark-blue sea, were funneling their way into the Straits of Gibraltar towards distant shores across the Atlantic.

As Karen and Dulac were taking in the sights, the cable car suddenly came to an abrupt stop.

A woman's loud shout filled the inside of the cabin. The passengers looked at each other with various degrees of anxiety, as the télébenne swung forwards and backwards like an out-of-control pendulum, each movement accompanied by more shouts. Suddenly a child started to cry, increasing the collective level of fear and sensation of unease. Her mother, embarrassed, tried to soothe the young girl, finally distracting her with a small teddy bear.

Dulac looked down. They were at least 100 feet off the ground, nowhere near one of the towers. Slowly, the swaying of the cable car subsided.

"This is why I don't ski Europe anymore," said Karen. "I hate these things."

"Probably just a power outage." Dulac tried to be reassuring. "I read somewhere they have many here."

After what seemed like an eternity, the télébenne started upwards again, slowly at first, then more quickly. A communal feeling of relief filled the cabin.

Dulac pointed to a small bronze plaque beside the door which read: "Von Roll, Switzerland."

"Even the Swiss aren't perfect," he said.

The cable car reached the top, the door opened and Karen, followed by Dulac, exited quickly.

"After we finish up here, I'm walking back down, thank you very much," said Karen with an air of determination.

"Why?" said Dulac. "They say lightning never strikes twice at the same spot."

"I'm not interested in testing that theory. Besides, I could use the exercise, and so could you." She glanced reproachfully at his stomach.

After enjoying the antics of the Barbary Coast macaques for half an hour, Dulac and Karen began their descent, occasionally stopping for a drink of water and to admire the sea daffodils, rest-harrows and other species of wildflowers along the narrow road. After two hours, they reached Main Street again and were looking for a restaurant when Dulac spotted Dickinson, seated at a table on the concourse. He was talking to his wife and they were with a man with crew-cut, brown hair and a burly build.

"Isn't that—?" started Karen.

Not wanting to engage in uninteresting discussions again, Dulac grabbed her by the elbow and hastened his step. They were about to pass by the table when Dickinson looked up and recognized them.

"Hello, ah . . . Mr. Dulac, I believe." Dickinson got up, smiling. "Won't you join us for a coffee?"

"Actually, we were about to—"

"Yes, why not?" said Karen.

Dulac shot an annoyed look in her direction.

"Please," said Dickinson, offering them two seats. "You remember my wife Mary, and this is my personal assistant, Bob Cummins."

"Hello," said Mary, with the practiced smile of a politician's wife, well-honed after thousands of hours of repetition.

The burly guy with a crew cut just nodded.

Dulac and Karen sat down. He couldn't help reflecting that Dickinson's bodyguard had been promoted to "personal assistant" for the occasion.

"We were all at the Captain's table last night," said Mary, probably more to make sure she was right in her assumption than to inform everyone else of the already obvious. "How did you enjoy the steak?" she said, turning toward Karen.

"Actually, I had the salmon."

"Oh, yes, and how was that?"

"A bit on the dry side," said Karen, feigning a modicum of interest.

The conversation moved from dull to duller when Dickinson summoned the waiter.

"What will you have?" said Dickinson to Dulac. "It's on me."

"No need, I—"

"I insist. What'll it be?"

Dulac hunched his shoulders. "Ah, coffee is fine."

"You're sure?"

"Sure."

Dickinson turned towards Karen. "Ms. . . . ?"

"Dawson. The same, black please."

Dickinson looked up at the waiter, who smiled perfunctorily and retreated. Dickinson turned towards Karen. "And what line of business are you in, Ms. Dawson?"

Karen shot a quick glance at Dulac, who smiled smugly. "I'm glad you asked, Governor. I teach animal mythology at La Sorbonne."

Dickinson drew back slightly, looking askance at Karen.

"Really? Animal mythology. I didn't know mythology was so . . . so compartmentalized."

Karen looked at Dulac, who shot her a "please-don't-go-there" look.

She glanced at her watch. "Actually yes, but it would take a bit of time to explain, and we have to go get some shopping done before re-boarding."

Dulac's face broke into a smile of relief.

CHAPTER 6

As he walked down the stairwell from deck five to deck three, Tariq suddenly felt a sudden spasm in his left leg. The pain always came back in the middle of the night, or early morning, depending on the level of humidity in the air.

Immediately the images of cell 306 of Islamabad Prison came back and flooded his brain, the dank, grimy walls, the rats, the smell of sweat and urine of the prisoners. But worst of all, he heard the screams again, over and over, his screams, although he'd tried to convince himself they weren't really his. Five years ago, he'd been arrested by members of the Directorate of Inter Service Intelligence, or ISI, Pakistan's infamous secret police, on charges of plotting against the government. Claiming his innocence, he'd continued to refuse to give them names of his collaborators even when they had hung him from the meat hook, wired his testicles to the batteries, and shot timed surges of electricity thru his quivering body. Unable to break his will, they'd beaten him for two days, on and off every three hours, until they'd broken both his tibias with their steel billets. After, they'd left him to lie in his cot without any medical attention, and although his right leg

27

had miraculously healed without distortion, his left tibia had reset at an angle, giving him a permanent and painful limp. The best way he could endure the pain was to take more and more frequent doses of Paracetamol. He groped into the left pocket of his white uniform, took out the bottle and opened it. He popped out two tablets and downed them quickly. After a moment, he resumed walking along the corridor to the deck, then right towards the stern. In the fading darkness, the ship's lifeboats appeared, suspended on their davits.

As he neared Lifeboat 9, he recognized Saquil, Youssef, Hassan and the other familiar faces, and felt a surge of adrenalin shoot up his spine. The operation they had carefully planned was going smoothly. Their mole Tajar Singh, Chief Security officer at P & W Cruise Lines, had hired eight security officers over the past six months, so as not to draw unnecessary attention from corporate. Now it was full action mode. There was no going back.

"*Salaam Aleikum*, Youssef," Tariq said in a low voice. "Everyone here?"

"*Aleikum Salaam*, Tariq. Yes, all are here," whispered Youssef.

"Good. Very good," said Tariq, trying to disguise his nervousness. He fixed his gaze on the young man with a pencil beard. "Saquil, get the guns." Tariq turned and eyed the man next to him. "Hassan, you'll hand them out to the men."

"Yes, Tariq."

Saquil went up the four stairs leading to the open lifeboat and went in. A moment later, he appeared with five Glock pistols, took them out of their plastic bags and handed them one by one to Hassan, along with the ammunition, as Hassan started distributing the weapons to the rest of the men. Saquil went back in, came out with the six Micro-Uzis and handed them to Hassan.

His job finished, Saquil closed the canvas top and descended the stairs back onto the deck.

He handed Tariq the last of the Glocks, with four clips of ammunition.

Tariq eyed his men one by one, as they huddled closely around him. Then he spoke, his voice hushed but firm.

"You all know what you have to do. Just like we practiced in Turbat. Najib, you and your men take control of the steerage room. Karim?"

"Yes, I know. I go down the stairwell and take control of the engine room, and—"

"And if someone gives you any trouble, any trouble at all, shoot him. We've got to show them who's in charge. That goes for everyone. We are at war. Understood?"

"Understood," his men chimed in unison.

"Good. Hassan, you and the others will lead the passengers to the amphitheater. Now go. May *Allah* be with you."

* * *

I've got to send a Security Alert. I've got to press that button. Hands in the air, flanked by his fellow officers, Captain Goran Peterson stood helpless before the two armed men. His rage mounted as one of them ran the barrel of his Uzi submachine gun along the curve of First Officer Sandra Brown's left breast.

"Nice." The short squat man dressed in brown fatigues grinned lecherously.

"There is no need for that." Captain Peterson tried to reason with the thin, dark-complexioned man in officer's whites. A mole in his own crew. How had that happened?

The thin man gripped the other man's shoulder and pulled him back. He stepped close to Peterson, the business end of his pistol inches from Peterson's face.

"You are very lucky, Captain. Next time you talk without permission, I shoot you. Understood?"

Peterson nodded.

"Good." The thin man waved his gun at the rest of the officers standing meekly in a row, their backs to the ship's command console. "That goes for everyone." He brought the microphone of his small lapel-hung VHF radio closer to his mouth. "Engine room secure?"

"Yes, engine room secure," answered a voice masked in static.

"Steerage room?"

No reply.

"Steerage room, do you hear me, over?"

"Yes Tariq, steering room is—"

"No names, asshole," he yelled into the VHF. "No fucking names!"

"Sorry. Yes, everything in steering area is secure."

"Good." The thin man with fine features and plastered-down black hair switched off his VHF and turned to Peterson. "So now you know my name, Captain. Yet it is a very common name." The hijacker smiled "Do you know how many Tariqs there are in Pakistan alone, Captain?"

"Should I care?"

"Wrong answer." Tariq stepped back and kicked Peterson in the groin. He doubled over in pain and fell to his knees, gasping for air.

The four other officers stood motionless as the squat man motioned upwards at them with the barrel of his Uzi. "Up, keep your hands up."

Now, thought Peterson. His back to the hijackers, Peterson grabbed the edge of the console and pulled himself up slowly, brushing with his left knee the SASS button hidden underneath the console. He turned and raised his hands again, facing the two hijackers.

"Anyone else feeling cocky?" Tariq waved his pistol at the officers. "No? Good. I want names and rank. Starting with the pretty lady here."

"Sandra Brown, First Officer," Officer Brown's voice trembled.

Tariq pointed his gun at the short, thirtyish balding man beside her.

"Tate, Jeremy Tate, Chief Radio Operator."

"Good. We need you." Tariq took two steps to the left and pointed again.

30

"Staff Captain Peter Rhodes," said the tall, lanky man with sandy brown hair.

"And you?" Tariq pointed his pistol at the last of the officers.

"Pierre Lanctot, Security Officer." said the man with sloping shoulders and a small, hooked nose.

"And of course Captain Peterson," said Tariq, looking at the captain. "Now that we are all well acquainted, my friends and I are going to help you run this ship." Tariq laughed in short raucous spurts, taking in bits of air between bursts. He turned and looked at the large command console, its impressive array of levers, buttons, monitors and screens fanned in an arc beneath the windows of the bridge. "So, Rhodes, which one is the steering lever?"

"It's the Azipod. Over there." Rhodes pointed to his left.

"That one?" Tariq aimed his pistol at the small, black spherical lever mounted near the edge of the console.

"Yes."

"So this controls the ship's direction and speed?"

"Correct."

Gun trained on Rhodes, Tariq moved up to the console, put his palm atop the round lever, turned it hard right on its axis and pressed it forward. The 45,000-ton ship started turning, slowly at first, then more quickly into an ever-tightening arc. "Amazing." He turned the lever hard left.

"Now look here, this is not a damn toy," said Peterson. "You can't just throw this ship around like in a video game, you—"

Tariq spun around, his black eyes hardened, his fine-featured face twisting into a mask of rage.

"You what?" He swung and hit Peterson in the face with the butt of his pistol. "Say it, Captain, come on, say it . . . Paki? Idiot? Bastard? What's on your mind, Captain?" said Tariq, the barrel of his Glock now inches from Peterson's face.

Peterson reeled backwards, trying desperately to stay calm.

"He doesn't listen, your captain." Tariq walked nervously back and forth before the officers, waving his pistol. Slowly the anger in his face melted away, giving way to an air of self-assurance and defiance. He stopped in front of Rhodes. "Tell me, Rhodes, as Staff Captain, you are second-in-command. Correct?"

"Yes," said Rhodes.

"So if anything were to happen to the captain here, you are fully capable to run this ship."

"I, I suppose," said Rhodes hesitantly.

"Good. Very good." Tariq paused for a moment, looking at the console. "So if I tell you what course to take, you or I, or anybody else can steer this ship. Correct ?"

"I, I guess—"

"Don't guess, Rhodes. Yes or no?"

"Yes."

Tariq turned and took a couple of steps towards the exit doors of the bridge. He stopped, raised his arm and spun quickly, aiming his pistol at Rhodes's face.

"So I don't need two captains aboard this ship, now do I?"

Rhodes stood trembling, blood draining from his face. "Please, I . . . I have young children . . . my . . ."

Tariq cocked his head slightly, swung his arm to the right and pulled the trigger. Twice.

CHAPTER 7

Caravan House, Southampton

Sitting alone in the dimly lit monitoring room of the P & W Cruise Lines' headquarters, Andrew Allin looked up from the GPS screen and towards the opposite wall at one of the five clocks indicating times around the world. 7.45 a.m., Greenwich Mean Time. Fifteen more minutes and his shift, the graveyard shift, would be over and his replacement Peter Nellis would come strutting cheerfully in and take over the monitoring of the company's ten ships across the Atlantic and Mediterranean.

Allin rose and walked over to the window overlooking Temple Place. Outside, the yellow lights of the square shone softly on the falling sheets of rain, occasionally whipped sideways by gusts of a budding Northeaster. Suddenly, in the window's reflection, Allin caught sight of the red flashing light. It was the Security Alert System at Sea, the system used to warn of a terrorist or piracy attack on a ship.

"Damn," he blurted, as he rushed back to his chair and sat before the SASS receiver. The monitor read: *Caravan Star.* ID number 3807 — 4 b. Position: Lat N46 47' 22" Long 22 26' 20". Time of incident: 6.47 a.m. GMT. 5.47 a.m. Ship's time.

Probably another false alarm. There's been three already this month. Allin pressed the reset button and the red light stopped flashing. Following protocol, Allin picked up the phone and dialed Chief Security Officer David Winston's home number. While he waited for Winston to answer, Allin took comfort in the magenta line drawn by the *Caravan Star*'s track across the GPS screen's map of the Atlantic. The *Caravan Star* was on course. Nothing seemed unusual.

"Yes?" said the drowsy voice.

"Sorry to disturb you, sir, I—"

"Who is this?"

"Allin, sir. It's the *Caravan Star*. She's sent out a SASS. Probably another—"

"I'll be right over."

* * *

Frozen in shock, Rhodes and the others watched in horror as Peterson, his uniform bloodied, his back against the console, slowly slipped to the floor. Sprawled askew, his legs and arms began twitching away the last spasms of his life until eventually he lay still, eyes glazed over, mouth agape. No one uttered a word. Rhodes, standing next to Brown, could feel her shoulders convulsing. After a moment, her shaking stopped.

"Get him out of here," Tariq ordered the squat man. "Put him in the life jacket box." He pointed at the steel box next to the glass doors.

The hijacker slung his Uzi over his shoulder, grabbed Peterson's legs and dragged him across the floor. He opened the lid, took out the life jackets and manhandled the lifeless body into the box.

Tariq looked on, expressionless. The squat man closed the lid and Tariq slowly turned to Rhodes. "Now, Captain, change course to 325 degrees. Speed 23 knots." He waved his gun at Rhodes, then pointed at the Azipod lever.

Rhodes felt his knees go weak. His right hand shook uncontrollably as he reached for the Azipod lever. Breathing deeply, he steadied himself on the edge of the console, took the lever with his left hand and moved it forward and to the right. The ship veered slowly to starboard. After a moment Rhodes brought back the lever to its central position and set the automatic pilot. He continued to look ahead in the darkness, not daring to move, his thoughts darting from one possible scenario to the next at light speed, searching for the best option. *I've got to send a SASS, this psychopath is going to kill us all.* Using the reflection in the glass window, Rhodes eyed Tariq discreetly. Tariq's gun was still trained on Rhodes as the hijacker looked at the monitors in turn, trying to read their functions.

"What's this one?" Tariq pointed at the dark-blue, radar-like screen with his pistol.

Rhodes turned slightly. "It's the forward-seeking echo sounder. It detects obstructions at sea level. Things like containers and reefs." Rhodes brought his knee up discreetly underneath the console, feeling for the SASS button. Nothing. He was standing too far right. He sidled to the left and tried again. Still no luck.

Tariq moved closer to Rhodes, observed the ship's speed and heading on the GPS chart plotter and smiled approvingly. "Good. That's very good," he said smiling. He reached into his vest pocket, pulled out a sheet of paper and handed it to Rhodes. "Read this. When I say so, you're going to set off the Fire Security Alarm and announce over the PA system exactly what's written here. One wrong word, one attempt to warn anybody and you're dead. Understood?"

CHAPTER 8

US Coast Guard Rescue Coordination Center, Alameda, California

"Just a minute David, I'll get Dan Hoffman on the line." Sitting in his third story corner office, Operational Commander John Kiefer put down his coffee mug, pressed the hold button on his phone and dialed the number for his counterpart, Operational Commander Dan Hoffman, Atlantic Region, Norfolk, Virginia. After a moment, the familiar, raspy voice came on the line.

"Hoffman here."

"Hey Dan, this is John."

"Hey John. What's up?"

"We've just received a SASS notification from P & W in Southampton. It was sent about 15 minutes ago by one of their ships, the *Caravan Star*. I have their Chief Security Officer David Winston on the line. Hang on a second and I'll put him back on."

Kiefer pressed the conference call button. "David, you still there?"

"Hello gentlemen, Winston here."

"Hi David, this is Dan Hoffman. Has the SASS been confirmed?"

"No. We don't dare call her. If we do, we—"

"Has she changed course?" said Kiefer.

"No. She hasn't altered from 271 degrees," said Winston.

"So it could be a false alarm," said Hoffman.

"Correct," said Winston, "but if it's not and we call her, we risk alerting the pirates and lose the element of surprise. They might panic and do something stupid."

"You're damned if you do and dammed if you don't," said Kiefer.

"What's her position, David?" said Hoffman.

"Wait a minute," said Winston. "She just altered course to northwest, heading 325 degrees."

"Towards the Azores?" said Kiefer.

"Yes," said Winston, "there's definitely something wrong."

"She could have a mechanical," said Hoffman.

"She would have notified us by now," said Winston.

"How many on board?" said Kiefer.

"Her manifest indicates 353 passengers and 154 crew. The *Caravan Star* is on a repositioning trip from the Mediterranean to the Caribbean via Cancun and Miami."

Kiefer rose from his chair and walked over to the wall-size map of the Atlantic on the other side of the room. "She's still far from the US coast, but we sometimes send units into the mid-Atlantic on Search and Rescue. Dan, what have you got in Section 3?"

"Nothing within range," said Hoffman. "The *Dolphin* is operating in the St Lawrence, and the *Sea Hawk* is in Groton for a refit. The *Vinalhaven* is patrolling off the Florida coast."

"Do you have anything in the Azores?" said Winston.

"Negative," said Kiefer. "The last squadron of F-22 raptors was pulled five years ago. The Air Force maintains only a skeleton staff and administrative personnel at Lajes to help refuel their C-130's."

"What about the US Navy?" said Winston.

"They usually won't respond until she's off the US coast, and only if she poses a clear and present danger to a US city," said Kiefer. "Anyway, this could be just another false alarm. We've had two already this month. To my mind, those SASS buttons are just too damn sensitive. Tell you what David, we'll try to locate her and keep an eye on her. Let us know if you get confirmation on the SASS. Anything to add, Dan?"

"Yeah. We'll calibrate with the French satellite command at Lyon and—"

"Gentlemen, I'm going to help you prioritize this," interrupted Winston.

"Say what?" said Kiefer.

"According to the manifest, we have a certain Governor George Dickinson aboard. He and—"

"The Republican presidential candidate?" said Kiefer.

"The very same. He, Senator Durward Easton and their wives are on our Five Star Gold Packages. They're celebrating the Dickinsons' 35th wedding anniversary. There are seventy-six other American passengers on board. Shall I send you the manifest?"

"Christ!" said Kiefer.

CHAPTER 9

Aboard the Caravan Star, stateroom 507-B

Tucked under the warmth of the duvet comforter, Dulac was enjoying the dreams of deep sleep when suddenly the loud sound of electronic static jolted him awake. Seconds later, the PA system outside their cabin crackled to life.

"Can I have your attention please? This is the Staff Captain speaking. As required by maritime safety law, this is an unscheduled fire drill. All guests and crew are required to report on deck wearing life jackets. Please identify the location of your muster station on the panel in your room and proceed with caution. I repeat, this is a drill only. We apologize for the inconvenience." The PA system clicked off.

Dulac looked at the bedside clock. 6.55 a.m. He glanced at Karen, her thick auburn hair covering part of her face in a sensuous swirl. Half awake, she mumbled, "What was that all about?"

"A fire drill."

"Just as I was getting back to sleep." She punched her down pillow.

Dulac donned his boxer shorts, turned on the light and went to the window. On the barely discernible horizon, a swath of fog had wedged itself between dawn's pale blue sky and the gray, roiling sea.

He stretched lazily and caught his reflection in the sliding door's windowpane. He didn't like what he saw. *Must have put on at least five kilos.* His face was puffy, his eyes were deep set in their sockets and a pallid, yellowish skin tone had replaced the usual ruddy cheeks. His Interpol colleague Gina Marino had been right when she'd told him he looked like a tired Michael Douglas. Dulac replaced an errant strand of sandy-gray hair and turned towards the bed. "So?" he said, eyeing Karen.

"You go ahead. I'll pass."

"Suit yourself, but they'll be checking all the rooms." He walked over to the door and studied the small wall chart showing directions to their muster station.

Karen threw away the cover in disgust. "Why now? Can't they do this at some civilized hour?"

"Wouldn't be unscheduled then, would it?"

"I suppose." Karen got up and reluctantly donned her olive-green nightgown.

"You're not going on deck wearing only that?"

"Why not? Surely this won't take long."

"Looks pretty windy out there."

Dulac went to the closet, pulled out the life jackets, a two-piece sweat suit and a sweater. "Here, wear this." He handed her his tan and blue sweater. "With your lifejacket over it, you'll be okay."

As Karen took the sweater and slipped it over her nightgown, Dulac couldn't suppress the thought of how only two layers of nondescript clothing were needed to hide an otherwise beautifully sculpted figure and transform it into matronly shapelessness.

"Not exactly Gucci-coordinated," she said, noting Dulac's air of amusement.

Dulac opened the cabin door. "*Après vous, madame,*" he said, ushering Karen into the hallway.

"Yeah, thanks," she said, with an air of resigned gloom.

They made their way down the narrow green corridor amid the other passengers of Deck Five. Even with the announcement of fire drill only, Dulac couldn't help noticing the anxious looks on some of the passengers' faces as they exited their rooms and joined the human flow on its way to the deck. At the end of the corridor, two crewmembers dressed in whites were keeping the swinging doors open as Dulac and Karen made their way through onto the deck. Outside, the early sunrays had burned off the fog, leaving only a churning silver sea. The air was raw and the teak deck glistened with a coat of morning dew. Shivering, Karen snuggled up to Dulac as they joined the pushing and shoving crowd of passengers milling about.

"Over here, please. Everybody over here," said a voice lost in the crowd.

Dulac tried to spot where the voice had come from. He looked about and after a moment saw a man, dark-complexioned, wearing a white cap and uniform, waving the people over to him.

* * *

Dulac grabbed Karen's elbow and led her through a group of passengers. "That must be our muster station."

"Ladies and gentlemen," said the man, "can I have your attention, please?" The group tightened around him. "First, I'd like to remind you that this is a drill only. As far as the staff is concerned, even if you've gone through this before, bear with me, as it does no harm to refresh your memory. We at P & W Lines take safety very seriously. Today, ladies and gentlemen, I'm going to show you the main fire exit locations on board and—"

"Excuse me," interrupted an elderly woman with a white-powdered face, "why can't we do this later during the day?"

Mutterings of approval ran through the group.

"Ma'am, I don't set the schedule," said the man, totally unapologetic. "I only follow orders. As I was saying, we want you to know the main exits. We'll start from the front of the ship and work our way to the back. Right now, I'll take a quick roll call." He grabbed his pencil and started down his list. "Adams—?"

Moments later, having gone through the list to his satisfaction, he said, "Now if you'll follow me, we'll go the front of the ship. Before we start the drill, the captain has a few words he'd like to say to you at the amphitheater."

Something grated in Dulac's ears. He couldn't quite identify it, but the annoyance was there.

"Terrific," said Karen. She turned to Dulac, "Do we get a refund for their ruining my night and probably the rest of my day?"

"Good luck."

They joined the crowd of passengers and staff and started towards the bow of the ship. As they walked along, Dulac glanced slightly to his right. "Strange," he said.

"What's strange?" replied Karen, annoyance in her voice.

"The sun is to our right."

"So?"

"We should be heading west. The sun should be rising directly behind us."

CHAPTER 10

On the bridge, 7.05 a.m. Ship's time

As he stood next to Tariq at the console, Rhodes glanced at the other hijacker, who was busy tying the other officers' hands behind their backs with plastic tie wraps and forcing them to sit on the floor. Rhodes thought of his antiterrorist training seminars in Southampton two years ago. Rule three—Never, never challenge their authority, the instructor had said. Then why had Peterson ignored this basic principle? Was it because he'd simply lost it? Odd for a man like Peterson, with his 20 years of service. Had he set off the SASS before being shot? If so, was Southampton acting upon it? His mind raced in different directions when suddenly Tariq spoke.

"You. Tate, is it?" He pointed his pistol at the Chief Radio Operator, sitting next to Lanctot.

"Yes."

"When is your next report to headquarters?"

"At 7.30 a.m. Ship's time. I text them basic information."

Tariq looked at the ship's clock: 7.15 a.m. "And what is in your report?"

"I give a weather summary, wave size and direction, confirm the ship's position and speed, our Estimated Time of Arrival and any problems since the last report. I—"

"The people in Southampton are monitoring the ship's direction and speed, yes?"

"Yes."

"Surely by now they've noticed the change of course." Tariq waved his pistol in front of Tate.

"Perhaps."

Tariq pressed the gun barrel to Tate's left temple. "Perhaps or surely?"

"Su . . . surely," said Tate, his face red.

"What are you going to tell them about the change of course?"

Tate hesitated for a moment, then said, "We're encountering heavy seas. We've rerouted temporarily for the comfort of the passengers. We do that sometimes."

"Good. You're a quick learner, Tate. I like that." Tariq walked over towards the far end of the console where the surveillance monitors showed their dull gray pictures of the different areas of the ship. He looked more closely at the deck monitors and watched as the passengers and crew proceeded towards the bow of the ship. Tariq brought his VHF radio closer to his mouth. "Deck Three, this is Bridge, do you copy, over?"

"This is Deck Three."

"Everything under control?"

"Everything okay."

"Deck Four?"

"All is okay. We are going to the front."

"Deck Five?"

"Okay."

"Good. Very good," said Tariq. "Proceed as planned."

* * *

"These damn fire drills, why don't they do them before we leave port?" said the middle-aged man with crew-cut, light-brown hair, walking next to Dulac.

"My first cruise," said Dulac, as they ambled forward amidst the drowsy and reluctant crowd.

Beside them to their left, rows of neatly stacked green recliner chairs lined the wall of the deck. To the right, some of the passengers were using the metal handrail for support.

"First time I've had one this early," said the man, a disgruntled look on his face.

"Kind of a rude awakening," said Dulac.

"I guess P & W is playing it safe."

Dulac shot a side glance at him. "What do you mean?"

"Their security officers are armed. Our guy has a short stock Glock in his VHF holder."

Dulac froze in mid-stride, looking at the man in bewilderment. "You saw a pistol on this guy?"

"Yup. With that short stock, it's gotta be a Glock. When I was stationed in Iraq, some of the officers in my unit used them. More compact, lighter than the Colts, they said. Anything wrong?"

"Damn right there's something wrong," said Dulac. "Before we left, I did an internet search on P & W's safety protocol. It says they follow IMO's recommendation against onboard personnel being armed. This is supposed to be a gun-free ship."

CHAPTER 11

USCG offices, Alameda, California

With 40 years of active service in the US Navy under his belt, Captain John Kiefer had not adapted easily to retirement. In fact, he hadn't adapted at all. Like many men used to the responsibilities and perks of command, he'd found the routine of walking the dog, mowing the lawn, doing the dishes and taking out the garbage mind numbing and stultifying. He felt still fully capable, yet so useless. Not a day would pass when he didn't relive, at least in part, some of his many missions commanding his last ship, the missile-equipped Arleigh-Burke Class destroyer Appomattox. That was all history now, but he'd let it be known among circles of his Navy buddies that he'd take anything short of kitchen patrol to get out of the house and feel useful again.

So when his friend Vice-Admiral Neil Wilkins had pulled a few strings and offered him a post as Operational Coordinator in the Coast Guard, Kiefer had jumped at the opportunity.

Even if the job didn't have the heavy responsibilities of his previous post, he found comfort in being part of one of his country's essential organizations, giving his life a renewed sense of purpose. Yet when times were quiet, which was often, he wondered if ever he would face any of the excitement of his old job. On that score, Kiefer was about to be more than pleasingly surprised.

Kiefer picked up the phone and dialed Admiral Lee Jenkins's direct number. It was definitely time to report to the boss.

"Hello sir. John Kiefer here. We have a problem."

Jenkins emitted a small guffaw. "Hey John. You sound just like the movie."

"Sir, there's a strong possibility we have a hijack situation on the *Caravan Star*. She's a cruise ship bound for Miami via Cancun. Governor George Dickinson, Senator Durward Easton and seventy-six other US citizens are among the passengers."

"Jesus. What do you mean a strong possibility?" said Jenkins, his voice now dead serious.

"She sent out a SASS about an hour ago. Since then she's altered course towards the Azores."

"Any other contact from her?"

"The last message from her was at 7.30 a.m. Ship's time. Her radio operator sent a text that the ship altered course temporarily to avoid heavy seas. According to our weather data, the waves are only two feet now at the ship's lat/long coordinates."

There was a moment of silence, while Kiefer waited for his boss's reaction.

"Good enough for me. We'll call Nancy."

* * *

As Secretary of the Department of Homeland Security, overseeing inter alia the US Coast Guard, Nancy Lombardi was arguably the second most powerful woman in Washington after Jane Winney, the Secretary of State. A *Summa Cum Laude* graduate from Yale Law School with an IQ in the high 150's on a bad day, Lombardi was the first woman to hold such a high US cabinet posting under both a Republican and a Democratic president. A fervent and tireless worker, the diminutive fireball of a woman headed the biggest US cabinet after Defense and Veterans' Affairs. Known in Washington's upper stratosphere of power for her long memory and short temper, one didn't disturb Nancy Lombardi without a compelling reason to do so, especially in the middle of the night.

"I'll advise the President," she said, after being briefed by Jenkins and Kiefer.

CHAPTER 12

Looking back amongst the flow of passengers and assorted crew members, Dulac caught sight of another man dressed in an officer's white uniform and nudged the ex-Army man walking next to him.

"Take a quick look to your right, at the guy wearing whites," whispered Dulac.

Army slowed and half-turned towards the rear. "Definitely a short stock Glock," he whispered to Dulac.

Suddenly everything became clear in Dulac's mind: the drill, the misnomer of the ship's bow, the course alteration, the pistols. He eyed Army, grabbed Karen by the arm and pulled her aside along the cabin wall. Army stopped next to them as the rest of the passengers kept walking.

"What's up?" Karen said, staring intently at Dulac.

"These guys aren't security officers." Dulac nodded discreetly towards the man in whites ahead of them.

"What do you mean?" said Karen, pushing a strand of hair from her face. She looked at the veteran, then back at Dulac.

"What makes you—?"

"I'll explain later." Dulac looked nervously around. "We've got to find a side entrance."

"But what do you——?"

"Just do as I say," said Dulac, his voice testy.

Dulac, Karen and Army started again, slowly, letting other people go by. They were about to reach the end of Deck Five, and in front of them passengers had stopped before a set of twin doors, waiting to enter. Above the doors, an arrow pointing downwards indicated "Amphitheater". Army stopped abruptly, as did Dulac and Karen.

"Am I thinking what you're thinking?" whispered Dulac to Army.

"If you're right and we go in there, we're screwed," said Army.

Dulac saw it first. They were a dozen feet away from a narrow corridor to the left, between two steel columns. "There. He pointed and looked fore and aft along the deck. The safety officers were busy talking to other passengers. Dulac shot a glance at Army, then grabbed Karen by the waist and pulled her into the corridor.

"Run," he said and they started to sprint down the corridor. Halfway down, the sign on one of the doors caught their attention: *Employees Only*.

"In here," said Army.

They stopped, opened the door and rushed in, closing the door behind them. Dulac groped for the light switch on the wall and finding it, flicked it on, revealing a set of lockers to the left, a cluster of mops and buckets to the right.

"What . . . what the hell is this about?" Karen bent over and put her hands on her thighs as she gasped for air.

"I've never heard a naval officer who keeps referring to the bow as the front of the ship," said Dulac. "Also, why is our security officer's gun in a VHF holder? If P & W has changed its policy on guns, can't it afford proper holsters?"

Standing next to them, Army breathed laboriously, obviously affected by the dash. "Maybe he called it the front to make it clearer for the passengers," he said. "By the way my name is Henry. Henry Porter. Folks call me Hank."

"Thierry Dulac, and this is Karen Dawson."

Hank eyed Dulac, who was breathing easily. "Say, you're in pretty good shape."

"Not really. I was in a lot better shape three years ago after my Interpol training at Lyon."

"So you're military, too?"

"Not really, but we get to practice on the range with our pistols."

"It's a pleasure." Hank proffered his right hand. "Corporal Henry Porter, formerly 82nd Airborne."

"Corporal."

Karen shot an alarmed look at Dulac and said, "Thierry, are you saying these guys are . . . are . . . ?"

"Hijackers."

"Jesus! But the fire drill. They—"

"It's fake," said Dulac.

"Come on, I mean, how can you be sure?" Karen looked for a bit of reassurance and found none. "It seems perfectly logical to me for them to gather us to inform—"

"It's fake, Karen." Dulac stared resolutely into her blue eyes.

Karen took a deep breath. "So if the fire drill is fake, as you seem to be so sure of, why are they bringing the passengers to the amphitheater?"

"To better control them," said Hank. "Remember the Moscow hostage taking? The last thing any hijacker wants are stray passengers running all over the ship."

Karen stood silent, paralyzed, staring at Hank.

"You mean, like us?" Her eyes were large globules of fear.

Hank nodded gravely.

"So what do you suggest we do now?"

"We gotta get help. Don't ask me how we're gonna do—" said Hank.

"My phone," interrupted Dulac. "My sat phone. I've got to get back to our room."

"Why?" said Karen. "I thought you said they would check every room."

"I've got to get my phone. Once they see we're missing from the manifest, the hijackers'll hunt us down. We've got to call the cruise line for help."

"I'm with you," said Hank.

"This is way over the top," said Karen. "I can't believe this is happening. There must be some other, logical explanation to all this. I'm sure this—"

Dulac grabbed her arms and stared into her scared eyes. "Listen, if I'm wrong, all we'll have missed is a bland lecture on ship safety. We can catch up on that later. If I'm right, we'll . . . we'll have to think of something." He turned towards Porter. "Hank, wait here with her. If I'm not back in ten minutes, you're on your own."

CHAPTER 13

Addington Manor, County of Hampshire, England, 9.45 a.m.

Sir Adrian Bolding, CEO and majority shareholder of P &
W Cruise Lines, preferred working the early hours of the day
at home, away from the hectic bustle and constant interrup-
tions at the company's headquarters.

Sitting alone in the cavernous dining room of his seventeen room, 16th century ancestral mansion, Bolding had
not slept well the previous night. The September sales report
had been tabled at the meeting of the executives the previous
afternoon. They were disastrous, down 20% from last year,
and down 15% from the month of August. Worse, according
to his contacts, Carnival and Norwegian's sales had increased
significantly during September. Looking up across the room
at the portrait of his grandfather and founder of P & W, Sir
Geoffrey Bolding, Sir Adrian was reminded of his responsibilities and duties as President and sole heir to the family
shipping line. Some days, and this was one of them, he wondered what would have happened if he hadn't caved into his
father's constant rebukes, and instead followed his dream of
becoming a violinist. He could still remember his father's
last speech to him, word for word. *Your duty to the family comes*

first, Adrian. Besides, do you really think you can keep Addington on a violinist's revenue? Let's be honest, Adrian, you're good, but not that good. You'll never be a star. Take it from me, make money first, then you can fiddle all you want.

Still, a first violin position in an orchestra . . . Too late now.

He parked that train of thought in a distant place and brought the coffee cup to his mouth. Just then his butler, Higgins, appeared in the doorway, phone in hand.

"Excuse me sir. It's a call from your office. David Winston wishes to speak to you. He says it's urgent."

Bolding waived Higgins over and took the phone.

"She's headed for a damn reef? A SASS? Why didn't you call me earlier?" said Bolding, getting up and throwing his monogrammed cloth napkin onto the table. "How much time till she reaches the reef?"

"About four hours. Sorry, sir. We're still not sure if—" said Winston.

"Bloody hell. That's all I need."

Bolding pressed the end-call button and eyed Higgins. "Get Jennings to bring the car. Now."

"Yes sir. Right away sir."

* * *

Half an hour later, dressed in an open-collared pink shirt, sleeves rolled up, Bolding sat in the windowless video conference room, tapping his fingers impatiently on the table while waiting for the monitor to come to life. Beside him sat David Winston, a worried and intent look on his flushed face, still burning from the rebuke he'd received earlier from his boss.

Bolding turned towards his newly appointed Chief Security Officer. "So Winston, second week on the job and you're in the arena with the lions."

"Yes, sir. Didn't expect it quite so soon."

Feeling his level of exasperation rise, Bolding reached across the table, picked up the phone and dialed his secretary's number.

"What's happening with that call to Sir Hays, Sheila?"

"He hasn't called back. I'll try again, sir."

Bolding hung up and turned towards Winston.

"Damn civil servants. All the same. You'd think that with the exorbitant salaries we pay them they'd be a little more responsive."

Fifteen more minutes, and the video screen finally flickered to life, Britain's Home Department emblem adorned the screen briefly, then gave way to the picture of two seated men. Bolding recognized one of them, the man with the slightly bulging eyes, the tight, thin-lipped mouth and the patted-down reddish hair, someone he knew only too well, his classmate at Eaton and an arrogant, smug sob. Sir Terence Hays, the Home Secretary, responsible for Britain's MI5, MI6 and New Scotland Yard.

"Good morning gentlemen, can you see us?" said Hays.

"Glad you could get back to us, finally. With me is our Chief Security Officer, David Winston."

"Quite," said Hays, "and to my left is Rear-Admiral Arnold Archibald, Commander Operations."

"Gentlemen," said Bolding, surprised. He hadn't expected Hays to escalate matters so quickly, especially all the way up to the level of a rear-admiral. He was about to find out why.

"Before we go any further," said Hays, "I would like to clear up a small matter of protocol. Sir Adrian, in future, let us contact the Americans, if you please. None of us appreciate being blindsided, especially the PM. Is that clearly understood by everyone?"

Bolding felt the blood rush to his face. Here was a bloody civil servant worried about being blindsided when Bolding was possibly facing the sinking of one of his ships and the drowning of passengers and crew. He kept his temper in check and said, "We were simply following IMO protocol. The *Caravan Star* is headed for Miami. So naturally we—"

"Well, fine and dandy, Adrian but the US coast guard and Navy know more about this than we do. You can maybe imagine that our chaps don't appreciate being told by a foreign state about what's happening to a ship under British registry." Hays turned towards Archibald.

"Quite," said Archibald. "We can coordinate things much quicker and more efficiently. Saves a lot of red tape, too."

Bolding thought quickly. This was not the time to get into a pissing contest with Hays and Archibald over protocol. Let Hays win this one. "We notified you as soon as we could. Next time we'll make sure you're in the loop from the beginning."

"Fine. Now then, Sir Adrian, what is the situation?" said Hays.

Bolding took off his reading glasses, rose from his seat and took short, quick steps to the far side of the room where a map of the Atlantic hung from the wall. With his right hand, he stretched up to a spot on the map. "The *Caravan Star* is approximately here," said Bolding, his small, rotund stature in net contrast with the height of the large map. "She's altered course north by northwest towards the Azores and increased her speed to 24 knots. After much discussion here, we decided to try and reach her by Inmarsat and high-frequency radio. She's not responding to either. The only communication we've had from her was the text report from the radio operator. The weather information was so wrong we believe he was trying to notify us of the attack."

"I see," said Hays. "Do we have any idea who is behind this?"

"Afraid not," said Bolding.

His expression somber, Hays looked at Archibald. "What have you got, Arnold? Anything within range?"

Archibald, a man with a round, fleshy face and a wisp of gray hair combed sideways, cleared his throat, "Our frigate *HMS Vixen* is nearest to the *Star*. She's about 250 nautical miles to the northeast. At 32 knots flat-out, she could intercept the *Star* in approximately 8 hours."

"Anything closer?" said Hays.

"We can send one of our Orion P-3 reconnaissance aircraft out of Gibraltar, but it can't do much except shadow the *Star* for a while until a more substantial unit gets involved. Besides, that would be getting pretty close to its range limit at this point."

"You've been in touch with the US navy, I believe?" said Hays.

"Not yet," said Archibald. "The chap who contacted us is a certain John Kiefer of the USCG, who is coordinating temporarily. I've placed a call to Admiral West of the US Navy. We're expecting a call back from him at any moment. He may have a ship closer to the *Star*."

Hands clasped in front of him on the table, Hays shifted his attention to the video monitor. "Adrian, is there any way of communicating with someone on the Star?"

"Since the ship's communication systems are shut down and she is well out of cell phone range, our only chance is that an officer—"

"We checked all the officers' satellite phones and no one is responding," interrupted Winston.

"Thank you, Mr. Winston," said Bolding, shooting a reproachful look at his overly eager young officer. "If I may finish."

"Sorry sir."

"I was saying that our only chance is that either a member of the crew or a passenger has a satellite phone in an unobstructed transmission and reception area," said Bolding. "Our people are cross-checking the passenger and crew manifest with the satellite phone companies' registries to see if we can get a match with one of them."

Elbows on the armrests of his chair, Bolding shifted slightly in his seat before resuming. "There is something everyone should be aware of. According to her current heading, the *Star* is headed straight for Torrais Reef off the island of Corvo. Unless she alters course, she will hit it in less than four hours."

CHAPTER 14

Aboard the Caravan Star, 7.55 a.m. Ship's time

"You had me worried," said Karen as Dulac rushed in, gasping for air, his brow covered in sweat.

"This only works with a clear view of the sky," said Dulac, showing them the black Motorola sat phone.

"Back on deck?" said Hank.

"We can try," said Dulac, "but reception will be better off the open platform at the stern."

Dulac opened the door cautiously and looked right, then left. No one.

They started down the richly carpeted corridor that ended in front of a pair of French doors. Dulac peered through. Inside, the dining room was empty, its indirect wall lights illuminating the mahogany-paneled walls with a soft, bluish glow. To the left, a marble-topped buffet bar in the shape of an "S" spanned the entire length of the room. To the right, the tables had been readied for what seemed like a breakfast setting.

"Must be one of the five smaller dining areas mentioned in the brochure," said Dulac to Karen and Hank. "Let's take a look."

They entered and were halfway through the room when a rotund man dressed in chef's whites came out of the swinging kitchen doors. "Sorry, we are closed until 8 a.m. The fire drill." The man waived his hands dismissively, turned and started to walk balk towards the kitchen.

"Hey!" Dulac shouted.

The man spun, startled. "Sir, we are closed. I cannot—"

Dulac moved in closer, towering over the short chef. "Listen to me. I'm an Interpol agent. The fire drill is fake. Hijackers have taken over this ship. Do you understand? Pirates. Hijackers."

The chef looked at Dulac in wide-eyed disbelief, then at Karen and Hank, who nodded in approval.

"Do you have a computer?" said Dulac.

"*Si*, but why—?"

"Where is it?" said Dulac, losing patience.

"I show you. Please follow." The chef led Dulac and the others into the kitchen, through its narrow passages lined with vast arrays of stainless-steel pots and pans, past three cooks whipping eggs in large saucepans. "Over here," said the chef, pointing to a computer on a small table.

"Try your internet connection," said Dulac.

The chef sat down and typed in his password.

Dulac, Karen and Hank gathered around and read over the man's shoulder. *Connection failed, try again later.*

The chef tried again. To no avail.

"They've closed down the router," said Dulac. "No one can call in or out."

"*Dios Mio!*"

"Where are the other cooks?" Dulac looked about at the near-empty kitchen.

"They went to the fire drill." The chef pointed to his helpers. "We stay behind for my egg soufflé. I—"

"Are there weapons aboard?"

"What do you mean?"

"Guns, pistols?" Dulac made a sign with his forefinger and thumb.

"No, No. Ees not allowed. We—"

"—have a gun-free policy," said Dulac. "What about flares? Surely you must have flares?"

"I no understand." Hunching his shoulders in ignorance, the chef looked at Hank, then Karen for help.

"*Fusas*?" Karen said. "No. *Bengas*?" Karen made a gesture of an explosion with her hands.

"*Si. Bengalas. Bengalas de securo.*"

"Where are they?" said Dulac.

"I have seen a box in the front, on the deck," said the chef. "Only officers can open them." He made a gesture simulating the turning of a key.

"Great," said Dulac. "Do you have something to break it open? A crowbar?"

The chef shrugged again.

"A, a *pala*?" said Karen.

"A *palanca*? No, we do not have."

"What about an axe? In case of fire?" said Dulac.

"*Si*, we have. Over there in the corner." The chef smiled in satisfaction and pointed to the glass-paneled box containing a fire hose and a small hatchet. "We have beeg ones on deck."

Dulac went over to the box, opened it and grabbed the hatchet. "This'll do," he said.

* * *

The Caravan Star's Luxor amphitheater

Dressed in officers' whites and standing in front of the amphitheater's doors, Omar and Saquil had just finished ticking off the names of the passengers and crew from their manifest lists. Feeling constricted in his too-tight uniform, Omar adjusted the belt of his trousers. As the crowd funneled through the entrance and into the amphitheater, he instructed the passengers and crew to seat themselves amidst the rows of comfortable, padded seats. "To the front. Lots of empty seats there."

As the last passengers made their way through, Saquil glanced at Omar's manifest sheet. "Any missing?"

"Seven on deck five, including four from the kitchen."

Saquil threw a concerned look at Omar. "You'd better round them up before—"

"We'll see what Tariq has to say."

"Really? I wouldn't wait around to find out if I were you." Saquil drew in a deep breath. He better than anyone knew how irascible and unpredictable Tariq could get if everything didn't go exactly according to plan.

"What about the others?" Said Omar.

"All passengers are accounted for except yours. Nebil and the others are already in the amphitheater."

Omar hesitated for a moment, then said, "Guess you're right. I'll see what's happening in the kitchen."

At that moment, a passenger in a gray sweat suit, his stomach bulging over the drawstring of his pants, stopped before them. "When do we get breakfast?"

Saquil looked at his watch. "This should not take long. I'd say in about twenty minutes."

The fat man, seemingly reassured, proceeded inside the amphitheater.

Omar handed the manifest sheet to Saquil, turned and started down the corridor leading to the deck. Saquil turned back towards the front of the amphitheater just as a man in officer's whites appeared on the stage, a hailer in hand. Hassan. *He's always on time.* Hassan brought the hailer to his mouth and waived his right hand in the air to get everyone's attention. "Please be seated and make yourselves comfortable. The captain will be here shortly."

As the last of the passengers and crew made their way through into the theater, Saquil entered and closed the doors. Then, his back to the doors, he discreetly locked them.

Saquil looked around. Except for Omar, the other hijackers were at their posts, standing in front of three of the four emergency exits. He walked a few steps and sat down in the aisle seat of the center section's last row. He glanced slowly left, then right. No one else was seated in the row. Saquil took the Glock from his VHF holster, cocked it and rested it on his lap.

CHAPTER 15

"What was that all about?" said Bob Lombardi to his wife Nancy, as she hung up the phone, got out of bed and put on her beige silk nightgown.

"That was Jenkins. He says a cruise ship has been hijacked somewhere in the middle of the Atlantic. Gov. Dickinson and Senator Easton and their wives are among the passengers."

"Wow!"

At that moment, their teenage son Matthew walked drowsily into the bedroom.

"What's all the noise about?" he said, rubbing his eyes.

"Just another run-of-the-mill national emergency," said Nancy. "Matthew, go back to bed."

"So you're not going to tell me what it is?"

"No, I'm not. Now go back to bed. You have a physics exam in the morning, don't you?"

"Yeah, yeah, yeah. Everybody ignores me in this house." Rubbing his eyes, he turned and shuffled slowly out of the bedroom.

Lombardi put on her slippers, went down to her mahogany-paneled office on the main floor, closed the door and sat down at her large desk. She turned on the light, picked up the phone and dialed the President's triple firewall protected encrypted number, to be used only in extreme emergency. After three rings, the familiar voice came on the line.

"Mr. President, Nancy Lombardi. Sorry to bother you at this hour but . . ."

* * *

The President began issuing orders the second Secretary Lombardi finished her briefing.

". . . And get West and Peters on board and tell them I said you'll take the lead. Keep me posted."

"Yes Mr. President," said Lombardi.

She hung up and phoned CIA Director Don Peters, Admiral Doug West, and her secretary Melissa Downs, instructing them to meet her at her office at Department of Homeland Security headquarters. Next, she called her chauffeur Bill Evans to bring the Navigator out front. Lombardi went back upstairs, changed into her two-piece blue suit, kissed her husband on the cheek, then went downstairs and out the front door. The Navigator was there, wisps of white fumes emanating from its exhaust.

Ten minutes later, Nancy Lombardi stepped out, looked into the automated iris recognition system at DHSHQ, and walked through the two sets of glass doors into the large circular hallway.

"Morning Keith," she said to the older, familiar night guard on duty.

"Morning Ms. Lombardi. A bit early today?" He said with a broad smile.

"That it is. Is Melissa in yet?"

"Yes ma'am. She arrived five minutes ago."

Lombardi walked past the security station to the elevators and pressed the up button. Moments later she made her way through the open office room of the fifth floor, past the empty cubicles to her corner office. Lombardi had convinced the President that she was in the best position to coordinate parameters and information between Homeland Security, the Navy and the CIA and she was lead of the *Caravan Star* case, at least for the present. She knew she had to establish her authority quickly, and the first opportunity presented itself now through protocol.

From the window of her office in the old naval compound taken over by DHS, she saw the lights of the navy-flagged limousine as it approached the security post, the sole entrance through the barbed wire and walled perimeter surrounding the complex. Lombardi smiled. Ten minutes later, her inter-office phone rang. "Yes Melissa."

"Admirals West, Turner and Mr. Peters have arrived. I've shown them to the conference room. Coffee is brewing. I've also ordered rolls and muffins."

"Great."

Lombardi got up, walked by the black-and-tan Western saddle mounted on a wooden buck given to her by George W. Bush, through the corridor to the conference room and entered.

The three men stood up in unison.

"Gentlemen. Sorry to get you up so early but the situation is critical."

"Evening Nancy, or should I say good morning," said CIA Director Don Peters, a tall, lean man in his mid-fifties, perfectly at ease in his impeccably cut single-breasted dark gray suit.

To Peters' left stood Admiral Douglas West, Chief of Naval Operations, a four-star admiral in his early sixties in his blue blazer Service Dress uniform. Lombardi couldn't help thinking the man's curved, hawkish nose, jutting chin and incisive, intelligent eyes befitted perfectly the head of the world's most powerful navy. Next to West stood Admiral Paul Turner, his face screwed up in a permanent scowl, head of Atlantic Region Fleet Forces Command.

"Grab yourself some coffee, gentlemen. I have a feeling it's going to be a long day." Lombardi's secretary walked in with a tray and deposited it on the small buffet along the wall. Lombardi took a mug of coffee, black, then sat down at the head of the oval walnut table, the distinctive crest of the Department of Homeland Security boldly inlaid in gold letters in its center.

"So everyone knows where I'm coming from," she said, "I just got off the phone with the President. He's asked me to give protection to the families of the American passengers, as we can't rule out a homeland attack on those folks. I've instructed my people to implement that order immediately. In parallel, the President wants us to, and I quote, 'Use all necessary means and forces to resolve this situation discreetly and quickly'."

Lombardi paused and looked at Peters, then West. "Gentlemen, I don't have to remind you that since we have American lives at risk in international waters, we have complete and unequivocal jurisdiction." She took a sip of her coffee. "Before we discuss options, I've asked Coast Guard Operation Command John Kiefer to join in by video conference." She pressed the monitor button and the screen on the wall facing her flickered to life.

"Good morning, John," said Lombardi.

"'Morning Nancy, gentlemen," said Kiefer.

"John, give us an update, will you? Where do things stand?" said Lombardi.

"Sure. Hang on a minute. I'll try to link my computer to your screen." Kiefer opened his computer, clicked on some keys and a few seconds later, the map of the North Atlantic showed up on the far wall across the conference room.

"Can you see the map?" said Kiefer.

"Perfectly," said Lombardi.

"I'll focus in on the ship's location."

Kiefer zoomed in and pointed with the cursor to a spot on the ocean. "The *Caravan Star* is approximately here," he said, "about ninety nautical miles southeast of the Azores, traveling at 24 knots, direction north by northwest 335 degrees. We've tried repeatedly to reach her and since she's not responding, we have to assume she's under the hijackers' control. We have no idea who they are or what they want."

"So we can't rule out a suicide mission," said Lombardi. She turned and eyed Peters. "Don, have you had time to gather any intel on this?"

Shoulders hunched, Peters leaned forward, resting his elbows on the table's edge. "Not much, but after I got your call, we did some research on files we have on the International Maritime Organization. According to what we could dig up on such short notice, apparently many cruise ship operators, including P & W Cruise Lines, have been caught out by the IMO doing insufficient background checks on their lower-end personnel. With the recession affecting the industry and reduced passenger flow-through, virtually all cruise ship operators have been under pressure to keep costs down in order to lower prices. Some of them have chosen to cut corners at the lower end. So this could mean these hijackers were on board from the beginning, before the ship left Southampton, disguised as maintenance personnel, dishwashers, whatever. They may also have come on board at Gibraltar when the ship called port there yesterday."

"Anything more specific?" said Lombardi, reclining slightly in her swivel chair.

"Not yet, but if they have weapons, and we have every indication they do since they control the ship, they must have had inside help to get those weapons past the safety checks and scanners of the *Caravan Star*," said Peters. "We'll be coordinating with the Yard in London to find out exactly who's on that ship, and how and when they got on. That's going to take time."

Admiral West turned to Admiral Turner. "In the meantime, Paul, what have you got within range of the *Star*?"

"I'll need the video screen," said Turner.

"Yes of course," said Lombardi. She glanced at the monitor. "John, if there is nothing else at your end, we'll have Admirals West and Turner take over from here. They can fill you in later."

"Not for the moment, Nancy," said Kiefer.

Seconds later the screen went blank.

Admiral Paul Turner opened up his laptop, pressed a button and the video screen came to life again. Turner scrolled down and a map of the Atlantic filled the screen. "The *Caravan Star* is approximately here," he said, pointing with his right hand to the small red icon. The British have a couple of ships that are at least 9 hours away, one here and the other over there." He pointed to two yellow icons. "Our missile cruiser *USS Anzio* is approximately here." He pointed to the green icon. "She's on her way to Toulon for NATO exercises with the French. We can divert her and providing the weather holds, she can intercept the *Star* in about three and a half hours. But we don't have a lot of leeway."

Lombardi eyed Turner. "Meaning?"

"Meaning that if the weather worsens, or if the *Star* increases her speed, the Anzio won't be able to make the intercept before she reaches Torrais Reef."

"Thinking positively and assuming the *Anzio* makes it in time, what then?" said Lombardi.

"We have a couple of options," said Turner. "We can have the *Anzio* drag one of her Kevlar towing cables in front of the *Star* in an attempt to snag her propellers. The timing has to be perfect, otherwise the cable sinks ineffectively. We also risk a collision when the *Anzio* crosses the *Star's* bow. We need a speed differential of 10 knots or more between the—"

"The other option?" interrupted Nancy.

"With the *Anzio's* power, we can bring her alongside the Star and literally shove the *Star* off course. We've done it before off the coast of Somalia."

"With a ship the size of the *Star*?" said Peters.

"As cruise ships go, the *Caravan Star* is on the small side at 720 feet long and 45,000 gross tons," said Turner. "A lightweight compared to the 200,000 GT behemoths of today. Besides, it really boils down to who has the greatest amount of horsepower. The *Anzio* has a bit of an edge over the *Star* on that score."

"A bit of an edge. If the weather holds. If the *Star* slows down. This sounds like far from a sure thing, Admiral. Anything else?" said Lombardi.

"Any other options are aggressive," said Turner.

"Such as?"

"Assuming the Anzio can reach the *Star* in time for an intercept, the *Anzio* carries some torpedoes that could be deactivated and aimed at the *Star's* stern, onto her propellers," said Turner. "With the deactivation, there would be no risk of breaching her hull."

"What kind of accuracy are we talking about?" said Lombardi.

"Depending how close the *Anzio* can get, I'd say at best about 40%."

"Is that all?"

"Yes."

"So it's pretty much hit-or-miss," said Lombardi." And correct me if I'm wrong, but you have no way of predicting how any torpedo hit will affect the *Caravan Star's* course."

"You could say that," said Turner, his scowl replaced by a look of embarrassment.

Lombardi leaned forward and clasped her hands, resting he elbows on the table. "I don't like what I'm hearing, Admiral. Not one damn bit." She eyed West.

"Admiral, get the *Anzio* on the *Star's* tail. In the meantime, I want you to give me some more options before I phone the President."

"We're doing our best, Nancy," said West.

Lombardi felt a surge of blood to her temples. "Your best? Admiral, I want to present the President with a credible, achievable solution to get control of this situation. Not some seat-of-the-pants ideas that might or might not work. The President will ask me what we're doing to save those eighty Americans and other passengers and we'd better have something more solid than what I've heard so far."

"We'll see what we can do," said West.

"By the way," said Lombardi, "something has been nagging at me since we began this meeting. If these guys are terrorists on a suicide mission as might be the case, why wait till the ship hits the reef? Why not just blow her up right now?"

Turner's scowl had returned. He pushed back his glasses further up the bridge of his nose. "It's not that easy, Nancy. Like most modern cruise ships, the *Caravan Star* has a double bottom and watertight compartments. The hijackers would have to have detailed knowledge of her construction and place bombs at strategic locations to sink her. Even then, it's far from a sure thing. On the other hand, if they run her aground on a reef, the reef will act like a giant can-opener and the ship will sink quickly. We all saw that with the sinking of the *Costa Concordia*. The hijackers know that too."

There was a moment of uneasy silence as everyone absorbed Turner's words.

"Anything else?" said Lombardi.

No one spoke.

Lombardi pushed back from the table and got up, then looked at her watch. "That'll be all, gentlemen. We reconvene here in an hour."

CHAPTER 16

Aboard the Caravan Star, 8.18 a.m. Ship's time

"So what's your plan?" Karen asked Dulac.

"They're going to check the manifests and realize some passengers are missing, namely us." Dulac eyed the chef and his assistant. "You—"

"My name is Alfonso. And he is Stephano, he is Peter, and that's Samir." He pointed to his assistants. "We come with you." Alfonso looked anxiously at Dulac.

"Not a good idea, Alfonso," said Dulac. "We'd just make a bigger target. Don't worry, they won't harm you since they have to eat eventually. You'd best stay here and play dumb, make as if you don't know. We're going to the stern to try to contact P & W. If we're lucky we'll get a hold of some flare guns on the way. Once we've contacted them, we'll come back and check things here." Dulac eyed Karen and Hank. "Any suggestions?"

They looked at each other and shook their heads in silence.

"Let's go." Dulac started across the kitchen towards the entrance of the dining room, hatchet in hand.

He stopped before the doors and peered through the window into the dining room. *"Merde!"* He put out his left hand in a gesture to stay back.

"What?" said Karen.

"One of them is coming this way," whispered Dulac. "He's sweeping the dining room with his gun to see if anyone is hiding there. They're onto us."

Dulac felt Karen's heavy breathing over his right shoulder. He moved slightly away from the door, and a dose of adrenaline shot up his back into the nape of his neck. His stomach muscles contracted, and the pounding of his heart resonated in his chest. Dulac tensed his grip on the hatchet's handle and raised it above his head.

"Jesus, you're not going to . . ."

Suddenly the door swung open and the man entered, his arms outstretched, both hands gripping his pistol. He started to turn. Dulac swung, catching the hijacker's skull dead center with the blunt end of the hatchet's head. The man looked at Dulac, eyes rolled back, his knees buckled and he crumpled to the floor.

Karen brought her hand to her mouth. "You've . . ."

Dulac knelt down and felt the man's pulse. "Just a concussion." He signaled to the cooks. "Tie him up and gag him. Can you hide him somewhere?"

"Si, si," said Alfonso. "We have a dry storage room."

"No good. Anywhere else?"

Alfonso looked at his assistant and hunched his shoulders.

"What about garbage bins?"

"Si, si. We have beeg ones," said Alfonso. "We put waste bags over him."

"Perfect," Dulac knelt down, removed the Glock from the hijacker's hand, felt his pockets, and pulled out four spare bullet clips. Dulac straightened his lanky frame and smiled at Karen. "Our odds just got a whole lot better."

* * *

72

The passengers' growing impatience was palpable as they waited for someone to appear on the stage of the amphitheater.

"What is taking them so long?" Dickinson's wife fidgeted with the hem of her sweater.

"I have no idea, dear." Dickinson looked around and behind him, searching for the safety officers who had somehow disappeared. "What do you think, Durward?"

"I'm getting fed up with this. I'll give them five more minutes, then we're leaving."

"This is unacceptable. We should go now." Dickinson signaled to the bodyguard on his left. "Tom, let's go."

"Yes sir."

Getting up was as far as they made it. Machine gun fire erupted from the stage and a shower of broken glass fell from the ceiling. The bodyguard shoved Dickinson back down in the seat and fell on top of him. Dickinson's peripheral vision showed him two men on the stage, firing at the chandeliers overhead.

Cries of panic filled the room, and the hijackers kept firing wildly at the ceiling, taking out all lighting except for the emergency exit lights and the indirect lights on the amphitheater's walls and leaving the room in murky darkness. The muted moans and cries of terrified women and children replaced the sound of gunfire. One of the hijackers raised a portable loudhailer to his mouth. "We control the ship. Do not leave your seats or you will be shot." The matter-of-fact tone of his voice was more convincing than any angry shout could ever be.

Dickinson hugged Mary closer to him and whispered. "Are you all right?"

"What's happening?" She crouched under the bodyguard's outstretched arms.

"Pirates. They've taken over the ship." He looked at Easton, huddling over his own wife, his back covered with glass. "Are you okay?"

"I . . . I think so."

Dickinson's bodyguard shifted his position slightly and Dickinson could tell he was trying to do some recon. Dickinson tried to do the same. Men and women cowered in their seats, their faces frozen masks of raw fear.

"Don't move and you won't get hurt." The man spoke in the same chilling matter-of-fact tone.

Dickinson shot another side glance at Easton, who was trying to console his crying wife Sandra. He turned back towards Mary.

"We'll never see the children again, will we George?" she said between sobs.

CHAPTER 17

On the bridge, 8.46 a.m. Ship's time

Rhodes stood at the console next to Tariq and looked over his shoulder for a moment at the other officers sitting on the floor, their expressions dulled with resignation. The squat man sat on a small chair, his Uzi across his lap, watching the officers with an air of contempt. The ship lurched slightly and brought Rhodes's attention back to the bow, just as a plume of spray broke over the Star's portside onto the deck. He looked up at the anemometer, South by Southwest, 54 knots. At that wind speed and angle, the Star was no longer impervious to the momentum of the building waves, and even with her four Vosper stabilizers, she was beginning to roll slightly.

Rhodes' anxiety burgeoned. Hugely top-heavy and essentially unseaworthy, cruise ships were not designed to face storms. At best, they had to avoid them. At worst, they had to outrun them. The *Caravan Star* was doing neither.

"You have been to the Azores, Rhodes?" Tariq's thin lips twisted his mouth into the form of a small, inverted crescent.

"A few times." Rhodes wasn't sure of the wisdom of talking beyond the strict minimum.

"I hear it is very windy there."

"Yes, quite windy."

"More than here, now?"

Rhodes looked to his right at the weather fax machine, the most recent weather map hanging from its slot. Those tight, stacked-together isobars around the Azores meant even stronger winds. "Today, yes." Rhodes hesitated, then continued, "Perhaps we should consider—"

"Good. That's very good." Tariq stared ahead, his air of quiet determination effectively answering Rhodes' query. "How much time till we get there?"

Rhodes looked at the chart plotter, moved the cursor to the Azores and pressed the ETA button. "In about three hours."

"Excellent."

Both men continued looking ahead as the weather worsened and the waves increased in size. The silence grew more and more uncomfortable as time went by. Finally Tariq spoke. "So, Rhodes, you have children, yes?"

"Two daughters."

"You are a lucky man."

"I believe so."

"I also had two girls. Once."

Tariq kept looking ahead, his expression now slightly pensive. Rhodes felt suddenly uncomfortable, not knowing if he should probe.

"Azalea and Hansa. They were killed in a raid against my villa by Pakistani government troops. Also my wife Zora."

"I, I'm sorry—"

"Don't be. In Baluchistan, death is a part of everyday life. It is all around us. We get accustomed to it."

Tariq's upper lip trembled slightly. For an instant his fine features softened, and Rhodes thought he saw an ounce of compassion in the man. "But they were so young, so beautiful, so full of energy . . . Anyway, it is not your concern." Tariq's face became hard again. He moved to Rhodes' left, picked up the manifest from atop the console and started to go through it. Suddenly he smiled, then emitted a loud whistle. "Interesting. Do you know the name George E. Dickinson?"

"Not particularly." Rhodes felt the blood rush to the tip of his ears.

Tariq aimed his pistol at Rhodes's head. "You are sure?"

"I . . . I think there may be some American politician—"

"Correct, Rhodes. An important American politician. He is a Republican candidate for the presidency, no?"

"Possibly, yes."

"Very, very interesting." Tariq broke out into a nervous, syncopated laughter. He turned and eyed the other hijacker. "Get up." The man sprang up from his chair. "Tie him," he said, looking at Rhodes. "I'm going to the amphitheater."

* * *

The bridge's glass doors opened. Tariq walked to the elevators and pressed the down button with the muzzle of his gun. While he waited, he suddenly felt a surge of elation invade his whole being. *I've done it. I control the whole ship. It was so easy. And now I have a bonus. Allah is with us, as this is His sign. Allah be praised.* He knelt, kissed the ground, and got up just as the overhead light signaled the arrival of the elevator.

He entered and an incomprehensible voice, masked in static, called on his VHF radio. "Repeat. I didn't get that. Repeat."

"Bridge, this is Luxor 2. Do you copy, over?"

"That's better. Go ahead."

"Omar went to find some missing passengers and kitchen staff. He hasn't returned. It's been over 20 minutes. He's not answering his VHF."

Tariq felt the blood vessels in his forehead fill up. "*Khara!* Did you send someone after him?"

"No. We didn't want to lose control of the—"

"I'm on my way."

CHAPTER 18

P & W Cruise Lines Headquarters, Southampton

In the company's main conference room on the third floor, 54 P & W employees stood shoulder to shoulder, making small talk and wondering exactly why they'd been summoned to an emergency meeting by the president's secretary. Rumors were already circulating that one of the company's ships was in trouble in the Atlantic.

At 10.15 a.m., Bolding walked in and stood at the head of the conference table, his curling gray hair slightly ruffled and a look of disquiet replacing his usual air of self-confidence. The room fell silent.

"Ladies and gentlemen, I'm sure some of you have heard that we have a situation with one of our ships. To make matters perfectly clear, I'd like to share with you as much information as I can, in order to dispel any false information or rumors." Bolding paused, looked about the room and continued. "Right now, as I'm sure some of you have noticed, the *Caravan Star* has altered course and is heading in the direction of the Azores. She was not scheduled to go there on this trip. To make matters worse, we've lost all communications with her, and she's not responding to her

Inmarsat or High Frequency radios. She has also issued a SASS."

Bolding paused again, taking time to scan the audience briefly. He took in a deep breath and continued. "So we are forced to conclude that barring a major breakdown, this unfortunately means she's been taken over by hijackers."

A murmur of shock and disbelief ran through the room.

Bolding continued, "So far, this is all we know. Now I ask all of you, that for the safety of all concerned including the passengers and crew, this information remain strictly contained within these walls and be kept absolutely confidential. It is of vital importance that no false rumors start circulating. We will keep you informed of any new developments. In the meantime, please go about your duties in a normal fashion. Any questions?"

A woman with wire-rimmed glasses and curly brown hair raised her hand.

"Yes Victoria," said Bolding.

"Mr. Bolding, do we have any idea who these people might be?"

"I'm afraid not."

Another hand shot up.

"Yes Robert," said Bolding.

"Sir, could she simply have a mechanical problem?"

"I'd like to think that, but as I said, the accumulation of coincidences makes it highly unlikely."

Another hand shot up.

"Yes Peter," said Bolding.

"So what is P & W doing about the situation?"

Some of his fellow co-workers turned and looked askance at Peter Winthrop, the Eastern Europe sales rep.

Bolding saw their look of reproach, but the last thing needed at the moment was ill-feeling among the employees. "Perfectly fair question, Peter. All I can say is that we've alerted the proper authorities including Home Office and the Navy. We will be looking at every option to keep the passengers and crew safe."

Bolding's secretary appeared in the doorway, signaling for Bolding to come over.

"Excuse me for a moment." Bolding walked across the room and joined his secretary.

"Sir," she whispered, "the receptionist says she's on the line with someone from the *Caravan Star*. Apparently, it's one of the passengers."

Bolding turned back to the room and dismissed the employees. "That will be all for now." Then, accompanied by his secretary, he exited the hallway and rushed up the stairs to the fifth floor and over to the receptionist's desk. Three other employees were huddled around and backed away as Bolding approached her desk. He grabbed a chair from an adjoining workstation and sat down in front of her. "Put him on speaker. And whatever you do, don't lose the call."

"Yes Mr. Bolding."

The receptionist flipped a switch and the speaker suddenly spewed out static and hissing white noise. Bolding leaned over, nearer the receptionist's microphone. "*Caravan Star*, this is Adrian Bolding. I'm chairman of P & W. Who is this?" Bolding scribbled a note, turned and handed it to his secretary, standing behind him. The only response was more static.

"Could you repeat that? I didn't get that. Please repeat."

"I'm Thierry Dulac." The voice sounded far away, as if drowned out by a strong wind. "I'm a passenger on the *Caravan Star*. She's been taken over by hijackers."

"Where are you on the ship? How many are there? What is the—"

"Whoa. Easy. I'm on deck with two passengers. The others have been corralled into the amphitheater. We managed to get away and we're calling you on my sat phone from the stern. It's very windy here."

"Mr. Dulac, any idea how many hijackers there are?"

"I'm guessing at least six. They're posing as security officers. We've just neutralized one of them in the kitchen. I don't have much time to talk. They're probably looking for us right now."

"Mr. Dulac, I've placed a call with Arnold Archibald from the British Navy to join us. You said you neutralized one of the terrorists. Are you armed?"

"We are now. With one of their Glocks and four clips of ammo."

"Have you people handled guns before, Mr. Dulac?"

"Henry Porter was with the 82nd Airborne. I am an Interpol agent with weapons training."

"Very good. Excellent, I—"

There was a clicking sound on the phone.

"Bolding, this is Archibald."

"Yes Admiral. We have a Mr. Dulac from the *Caravan Star* on the line. For your information, Mr. Dulac, the *Star* is headed for a reef off the Azores. If she doesn't alter course, she'll hit it in less than three hours. We've had no contact from these people. I'm afraid it's beginning to look like a suicide mission."

"Great. Just pissing great."

Bolding covered the phone with his hand and signaled his secretary to come closer. "Have Winston get in touch with Watters and inform him of the situation. Get them on the line."

"Yes Mr. Bolding."

Bolding returned to the conversation between Archibald and Dulac.

"Where are you aboard the ship?" said Archibald.

"We're at the stern."

"Any sign of the hijackers?"

"None. That is, apart from the one we . . . ah, neutralized."

"I see. Mr. Dulac, for your information we've been in —"

"You're fading. I didn't get that. Could you repeat that, Admiral?" said Dulac.

"I'm saying we are in touch with the American Navy and the missile cruiser *USS Anzio* is on its way," said Archibald. "Help is coming, but unless the *Star* slows to 17 knots, the *Anzio* won't reach her before she hits the reef. We must find some way, or someone to slow her down."

"I didn't get that last bit. Please repeat."

"I said we must slow down the *Star*," said Archibald.

"OK. How will you do that?"

"Sir Adrian?" said Archibald.

"Mr. Dulac, I've just had David Winston place a call to our Chief Engineer Egan Watters. We must assume that the bridge is heavily guarded, so that option is out," said Bolding. There was a clicking sound. "Mr. Winston, are you on the line?"

"Yes. Mr. Dulac, this is David Winston. I have our Chief Engineer Egan Watters on the line. I have already briefed him about the need to slow down the *Star*."

"Hello, Watters here." Watters' voice was high-pitched, almost childlike.

"Mr. Watters, Adrian Bolding. We have one of the passengers of the *Caravan Star* on the line. A Mr. Dulac. He needs to know how to slow down the —"

"Wait a second," interrupted Dulac. "Are you saying you want *me* to slow this ship down?"

"We don't have anybody else but you and Mr. Porter, Mr. Dulac."

"Jesus." Dulac turned to Karen and Hank. "They want us to slow down the ship." They looked at each other in silent disbelief, the groaning of the wind howling over the superstructure adding to the drama of their predicament.

Watters' high-pitched voice interrupted the low frequency static over the sat phone. "Mr. Dulac, is it?"

"I'm having trouble hearing you. Say again." Dulac turned slightly to shield the phone from the wind and moved towards the ship's railing.

"Can you hear me now?"

"Yes, that's better."

"Watters here. Are you familiar with how a ship is powered?"

"Vaguely. I think it's like trains. Diesel motors supply the power to electric generators, which in turn drive the propeller shafts. Hang on a second, Porter needs to hear this." He waved Hank over to join him and listen in.

"Very good," continued Watters. "In a nutshell, that's exactly how it works. It's done through a series of frequency converters and drives. In the case of the *Star*, there are two banks with two Wartsila diesel motors per bank, and each bank has its corresponding generator, which is controlled electronically by a cycloconverter which measures the amount of electricity needed by the electric motors of the Azipod system, and in turn—"

"Yes, yes, Mr. Watters, get to the point." Bolding interrupted impatiently. "How can Mr. Dulac and Mr. Porter slow down the ship?"

"I'm assuming the hijackers are guarding the engine room's computers," said Watters. "That's the brains of the system. But if they can find their way to the aft section of the engine room, below Deck 1, the cycloconverters are near the stern, away from and out of sight of the computer control center. If someone were to knock out the cycloconverter of one bank, that would disconnect the generator from the Azipod, then trip the shutoff valves of the corresponding two diesels, which will then stop."

"So the ship would be left with only one bank?" said Bolding.

"Correct. She will slow to about 14 knots."

"Assuming Mr. Dulac and Mr. Porter could find their way down to the engine room," said Bolding, "how would they recognize the cycloconverter?"

"It's a green box mounted on a metal frame, about shoulder height, next to the rear of the Wartsila aft diesel. You will see heavy-duty pipe housing for the electrical cables, leading to and from it. The box has a transparent plastic window cover," said Watters.

"Wait a minute, wait just a damn minute," said Dulac. "I didn't say I would do this. I—"

"Sorry, no you didn't Mr. Dulac," said Bolding. "But time is getting short and we really have no one else to turn to."

There was a long moment of uneasy silence. Dulac looked at Hank, who nodded in approval. Finally Dulac spoke.

"Well, I guess you're right."

"Fine," said Bolding. "Now Mr. Watters, how do we get them to the engine room? Presumably the hijackers have secured it."

"Apart from the two main entrances fore and aft, there are three escape ladders," said Watters. "One is near the bow on Deck Three. Its entrance on the deck is a hatch marked with a red X, stamped "authorized personnel only". One is amidships, near the entrance to the kitchen. At the stern, there is a ladder in a circular stairwell, next to the life jacket boxes in the pool area. Its entrance is also a hatch marked with a red X. Where are you now, Mr. Dulac?"

"Near the stern."

"Then use that ladder. It's also nearer the port motor bank," said Watters.

"And how do I disable this, this cyclo-whatever?" said Dulac.

"Cycloconverter. If you have time, open the plastic cover and remove some of the circuits."

"And if I don't?"

"Hit it. Hard."

CHAPTER 19

Aboard the USS "Anzio"

At 52 years of age and with 30 years of naval service under his belt, Captain Ed Donnelly had seen his fair share of action during years when the US Navy, although not officially engaged in major conflicts, had nevertheless been involved in various skirmishes in hotspots across the globe. After numerous escort missions in the Middle East as a lieutenant aboard the USS Stark, he'd seen combat in the Gulf War initially as first lieutenant, then as captain of the frigate USS Jensen. Using unusual and bold tactics during the battle of Bubiyan, he'd sunk three Iraqi patrol escorts and helped destroy what was left of the hapless Iraqi navy, all without a single casualty aboard his ship. Thus his obtaining command of the Ticonderoga-class missile cruiser USS Anzio five years earlier had been seen by his contemporaries as a natural progression in his illustrious career, and a just reward for his exceptional leadership skills and intuitive acumen in the heat of conflict.

In dissimilar yet high-stakes circumstances, some of Donnelly's qualities were about to be tested once again.

Donnelly had just finished briefing his officers on the *Anzio's* new mission. He dismissed them, left the officers' mess room and made his way to the port side ladder leading up to the bridge. As he climbed up the steep ladder, he grabbed the steel railing now and then, helping himself upwards and steadying himself as the ship swung onto its new course. Slowly, the *Anzio's* side-to-side rolling subsided and was replaced by a pitching motion. Taking a breather on one of the inter-deck platforms, he looked out one of the portholes and saw the bow cleaving the waves effortlessly, sending plumes of water over the ship's flared topsides. He reached the top onto the small metal landing and paused, catching his breath. His 220 pounds over an only 5' 8" frame were starting to take their toll, confirmed by counts of high blood pressure and bad cholesterol. He tucked in his shirt, opened the door and entered. On the bridge the crew were busy at their various tasks. The helmsman, his eyes glued to the oncoming waves, was making small corrections to the helm in an attempt to reduce the pitching motion of the ship. The navigator, a tall, bald African American, was plotting waypoints on the chart plotter. The three watch officers were scanning their respective watch horizons with their 7X50 Marine Special Issue Steiner binoculars. They all turned, stood at attention and saluted Donnelly.

"At ease, gentlemen," he said, and they resumed their tasks. He went to the port side of the bridge and looked aft. The Anzio's propellers were churning a 50-foot-wide undulating snake of bubbling froth, its twin 90,000 HP GE LM 2500 Gas turbine engines pushing her effortlessly at 29 knots. He turned towards the portside watch officer.

"Mind if I borrow these?" asked Donnelly, eyeing the officer's binoculars.

"Yes sir, I mean no sir." The young blond-haired man handed his binoculars to Donnelly. He brought them to his eyes and looked off the bow. The driving rain and low clouds were making the horizon almost impossible to detect amongst the oncoming waves. Donnelly knew that when they neared the Azores the waves, due to the ocean's shallow bottom, would become as powerful and tightly packed as a herd of charging elephants.

"Not good." Donnelly handed the binoculars back to the watch officer, turned and walked over towards the navigation station, where Ensign John Eaves was busy looking at the latest radar weather picture.

"What do you have, Eaves?" Donnelly's anxiety mounted when he saw the young ensign's preoccupied look.

"The depression is moving quickly across the Azores. These are the isobar charts of two hours ago." Eaves handed Donnelly two faxes. "And here's what we received 10 minutes ago."

"Christ!" Donnelly looked at the latest fax. "Those isobars are packed steeper than a cliff off Everest."

"There's a 20-point pressure drop from this one to—"

"I can read, Eaves."

"Sorry, sir."

Donnelly walked back to the helmsman. "Give her a couple more knots, to 31."

"Yes sir." The young helmsman nudged the throttle lever slightly forward.

Donnelly leaned into the radio operator's cubicle. "Get me Admiral West on the line, Ensign."

"Yes sir."

CHAPTER 20

Caravan Star's Deck Five

After the call with Bolding, Dulac, Karen and Hank conferred in a sheltered nook of the deck, trying to figure out
a place to hide.

"We've got to keep out of range of those cameras."
Dulac pointed to a camera on the top of the metal support
beam. "As far as I can make out, there's one at every fifth
column along the deck."

"Where are we going?" Karen asked.

Dulac pointed to the row of lifeboats, hanging on their
davits along the side deck. "You guys are going in one of
those. As good a place to hide as any. Besides, you'll have a
head start on everybody else if we hit that reef."

"Fantastic. Your confidence is just, well, contagious."

"What about you?" Hank looked at Dulac.

"I'm going below to the engine room. Here, take this."
He handed Hank the sat phone. "It's no use to me below
deck."

"I'm coming with you, Thierry," Karen said.

"Forget it. You'll only be in the way. Besides—"

"I can't just sit here and wait."

"I'm coming too. Besides, we'd be sitting ducks in one of those." Hank pointed to the lifeboats.

"Karen, I'm going to have a hard enough time avoiding those cameras alone. If—"

"We're coming."

* * *

Luxor amphitheater

Except for an occasional subdued exchange between passengers, the amphitheater was relatively quiet. People were trying to comfort each other, trying to guess what the hijackers would do next. Dickinson, for want of anything else to do, had meticulously begun to remove all bits of glass from his clothes and seat.

Easton, holding his wife Sandra's both hands in his, leaned over and whispered to Dickinson. "They can't keep us here forever."

"These scumbags want money," said Dickinson from the corner of his mouth. "They're probably negotiating with the cruise line right now. P & W has got to have insurance for this kind of situation. They'll have to pay."

"I hope you're right, George." Easton looked a bit doubtful. "In the meantime, there's not much we can do except wait and see."

"In these situations, it's best to try and stay unnoticed, or so I've been told," said Dickinson.

"Yeah, sort of stay under their radar."

Saquil stood motionless on the stage with his loudspeaker slung over his shoulder. Hassan, his Uzi at the ready, paced nervously back and forth on the stage, sometimes crossing in front of Saquil, sometimes behind him.

Suddenly Tariq burst onto the stage, pistol in hand, and, limping slightly, rushed up to Hassan. "Where is Omar?" said Tariq, his face inches from Hassan's.

"He . . . He still doesn't answer. I tried just—"

"Where was he going?" said Tariq.

"To Deck Five, I think," said Hassan.

Tariq handed Hassan the Glock and grabbed his Uzi. "Here, take this. Start on Deck Five and work your way up to the bridge. Find him."

"Yes Tariq." Hassan hurried off the stage and disappeared.

Tariq slung the Uzi over his shoulder and turned to Saquil.

"Give me that hailer." Tariq grabbed the loudspeaker from a bewildered Saquil. Tariq turned, walked to the front of the stage brought the hailer to his mouth.

"Listen to me. Listen carefully. I want Governor George Dickinson, Senator Durward Easton and their wives up here now."

"Stay low." Dickinson whispered to Mary from the side of his mouth. "They don't know who we are."

Tariq looked left and right, then up and down the rows of hostages from front to rear. Nobody moved.

"No? Oh, I see. I'm *sooo* sorry. My fault. I guess I didn't make myself clear." He slammed the loudspeaker down onto the stage, and in a quick, fluid motion unslung the Uzi from his shoulder and squeezed a spurt of automatic gunfire just above the heads of the hostages.

Muted cries of terror sprang from the amphitheater below.

Tariq grabbed the hailer. "Last chance," he yelled. "Next time I shoot low."

"Damn." Dickinson turned and shot a side glance at Easton. "Durward, unless we go up there, this maniac is going to slaughter a whole bunch of people, and we're just as likely as not to be in that bunch."

Dickinson, his bodyguard, Easton and their wives rose slowly from their seats in the middle section of the theater and made their way towards the aisle.

"Ah, that's better." Nothing like a bit of friendly persuasion to get things going." Tariq put down the hailer and broke into syncopated bursts of laughter.

Dickinson's bodyguard in the lead, they walked up the stairs onto the stage, where Saquil led Dickinson to the center. Once there, the bodyguard stood between Dickinson and Saquil.

Tariq took two steps towards the bodyguard, cocked his Uzi and pointed at the man's head. "Off the stage. You have three seconds."

The bodyguard backed away, his face contorted by anger and frustration. He turned slowly and walked down the steps off the stage.

"The rest of you, over here." With his Uzi, Tariq waved the others over to stand next to Dickinson.

"That's better. Much better." Tariq brought the lapel VHF close to his mouth. "Bridge, this is Tariq. Everything okay?"

"Everything is under control."

"Get me the ship's radio operator on the VHF."

"Yes Tariq."

Moments later, Tariq heard a voice on his VHF: "Tate here."

"Tate. Yes, that was the name. Listen to me very carefully, Tate. First you are going to switch on the stage camera on the amphitheater and link it to the bridge Inmarsat image hook-up. Got that?"

"Yes sir. You want the stage to be visible on the bridge monitor."

"Correct. Then you are going to turn on the Inmarsat system, and contact P & W's offices in Southampton. Have them get Adrian Bolding on the other end for a videoconference hook-up. Is that clear?"

"Yes sir. Very clear."

"Call me on my VHF when you have him online."

"Yes sir."

Tariq turned to Dickinson, Easton and their wives and led them to a spot to the left of center stage, "Stand here. Then he eyed Saquil. "Get the board and easel."

"Yes Tariq." Saquil turned and started off the stage.

Tariq, his Uzi cradled in his left arm, reached into his pocket with his right hand and took out the bottle. With difficulty, he opened the lid and popped two pills into his left palm, grabbed them and downed them. Then he turned to Dickinson and broke into another burst of laughter. "So Governor, as you say in America, it's show time."

CHAPTER 21

Department of Homeland Security Headquarters

Admiral West sat next to Rear-Admiral Turner across from the head of the conference table. He looked at the clock on the opposing wall, then glanced at his watch as if to check its accuracy. "She's not going to like this," he said.

At that moment, Lombardi, her short build accentuated by her two-piece suit, walked briskly into the room and sat down at the head of the table.

"So gentlemen, what have you got?" She crossed her arms on her ample, low-slung bosom and reclined in her swivel chair.

West cleared his throat. "Well Nancy, first the bad news. The weather has deteriorated around the Azores and with the *Star's* current speed, it's going to be difficult for the *Anzio* to get there in time."

"Difficult, or impossible? Call it straight, Admiral." Lombardi leaned forward against the table with her elbows, hands clasped.

West took in a deep breath. "I'll stick with difficult."

"And the good news?"

"We had a call from the British," said West. "They're in contact with someone, a passenger onboard the *Star*."

"So?"

"He's going to try to slow down the ship."

Lombardi reclined in her chair again, crossed her arms on her chest and looked askance at West. "Really? How the hell is he going to do that?"

West pursed his lips. "The plan is he'll break into the engine room and sabotage two of the four diesels."

There was a moment of silence. Lombardi uncrossed her arms, set her hands down flat on the table, and raised her head slightly. She shot West a doubtful glance.

"So you're telling me, Admiral, that your plan, the Navy's plan, is resting on one passenger? On his attempt to slow down the ship?"

"Well, yes, but not exactly—"

"Exactly what?"

"We were going to send a C-130 to drop some heavy-duty fishing nets in front of the *Star* but that option is out now."

"Why?"

"According to her position and the isobar chart, the *Star* must already be into some pretty heavy seas. We can't stop her altogether. If we do, she'll lose steerage and, well, these cruise ships aren't the most seaworthy of vessels."

"I'm reading between the lines, here, Admiral," said Lombardi. "Are you saying she could capsize?"

West eyed Turner. "It's happened before," Turner admitted.

Lombardi pushed herself away from the table, got up and started pacing slowly back and forth, her hands clasped behind her back. She shot an occasional glance at the seated officers.

"So here we are, with a bunch of hijackers whose demands we don't yet know, aiming a cruise ship onto a reef, and we don't dare stop the ship for fear she'll capsize." Lombardi stopped and banged her right fist on the conference table. "Any other good news, gentlemen?"

"I understand your frustration, Nancy," said West. "Believe me, we're doing everything we can. We contacted the Portuguese authorities in Lajes and they promised to send help if the *Caravan Star* should—"

Lombardi stopped and threw a baleful glare at West. "Whoa, just hold on. This is really not good, Admiral. Not good at all. Here we are, the biggest, most powerful navy in the world, and you're telling me we can only sit by the sidelines and hope that one lucky passenger stops a ship from running aground. I'm sure the President will be thrilled to hear this. In the meantime, gentlemen, I recommend that you come up with some other, more productive alternatives. We reconvene in an hour."

Lombardi turned and was halfway to the door when Turner started to speak. "Nancy, we have—"

West grabbed Turner's right forearm and squeezed it hard. "Not now," West whispered out of the side of his mouth.

Lombardi stopped in mid-stride and turned towards the seated admirals. "Yes?"

"Ah, we, we fully sympathize with you, Nancy," said Turner. "We'll keep you posted as the situation evolves."

CHAPTER 22

Caravan Star's Deck Three

The rain had gone from a drizzle to a downpour, and because of the wind's angle, Dulac, Karen and Porter were soaked to the bone. To make matters worse, the seas had become confused and jerky, escalating the ship's rolling motion. The wind howled eerily around the ship's deck columns and life-boat davits as they made their way carefully along the deck towards the stern, trying to avoid the video cameras on the columns. At last, they reached the stern and stopped under the metal overhang of the steps leading to the sky deck.

"There it is." Hank spotted the emergency hatch leading to the engine room below and pointed. They walked over and Hank bent down to loosen the metal clasps of the cover. He opened it and Dulac peered inside. A faint light shone from below, from the depth of an otherwise dark, narrow and circular stairwell. Dulac looked at Karen, shivering, an expression of dread on her face.

"You're sure you want to go down in there?"

"I get claustrophobic."

"Great. Hank?"

"I'm good."

Dulac stared at Karen. "So?"

She stood shaking and unsure for a moment. Then she straightened her back. "I'm coming down. At least I'll be warm."

"Fine. Let's go." Dulac grasped the edge of the opening and started backwards down the ladder, one hand on the metal rail. The others followed, Karen first, then Hank, step by step, slowly. As they made their way down, the light below became gradually brighter.

"Let's wait a second," Karen whispered. "I'm getting dizzy."

Dulac stopped and looked up over his shoulder. Behind him, Karen and Hank were all but blocking the faint shaft of light coming from above. A low-pitched murmur of sound hummed below them.

"You guys okay?" whispered Dulac.

"I'm fine," said Hank.

"Karen?"

"How much further?"

"We're getting closer to the engine room. I'd say another twenty feet."

"Let's go. I've got to get out of this, this damn coffin."

They started down again and the humming became a whirring sound, louder and higher pitched. Suddenly, the light became bright. Dulac turned upwards towards Karen. "We've reached the ceiling of the engine room. From now on, we'll be in plain view of anybody down there."

"Fantastic," said Karen.

From their position, they could see the vast engine room stretching below them, and the rest of the steel stairwell leading to the floor. The mammoth, twin sets of Wartsila diesels whirred effortlessly amidst an array of complex piping and electrical conduits linking the diesels to the electrical generators. To the left of the diesels, along the wall, stretched a U-shaped computer console with switches, dials and controls. The room seemed eerily empty of human presence.

Dulac started slowly down again and said, "they must be keeping the engine room staff in a separate—"

Suddenly, Dulac spotted a man holding an assault rifle coming from behind one of the diesels. The hijacker turned left and started walking down the aisle between the two sets of diesels.

"Back. Get back up," whispered Dulac urgently.

They backtracked carefully up the ladder, past the edge of the ceiling into the darkness.

Dulac checked the slider of the Glock and looked down. The man walked next to the ladder at the foot of the stairwell, then stopped. Dulac held his breath, clasped the Glock with both hands and aimed at the man's head. *Look up and you're dead.*

The hijacker slung the strap of his assault rifle on his shoulder, lit a cigarette, then resumed walking again.

"Close," whispered Dulac. After a moment, they slowly started down again and reached the floor. He looked about. No one.

"No point in all of us going to find that cycloconverter," said Dulac.

He pointed to a corner space between the port diesel bank and what appeared to be a long metal closet.

"You guys wanna wait there?" said Dulac.

"Sure," said Hank.

Karen just hunched her shoulders.

"I'll take that as a yes," said Dulac.

He turned and started slowly towards the stern, between the banks of diesels, panning with his Glock as he went. *Green box, where the hell is the green box?* The length of the diesel banks seemed endless. He shot a quick glance behind him. No one. Finally, he neared the rear of the aft most port diesel, and there it was, just as Watters had said. A small green box mounted on a gray . . .

Dulac saw the submachine gun barrel at right angles to him just before the man stepped out from behind the Wartsilla into the aisle, twenty feet away. As the man caught sight of Dulac and started to swing his Uzi, Dulac fired four quick shots into the man's chest. The man screamed and lurched backwards onto the floor, spraying the ceiling wildly with a burst of bullets.

Dulac thought quickly. The other hijackers would be onto him in a second. No time to remove the cycloconverter circuits. He aimed at the box and fired. The plastic cover flew into pieces, emitting a blue flame as electric sparks shot in every direction. A green smoke engulfed the burning plastic. The man on the floor lay motionless, his legs sprawled, a pool of blood forming on the floor next to his chest. Dulac spun around and started running back towards the ladder. He didn't notice that the port bank of diesels had become silent. Still running, Dulac caught sight of the stairwell's cylindrical shape. *Where's Karen? Hank?* Then he saw them starting up the stairs at the bottom of the stairwell. Machine gun fire erupted from behind him and bullets began ricocheting off the ladder and the diesels' cowlings. Dulac shouted. *"Quick! Let's get the hell outta here!"*

They scrambled upwards, first Harry, then Karen, then Dulac. They barely reached the ceiling of the engine room when the stairwell went pitch black.

"Shit! They've shut the lid," said Hank.

Gunfire bursts exploded from below, bullets ricocheting off the metal steps and railing of the stairwell.

"We're trapped," said Karen.

"Maybe," said Dulac.

"What do you mean? They've shut the damn lid," said Hank.

"Keep climbing," Dulac ordered.

"What?" said Hank.

"Just do as I say!"

The gunfire from below stopped.

"Let me pass." Dulac moved alongside Karen.

"I'm going to be sick."

"Just concentrate."

Dulac had just squeezed past Karen up the narrow ladder when a hissing sound came from below.

"What the hell is that?" said Karen.

Steam started filling the stairwell.

"*Owww!*" she yelled, as searing hot water hit her left ankle.

"They're using wash-down pressure hoses," said Dulac. "Here, take the Glock and fire. That'll keep them honest."

Karen took the pistol and fired randomly below. The hissing sound stopped.

"I'm at the top," said Hank.

"Do you feel some kind of locking mechanism?" said Dulac.

"There's a wheel."

"Before you turn it, try pushing up first."

"I'll be damned. It's not locked." Hank opened the hatch.

"I hoped to hell that was it. The wind and wave motion caught it and flipped it shut."

They climbed out of the stairwell onto the deck. Hank closed the hatch shut and locked it.

CHAPTER 23

His tie askew, Winston rushed into Bolding's office. Bolding was on the telephone and looked up in annoyance at Winston. "I'm with the insurers. Unless—"

"Excuse me sir, It's the *Star*, sir, I—"

"I'll call you back." Bolding hung up and looked expectantly at Winston.

"They've turned her Inmarsat telecom system back on." Tate was on line. He has instructions from the hijackers to get you on the video hook-up and call him back."

Bolding stood and started towards the door.

"Good. Come with me." He issued orders to his secretary as they passed her desk. "Get the video technician to meet us in the conference room and call Sir Terence Hays to let him know we'll patch him into the videoconference."

"Yes sir."

"Should we call the Americans?" Winston could barely keep up with Bolding's quick pace. "They might—"

"No. First let's see what these buggers want."

"Yes sir."

101

"Any news from those passengers? What's that man's name again?" asked Bolding.

"Dulac, sir. No news. But according to our chart plotter tracking, the *Star* has slowed down. She's currently doing 16 knots. "

"What about her course?"

"Still the same at 341 degrees. At her current speed, she's a bit less than 2 hours away from the reef."

Bolding and Winston took the elevator to the fifth floor and the videoconference room and sat down. Minutes later, the technician entered and immediately started connecting cables and flipping switches from behind the master control unit. He then looked at Bolding, a smile of satisfaction on his face.

"Everything ready?" Bolding started unbuttoning his jacket.

"Yes sir," said the technician. He looked at his watch. "I'm told Sir Hays will join us in five minutes. Then we'll connect with the *Star.*"

While the three of them sat waiting for the Home Office to make the connection, Bolding drummed his fingers impatiently on the table.

"How did it go with the insurers, sir?" said Winston.

"The bastards won't spend a farthing unless they have confirmation of an act of piracy. Since these hijackers haven't made any demands, we're in limbo."

"That may change soon," said Winston.

The video screen flickered to life and the image of Sir Terence Hays appeared.

"Good to see you, Terry," said Bolding. "I have Winston with me. Are we ready?"

"Let's get on with it," said Hays. "We have a meeting of the exec in twenty minutes. After that I have to brief the Prime Minister."

Bolding nodded to the technician, who adjusted the image sensors of the monitor. After a moment, the image of Hays disappeared, to be replaced by the picture of the

Star's bridge. From the vacillating image, Bolding could barely make out Rhodes, seated on the floor. The camera moved slightly and he recognized Tate and Brown. He looked for Peterson.

"Can you see us?" said Tate.

"Pretty well," said Bolding. "Where is Peterson?"

"He's . . . He's dead."

"What? Did you say he—?" Before Bolding could finish, the image vacillated again and another picture replaced the one of the bridge. Bolding recognized the Luxor amphitheater, with its mauve velour walls and steeply sloped seating. Except for the lighting of the stage, the amphitheater was barely lit. Only the emergency lights at the exits still shone, giving the room a funereal appearance. Onstage, a thin, dark-complexioned man in white officer's dress was standing beside an easel, the stage lights shining off his jet black, oily hair. On the other side of the easel, another man had his submachine gun trained on what appeared to be four hostages, standing in a row.

The thin man beside the easel spoke. "Bolding, can you see me?"

"Ah, yes. I'm afraid you have me at a disadvantage. I don't know your name."

"Please repeat."

"I don't know your name."

"You'll know my name in due course." The man's voice was strained and aggressive.

"I assume this is about—"

The camera focused on the hijacker and the man's head tilted back slightly, his chin jutting forward in an air of defiance. "You should assume nothing Bolding, nothing."

"If we—"

"Shut up and listen, Bolding. So you're wondering who we are? What we want? I'll tell you. The whole world will know who we are. Our people have suffered long enough, and the Pakistani government does nothing. Do you understand? *Nothing*. My wife and daughters were murdered by

Pakistani forces. Right in our home." The man paused, visibly overcome. After a moment, he regained his composure. "My two nieces, they were raped by eleven Pakistani officers and left to die on the streets in Karachi. My brothers rot in their jails. Their only crime was to want justice." He shook his right fist in the air. "We want justice now, Bolding, and we will get it." He turned, took two steps towards the easel and picked up the marker on the easel's tray. He wrote quickly on the sheet of paper, then turned to face the camera again. "You're wondering what this has to do with your ship, Bolding?"

Bolding looked at Winston quickly, then back at the monitor.

"Yes, I am."

"Nothing personal, Bolding." The man crossed his arms imperially over his white uniform. "We are the Baluchistan Tigers and we need money. That's what you can tell your reporters, or to whomever you want. Money buys justice, Bolding. You, of all people, should know that."

"I'm afraid I don't follow."

"Do you remember that article last year in the *Daily Mirror*? Of course you do. The rape charges brought against your son by the daughter of Sir Jeffrey Evans?"

Bolding felt his face redden, "Leave my son out of this. The matter was settled out of court without any admission of guilt."

"Point proved, Bolding. Money buys justice." The man smiled. He turned and flapped the back of his thin hand on the page of the easel. "You will wire transfer these sums to the banks I have written down here, Bolding, and the Pakistani government will free the seven Baluchistan hostages it holds in Islamabad prison. Otherwise many will die, that I promise you." He turned and pointed to the hostages. "The Governor here, the Senator and their wives, they will be first. Do you understand, Bolding? Am I making myself clear?"

"Very clear."

"Good." The hijacker turned and pointed back to the easel.

"I will go through our demands slowly, Bolding, so you and your government officials listening in can be certain they're recorded them clearly. Ready?"

"We're ready." Winston even grabbed a pad of paper and pencil.

"Good. One: the sum of 20 million US Dollars will be wired to the Saman bank in Tehran. The manager is Mr. Sirhan Aswaled and he will send confirmation to our agent upon receipt of funds. Two: the sum of 20 million US dollars will be wired to Sili Bank, Pyongyang, North Korea. Mr. Kwan Sung will confirm receipt to our agent. Three: 20 million US dollars will be wired to Banco Cuscatlán of Costa Rica. Our agent Leon Binagro will confirm receipt of all funds to me via sat phone. Four: I want confirmation of the freeing of my seven Baluchistan brothers from *Dera Ismail Khan* Prison."

The man looked at his watch. "You have exactly two hours to comply with our demands. Otherwise your lovely ship here will be destroyed on Torrais Reef and many will die. Is that clear?"

"You actually believe we can get $60 million together in two hours?"

"Actually, I believe you can do it in one hour and 59 minutes."

"Even if we agree, we can't possibly raise that kind of money in such a short time." Bolding turned and looked at Winston again, then back at the monitor. "And I think you know this. Besides, we have no influence whatsoever on the Pakistani government or their internal policies. You know that too. Surely you can't—"

Suddenly the other hijacker, carrying a VHF and standing behind the thin man, waved his hand at the thin man and shouted. "Tariq, Tariq, it's Najib in the engine room. They've killed Jawab."

The thin man spun around. "What?"

"Three of them."

"Who, what three? Saquil, what are you talking about?"

"Three passengers. They were not checked in at the amphitheater. They shot Jawab in the engine room. They sabotaged the motors and escaped to the upper deck."

Tariq grabbed his lapel VHF. "Hamed?"

Bolding heard a screeching sound from Tariq's VHF radio.

"You and Beza find those fucking passengers. I want them dead, understand? Dead!"

"So the name's Tariq, is it?" interrupted Bolding.

Tariq spun back and looked in the direction of the amphitheater's camera.

"What?"

"As I was saying, we cannot consider paying you a ransom without—"

"So you think I'm bluffing?" Tariq, his face steeled, cocked his head sideways.

"I didn't say that," said Bolding. "I meant we'll have to get our insurers involved before—"

"So Bolding, you think I'm not serious?" Tariq's voice went an octave higher.

"I'm sure you are, but realistically—"

"Maybe you think you can buy time until help arrives? Do you think I'm that dumb, Bolding?"

"I was merely pointing out to you—"

"Your Captain Peterson, he didn't think I was serious." Tariq's voice had become almost hysterical. "He thought I was bluffing. He's dead. Now you don't know me, Bolding, so naturally, you don't think that a simple Paki peasant can be serious when he asks for 60 million dollars of ransom money from a rich, upper class British nobleman such as yourself, eh Bolding? But you're wrong. Dead wrong. Here, let me show you how serious I am." Tariq limped quickly up to Saquil, grabbed his pistol from the holster, then went to Dickinson's wife and pressed the barrel of the pistol against her left temple. "This is how serious I am."

"No, no. Wait! We'll find a way. We'll pay—"

Tariq cocked his head slightly, looked at the camera and smiled. There was a loud explosion and the woman's head jerked sideways. Her knees buckled and she fell to the floor.

For a long moment, the camera remained fixed on the woman. She didn't move.

"Good God!" Bolding's face drained of color.

The others on the video call didn't say a word. They were all dumbstruck, paralyzed, absorbing the horrendous act they'd just witnessed, watching a pool of blood form around the woman's head. Dickinson fell to his knees beside her, his face a mask of disbelief and pain. *"No, No! Mary, No!"* He looked up at Tariq. "You murderer, you goddam bastard."

Dickinson lunged at Tariq, who hit him in the face with the butt of his pistol. The governor reeled backwards, then knelt down again, cradling his dead wife in his arms as he moaned. *"Mary, Mary. No, Mary, no."* Saquil grabbed him by the shoulders and tried to drag him away as Tariq started to leave the stage, leading the other hostages at gunpoint. Dickinson still held his wife, rocking her body in his arms. "You bastard. You'll pay for this," he shouted to Tariq.

Tariq turned and walked over to Dickinson, aiming the Glock at Dickinson's head. "Up, old man, or you get it too."

Dickinson got up. His face was contorted in pain, his shoulders convulsing, and he tried to lurch at Tariq again. Easton grabbed him and pulled him back among the other hostages. Tariq waved his pistol nervously at Easton and the others, "Everyone off, off." He motioned them down the steps and off the stage.

* * *

Hays, Winston and Bolding sat transfixed, staring at the video screen in silence. Finally, Bolding mustered the courage to speak, "Tariq, this is Bolding. Do you hear me?"

Tariq turned towards the camera. "What?"

"Please, no more killings. I'll get you your money."

"I have no doubt of that, Bolding." The screen went dark.

CHAPTER 24

Aboard the USS Anzio's bridge

Donnelly scanned the horizon through the ship's tri-pod-mounted telescope. The ensign to his right called out.

"Captain, I have the *Caravan Star* on radar."

Donnelly replaced the plastic protector of the telescope eyepiece and looked at the radar screen a few feet away. "What's her heading?"

"She's on three-four-one."

"How far?"

"30.6 nautical miles off our port beam."

"Speed?"

"She's slowed to 15 knots."

Donnelly looked at the *Anzio's* GPS: 28 knots and clos-ing. He took a closer look at the white blip on the radar screen, moving slowly towards the center of the screen and the *Anzio's* position.

"Think we'll make it?"

"I think so, sir. But it'll be close."

Donnelly picked up the phone and called the engine room.

"Harrison."

"Donnelly. Can you give me some more juice?"

"We've got a bit of vibration in the port turbines, Captain," said Harrison.

"I need a couple of knots more."

"Right. She'll take it, but not for long."

Donnelly went to the right of the console to the remote-control throttle and pushed the handle all the way forward.

CHAPTER 25

Bolding, Hays and Winston were still in a state of silent shock when Allin appeared at the doorway of the conference room.

"What now?" said Bolding.

"Sorry sir, it's the US Navy. An Admiral West, I believe. He's with some woman from Homeland Security. I told them you're in a videoconference with Sir Hays and they want to join in."

Bolding looked at Winston. "Might as well let them know." Bolding's voice cracked under the strain. "Terry?"

"Yes," said Hays.

The video technician went to the monitor and adjusted the channel. The screen flickered and images of Admiral West and Lombardi, seated at a table, appeared.

"We were about to call you," said Bolding. "It . . . it was terrible. The hijackers. We were in a videoconference. He, he just murdered her. Right in front of us." Bolding couldn't continue. His voice choked with emotion and his lower lip trembled.

Hays picked up in Bolding's place. "They shot Dickinson's wife in cold blood. These pirates call themselves the Baluchistan Tigers. They want 60 million US dollars within two hours. And they want seven prisoners freed from Islamabad prison."

"Jesus!" Lombardi looked at West, then back at the camera. "Send us the tapes of the video conference. We'll have our people look at them immediately. How did you leave it with the hijackers?"

"I said I'd find the money. Somehow." Bolding recovered enough composure to speak. "God knows how we're going to meet their demands to free the prisoners. I'm just hoping these psychopaths won't kill anybody else."

"I understand." Lombardi turned towards West briefly. "Please know you have the full support and force of the United States and her Navy at your back. In the meantime, gentlemen, we have good and bad news. First the good. As you are no doubt aware, the *Caravan Star* has slowed to 15 knots. It gives us a small window of opportunity before she hits that reef."

"And the bad?" said Bolding.

"Although the *Anzio* is closing fast," said West, "her captain says that unless the weather gets any better, he won't be able to push the *Star* off course. The seas are too rough and we risk losing both ships if we have asynchronous contact between them."

"So what can you do?" said Bolding.

"We're looking at other options," said West.

"Such as?"

"If she gets there in time, the *Anzio* can outflank the *Star*, cross her bows and drag cables into her propellers."

Bolding threw a skeptical look at Winston. "Really?"

"The biggest problem we see is maintaining the element of surprise," said West. "If they see us coming, the hijackers might do something stupid."

"Such as kill more people," said Hays.

"Yes," said West. "But I'm afraid we don't have a hell of a lot of other options."

"But they want money. Once we get them the money—"said Bolding.

"What about their other demands, freeing the prisoners from Islamabad prison," said Lombardi. "Do you have anyone working on that, Sir Terence?"

"I've put a call out to the Pakistan Ambassador, but I'm not very optimistic. Even if we were to convince Islamabad, which is highly unlikely, we can't do it in two hours."

"I'm sorry, but there's no guarantee they'll be satisfied with only the money," said West.

There was a moment of silence. West had spoken what everybody else thought and dreaded.

Finally, Bolding spoke. "So what can we do now?"

"How secure is this videoconference?" said Lombardi.

"Hays here. Its triple firewall protected and encrypted by MI6. We can't get more secure than that."

"Fine. I ask that everyone in the room to leave or disconnect, except you, Sir Adrian, and you, Sir Terence."

Bolding signaled Allin and the technician to leave.

"Done."

"Sir Terence?"

"Also."

"Gentlemen, have you heard of Sleeping Beauty?"

Hays smiled wryly. "I presume you aren't referring to the Disney film."

"Not quite," said Lombardi. "Sleeping Beauty is the codename for a joint US Navy and Army terrorist control experimental program. It's a gas that's been developed in complete secrecy as a method of neutralizing terrorists while avoiding loss of life of hostages."

"Sounds vaguely familiar," said Hays. "I'm thinking of the Russian hostages taken in Moscow in 2002. If my memory serves me right, the Russians used gas and over 100 hostages died because of inhaling the gas."

West adjusted his bifocals. "You're not far off the mark, Sir Terence. It was actually 120. We've come a long way since 2002. The gas we've developed is a derivative of the Fentanyl the Russians used, but without its side effects. It's called Bezorban."

"So what has this to do with the current situation?" asked Bolding.

"The *Anzio* is equipped with Bezorban, to be used in extreme circumstances only. We are equipped to use it against any terrorist force, if justifiable," said West.

"In extreme circumstances? If justifiable?" said Bolding. "I'm under the impression there are still some heavy risks here. Risking the lives of 500 passengers and crew is—"

"We think saving the lives of the passengers of your ship, captured by terrorists on a suicide mission, fully justifies its use," said Lombardi. "Especially when the terrorists are led by a psychopath who just killed a woman with a head shot right in front of your eyes. I don't need to tell you what that means, do I? That he won't hesitate to kill everyone on that ship."

Bolding clung to hope. "But they want money. Once we get them the money—"

"And again—there's no guarantee they'll be satisfied with money only," said West.

"We'll have to think about this," said Bolding. "In any case, what would be your plan if we were to agree?"

"The plan is for the *Anzio* to get within helicopter range and then send a team of Navy Seals equipped with canisters of Bezorban onto the deck of the *Star*. We calculate it will take about ten minutes for the gas to take effect after the Seals blow it down the Dorade vents with portable compressors, into the ventilation system of the ship. After we take control, we can administer the opioid reversal drug Naloxone to those who need it. The *Anzio* has 200 doses of the drug to counter the effects of the Bezorban."

"Well, as I said, I'll have to discuss this with Home Office, won't we, Terry?" said Bolding.

"I see this as a matter of Internal and Foreign Policy," said Hays. "There are possibly legal implications if—"

"Gentlemen, I think you misunderstood me," interrupted Lombardi.

"I beg your pardon?" said Hays.

"We're calling to keep you informed. The decision has already been made."

Bolding and Hays didn't react. Finally Bolding broke the silence. "Is there no other way? I mean this sounds rather risky. I would—"

"Believe me, Mr. Bolding," said West, "there's no other way unless the *Star* changes course. Right now, we have no indication of that."

"I see," said Bolding, with an air of resignation. "Let us know when you have further developments. We'll do the same. Terry, will you call the Pakistani government about freeing the prisoners?"

"I'll try, but I'm not very optimistic."

"Let me know. I'll call our insurers concerning the ransom."

Bolding shut down the video screen.

CHAPTER 26

On the stern deck of the Caravan Star, 10.15 a.m. Ship's time

Rivulets of rain, funneled by the wind, ran down the sides of Deck Five, onto the stern area of the ship.

Dulac, Karen and Hank tried to find protection from the increasing gale behind one of the wider metal columns.

"They're bound to be looking for us," said Dulac. "We've got to find a place to hide." He looked at Hank, then Karen, shivering in her wet sweater and dressing gown. "Any ideas?"

"What about in those?" Karen eyed one of the lifeboats. "At least we'll be warm."

"I've changed my mind. That's the first place they'll check." We'd be sitting ducks there."

"So what *do* you think?" asked Hank.

"We've got to get P & W back on the sat phone again, and we've got to find a safe spot where we can try to call them," said Dulac. He looked astern. He spotted a small bar covered with a canvas canopy next to the pool. The wind played hell with the canopy, but it was the only obvious possibility. *Not perfect, but it'll do.*

Dulac pointed to the bar. "Let's go."

They ran across the deck to the bar and ducked underneath its counter for protection. Wind and rain swept around the sides of the bar and under the counter. Overhead, the canopy buffeted about like a large flag, ready to rip into shreds at any instant. They huddled closer to each other and tried to stay warm. Dulac saw that Karen was showing the first signs of mild hypothermia.

Dulac looked at Hank. "Give me the sat phone."

Hank reached into his pajama pants pocket. "Shit!"

"What?"

"It was here. It must've fallen out when—"

"*Merde.*" Dulac looked up and back into the direction of the escape hatch. Nothing. "We can't stay here. They know we're at the stern, and they're probably working their way aft right now."

"What do we do?" said Hank.

"They'll check every corridor, nook and cranny, hallway and lifeboat, and work their way astern from the center. That's what I would do."

"So what options do we have?" said Karen.

"We've got to buy time until the American warship gets here," said Dulac, looking forward towards the deck. "Somehow we've got to get past the hijackers, to the bow."

"What for?" said Karen.

"If we can get by them, they won't know where to look next."

"And how do we do that?"

Rain dripped from Dulac's nose and eyebrows. He got closer to Karen and looked into her frightened eyes. "What's the most miserable, unlikely place to be on the ship when it's howling and raining nails?"

"Right here?" Karen shivered, her wet hair plastered down onto her head.

Dulac rose slightly and pointed to the open sky deck above.

"You've got to be kidding!"

* * *

116

The squat man rose abruptly from his chair and the glass doors opened. Tariq appeared and shoved Dickinson, Easton, his wife and three other hostages onto the bridge. Dickinson was shaking. Only his right arm draped over Easton's left shoulder kept him standing. "You'll pay for this," Dickinson promised Tariq. "I'll make you—"

"You'll make me what?" Tariq pressed the barrel of his Glock against Dickinson's forehead. "Sit down, old man. Hands behind your back." He motioned with his pistol for Dickinson and the others to sit next to the officers. "Tie them up," he ordered the squat man. He eyed Rhodes, who was sitting next to Sandra Brown. "You, Rhodes, up here with me."

With difficulty Rhodes, hands still tied behind his back, got onto his knees then rose. He went beside Tariq next to the console.

Just then, a huge wave hit the *Star* and she shuddered.

Tariq glanced at Rhodes and said, "A bit nasty out there, eh Rhodes?"

Rhodes looked at the digital anemometer: 55 knots. "It's getting pretty foul."

"When do we get to the Azores?"

Rhodes looked at the GPS readout. "In about an hour and 15 minutes. We'll have to alter course to avoid hitting—"

"We're right on course, Rhodes. Right on course." Tariq looked straight ahead into the growing storm.

CHAPTER 27

Southampton, P & W Headquarters

Bolding relayed the details of the hijacker's demands to P & W's insurers as soon as he returned to his office. He didn't like their response. While he waited for Hays to come on line, he scribbled a note on his pad and signaled his secretary over. "Get the Americans back online for a videoconference."

"Yes sir."

The phone line came to life. "Hays here."

"Yes Terry, it's Adrian."

"Did you get the money?"

"The P and I Club deny coverage and the War Risk people won't budge. They'll only reimburse what we pay out if the method of payment is in line with the conditions of the policy."

"Buggers. They're all the same," said Hays. "You pay for their umbrella, and they take it away when it rains."

Bolding looked at his watch. "We're running out of time."

"Adrian, surely you have reserves for this kind of contingency?"

"Terry, there is something you must understand. The situation at P & W is, well, not that comfortable, shall we say."

"We're talking about human lives, Adrian. Besides, I don't have to remind you that the Somalians get ten times that amount of money for hijacked cargo ships every year."

"I know all that, Terry. And I'd pay if I could. But I don't have it. I simply don't have it to pay."

There was a moment of heavy silence.

"I was afraid of that. How much time?"

"About an hour."

"Damn. What is the situation with the *Anzio*?"

"I've called for a videoconference with the Americans again."

"Put me through when you have them online. Just to let you know Adrian, I've spoken to the Prime Minister and he agrees that we can't let this situation deteriorate any further."

"But I can't come up with the money, Terry, I—"

"We'll get the money, Adrian. The Government will get the money."

* * *

Bolding hung up. Five minutes later his secretary showed up at the doorway.

"I have Admiral West and Secretary Lombardi ready for the video," she said.

"Get the Home Office hooked up and phone Sir Hays. Get Winston to join me in the conference room."

"Yes sir."

Bolding rose, walked over to the conference room and sat down.

A few minutes later, Winston appeared and joined Bolding around the table. They waited until the video monitor flickered to life.

"Secretary Lombardi, Admiral. Sir Hays is about to join us. I have my Chief Security Officer David Winston here with me now."

Winston gave a quick nod. "Secretary Lombardi, Admiral."

Bolding looked at the clock on the wall behind the video monitor: less than 50 minutes.

The video screen flickered again and Hays joined in, "Secretary Lombardi, gentlemen. Any news from the *Anzio*?"

"She has the *Caravan Star* on radar, but no visual contact yet," said West. "She hasn't altered course."

"We have a decision to make concerning the hijackers' demands," said Bolding.

"Surely you're not considering payment." Lombardi's voice made it clear she wasn't asking a question.

"That's easy for you to say," said Hays. "The *Caravan Star* is a British ship, flying a British Ensign, run by a British company. We—"

Lombardi took over. "Don Peters had his people scan the videos and got some info on these Baluchistan Tigers. According to his intel, the leader of this hijacking is a certain Tariq Assirgan, wanted by the Pakistani government in relation to the planning and execution of three suicide missions in Islamabad. And that's only in the past 18 months. They've killed a total of 156 innocent people so far. Peters says he can't rule out they're on another suicide mission."

"Or Jihadists out to kill unbelievers," added West.

There was a pregnant silence, as each the participants eyed the opposing parties of the videoconference.

Finally Hays spoke. "Ms. Lombardi, Admiral, let me be very clear. While the British government does not officially pay ransom to terrorists, we have set aside $60 million in a Swiss trust account for Mr. Bolding here to pay the pirates. We have no indication that these are anything but pirates, and we have every indication they will not negotiate. If the US government decides to proceed with Sleeping Beauty, it does so at its own risk and peril, and shall bear the entire responsibility of so doing."

There was another pregnant silence, as all digested the impacts of Hays's statement. Finally Lombardi spoke. "Is this how the British government plays cover their rears, Terry, or just you?"

"Now look here, Secretary Lombardi—"

"So what you're telling us, Terry, is that you're willing to risk these fanatics murdering the entire crew and all the passengers? Or them drowning if they manage not to get murdered? Is that what you're telling us?"

"I didn't say that, Secretary Lombardi," said Hays.

"Oh really? Then please. Explain."

"We have no knowledge of Bezorban's side effects," said Hays. "Even you admit you don't know the full consequences of its use. As you mentioned earlier, you will use it only in extreme circumstances. We have every indication that if this Tariq gets his money, he'll back off. Why would he—?"

"Terry, you are *not* that naïve," interrupted Lombardi, "It's far more likely he wants to do both. Get the money *and* kill the passengers."

Another pregnant silence.

Lombardi looked at West for a moment, then turned back towards the video screen. "Gentlemen, we consider having two people murdered and the lives of the other passengers at high risk to be extreme circumstances."

Hays sat back and took in a deep breath. "It's your decision Admiral, Secretary Lombardi. We can do nothing to stop you. I'll advise the Prime Minister accordingly. In the meantime, our government will try the other route. Adrian, tell the pirates they'll get their money as soon as they alter course."

CHAPTER 28

On the sky deck of the Caravan Star

Wet and cold, Dulac, Karen and Hank huddled together, shivering behind the two-sided metal enclosure next to the door, trying to get some protection from the 50 knots wind and sheets of pelting rain.

"Can't we go inside?" shouted Karen.

Dulac reached over and tried the door handle. "It's locked."

"Now what?" said Karen.

"We have no choice," said Dulac. "The only way is to keep going across the sky deck to the bow, then down the open stairs to the lower deck."

"Just fantastic," said Karen.

"Any other ideas? Hank?"

Hank exhaled a sigh of doubt. "We can try the other doors on the way. Who knows, we might get lucky."

"Let's go," said Dulac. "The longer we wait, the colder we get." He turned to Karen. "Stay close behind me, keep low and walk with a wide stance: the deck will be like a skating rink."

* * *

Standing next to the ensign on watch, Donnelly looked at the anemometer: 61 knots. They were in a full gale. To his left, watch officer Dick Hunt looked alternatively at the ship's compass and the bow, as the Anzio reared up now and then like a bucking stallion in slow motion.

His eyes still glued onto the anemometer, Donnelly asked Hunt, "What's your speed over ground?"

"Down to 17 knots, Sir."

"Damn." Donnelly glanced at the radar screen, the white dot representing the Caravan Star was now within the 18-mile circle from the Anzio. He grabbed the 7 x 50 powered telescope and adjusted its eyepiece. He nudged the telescope slightly upwards, then to the right, then left. "That's her," he exclaimed. "That's the Star. Bearing 165 degrees. There she . . . shit, lost her again. This bloody weather isn't helping one goddamn bit," said Donnelly. He glanced at the radar again, showing the outline of the Azores, the island of Corvo and the jagged outline of the Torrais reef. Inside the 16-mile circle, the white dot was moving inexorably towards the reef, as if drawn to it by a magnet.

"She's heading straight for it," said Donnelly. He turned and went to the navigator's station. "Give me an intercept time for us, and the collision time for the Caravan Star to the reef," he said to the navigator.

The navigator punched numbers into this computer and after a moment said, "the Star has 47 minutes till collision."

"And our intercept time?" said Donnelly.

"We have two options."

"Which are?"

"The direct intercept course takes us across some shallow water over there," the navigator said, pointing to his GPS chart. "Normally we would swing 20° to port to avoid those poorly charted waters. But if we take the direct route, we can intercept in 35 minutes."

"And if we don't?" said Donnelly.

"Fifty-eight minutes."

CHAPTER 29

On the Caravan Star's bridge

Tariq looked at the squat man, then pointed to Tate.

"Get him up. Untie his hands."

"Yes Tariq." The squat man rushed to obey.

"You. Check for a message from Southampton."

Tate went to the radio operator station, sat down and opened his computer. He turned toward Tariq. "No messages."

"Nothing?"

"No sir."

"We'll see about that. Get Bolding on the—"

The squeal of a high-frequency radio interrupted Tariq. A voice distorted by static hailed the ship. "*Caravan Star, Caravan Star*, this is P & W Southampton. Do you copy, over?" Tate recognized Allin's high-pitched voice. "This is the *Caravan Star*. We read you six on 10. How do you read me, over?"

"Seven on 10. I have Sir Adrian Bolding on the line. I . . ."

Tariq grabbed the microphone. "Bolding, this is Tariq. I have no messages from my agent. Where is my money? Time is running out."

Heavy static screeched.

"Repeat, Bolding."

"We have your money. I have confirmation from the Home Secretary. 60 million dollars is in a trust account in the Bahamas under . . ."

"In the Bahamas? Do you take me for a fool, Bolding?"

"What do you mean?"

"The Bahamas? A British protectorate?" Tariq yelled, microphone in hand, pacing rapidly back and forth in front of Tate. "I suppose I just go to Nassau on a holiday to collect?"

"No, no. The trustee can wire the funds from Guaranty Trust Bank to anywhere in the world."

"And who is this trustee?"

"Your man in Costa Rica. Leon Binagro."

"Tell me Bolding, what guarantee do I have that you do not have another trustee, a Bahamian trustee, under your instructions, whose authorization is needed before the bank can release the funds?"

"Well . . . I . . ."

"Unacceptable, Bolding. You had my instructions and ignored them, Bolding. Now more passengers will die."

"No, no, wait. Listen. You must give us more time. We cannot get the funds transferred to North Korea before noon. The bank in Tehran is closed until 2 a.m. your time."

"Then transfer the $60 million to Costa Rica. Get Binagro to call me on the sat phone when the funds are received." Tariq looked at his watch. "You have 41 minutes."

CHAPTER 30

West and Turner sat across from the video screen, their eyes riveted to the high-scale map on the screen. Lombardi paced nervously back and forth, alternating her tense gaze between the map and the admirals. The screen showed the Caravan Star closing in on Torrais Reef, and further up on the screen, the Anzio on a course to intercept her.

"Can she make it?" Lombardi didn't slow her pace.

"Not unless the *Anzio* takes a straight course across Selkirk Passage," said Turner.

"So what's the problem?"

"I've spoken to Donnelly," said Turner. "It's low tide. He won't risk his ship running aground in such shallow water with those large waves. Even if they come down, it's pretty tricky. He'll know definitely when they get closer."

Lombardi looked at the video screen just as the *Anzio* started altering course slightly to port.

"How much time until the *Star* hits the reef?" said Lombardi.

"About 39 minutes," said Turner. "The men aboard the *Anzio's* helicopter are ready to take off. They need 12 minutes to reach the *Star*, another five minutes to pump the Bezorban into the *Star's* Dorade vents. Then ten minutes for the Bezorban to take effect, so the Seals can take control of the bridge and alter the *Star's* course."

"That's cutting it real close," said Lombardi eyeing West, then Turner.

"That's if all goes well," said Turner.

Lombardi looked at her watch. "So we have less than 12 minutes to decide."

"And counting," said West.

Lombardi walked to the window and looked outside. A slight rain began to wet the asphalt parking area below. She issued the order without turning. "Send the chopper." She paused for a second and continued. "And God help us all."

CHAPTER 31

On the Caravan Star's bridge

Tariq brought his lapel mike closer to his mouth. "What's happening? Where are those passengers?"

"We checked all the rooms and corridors. We checked all the lifeboats even. There's no sign of them," said Jawal.

"Where are you?"

"At the back. We found a sat phone on the deck. It must belong to one of them."

Tariq looked at his watch. "Listen to me. We have 31 minutes till we hit that reef. You don't come back until you find them. Understood?"

"Yes, Tariq."

* * *

"Thierry, I'm freezing." Karen had to yell to be heard as she struggled to keep her balance in the raging gusts. Spray flew over the bridge and onto the sky deck. "I can't go on."

Dulac turned and grabbed Karen's left arm. "You have to! We're almost there! We're near the end of the sky deck, we'll get shelter over there." He pointed to a small metal structure dead ahead.

"What if we can't get down from there?" Both Karen and Hank looked at Dulac, who didn't answer.

A series of faint *pops* erupted from the rear, almost inaudible in the howling wind. They turned to see two hijackers shooting at them from the aft end of the sky deck.

Dulac looked around. A large wooden box was to his left, about a dozen yards away next to the shuffleboard lanes.

"Go!" Dulac pushed them in the right direction.

They dashed for the protection of the box, making it just as a burst of gunfire broke out from the front of the sky deck.

"Jesus! We're trapped!" Hank risked a glance from the side of their meager shield.

Dulac grabbed the Glock from his pocket and opened fire, alternating between the bow and stern. Bullets riddled the wooden sides of the box. Dulac looked aft and saw the two men astern split up, to widen their angle of fire.

"We're screwed," said Hank, as the three looked nervously about for another shelter.

At that moment, something off the ship's starboard side caught their attention. It was a dark object, its shape initially obscured by the thick clouds. Suddenly they recognized the unmistakable shape of a helicopter, closing in fast just above wave height. "Great timing," Dulac said.

The helicopter reached the ship and slowed, returning fire as the hijackers at the front of the sky deck peppered the sky with bullets. It neared the *Caravan Star's* helipad at the bow. In only a moment, the chopper was down and out of sight, hidden by the sky deck.

"Now's our chance," said Dulac. "They're busy trying to get the chopper."

He rose from his crouch, panning with his Glock. Shots erupted from the aft portion of the sky deck. Dulac pointed to a metal ramp at the sky deck's front. "That must be the staircase leading down," he said. "Go. I'll cover you."

Karen looked hesitantly at Dulac, then at Hank.

"Now!" yelled Dulac. He opened fire towards the rear of the sky deck.

* * *

From the bridge, Tariq saw the helicopter lower onto the helipad.

"What the . . . ?" In an instant, eight Navy Seals were on deck, their faces hidden by gas masks. Some carried canisters, the others shooting towards the bridge. Before Tariq could even speak, three SEALs held open canisters to the opening of the Dorade vents. Others pressed compressors next to the canisters.

"They're gassing us. Open the glass doors!" Tariq yelled. "Kill those bastards."

Tariq grabbed his pistol from the console, then brought his lapel mike close to his mouth. "Amphitheater, engine room, steerage room! Get out! Repeat. Get out now! They're going to gas the ship. Get . . ."

"Tariq, this is Jawal. What's happening?"

"We're under attack. They have gas. Get the men outside and come to the bridge. Hurry."

CHAPTER 32

Homeland Security Headquarters, conference room 3B

Lombardi looked anxiously at the radar image of the Azores displayed on the wall-mounted video monitor. The icon representing the Caravan Star appeared to be on the top of Torrais reef.

Admiral Turner, his sat phone pressed to his ear, put his hand on the mouthpiece before speaking. "Donnelly says they're onboard. They're pumping the gas and proceeding to the bridge. They've met heavy gunfire."

"Any casualties?" said Lombardi.

"Not so far," said Turner.

"How much time before the reef?"

Turner looked at the radar. "About 18 minutes."

"Jesus." Lombardi felt a twinge of pain across her chest. An image of the *Caravan Star* hitting the reef flashed across her mind, followed immediately by the image of 500 unconscious passengers and crew piling up pell-mell as the ship rolled over and capsized. It'd be the *Costa Concordia* all over again. Or worse. Lombardi stood up and started pacing again, this time in front of the monitor. She turned to Turner. "What's the situation with the Portuguese?"

"They sent three helicopters and four Coast Guard patrol boats from Lajes. Problem is, with those waves the boats won't be able to get closer than 200 feet from the reef."

"Terrific. Just terrific."

"We're doing everything we can."

Lombardi walked to the window again and looked out. A gentle breeze tickled the leaves of the acacia trees in the yard below. If the plan succeeded, the *Caravan Star* would be out of harm's way within the next ten minutes. If it failed, many passengers and crew would drown. As head of the operation, her neck was the one on the chopping block.

CHAPTER 33

On the bridge of the Caravan Star

The squat man stood behind a metal column near the bridge's entrance and returned fire. The SEALs slowly forced him back. A windowpane next to Tariq fractured into a mosaic of broken glass, shattered by ricocheting bullets.

"Get up," Tariq ordered Dickinson and the other hostages. He was about to march them outside in front of him when the Inmarsat radio came to life.

"*Caravan Star*, do you copy, over?" Tariq recognized Binagro's voice. Tariq walked back and picked up the microphone on the radio operator's desk, keeping his gun trained on the hostages.

"Tariq."

"Leo. We have the money."

"All of it?"

"Sixty million US, deposited in the Costa Rican account."

"*Allah* be praised!" Tariq smiled, a smile cut short by a burst of machine gun fire close to the bridge. "I've got a problem here."

"Sounds it," said Binagro.

"Our wings. Did you get them?"

"They're waiting in Corvo."

"I knew I could count on you." Tariq dropped the microphone onto the desk.

Suddenly the squat man entered, wobbly, a stream of blood dripping from his left arm.

"They're blocking the entrance below. What do we do?"

"We've got to get out of here. The gas." Tariq started to cough. "We'll go down the other side of the bridge." He turned to the officers sitting on the floor, some of whom had already passed out. "Anyone tries to follow, he's dead, understand?"

Tate nodded weakly.

"Let's go." Tariq prodded the six hostages to the other side of the bridge with his pistol. He pointed the Glock at Easton's wife's head. "Senator, try anything and your wife gets it first."

* * *

Luxor amphitheater

With the hijackers gone, a group of passengers rushed to the heavy wooden doors of the main entrance and tried breaking it down, but to no avail. Women and children coughed as the gas spread quickly. Some tried to breach the emergency exits, only to find the hijackers had locked them also. They were trapped. The sweet odor of oranges grew more pungent. Passengers began to pass out. Panic mounted, nearing eruption.

A passenger began to shout. "Light a fire! Light a fire! We're being gassed. Get stuff to light a fire. It'll trigger the sprinklers and the water will dilute the gas."

A young man with a goatee rushed to the stage and tore down one of the side curtains. Others fell unconscious and slumped in their chairs as the Benzorban depressed their central nervous systems and slowed their respiratory functions. Soon, the amphitheater was filled with unconscious passengers, some fallen in the aisles, others on the stage or slumped in their seats, mouths agape. A few passengers still walked around, their faces blank, trying to fight the paralyzing effect of the gas by staying in motion.

* * *

On the sky deck, Dulac, Karen and Hank reached the metal enclosure of the foremost staircase, leading to the decks below. Dead ahead off the ship's bow, surged the high, dome-like shape of Corvo, its dark cliffs now clearly visible through the driving rain and clouds.

Dulac heard bullets ricocheting off the enclosure. He looked aft. The two terrorists were closing in. Dulac tried the door of the staircase.

"It's open. He motioned Karen and Hank forward. He shut and locked the metal door behind them. They started down the narrow metal steps to the deck below. Karen stopped abruptly. "What's that smell?"

Dulac started to feel dizzy. "Smells like some sort of gas. We've got to get out of here fast."

They scrambled down the stairs to the next level. The door in front of them indicated they'd reached Deck 5.

A gust of wind tore the door from Dulac's hands as soon as it opened and flipped it back onto the wall with a crash. They stepped outside and Dulac looked aft, then forward. A huge mass of land obliterated the horizon dead ahead of the ship.

No one spoke. Dulac looked left across the open corridor and saw two of the hijackers, guns drawn, herding six hostages in front of them.

The armed men looked right at Dulac and for a split second, the members of each group eyed the members of the other group with equal surprise and indecision.

"That's them! They killed Jawab." The hijacker shoved Dickinson aside and started shooting.

Dulac, Karen and Hank jumped back from the corridor, out of the line of fire.

The squat pirate started after them, the other shouting after him. "Get back! There's no time!"

The squat man didn't listen. He kept going, spraying the corridor with gunfire, bullets ricocheting off the metal columns. When he stopped to reload Dulac saw his chance and broke cover. He took aim and fired three shots. The squat man looked at him in surprise. The he dropped to his knees and fell forward, still clutching his Uzi.

The remaining hijacker froze in place for a moment, glaring at Dulac. Gunfire erupted to the terrorist's right and he swiveled to return fire. Caught in the crossfire, two hostages fell to the ground. Four others screamed in panic and fled down the corridor towards Dulac. The hijacker took aim and fired, hitting a small woman in a gray jumpsuit in the leg. She fell, screaming and clutching her left leg. Dulac fired back at the tall man, who was receiving heavy gunfire from his right.

"*Help me, please, someone help me!*" The injured woman stretched her left hand out in Dulac's direction.

"Jesus!" said Karen. "We've got to do something."

Dulac eyed Hank. "Grab her and pull her back. I'll cover you."

Hank crawled on his stomach and grabbed the woman's hand, pulling her back to safety. The other hostages fled down the corridor, past Dulac, Karen and Hank. The tall man fired again but missed.

Hank checked the woman's leg. "She's losing a lot of blood."

"Can you make a tourniquet?" asked Dulac.

"I'll do it," said Karen. "Done this before."

"Good," said Dulac. "I'm going to get that sonofabitch."

He thought fast. Fighting his way down the corridor was not an option. No protection. He checked the Glock. Five bullets left. He had to cross over to the other side to get a better angle.

The firing from the tall man's right had become sporadic. Dulac saw his opportunity and sprinted across to the other side of the corridor. He huddled behind a column and saw another passageway, one that led to the deck. *I can get behind the bastard!*

Suddenly he heard the dull sound of grinding and felt the whole ship start to vibrate.

Low at first, the sound became deeper, louder, and the vibrations increased. Dulac's right shoulder pressed against the wall of the corridor. He felt dizzy for a moment but tried to shake it off.

We've hit the reef!

He felt the ship slow to a halt. The pressure on his shoulder eased and Dulac got up and started down the passageway to the deck. He felt the dizziness return, stopped and leaned against the corridor's wall. After a moment, he started towards the deck again. The gunfire was getting louder. He looked left down the deck and saw the tall hijacker, alternately darting behind the cover of a metal column and firing at the Seals. He was 20 feet away, his back to Dulac, oblivious of his presence.

Dulac took a wide stance and tightened his grip on the Glock, aiming squarely at the middle of the man's back.

"Drop it!"

The man turned, swinging his Uzi.

Dulac fired two shots.

Then everything went black.

CHAPTER 34

Onboard the Anzio, a half-mile astern of the Caravan Star

Donnelly peered through his binoculars. "She's hit! She's hit the reef!" He grabbed the VHF and called the chopper pilot. "Becker, do you copy, over?"

"Yes, Captain, this is Becker. Loud and clear. Over."

"What's your situation?"

"The *Caravan Star's* hit the reef. My men are facing heavy gunfire at the bow. We're hovering to cover them."

"What about the bridge?"

A waving hand in Donnelly's peripheral vision caught his attention. The radioman. "Sir, I have Admiral West on the line." Donnelly grabbed the microphone.

"Donnelly."

"We're watching the satellite tracking. The *Caravan Star* isn't moving," said West.

"She's on the reef. Becker is hovering over her in the chopper."

"Damn." Short pause. "Are you in control?"

"I didn't copy that. Please repeat."

"Are you in control?"

"Negative. No report from the bridge. I—"

The ensign signaled Donnelly with the portable VHF. "Sir, the *Caravan Star's* sending a Mayday on channel 16."

"Mayday, Mayday, Mayday, this is . . . this is . . . *Star*, do you copy, over?"

Donnelly grabbed the microphone. "*Caravan Star*, this is the *Anzio*, over."

"Jones, sir. I'm on the bridge with Edwards. She's aground. The ship's officers are unconscious and they don't look good."

CHAPTER 35

Department of Homeland Security, Washington

West finished briefing Lombardi on the latest information on the Star.

"Shit, shit, *shit!*" Nancy Lombardi banged her fist on the table and glared fiercely at West. "How fast can we get the Naloxone to those hostages?"

"According to our test info, most people won't need it."

"Most people? Great. Then all we have to worry about are the ones who do, right, Admiral?"

"Of course. We're doing all we can. We—"

"Yes yes, I know." She looked at the monitor. "How far is the *Monterey*?"

"About 20 miles off. She sent her chopper with 10 SEALs and 100 doses of Naloxone. They have two doctors on board. They're waiting for Becker's instructions."

"So between the *Anzio* and the *Monterey* . . ."

"Madam Secretary, we don't have control of the *Star,*" said West.

A secretary rushed in. "Sir, I have Captain Donnelly on the line."

"Transfer him to the speaker phone," said West.

They heard a gurgling noise masked in heavy static, then a voice came on the line.

"Admiral, this is Donnelly. I—"

The radioman interrupted. "Sir, it's the Caravan Star again."

"I'm going to have to call you back, Admiral. I have the *Star* on VHF."

Donnelly turned to the ensign. "Put them on."

"Egan here, sir. We have control of the bridge, Decks Three, Four, Five, Six and the engine room, Captain."

"Good work, Egan. What about the rest of the ship?"

"The men are mopping up, sir. So far, no resistance."

"Casualties?"

"Four hijackers dead. Two are in pretty bad shape. We have three SEALs with non-life-threatening wounds and one with a stomach wound. Also one man with an apparent heart attack. They've given him a defibrillator boost and he seems to be okay. We're evacuating them to Lajes."

"What about the passengers and crew?"

"The *Monterey's* helicopter is hovering on standby. They'll take care of passengers and crew, and distribute the Naloxone as needed. The Portuguese helicopters will also help evacuate."

"Good. From where we are, the *Star* seems to be listing."

"Affirmative. I can feel heeling from the bridge."

"Listen to me Egan. I want you to look at the instruments and tell me by how much. You'll find an inclinometer somewhere on the console. It's gradated in tenths of degrees."

"Where, sir?"

"Near the Azipod lever, the one that steers the ship."

Brief silence.

"I think I've found it sir. It indicates 4.6 degrees ST."

"Good," said Donnelly. Donnelly knew the chopper's limit for a side-slope landing was 10 degrees. Beyond that, evacuation could only be done when hovering, two passengers at a time. "Keep an eye on it and relay the info to Becker and the other choppers. Check back with me in twenty."

"Roger that, sir."

Egan checked back in precisely twenty minutes. "Sir, the hijackers are contained. Six dead, two badly wounded. We're evacuating passengers on the *Monterrey's* chopper now. The Portuguese helicopters and our chopper are on standby in Corvo for the next run."

"How many evacuated so far?"

"One hundred twenty, sir."

"Degree of list now?"

"8.5 degrees with high winds. Not safe to land, so the pilots are hovering and lifting two at a time."

"Unfortunate but unavoidable. Overall status?"

"We have passengers in the water. They decided not to wait for the choppers and took to the lifeboats. Three broke loose at launch. We did our best but we're in heavy seas. Doesn't look good, sir."

"Jesus."

"Also some passengers didn't react well to the Naloxone. We're flying them to the hospital in Lajes.

"Total casualties?"

"Twelve confirmed deaths not counting the hijackers, sir."

Donnelly grimaced. "Christ. Get the remaining passengers and crew off with all speed. I'm sending more boats to pick up survivors. Keep me posted."

"Roger that, sir."

CHAPTER 36

Santo Espirito Hospital, Terceira, Azores. 18 October, the next day

Dulac awoke, looking up at a drab green ceiling he didn't recognize. His left hand hurt so he looked down. Ah! No wonder. A transparent bag of serum hung on a support to the left of the bed, dripping into the IV tube protruding from his wrist. He shifted to the right and saw Hank, semi-reclining in an adjacent bed, reading a newspaper. With considerable effort, Dulac propped himself further up and sat upright.

Hank put down his newspaper and looked at Dulac. "How are you doing?"

"Not great. What happened?"

"You passed out on the deck after the ship hit the reef. They say the gas can kick in as much as twenty minutes after inhaling it."

"The last thing I remember was firing at the tall hijacker. Did I get the sonofabitch?"

"Don't know, but I heard one of them was operated on yesterday and he's here under police custody."

"What are you in here for?"

"Nausea from the gas. They're just keeping an eye on me for a while to check for other side effects."

"What about Karen? How is—"

The phone beside Dulac's bed rang. He leaned over and picked up the receiver.

"Hello?"

"Hello Thierry, it's Marie. I've been trying to reach you for the last two days. When I couldn't reach you on your phone, I got your coordinates thru P & W lines. I didn't know about the hijacking until this morning. They didn't give me a lot of details. Are you all right?"

"I'm ok. Just a few side effects from the gas."

"Where are you?"

"I'm in Espirito Santo Hospital in Lajes. Probably here for a bit while they check me out."

"Where can I reach you?"

"This number, my cell."

"Good, good. Call me when you have news. Love you."

"Love you too."

Dulac hung up and turned towards Hank.

"Where's Karen?"

Hank hesitated and looked uncomfortable. "They couldn't tell you. You were unconscious . . . she . . ."

Dulac felt his nerves tighten. "Tell me what?"

"Right after you rushed the two hijackers pinning us down, another one came up from behind and opened fire on me and Karen. Before the SEALs nailed him, she took two bullets, one in the thigh and the other in the abdomen near the spinal cord. They operated on her yesterday."

Dulac felt his jaw go slack. "Good God. How is she? Where is she?"

"She was in intensive care yesterday. Better ask the doctor for details." Hank shook the newspaper slightly. "We were the lucky ones."

"How's that?"

"Here, read this." Hank handed him the newspaper.

He stared at the bold headlines of 18 October *Herald Tribune:*

144

HIJACKED CRUISE SHIP HITS REEF.

At 11.45 a.m. local time yesterday, the cruise ship Caravan Star, carrying 527 passengers and crew, ran aground on Torrais Reef off the Island of Corvo in the Azores. The ship had been hijacked earlier that day by a terrorist group calling themselves the Baluchistan Tigers, a spokesman for P & W lines said. In a dramatic rescue operation, the crew of USS American missile cruiser Anzio, which had been tracking the cruise ship, helped save the lives of the majority of the passengers and crew after the ship hit the reef. P & W listed twenty-seven fatalities at this time and would not release their identities until notification of next of kin.

"Jesus." Dulac brought his left hand up to his forehead and felt a lump.

"I heard the doctors say you must have hit your head on something when you fell. Funny, isn't it?" Hank looked down at the front page. "They don't mention anything about the gas."

"The Navy is probably trying to keep a lid on it as long as possible. That lid will blow sky-high once reporters start interviewing passengers."

CHAPTER 37

Washington, DC

The President summoned Lombardi to a 10.00 a.m. meeting, she did not want to be late for, especially since the President had the habit of arriving early. She entered the small conference room next to the Oval Office. Admiral West and Admiral Turner were already there, sullen expressions on their faces. Also present were Jane Winney, Secretary of State, Nick Winters, Presidential Press Secretary, and Attorney General Calvin Smith.

The meeting was not going to be pleasant. Lombardi steeled herself and walked to one of the remaining seats. "Good morning." She tried to retain the right mix of gravity, humility and self-confidence in her voice.

The President entered the room just as she was about to sit down. The attendees stood up in unison. "Mr. President."

The President nodded. "Good morning ladies, gentlemen." He was not smiling. He sat down and rolled up the sleeves of his blue shirt. "Now then, where are we on this?" He eyed Lombardi. "Nancy?"

Lombardi put on her glasses and opened her laptop. "Mr. President, according to the information I have, we were able to successfully airlift 488 passengers and crew from the *Caravan Star*. I—"

"How are they doing?" interrupted the President.

"We have news from Lajes that most have fully recovered and are being taken care of by the Portuguese authorities. They in turn are coordinating with P & W for the passengers' return home."

"Most meaning what exactly?" The president's tone was anything but friendly.

"From the latest report I have, 422 passengers and crew have recovered."

"And the casualties?"

"There will be a coroner's inquest as to—"

"How many dead, Nancy?"

"Not counting the seven dead hijackers, but including Captain Peterson and Mary Dickinson, the Governor's wife, twenty-seven, Mr. President. Some were quite elderly and could have had strokes or heart attacks, and—"

"And the others died from the gas." The President's cold eyes fixed West for a moment, then Smith.

"Mr. President," started Smith, "I—"

Lombardi interrupted Smith. "Mr. President, autopsies will be carried out in Terceira to determine the exact causes of deaths."

The President turned slightly and eyed West. "What about these hijackers, Admiral? What information do we have on them?"

"Mr. President, I don't have much more than what was said at the last meeting. I'm waiting for a full intel report from the CIA."

"Fair enough, Admiral. Now let's get back to Sleeping Beauty." The President turned to Winters. "Nick, once the press grabs this, they'll crucify us. What about damage control?"

"Mr. President, we took the calculated risk of using the gas in order to save the lives of the majority of the passengers and crew. I think we can positively affirm we succeeded in doing just that. I've prepared a series of press releases for your approval."

"I agree," interjected West. "We had no other option. After they murdered Peterson and Dickinson's wife, we simply could not take the risk they would kill other passengers."

"Twenty-seven lives and counting is a pretty high price." The President eyed Lombardi. "I'm sure some folks will say the use of the gas wasn't necessary. Especially our British friends."

"Hindsight is always perfect, Mr. President," said West.

"Tell that to the ratings people." The President addressed the Attorney General. "Calvin, what is our legal situation?"

"Mr. President, apparently the class-action boys are already racing to Lajes in their private jets to sign up the passengers and crew. Since the US government has the deepest pocket in the world, I'd say we can expect a couple of billion dollars' worth of lawsuits minimum for starters."

"Any news from the British?"

"Just confirmation of what they told Admiral West." Smith eyed the Admiral briefly. "They hold the US entirely responsible for this action. No complaints from the Russians or anybody else about a breach of the Chemical Weapons Convention."

"Not even the Russians?" said Winters. "After the accusations we levelled on them for the Moscow situation, surely they're about to scream bloody murder."

The President shot a quick glance at West, then to Winney, then to Smith.

He turned to Winters. "Not really, Nick."

CHAPTER 38

Southampton, P & W Headquarters

Bolding called a meeting of his senior officers to weigh the full measure of the catastrophe. Tie askew, jacket unbuttoned, he rushed into the conference room, where sat Dirk Owens, VP Operations, David Winston, VP Security, Jane Davies, VP Personnel and Communications, and Allister Mills, VP Finance and Administration, their somber expressions testimony to the gravity of the situation.

"Now then, let's see what we can salvage from all this." Bolding eyed Davies. "Jane, how many casualties?"

Davies looked at her report. "We have 21 confirmed passenger deaths, and six crew members. Their bodies are being flown to London first. Then they will be flown to the appropriate destinations. All next of kin have been notified."

"I want a representative of P & W to accompany every one of those coffins," said Bolding. "The least we can do is to show compassion here."

"Yes sir."

Bolding turned to Owens. "Dirk, what's the situation with the *Star*?"

Owens cleared his throat. "We've left a skeleton crew aboard to take care of essentials, and to make sure the bilge pumps keep working. According to information received this morning, the Star has an 11-degree list to starboard, and she's wedged between two reefs. Initial damage report indicates a 20-foot-long gash on the port side, one foot wide, just below the waterline but above the double bottom. Right now the pumps are keeping up, but if she lists any further, all bets are off. The insurance marine surveyors are scheduled to arrive in Corvo this afternoon."

"So it's too early to know if she can be salvaged?" said Bolding.

"Correct. We'll have a better idea by this evening."

Bolding eyed Mills. "Allister, what's the financial impact of this so far?"

Mills looked uncomfortably at Bolding, then the others. "As expected, sales have dropped, but frankly I didn't think they'd slide this much. Yesterday alone, we had 12 tour operators cancel. I've tried to stop the hemorrhaging by offering discounted tours but no one is interested." Mills paused for an instant, then continued. "Also, we have a serious cash-flow issue."

"How serious?" said Bolding.

"Our lines of credit are fully used up. We need five million pounds by next week."

"What about our insurers?" interjected Owens. "Any news from them?"

"I can answer that," said Bolding. "They're about as cooperative as a bull in a rodeo. They mentioned something about a late premium payment issue." Bolding looked at Mills. "Do you know anything about that?"

Mill's face flushed. "We, we might have dragged our feet a little."

"Well, that's moot anyway. If we need cash, I'm going to make them an offer they can't refuse."

* * *

The next day, Bolding sat in the offices of Lloyd's. P & W's Solicitor Andrew Toombs, of the firm of Avery, Hawkins and Toombs, sat beside him. Philip Dunmore, Lloyds' VP Maritime, and Lloyd's solicitor James Brett sat across the table facing them.

Four copies of P & W's maritime insurance policies, bound in metal coils and plastic transparent covers, lay spread out on the conference room table. All four copies were earmarked with yellow and red stickers.

"We won't need those," said Dunmore. "We have our own." He smiled and pulled out three documents from his briefcase.

"Suit yourself," said Bolding. "I've asked you to come because P & W wants to make sure we settle this matter quickly. At least the portion of the claim that can be evaluated now."

"I must say this is most unusual, Mr. Bolding," said Dunmore, "as your policy states at page 104 that the insurer retains the right to fully assess all damages before—"

"I'm aware of that," said Bolding.

Dunmore eyed Brett quickly before returning his gaze upon Bolding. "Then I'm not quite sure I understand."

"It's quite simple. We're prepared to make a deal in exchange for fast payment."

"I see," said Dunmore, "but we have a firm corporate policy to—"

"I'm willing to knock off five million pounds from Lloyd's last payment in exchange for a payment of the same amount now. That's a substantial reduction from what you owe us under contract anyway." Bolding glanced at Toombs. "If you agree, Mr. Toombs here has drafted the appropriate waiver and sign off for the five million pounds."

Dunmore looked unimpressed. He turned to Brett. "I believe you have something to say, Mr. Brett?"

Mr. Brett instantly submerged himself in his file. He flipped through documents rapidly. "According to our records, P & W is late on three premiums of the building insurance policy for P &W's headquarters here." Brett looked up. "Are you aware of this, Mr. Bolding?"

Bolding regained his composure quickly. "I'll have it corrected immediately." He leaned forward to grab the phone.

"I'm not sure that will do any good." said Brett. "You see, Sir Adrian, there are cross-default clauses on both of our maritime and building policies, meaning if an insured defaults on one, it automatically suspends the other policy until payment of the defaulting policy is made. If an incident occurs before the default has—"

"Come now, Mr. Brett," interrupted Toombs. "We both know that these clauses have been stricken down by the courts as unconscionable and unreasonable."

"On a case-by-case basis," said Brett.

Bolding flung an angered look at Dunmore. "Are you telling me that Lloyds won't pay?"

Dunmore's expression hardened. "I never said that, Mr. Bolding. But you see, I'd be rightly criticized by our people if I were to comply to your demand of five million pounds up front, with Lloyd's later taking a position that your company, after three warnings of non-payment, has in fact defaulted not only on the building policy but on the maritime policy also."

"Christ!" said Bolding.

Bolding turned and glanced expectantly at Toombs.

Toombs pushed away from the table. "I'd like to discuss this in private with my client."

Bolding rose, throwing a glacial glower at Dunmore. "Excuse us." Bolding and Toombs left the room and headed to a secluded spot across the hall.

"Bastards. I knew something was wrong when Dunmore showed up with Brett."

"I'm assuming what they said about the non-payment is—"

"Probably true," said Bolding.

"I'm at a loss here."

"We're facing serious financial issues. We've been dragging our feet a little with non-pressing creditors. I never thought to look at the cross-default clauses."

"I see."

"I don't think you do."

CHAPTER 39

Santo Espirito Hospital, Azores

Dulac took the elevator up to the ER on the third floor. His mind kept replaying the nurse's synopsis of what to expect. She's very weak. She is under heavy sedation. And she may not recognize you.

That third possibility scared him most. He got off the elevator and followed the signs towards room 328. Peering through the open doorways of rooms on the way, he could see the occasional unoccupied bed, recently vacated by occupants either now on the road to recovery, or in the morgue. He hastened his pace, trying to suppress his fleeting bursts of curiosity mixed with morbidity. He reached room 328. The door was slightly ajar, so he took a deep breath and entered.

He hardly recognized her. Her gaze was fixed toward the ceiling, her complexion a deathly gray. Neither the deep black pockets under her eyes or the drawn lines rising from the corners of her open mouth did a thing to reassure Dulac she'd recover from this. For a second, he feared the worse, until he saw the barely perceptible rise and fall of the sheets on her torso.

He stood back in shock, wondering if he should intrude further, when Karen turned her head slowly towards him. She stretched out her left hand in invitation to his, her eyes a silent expression of pleading and resignation.

Dulac fought back tears as he took her hand, brought it to his lips and kissed it.

"Hello Thierry," she whispered through a faint smile, the muted sound coming from deep within her chest.

"Don't speak. I just came to say hello. You're doing fine." She smiled again and nodded slightly. She squeezed his hand with both of hers. "You've got to rest for now. Then we'll get you home. If it's ok, I'll just stay here awhile."

She nodded.

Dulac sat down in the worn leather seat, looking at the monitors. After a while, a nurse came by and whispered it was best to let Karen rest alone.

Dulac looked at Karen as she slept peacefully. He backed out of the room slowly and headed to the elevator. As he waited for the doors to open, pangs of guilt overtook him. He was the reason Karen was here. He shouldn't have left her and Hank alone. He'd acted on impulse instead of reason. Had he stayed and defended her, chances were she wouldn't have been hurt at all.

CHAPTER 40

Dulac had visited Karen every day, and after the third day, she'd been moved from Intensive Care to Recuperation. She was out of danger and the doctor's prognosis for a complete recovery was most encouraging. After four days, Dulac had shown no significant after-effects from the gas and had been discharged from the hospital.

He'd taken the Thursday flight from Ponta Delgada to Paris, then the next morning's TGV train to Lyon. Forty minutes after his arrival at the Gare de St Exupéry, he entered the Interpol General Secretary's office.

Its present occupant was Annette Arlberg, a svelte Norwegian with finely chiseled facial features bare of makeup and blonde hair cut shoulder length, who looked every bit the ideal of Scandinavian good looks and great health. Disillusioned by the crassness of the legal world, she'd jumped ship from the prestigious family law firm of Arlberg and Olafsson thirteen years before and through her father's connections, gotten a job at Interpol in Lyon. Gradually she'd climbed the ranks, starting as research assistant legal, then agent, and finally to General Secretary a year

156

ago when the previous incumbent had lost the confidence of the General Assembly.

In some ways, Dulac felt a kinship with Arlberg. He too could have practiced law in his native Montpellier instead of choosing a vocation in law enforcement. He too had forsaken a lucrative career path for the bringing to justice of international criminals. In other ways, Arlberg was an enigma. An unknown quantity. Somehow he knew the feeling was mutual, or at least devoid of the outright hostility he'd experienced with her immediate predecessor Richard Harris. A cold shiver ran up his spine as he consciously blocked further thoughts about Harris.

"Please." She motioned Dulac to one of the Art Deco seats across from her desk.

Dulac sat down.

Arlberg flipped a strand of hair back behind her left ear. "How do you feel?"

Dulac shrugged. "Tell you in a month. The quacks at Lajes say my early symptoms should eventually disappear."

"Symptoms?" A small frown creased Arlberg's tanned forehead.

"They say the first month is critical. Memory loss, dizzy spells may occur."

"I see. And so far?"

"Nothing much. Just a bit of dizziness in the morning."

"That's encouraging. Tell me, can you . . . ?"

"Get back to work?"

Arlberg put up her right hand defensively. "I don't want to push you."

"As a matter fact, they said the sooner the better."

"Good." Arlberg crossed her legs and reclined in her seat. "By the way, I heard your friend wasn't so lucky."

"One of the hijacker's bullets grazed her spine." Dulac felt a tinge of guilt returning.

"How is she doing?"

"Better. The doctors are saying there's a good chance she'll recover completely."

Arlberg took a pencil from her desk and started twiddling it between her fingers.

"Any thoughts on the hijacking?" she said.

"Very simple. Those hijackers couldn't have pulled it off alone. They must have had inside help."

Arlberg crossed her arms on her chest and walked back and forth, gathering her thoughts. "That seems to be the position of Scotland Yard and the Americans as well."

"What do you mean?"

"I've had a call from Nancy Lombardi, Director of Homeland Security."

"Oh?" Dulac's interest rose sharply.

"She says she's still responsible for the case on their side."

"I'm surprised. Why not the CIA, or the FBI?"

"Because of the deal they've struck with Scotland Yard. Problem is there is no way the Brits are going to let the CIA, or the FBI for that matter, roam their pastures, possibly pick up info on sensitive, confidential data along the way. As a compromise, Lombardi suggested to the Yard that Interpol get involved instead, which the Yard has reluctantly agreed to."

"I'm assuming you have also."

"Yes. Scotland Yard has put a certain inspector Harry Wade in charge at their end. They've put out a warrant for the arrest of the missing security officer, Tajar Singh. "

"Who are you thinking of assigning at our end? Lescop is due for something challenging." Before the phrase was complete his brain told Dulac he shouldn't have asked. From the way Arlberg looked at him, he knew that suggestion wasn't going to fly.

"I would prefer you took the case."

Dulac looked askance at Arlberg. *No way I'm working with the Yard again!* "Why me? Just because I was on the ship?"

"I have my reasons. Besides, you know the territory, so to speak, you've worked with the Yard before."

"Not the most pleasant of experiences."

"Really? And how is that?" Arlberg leaned slightly back towards the wall.

"You weren't around then, but the Hidalgo case comes to mind. The Yard took, shall we say, a more bureaucratic approach to the case than we did. That nearly lost us the case. I got the distinct impression they were paying lip service to my being there. And the cherry on the cake was when they took all the credit. Didn't even mention Interpol."

"I'd be lying if I said this is looking any different, but at least we'll be in the front row." Arlberg went to her desk, picked up a file and handed it to Dulac. "Here is what we have on Wade."

Dulac opened the file. From the photo, Wade looked middle-aged, mid-fifties at a guess, with a dour expression probably acquired through years of working with and around criminals. His mouth was only a slit but he had a remarkably rosy complexion for a man his age, with disproportionately large ears for his smallish head. Dulac started to glance through Wade's history, professional and personal.

"... 47 years old, divorced, three children, indeterminate sexual orientation ..."

Dulac emitted a guffaw and eyed Arlberg. "Indeterminate sexual orientation? What the hell does that mean?"

"Well, we can't really put on paper that he's switched from sail to steam, so to speak, now can we?"

"Delicate subject."

"Yes. But every bit of information helps."

Dulac read on. "So he has a gambling problem also."

"I would call it an issue. So far, he's been able to settle his debts with the London bookies without having to remortgage his house or sell major assets."

"Great."

"Read on. He has a crime-solving rate of eighty-nine percent."

"Almost as good as mine. Dulac smiled wryly, knowing full well Wade had a file on him and was going through the same exercise.

"Don't expect a warm welcome, but do try to be a bit diplomatic, Dulac."

"Diplomacy was my father's profession. Not mine."

* * *

Dulac left Arlberg's office and took the elevator down to the third floor. He got out, turned left and walked briskly past the open offices. He stopped before his assistant's desk, smiled at Kim Young Soo and asked the young Korean woman to summon Lescop to his office.

A few moments later, agent Daniel Lescop, a short, trim balding man of forty-something entered Dulac's office. Dulac pointed to a seat in front of his desk and Lescop sat down.

"The Iron Lady wants me to head the *Caravan Star* investigation." Dulac stood and looked distractedly out the window behind his desk.

"But you said I'd be the lead agent . . ."

Dulac turned back to Lescop. "She overrode my decision. I thought I'd let you know it wasn't my doing."

"I . . . well, thanks anyway," said Lescop, a look of resignation on his thin face.

"So I'm going to let you find another agent to do the digging work on the Bacarat case and bring you aboard the *Caravan Star* case. You'll still remain lead agent on Bacarat of course."

Lescop looked confused. "I, I don't understand. Isn't that against her instructions?"

"Not really. Just bending them a little. She didn't say I couldn't choose you to second me. Anyone you want to consider for Bacarat?"

"I think Seegers is available. He's just off the Alexia investigation. The Italians dropped all charges."

"I'll send him a note. Brief him on the file, then you're mine."

"Thanks. You won't regret this." Lescop rose and shook Dulac's hand enthusiastically.

"That remains to be seen. By the way, cancel any dates with wives and mistresses for the next few days."

Lescop looked quizzically at Dulac.

"You're going to Costa Rica tomorrow. I've arranged for you to be present when the San José police arrest Leon Binagro as accessory to the *Star* hijacking and for laundering the ransom money. If you have to reach me, I'll be at Scotland Yard, with a certain inspector Harry Wade."

"Going to have it out with the Brits, eh?" said Lescop, with a look of mirthful sympathy on his face.

"Something like that."

CHAPTER 41

Heathrow airport, 25 October, 10.50 a.m.

As the Airbus 330 descended through the clouds and hit a series of air pockets, Dulac instinctively grabbed the armrests of his seat. Ça commence bien! Moments later the plane bounced on touchdown, swayed slightly left, then right, before straightening out, slowing and taxiing to the tarmac. Dulac unclenched his sweaty hands from the armrests, his jarred nerves uncoiling gradually from around his chest, his misery coming to an end.

Half an hour later, Dulac cleared customs and wove his way through the crowd of friends and relatives greeting passengers. He didn't really believe someone would have been sent to pick him up, but he looked about just in case anyone was carrying a placard with his name. They weren't. Overnight bag and laptop in hand, he went outside to the taxi stand and waited his turn in the bone-chilling sprinkle of rain.

"Where to, guv?" The driver's words were barely intelligible as he didn't bother to turn towards Dulac.

"10 Broadway."

"Going to play in the Yard, are we?"

"Yep." Dulac stared out the window.

* * *

The taxi joined the flow of morning traffic onto the busy A4, through Chiswick and along the Thames. Moments later, Dulac caught a glimpse of the Royal Albert Hall to his left, soon followed by the posh mansions of the Belgravia district, one of the world's priciest pieces of real-estate and London residences to more than a few sultans and emirs. When the taxi reached Duke of Wellington Road, traffic had coalesced into gridlock, and the smell of diesel fumes slowly permeated the inside of the cab. Gradually the traffic started inching forward again and twenty minutes later, the cabbie stopped before an array of red vehicles parked in front of a tall rectangular building of glass, granite and steel.

"Here you are, Guv. That'll be fifty-one quid."

"Sorry?"

"Pounds. Fifty-one pounds."

Dulac reached into his left pocket, opened his wallet and took out a wad of twenty-pound notes. "What's with the red police cars?" Dulac was unable to contain his curiosity.

"The Diplomatic Protection Group Patrol. We call them DIPATS for short. They're supposed to protect the policemen and diplomats from terrorists."

"Policemen protecting policemen. Interesting concept."

"And my taxes are paying for it." The driver grunted his disapproval.

Dulac paid the cabbie, grabbed his computer and overnight bag and made his way up the granite steps. He showed his Interpol card to one of the DIPATS, who ran a scan through the card identifier. After a moment, he returned the card and nodded an OK to Dulac, who went through the revolving doors to the reception desk.

"I'm here to see Inspector Harry Wade." Dulac showed his ID card to a woman wearing glasses as thick as the bottom of a Tanqueray bottle.

"Is he expecting you?" She peered closely at the card.

"Hope so."

Dulac waited as the woman took a series of calls. Finally she called Wade's office and announced Dulac. After a moment, a tall, slim brunette with an easy smile appeared at the front desk.

"Mr. Dulac?"

Dulac nodded.

"Please follow me."

They took the elevator to the sixth floor. The doors opened and Dulac followed the woman to a small office amid an array of even smaller offices lining the windowed wall. A man with short-cut brown hair and a furrowed face rose from behind his desk to greet him. *Looks older than his photo.* As he entered Wade's office, Dulac's attention was immediately drawn to the framed certificates of varying sizes adorning the wall behind Wade.

"Ah . . . Mr. Dulac." Wade proffered a hand, "Sorry I couldn't meet you at Heathrow. How was your flight?"

Dulac doubted the sincerity of the apology. "Lumpy."

"Yes, well, these days, the weather doesn't help. Please." Wade sat down and offered Dulac one of the chairs in front of the desk. "So what can we do for you, Mr. Dulac?" said Wade perfunctorily.

"For starters, I'd like you to bring me up to speed with everything you've got on P & W, its officers, personnel records, critical path analysis leading up to and including the hijacking, onboard video and voice transcripts of the *Caravan Star*, transcript—"

Wade put up his right hand in protest. "Not so fast, Mr. Dulac. As far as we're concerned, you're support only. We'll call you when—"

And here we go. Hidalgo all over again. "Inspector, before we get started, let's clear up any misunderstanding, shall we?" Dulac looked fixedly at Wade. "I don't want to get all legalistic, but since you brought it up, Article 23 of the Interpol-Britain Cooperation Agreement gives me complete investigative powers on cross-border crimes. Since the *Caravan Star* was hijacked on the open seas and acts of piracy, sequestration and a number of murders were committed on that ship, Interpol has the right to all the information you have, including any data in HOLMES 3."

"You know about HOLMES 3?"

"Home Office Large Major Enquiry System. It replaced obsolete and non-intuitive HOLMES 2 a month ago. Much more powerful."

Wade eyed Dulac with a curious wariness. "I see you're well informed."

"I try. So when is your next Major Incident Room meeting?"

"Out of the question. We don't have enough—"

"What about this afternoon?"

"Impossible. We—"

Dulac rested his right forearm on Wade's desk and leaned toward him. "I need to get up to speed quickly, Inspector."

"I realize that, but there are certain internal protocols we need to observe before we can—"

Dulac needed to block Wade's evasiveness quickly. "Let me help you prioritize this, maybe with a call to Sir Terence Hays. I spoke with him while I was on the *Caravan Star*. I'm sure he'll—"

"Be my guest." Wade pushed the phone in Dulac's direction.

Dulac picked up the phone and dialed Gina's number. After three rings, she answered.

"Yes, it's me. Dulac. Please get me Sir Terence Hay's number. I'll wait."

Wade reached over and cut off the connection. "Listen, let's try not to get off on the wrong foot, shall we Dulac? I have a lunch meeting in 10 minutes. I'll see who's available this afternoon. Shall we say 1.30?"

CHAPTER 42

Centre de Rééducation Fonctionnelle, Paris, 12.45 p.m.

The nurse brought the lunch tray on the small wheel board table and swung the table over Karen's bed.

"And how is Madame Karen this morning?"

"Fine." Karen felt tingling in her left leg as she pushed herself up into a sitting position. She looked quizzically at the plate's metal cover.

"Quiche and potatoes." The nurse smiled as she removed the cover.

"Again?"

The nurse shrugged and went to the window to adjust the blinds. "A little more light?"

"No thanks. I'm quite tired actually."

"You must not sleep so much. Dr. Bouliva says it is not good for you."

"Easy for him to say. He's not the one who can hardly walk."

"You must think positively, positive thoughts. Things will get better." The nurse opened the blinds. "You must have faith. Last week, Mr. Dompierre started to walk again with the crutches."

"And how long has he been here?"

The nurse looked pensively upwards. "Oh, about a month. But you are much younger. You'll see, you'll walk better soon."

"I hope you're right."

The phone on the bedside table rang. Karen picked up the receiver.

"Hello?"

"It's me. Just wanted to touch base. How are you doing?" said Dulac.

"Thierry. Just a second." Karen turned toward the nurse and smiled. "That'll be all, *merci*."

The nurse turned quickly and walked out.

"Apart from the tasteless meals, not bad. Where are you?"

"At the Asquith Hotel, in London. I'm finishing a terrible lunch and about to return to the Yard."

"Can't be worse than here."

"Sounds as if you're getting better already."

"If tingling in my left leg can be considered getting better, yes." She pushed the table away from the bed. "How goes your investigation?"

"I'm about to find out what the Yard has. A certain Harry Wade is in charge. Not very cooperative."

"Try to be diplomatic, Thierry."

"That's exactly what Arlberg said. Too late for that."

"So when can I see you?"

"Hard to tell. Could be a few days, a week maybe. Depends on how many barriers they put up."

"I miss you."

"And I you. I've got to go. Call you soon."

* * *

Scotland Yard, 1.30 p.m.

Dulac stepped out of the elevator on the sixth floor and turned right towards Wade's office. The smell of freshly brewed coffee wafted through the air as Dulac made his way along the open cubicles, where constabulary personnel occasionally looked up from their computer screens and gave Dulac an inquisitive glance. For all the excitement, he could have been at the office of a mortician.

"Mr. Dulac." Dulac looked right. It was the tall brunette, Wade's secretary, walking at a brisk pace along one of the side corridors. "They're waiting for you in the Major Incident Room. Please follow me."

They went to the far end of the corridor, arriving in front of two wood panel doors. The young woman inserted a plastic key into the security slot next to the doors. A green light flashed and the left door opened. Dulac entered and the door closed automatically behind him. The room was lit in blue neon lights, and an array of large video screens adorned three walls. The fourth wall was reserved for pictures of Sherlock Holmes, as depicted by various actors in the celebrated detective's filmography. Dulac immediately recognized Jeremy Brett, Peter Cushing and Basil Rathbone. With the high resolution of his photo, Benedict Cumberbatch was clearly the latest addition. In the center of the room, men and women were seated at small tables, some looking at their laptops, others in hushed discussions with their colleagues. Dulac spotted Wade, seated, talking to two men.

"Ah, Inspector." Wade rose from his chair. "Meet Jonathan Coe from Workflow Management, and Simon Potter from Task Management." The two men rose and smiled mechanically. "Please." Wade motioned Dulac to a chair next to him.

"Gentlemen." Dulac walked over and sat down next to Wade. "What about Document Management and Critical Path Analysis?"

"I see you know Holmes well, Mr. Dulac," Wade said. "It's a little early for that input at this time."

"Let's see what you've got." Dulac thrummed the fingers of his right hand on the table.

"Jonathan?" said Wade.

"Right," said Coe. A tall man with hollow cheeks and wavy brown hair tapped keys on his computer's keyboard. The first of the PowerPoint slides appeared on one of the large video screens on the far wall, captioned as *Caravan Star*. The explanatory text read "Events 36. DRE impression parameters."

"Presumably you know about the DRE, Mr. Dulac?" said Coe.

"Dynamic Reasoning Engine. The so-called computer with a mind. You're going to tell me that . . ."

"I'm only here to let you know we will be using it down the road," said Coe. "We don't have enough relevant facts or data quite yet."

"I'm anxious to find out if it can handle paradox," said Dulac.

"What do you mean?" said Coe.

"Simple. Paradox: a statement seemingly self-contradictory or absurd, but possibly well-founded or essentially true. Or, if you wish, a conflict of preconceived notions of what is reasonable or possible."

Coe stood mute. He looked at Dulac, then the others.

"Yes, well, I guess it's all a matter of perspective, isn't it?" said Wade, in an effort to rescue Coe from his momentary paralysis.

"My point exactly," said Dulac. "Thank you, Mr. Wade."

Wade turned to Potter. "Simon?"

Potter turned on his computer. The slide changed to another image, also captioned *Caravan Star*. The explanatory text for this one read "Task Management" followed by a detailed chart with boxes and names.

"How many investigators have you assigned?" Dulac asked Wade.

"Two. And three assistants."

"I don't see my name in any of the boxes." Dulac looked pointedly at the screen.

"This is primary functionality, Mr. Dulac," said Potter. "We will of course call upon you when we feel there is an Interpol parameter and . . ."

"No, you will not. Because I—and Interpol—will already be in control of this operation. Every aspect of it."

"I beg your pardon?" said Potter.

Dulac noted the frowns of disapproval and could not have cared less. "Again, read your Interpol cooperation agreement. Quote: 'Article 23 (c), (ii). Whenever a major crime becomes trans-border, Interpol shall coordinate all investigation activities and take whatever action is necessary to take control of the investigation.'"

"But that's—"

Dulac continued, ". . . and subsection (e) (i): 'The investigative forces of Great Britain shall provide assistance deemed necessary by the Interpol agent in his investigation'. I assume that's clear enough for you gentlemen?"

"Well, that's all fine and dandy Mr. Dulac," said Wade," but we have already begun and as you can see, tasks have already been attributed and the investigation is well under way."

"I haven't seen anything tangible yet."

"That's because you haven't let us show you." Potter regained his composure. "Perhaps the next few pages will help."

"Fair enough. Go ahead," said Dulac.

Potter tapped on his computer keyboard. "Here we have the result of background checks on all security personnel on board *Caravan Star*. Seven people have false identities. All were hired through the previous security officer aboard the *Caravan Star*."

"Previous?" asked Dulac.

Potter continued. "David Winston replaced a certain Tajar Singh, two weeks before the *Caravan Star* sailed out of Southampton. Singh was on sick leave."

"And obviously you haven't been able to locate him."

"He's vanished," said Potter. "He and his family have been living in Southampton for the past seven years. Two kids in school. During his four years at P & W, good track record. Sixteen days before the hijack, he didn't report in. Family and friends haven't heard from him since."

"Any leads?" said Dulac.

"None. We put out an all points on him. We suggest you do the same at Interpol."

"How did these guys get their guns past the metal detectors?" said Dulac.

"Still baffled by that," said Wade.

"We had our people check all cameras and screening devices for entry aboard the ship," said Potter. "They are at present one hundred percent operational. We checked the security logs and there was no interruption from the time the *Caravan Star* set sail from Southampton. To our knowledge no one boarded her in transit, so we must presume the hijackers boarded at Southampton. We're still waiting for the results of the onboard video cameras."

"What about the people at P & W? What's the intel on them?" said Dulac.

"It's a rather delicate matter." Wade looked uncomfortable. "You see, there is a . . . call it a connection . . . in this matter between P & W and the Home Office."

"Meaning?"

"It's not up to me to elaborate. Let's just say we can't walk into their offices and start asking questions without reasonable cause," said Wade.

Dulac looked incredulously at Wade. "Really? So you don't intend to investigate P & W's officers?"

"Not for the moment. We've asked for certain information from P & W and so far, they've been quite cooperative. From what we've seen, we have no reason to suspect any foul play on their part. At worst, P & W has been lax in its hiring practices. If we were to investigate every shipping line on that basis, we . . ."

"We're talking about the death of twenty-seven people, Mr. Wade," said Dulac.

"Well, as I say, we don't have any reason to believe in—"

"Any foul play."

"Apart from Singh, at least not for the moment." Wade turned to Coe. "Jonathan, perhaps you can update us on workflow management."

Coe tapped his computer's keyboard and the video monitor showed a new image titled *Caravan Star: Workflow Management.* "Here we have the management chart with all potential agencies that have information on the case. As you can see, it's pretty broad-based and includes data from British, American, Russian, even Pakistani agencies. As the information gets typed in from the various services, Holmes 3 analyzes the relevancy of the data source in different categories, from 1 to 6, one being most relevant, six being basically irrelevant areas. The first four categories are classified by selection of categories, such as profile, fingerprints, past criminal records, memberships of organizations, criminal or not, etc. Then weaponry owned or used by the individual, individuals or organizations and their likely provenance and—"

"Tell me, Mr. Coe," interrupted Dulac. "Can I input data from right here, in this room? For instance, a person's name?"

"Of course."

"And will Holmes 3 analyze the relevance of the name it categorizes?"

"Absolutely. We can give it a go. Right now. What's the name?"

"Try Adrian Bolding. Sir Adrian Bolding."

"Now really Mr. Dulac," interjected Wade, his air one of contemptuous reproach. "This is no time to jest. I—"

"Humor me." Dulac's tone wasn't a request. Coe punched in Bolding's name. The video flickered for a moment and the information came on line:

Sir Adrian Bolding — Born Southampton 13 August 1958, attended Eaton and Oxford, divorced, son Mark aged 22. CEO of P & W Lines, shareholder of 19.5% class A voting shares, and 35%. Class C non-voting shares. Board memberships: P & W, P & W International, Frankfurt Trust, Bankers' Trust, Barrick Gold Canada. Weapons owned: four 12-gauge Browning shotguns. Registered use:

hunting. One Smith and Wesson .38 revolver. One .22
Remington High Power rifle. Registered use: target practice.
All corresponding registrations and licenses are current.
Subject's Classification: 3.

Dulac looked at Wade, whose rosy cheeks were slowly turning purple. "Well, Mr. Wade. It seems Holmes 3 doesn't agree with you."

"Could be because of the guns," said Wade lamely. "Besides, the computer has been known to err on the side of caution."

"Or it could be something else since Holmes 3 has an intuitive capacity. In any case I don't need probable cause, so I think I'll pay the people at P & W a visit."

Wade looked askance at Dulac and heaved a long breath of exasperation. "I suppose it won't do any good if I say you'll need to have someone from the Yard with you."

"I'm a big boy, Wade. I don't need a babysitter." Dulac got up to leave. "As you were saying, let's not get this wonderful relationship off on the wrong foot."

CHAPTER 43

P & W Headquarters, next day

Dulac had managed to schedule a meeting with Bolding at 11 a.m. After a one-and-a-half-hour train journey to Southampton, Dulac took a cab, destination Caravan House, P & W's headquarters. As the cabdriver wove in and out of the morning traffic in pouring rain, Dulac rubbed his arthritic hands vigorously and reminded himself why he disliked Britain. He reached in his coat pocket, grabbed the plastic bottle and extracted an anti-inflammatory pill, which he swallowed with difficulty. After a moment, the pain subsided slightly. The rain increased when he opened the taxi door. Of course. He grabbed his satchel and dashed up the steps to Caravan House's glassed entrance. Inside was an information booth at which sat a plump woman with a significant double-chin. She raised her eyes from her desk and inspected the soaked Dulac.

"P & W's offices are . . . ?"

"Fifth floor. Take the elevator to your left."

"Thanks."

Moments later, Dulac stood in front of dark mahogany doors embossed with the bronze inscription, "P & W Cruise

Lines PLC". He entered and asked the receptionist for Sir Adrian Bolding. Shortly thereafter, a petite woman with an oily complexion and a welcoming smile proffered her right hand. "Mr. Dulac, I'm Sheila Brown. Sir Adrian is expecting you. This way, please."

Dulac followed her across the open room, where men and women were busy at their computers and telephones.

"Our booking agents." She gave Dulac a quick side glance.

"Business is still good?"

"Oh yes. Very good."

Dulac made a mental note of the contrived answer. They stopped in front of another mahogany door at the far corner of the room. The secretary knocked.

"Come in." The voice behind the door was firm and commanding.

Sheila Brown opened the door. "Sir Adrian, I have a Mr. Dulac, inspector from—"

"Of course. Come in, Inspector. Finally we meet." Bolding rose from his seat and make his way around the large desk. From their exchange during the hijacking, Dulac had not expected such a short person. Bolding's deep, baritone voice seemed incongruous with his small stature.

"I can't thank you enough for what you did on board the *Star*. That took a lot of courage," said Bolding.

"Well, I was going on instinct alone. I guess E for effort doesn't cut it."

"What do you mean?"

"The ship still landed up on the reef."

"Yes, I suppose. But many lives were saved. Please, have a seat, Inspector. Coffee, tea?"

"Coffee, black."

"The usual for me, please Sheila." The secretary turned to leave and closed the door behind her.

"Now then, I gather this isn't only a social visit."

"Correct."

"Then how can I be of help, Inspector?" Bolding smiled.

Dulac opened his computer on his lap and looked up at Bolding. "We have a problem. I don't think the hijackers pulled this off without inside help. There is lot of, shall we say, convergence, such as the convenient disappearance of your safety officer Tajar Singh, the smuggling of weapons on board, the lack of screening of your safety personnel. In our trade we call it convergence."

"Yes, I suppose. You'll know a lot more when you find Singh, of course." Bolding leaned back in his chair and tapped his fingers together in the form of an arc.

"I'm not waiting for that to happen."

Bolding stopped smiling. "I see. Then how can I be of assistance?"

"I'd like to start with your officers. I'd like to talk to each of them. By the way, what's the status of the ship? Will she be re-floated?"

"We're discussing that with our insurers at this very moment."

"I've heard they might refuse to pay."

Bolding's face reddened. "Oh? And where did you hear that?"

"Not important. Judging from your reaction, there's obviously truth to the rumor."

"This is a private matter, Mr. Dulac."

Dulac paused a moment before leaning forward. "Mr. Bolding, let's get one thing straight. There is nothing private in the murder of two people, the deaths of twenty-seven passengers and the taking of hostages by armed terrorists."

"I fail to see what our insurance problems have to do with—"

"Nothing is private, Mr. Bolding. It will be best if you simply accept that." Dulac relaxed his posture and leaned back into his chair. "First, I'd like to talk to the Staff Captain the one that replaced Peterson." Dulac looked at his computer screen. "Peter Rhodes, I believe is his name."

"Actually, he's on sick leave. He's suffering from severe post-traumatic stress. I doubt you'll be able to get anything from him."

"Where is he?"

"At Southampton General."

Bolding's secretary walked in and deposited a tray with two coffees on the table beside Bolding's desk.

"Thanks Sheila," said Bolding.

"You're welcome sir," She smiled and walked out.

Bolding picked up his cup and took a sip of his coffee.

Dulac looked at his computer screen again. "What about First Officer Sandra Brown?"

"She's on sick leave also. She's suffering from the side effects of the Bezorban."

"Are there any of the ship's officers on the premises?"

"Jeremy Tate, the radio operator. I can send for him if you wish."

Dulac looked at his watch. "Please. Perhaps I can buy him lunch."

"I'd join you but I have a previous luncheon engagement. I'll see if he's free." Bolding picked up the phone and dialed Tate's extension.

Dulac leaned over and picked up his coffee.

Moments later, a thirty-something man wearing an open-collared blue shirt entered Bolding's office.

"Jeremy, please meet Inspector Dulac, from Interpol. He's got questions about the hijacking."

Tate hesitantly offered Dulac his right hand.

"Are you free for lunch?" asked Dulac.

"I . . . I was planning on having my sandwich here but—"

"Can you recommend a restaurant nearby?"

"Well, there's the dining room at The Lancet Hotel."

"Good." Dulac closed his computer and got up to leave. He eyed Bolding. "I'll need your security staff employment records for the *Caravan Star* for the past two years, along with the CV's and employment records of all P & W's officers."

Bolding bolted up from his seat. "Now see here, Mr. Dulac—"

"Oh, and before I forget, I'll also need the videos from aboard the *Caravan Star* during the hijacking."

"The Yard already has those. Surely, you're coordinating with them?"

Interesting. "Of course." Dulac said smoothy. "I just thought you might have a copy handy and that I'd take a peek while I'm here."

Tate and Dulac went downstairs and hailed a cab, which wound its way through the busy docks area towards their stated destination. On route, Dulac recognized the unmistakable, dark-blue hull of the *Queen Elizabeth II*, her elegant silhouette and nautical lines in marked contrast with those of the white behemoths berthed in front of and behind her.

Tate saw him looking at the beautiful vessel. "Probably the last time we'll see her."

"Oh, why is that?"

"Rumor has it she's been bought by some rich Arab who wants to transform her into a floating hotel."

"Like her sister ship the *Queen Mary*. So apart from the cruise ships, what is there to see in Southampton?"

Tate shrugged. "Nothing much."

"Really?"

"Well, if you're into planes, there's always the Aviation Museum. Southampton is where the Spitfire was manufactured during WWII."

"I gather you're not from Southampton," said Dulac.

"London."

They left the docks area and the cab took a right along Muir Street. Moments later, they crossed the bridge over the Itchen River and entered the city's historic section, past the decaying remnants of its medieval wall. A couple of intersections later, the cab stopped before a Tudor-style building, incongruously flanked by two pseudo-medieval turrets. A gold-lettered sign between the turrets read *Lancet Hotel*. Dulac paid the cabbie and they walked through the small lobby. Tate opened the stained-glass doors into the dining room.

Inside, patrons were taking an early lunch.

"Over there." Dulac pointed to the small alcove.

Tate and Dulac sat down. A young waiter with a nonchalant stride approached and inquired in a Cockney accent. "Gentlemen, what'll it be?"

"Bitters with a twist of lemon," said Tate.

"Same," said Dulac.

"Right." The waiter handed them the menus.

"What do you recommend?" Dulac scanned the options.

"The fish and chips are quite good actually. So are the lamb chops," said the waiter.

"I'll have the chops," said Tate, "medium rare."

"Same," Dulac handed the menus back to the waiter."

"Out in a flash, gents," the waiter assured them as he left.

Dulac eyed Tate. "So how long have you been at P & W?"

"Just over two years."

"And before that?"

"I was with Carnival for six years. Joined them out of the Academy."

Dulac heard warning bells in his head. Something had to have happened to make Tate leave Carnival for P & W. That would have been like going from Manchester United to some local soccer club.

"That's a bit of a change, I'd imagine. P & W's culture is quite, ah, different, isn't it?"

Tate crossed his arms protectively. "They're more human at P & W."

"Good place to work?"

"If you don't mind the long hours."

"How's that?"

"We're a bit short-staffed at the moment."

"Just the radio operators or all around?"

"I'd say all around."

The waiter arrived with their drinks. Dulac took a swig of beer and eyed Tate. "Do you mind talking to me about the hijacking?"

Tate sighed deeply. "I guess it's unavoidable, isn't it?"

"Afraid so. You see I—" Dulac's cell phone rang. He looked at the screen. Lescop.

"Sorry, got to take this. Yes Daniel."

"I'm at the Mirador hotel in San Jose. I have good news and bad news."

"Whatever."

"I went with inspector Juarez to arrest Leon Binagro this morning at his office."

"And?"

"We found him sitting at his desk. Dead. Shot twice in the head."

"*Merde*," said Dulac. "And the good news?"

"Someone must have disturbed the killer because he didn't have time to take Binagro's files with him. I was able to convince Juarez to let me download a ton of stuff on wire transfers relating to the hijacking."

"Good work. Anything else?"

"No point in me staying here until they get more info from their forensics people. They say that could quite a while. I've told them to keep me in the loop."

"Fine, see you back in Lyon then." Dulac pressed the end-call button.

The waiter arrived with their food.

"So Jeremy, any side effects from the gas?"

"At first, I had a few bouts of dizziness. Seems to be getting better though."

"I had the same. They're gone now. Tell me, let's talk about the hijacker Tariq. He—"

"Bloody psycho. He killed Peterson over nothing."

"Jeremy, what I'm after is this. Did Tariq seem to have any familiarity, did you notice any signs of acquaintance with any of the officers or crew of the *Caravan Star*?"

"You're saying he might have had a contact on board?"

"Don't you think it's possible, likely even?"

"I guess, but I didn't notice any sign of familiarity or—"

"Complicity?"

"Nothing comes to mind. Oh, but one thing."

"Yes?"

"I remember being surprised the whacko guy who shot Peterson knew the ship's speed and track were being monitored at Head Office."

Dulac pursed his lips and raised his eyebrows slightly. "Interesting. Very interesting. Were all the radio and video transmissions to and from the *Caravan Star* done through you?"

"Yes."

"They're all recorded?"

"There are two copies. One on the *Caravan Star* and the other here at Head Office."

"Where in Head Office?"

"In the archives section, on the first floor."

"So I could get a copy?"

"With the proper authorization, I suppose."

"And who is in charge of archives?"

"Emma Watson."

"Is she in today?"

"No. She's on partial maternity leave. She only works Thursdays and Fridays. She'll be in tomorrow."

CHAPTER 44

P & W Headquarters, 1.55 p.m.

Bolding found a letter marked Personal and Urgent on his desk when he returned from lunch with his Vice-President Finance Mills. He opened it and started to read. His left hand started shaking when he put the letter down on his desk. His heart pounded and he felt his blood pressure skyrocket. He reached in the desk drawer for his bottle of hydrochloro-thiazide pills. Bastards. Bolding dry-swallowed a couple of pills, picked up his phone and dialed the Home Secretary's number. "Sir Terence Hays, please. Adrian Bolding calling."

Bolding tapped his fingers impatiently on his desk. He didn't have to wait long.

"Hays."

"Hello Terry, it's Adrian."

"How goes the battle?"

"Not well. I think we should meet."

"What's this about?"

"Not over the phone. It's urgent, Terry."

"I see. Then why don't you drop by the cottage for sup-per? Pamela is preparing a roast. You can take the afternoon train and I'll pick you up at Holbrook station."

"I'll drive down. It'll be quicker. I've got to see Toombs first."

* * *

Bolding's Bentley drove up Hays' pink gravel driveway three hours later. The English Baroque manor Hays called his cottage came majestically into view.

The car stopped, and Bolding's chauffeur got out to open the rear door. Simultaneously, an elderly man dressed in butler's uniform shuffled his way down the steps of the portico and greeted Bolding.

"Good afternoon, Sir Adrian. Sir Hays begs your pardon, but he's busy on an urgent call. He asked me to show you to the East Salon. How was your trip?"

"Fine, Humphreys, fine."

Humphreys shuffled back up the wide limestone stairs and led Bolding past the hallway, adorned with traditional, unsmiling portraits of Hays's ancestors, onwards to the East Salon.

"Tea? Coffee, Sir Adrian? Or perhaps something a little stronger?" A wry look illuminated Humphreys' small, birdlike eyes.

"Black coffee will do."

"Please." The butler motioned towards the large, dark green sofa. He bowed slightly, then turned and shuffled out of the room.

Bolding walked about the room, trying to work off his anxiety. The walls were covered with light beige velour, decorated with gilt-framed paintings of hunting scenes. A half-sized bronze statue of a plump, Rubenesque nude, holding the forbidden fruit stood in one of the corners, the biblical snake wound around her thick, muscular calves.

He sensed someone behind him and turned to see Hays entering the room.

"Ah, Adrian. Sorry. Had a conference call I couldn't get out of. Pamela is at the hair salon. She'll be back in a bit."

"Good of you to see me, Terry."

"Please." Hays offered Bolding the sofa and sat down in the causeuse across from him. "Now then, what is this about?"

Bolding cleared his throat and took out a folded letter from his breast pocket. "I received this in the mail today." He handed Hays the letter.

Hays reclined in the causeuse and crossed his legs as he read. A frown etched itself onto his forehead.

"Lloyds called the cross-default and sent a copy to our bankers, Berkeley's Trust. Berkeley's putting P & W into default for not keeping up the insurance. I have 48 hours to come up with 68 million pounds. They're completely insane."

"Obviously you've had your lawyers look at this," said Hays.

"I saw Toombs earlier this afternoon. He says we have a valid case on the cross-default but that I have to buy time. If the banks start putting liens on the ships, the news will spread like wildfire. And the news is spreading already."

"What do you mean?" said Hays.

"I'll get to that. Terry, I just don't have the 68 million. I need the government's help. Surely it is in the interests of Her Majesty's government not to have one of the premier flag bearers of the British cruise fleet—"

"Adrian, we've already paid $60 million for the ransom. Unofficially, of course."

"I'm very grateful, but that was then. This is now."

Hays shuffled uncomfortably in the causeuse. "Paying out a ransom is one thing, but the government injecting the taxpayers' money for a bailout is quite a different kettle of fish."

"Governments do it all the time! If it weren't for the French government's intercession, the French cruise ships would be rusting in dry-docks at St. Nazaire as we speak."

Hays got up and walked to the window. He turned and faced Bolding. "Times are hard at Downing, very hard. I don't know. I have to think about this before I even bring this to Cabinet. You know these things take time, Adrian. Surely you can get some kind of temporary financing."

"That's the best you can do?"

"Under the circumstances, yes."

"I see."

"I wish I could be more encouraging but you must understand my position."

"Can you at least promise to bring it up before Cabinet?"

Hays drew in a deep breath. "I suppose I can put it on tomorrow's agenda. We have an emergency meeting on the Iran nuclear situation. I'll have to see how that goes. You can well imagine this might not be the best time to bring up your problem."

"I'll take my chances. Obviously, I'll be available if you need me to—"

"We'll see, Adrian, we'll see."

"Much appreciated. That brings me to another subject. There's an Interpol inspector. The one that was on the *Caravan Star.*"

"You mean Dulac?" said Hays.

"He's been poking around at P & W's offices. He even knows about my problem with the insurers. He's asking for our personnel records, financial statements. He's going on a fishing expedition. That's the last thing I need right now."

"So what do you want me to do?"

"Get him out of here. Get him off my back."

"That's a bit delicate, don't you think? I can't very well be seen to be interfering with any investigation. Particularly not an Interpol investigation."

"Yes, I know, but at least your chaps at the Yard could slow him down a little. Maybe call him into a few meetings in London. That sort of thing. It does no good whatsoever for company morale for employees to see a police inspector poking about the office."

"I'll see what I can do."

Hays stood next to the window, pushed aside one of the burgundy-colored velour curtains and looked outside. A silver Rolls came to a sedate stop in front of the porch.

"Ah, here's Pamela," he said.

CHAPTER 45

P & W Headquarters, the next morning

Bolding's secretary stepped into his office. "Mr. Dulac to see you, Mr. Bolding."

"Not him again. He was here yesterday. Now what does he want?"

"He says you promised him some documents. I—"

"Show him in," said Bolding wearily.

Bolding didn't bother to rise from his seat when Dulac entered. "I haven't had time to get the documents. I have more urgent matters to deal with at the moment. Besides, Scotland Yard has already requisitioned the security officers' files."

"What about the rest of the documents?"

"I'm telling you, Dulac, I simply don't have time."

"There are other ways, more formal ways. They're called search warrants, I believe."

Bolding bolted from his chair and stepped up to Dulac, within inches of his chin. "Listen to me. No threats." He pointed a forefinger menacingly. "I'm really not in the mood. You're going on a fishing expedition, Dulac, and I don't like it. Not one damn bit."

Dulac backed away, putting up his palms. "Whoa, Easy. I'm just trying to connect the dots. Which I will do, with or without your cooperation and approval."

"Do you have one shred of evidence of a conspiracy?"

"You mean other than your missing security officer going conveniently absent two weeks before the hijacking and his hiring of fellow Pakistanis?"

"Until you find him, you're shooting in the dark with a blindfold on."

Bolding went back to his chair, sat down and opened a file. "Now if there is nothing else, I have work to do."

Dulac was unfazed and unimpressed. "Surely you agree that it takes more than one man to get those weapons on board and bypass the security systems of your ship. Besides, how did those hijackers know precisely when to take over and which areas of the ship they had to control? How did they coordinate the ship hitting the reef exactly when they had a jet waiting at Corvo? Without help from inside your company, those hijackers would've had to have had a lot of dumb luck, don't you think?"

Bolding looked up. "Fine and dandy. I just haven't had the time to analyze the logistics of the hijack, which you've seemingly thought about in great detail."

"It's my job."

Dulac had obtained precisely the right amount of reaction he wanted from Bolding. For the present, he was satisfied with that. Without a search warrant, he was skating on thin ice, and he knew the last thing Bolding wanted was an out-and-out investigation. Both men knew the difference between Bolding's sharing of information however reluctantly and, if push came to shove, the disruptive effects of a formal investigation. He thought of bringing up the sale of Bolding's shares but resisted the temptation. He'd destabilized Bolding enough. Dulac switched tactics. "For starters, let's keep it simple, shall we? You keep copies here of the ships' video feeds. Any problem in my taking a look?"

Bolding pursed his lips. "See Emma Watson downstairs, first underground level." Bolding pointed outside the door.

"Fine. I'll do just that." Dulac closed his computer and put it in his satchel. "Thanks for your cooperation." He smiled and walked out.

* * *

Dulac went to the first underground level. He followed the signs to Archives, an open room containing large gray metal cabinets. When he entered, he saw a petite woman with curly gray hair behind a desk, busy at her computer The sign on the desk read *Emma Watson, Archivist.*

"I'm Thierry Dulac, from Interpol. I'm here to see the videos from the *Caravan Star* during—"

"Yes, I know. Mr. Bolding called me." She pulled three CDs from the side drawer of her desk. "The audios cover three-day periods of incoming and outgoing transmissions of the Inmarsat system. The videos are taken from the various monitors aboard ship."

"CDs, eh?"

"We're in the process of modernizing the equipment aboard the ships."

"I see. So there are some blanks on those recordings?"

"Yes. During the time the hijackers closed down the Inmarsat system."

"What about onboard audio transmissions?"

"You mean by VHF?"

"Exactly."

"Those aren't recorded." She handed him the CD s. "You can view them over there." She pointed to a desk with a computer on it.

Dulac bent over slightly and smiled at Watson. "This is going to take a lot of time. It would be a lot simpler and faster if you were to make me copies so I could look at them on my own. I'd really appreciate it."

"I couldn't do that without proper authorization. I'd have to call Mr. Mills."

"Could you do that?"

Watson dialed and moments later put down the receiver. "He's not in. He's—"

"Listen, I guarantee you these won't leave my sight. An Interpol inspector is bound by the same confidentiality rules as any other police officer." Dulac could see her resistance starting to melt. "I'll take full responsibility. You have my word."

"Well, I guess you'll obtain them sooner or later anyway." She looked at her watch. "Besides, I've got to lock up in 10 minutes."

"This way, I won't have to come back and waste a lot of your precious time."

After a long moment's hesitation, she finally gave him a look of acquiescence and went to the central computer. Minutes later, she came back and handed the copies to Dulac.

"You had better keep your word. I could get fired for this."

Dulac gave her another comforting smile. "Thanks. I'll make sure you won't."

* * *

Dulac was on his way back upstairs to see Bolding, CDs safely in his satchel, when his cell phone rang.

"Dulac."

"Wade here. We're meeting in the Major Incident Room this afternoon. It would be in your interest to attend."

"I still have business to finish here. Plus, I—"

"Shall we say 3 p.m.?"

Puzzled, Dulac looked at his watch." I guess I could make the 1.00 p.m. train to London."

After a steak and potatoes washed down by a glass of red wine at Southampton Central station, Dulac took the express to London, arriving an hour and a half later at

Waterloo Station. He grabbed a cab to the Yard, rushed up the steps to the entrance, and flashed his Interpol card at the security guards. Moments later, Wade's secretary entered her card into the MRI safety slot and let Dulac enter the room. Except for a woman sitting next to him concentrating on her computer screen, Wade was alone.

"Ah, Dulac, glad you could make it," said Wade. "Meet my assistant Wendy Lord."

Dulac nodded.

"Sorry to be interfering with your schedule, but we have some information you should be aware of," said Wade.

"Must be important."

"This may or may not have a bearing on our investigation, but I feel it's my duty to inform you. Due to the confidential nature of this information, I couldn't disclose it over the phone."

Dulac put his computer down beside the foam-backed chair and sat down.

"As guardians of the public interest, the Yard does occasional spot checks on the market transactions of the Cabinet members."

"Don't they have to put their assets into trusts?" said Dulac.

"Only the Prime Minister. The other cabinet ministers are not bound to do so."

"I see."

Wade nodded to his assistant, who turned on the projector. A picture showing reams of financial transactions came into focus on one of the large video screens across the room. A line was highlighted in yellow. "STH 60,000 class A shares P and W. Sold—(date) @ 3.75 pounds per share."

"I gather that STH means Sir Terence Hays?" said Dulac.

"Correct."

"That's exactly a week before the hijack."

"Correct also." Wade's face had turned pinker than usual. "Perhaps purely coincidental. As you can see, Sir Terence Hays bought and sold other stocks during that week."

"Or it could be an attempt to mask dubious transactions. Trouble is we know at Interpol that Bolding sold 20,000 shares the week prior," said Dulac. "Both Hays and Bolding must be prescient, or . . ."

"Of course, the fact that P & W seems to be in financial difficulty doesn't make the picture any rosier."

"The term *insider trading* comes readily to mind," said Dulac.

"If Hays, who happens to sit on P & W's board, or anyone in a position of authority had wind of the company's financial difficulty before it became public and traded shares based on that knowledge, yes."

"Most difficult to prove in court. But thanks for the heads-up."

"We heard you obtained copies of the *Caravan Star's* onboard videos. See anything of interest?"

"Don't tell me. The archives clerk at P & W panicked and phoned you. Or was it Bolding?"

"We have a set. We can compare notes."

"We'll see."

A triple ridge frown started to form on Wade's forehead.

"Mr. Dulac, we seem to be at cross purposes here. I think I have been more than forthright in supplying information to you, and I expect the same in return. I want your complete cooperation in this file."

"Fine. Tell you what. When you hand me the personnel files on the *Caravan Star's* officers you took from their offices without advising me or sharing with me, we'll talk about cooperation."

Wade's complexion went one shade darker pink. "We were going to inform you as soon as we had them analyzed."

"Sure, you were."

Wade stiffened in his chair. "I don't have to justify our methods of investigation to you, Mr. Dulac. Since we're on that subject, I would appreciate you giving us a detailed and comprehensive plan of your investigation. I—"

"Can't do that."

"Why not?"

"Don't have one."

"Suit yourself. But I won't have you jeopardizing the legality of our investigation by contaminating evidence—"

"Such as taking copies of CDs handed over voluntarily by P & W's officers. I don't think so. With all due respect, this is my ninth investigation under British law. I think I've gotten the hang of it by now. But thanks for the heads-up. I'll let you know about the CD's as soon as I've looked at them."

* * *

Bristol Hotel, London

Sitting at the desk in his room, bleary-eyed and tired, Dulac opened his laptop and inserted the fourth Video CD. As the screen came to life, he read the inscription at the bottom right-hand corner. Video camera two, bridge, eight — from — to —.

Finally, data on the hijack. As the video of the hijackers taking over the bridge played, Dulac looked attentively at the expressions on the faces of every officer as they stood, hands in the air before the terrorists.

Nothing suspect. They all look genuinely scared. He closed his computer, changed his shirt, and took the elevator down to the restaurant for a quick sandwich.

He started on another CD when he returned, viewing CDs from all over the ship to see if he'd missed anything. The on-deck videos of the hijackers disguised as safety officers herding passengers to the amphitheater played in front of him. For a brief moment, he saw himself, Karen and Hank making the dash down the corridor and entering the closet. *Lucky for us they weren't looking at the monitors.* Dulac got up, went to the minibar, poured himself a scotch and water, then reviewed the last of the CDs. He tried to focus on the hijackers as they appeared in turn on the screen, and the images became fuzzy. *Not enough resolution with my computer.*

I'll get Gina to look at this. He put in the second last CD and watched the hijackers making their demands at the Luxor amphitheater. Tariq was pointing at the other hijacker, who had just finished putting up an easel when the computer screen went blank. He tried removing and re-inserting the CD. Same result. He put in the last CD which recorded a gun battle between the hijackers and Navy SEALs. Finally, the *Caravan Star* came to a jarring stop on Torrais Reef. Dulac took out that CD, reinserted the previous one and tried scanning the CD again. He looked at the elapsed time on the right-hand corner. There was a jump in the timeline between the previous scene and the last one.

Someone has erased part of that scene.

His cell rang. It was a text message from Arlberg. *Imperative meet my office Lescop and Gina tomorrow 1.00 p.m. Be there. A.*

CHAPTER 46

Piccadilly Circus, London

A man with a dark, pockmarked complexion stopped his car next to the public pay phone, turned up the collar of his raincoat and stepped out into the rain. He entered the phone booth, inserted the cash pay card and dialed. A voice came on the line after the third ring.

"Hello?"

"Zabin."

"I told you not to call me at home," said a voice in hushed tones.

"Tariq survived. He's out of intensive care. They're going to send him to London." Silence. "Did you hear me? They're going to . . ."

"Damn. Anything we can do at this end?"

"I'm getting on it now."

"You realize that Tariq must never reach British soil."

"Fully. There's also other bad news."

"Yes?"

"The hit man screwed up the Binagro operation."

"What do you mean?"

"Binagro was terminated, but the hitman was interrupted by a San Jose police officer patrolling the building. He had to leave before destroying the data on Binagro's computer."

"Who has it now?"

"The Costa Rican police. They gave copies to an Interpol agent by the name of Daniel Lescop. He's back in Lyon. We checked the line of authority structure. He reports to Thierry Dulac."

The man in the raincoat hung up, turned up his collar and went to his car.

CHAPTER 47

Centre de Rééducation Fonctionelle Port-Royal, Paris, 27 October

During his flight from London to Paris, Dulac realized he had just enough time for a quick visit with Karen before taking the TGV to Lyon for his meeting with Arlberg that afternoon. Holding an assortment of flowers he'd bought at the hospital gift shop, Dulac entered the elevator and pressed the button for the fourth floor. Moments later, he stepped out and followed the arrows down the corridor to Room 419. He peered into the room discreetly before making his presence known. Karen, dressed in a blue hospital gown sat propped up in her bed, reading a glossy magazine. Dulac knocked gently on the doorframe and walked in. "Bonjour, it's me."

Karen put down her magazine, took off her reading glasses and turned towards Dulac. "I think I know you, don't I?"

"Okay, okay, so I should've phoned earlier."

"Not unless you wanted to."

He proffered the bouquet. "Amends."

"How sweet of you." She smiled, took the flowers and smelled them.

He bent over and kissed her. "How's my girl?"

"The doctors say I'm making great progress. I can walk for 10 minutes now. Want to see?"

"Sure."

Karen put aside her magazine, threw back the covers and swung her legs onto the floor. "Help me put on my slippers."

Dulac knelt down and put the slippers on her feet. He couldn't help noticing her calf muscles had shrunk considerably.

"Pass me my dressing gown, will you?"

Dulac handed the robe to Karen. She got up, slipped it on, and steadied herself on the metal bed frame. "Here goes," she said. Hesitantly at first, she started towards the doorway. Dulac reached out and took her left arm, but she shrugged free. "Thanks, but I must do this on my own."

"Okay." Dulac let go of her arm and walked beside her.

"Enough of me. What about you?"

Dulac took a deep breath. "More loose ends."

"Any news from Lescop?"

"He's back from San Jose. I'll be seeing him in Lyon. He's got some info on the ransom money transfers."

"Sounds promising."

"Wouldn't count on it. The hijackers had all the time in the world to launder that money squeaky clean by now."

Karen started to lose her balance and Dulac grabbed her left arm.

"Easy now."

"I'm . . . I'm good. Just a little wobbly at times."

They reached the end of the corridor and Dulac spotted a parlor to the right.

"Why don't we rest here for a moment?"

"Fine."

They walked over to a small sofa and slumped into it, sitting in silence for a moment, neither of them seemingly knowing what to say next.

"Penny for your thoughts?" said Karen finally.

"It seems every time we see each other, it ends up in a minor disaster. Last year I dragged you into the investigation of the Pope's kidnapping. Before that, I pulled you into the murder investigation of two archbishops. Now this."

"Never a dull moment with you around."

"Except this time, you end up in the hospital. I can't help thinking I'm responsible for you being here."

"Aren't you being a bit hard on yourself? After all, I invited you."

"If I had only listened to Hank—"

"Thierry, there is no way you could have done more than he did. We never saw the guy until he started shooting."

"I might have seen him first."

"And maybe not. No, I think we're both skirting around the main issue, Thierry, and I think you know that."

"Meaning?"

"I've been giving our relationship some serious thought, Thierry. And though I'm very fond of you, somehow I still have the feeling I hardly know you."

Dulac scratched the back of his nape. "Fair enough." He paused or a moment before continuing. "I've been meaning to ask. Did taking the post at La Sorbonne, did that have anything to do with . . . ?"

"With wanting to live nearer to you? Partly, yes. It's also a great opportunity to work with Professor Levasseur. He's the world expert on Greek animal mythology."

Dulac took Karen's hands in both of his "Now that you're back in Paris, it'll be lot easier to get to know each other better."

She leaned her head towards him. "I hope so."

An elderly woman using a walker shuffled into the room, smiled at them and slowly let herself down into one of the leather seats facing them.

Karen whispered into Dulac's ear. "Let's continue this later."

"Sure."

He looked at his watch. "I have to catch the 11 a.m. TGV to Lyon. Arlberg is ready to bust a gut."

"It's time I got back to my room anyway. I'm feeling a little tired."

He helped her up, put his arms around her hips and pulled her close. "Don't worry. We'll work this out."

CHAPTER 48

Interpol Headquarters, Lyon

As he left the elevator, Dulac suddenly felt the oppressiveness of the overheated room. He took off his jacket, slinging it over his right shoulder and walked across to the far corner, to Arlberg's office. The door was open. She looked up from the papers on her desk as Dulac entered, her face a scowl of disapproval and reproach.

"About bloody time."

"I got called into the Yard by Wade. It was worth it."

"I'll be the judge of that. Before we join Gina and Lescop in the conference room, I received a call from Hays yesterday. Care to guess what about?"

Dulac scratched his scalp. "Probably says I'm on a fishing expedition, and although I'll never admit it, I wouldn't say he's entirely wrong."

"He says you're interfering with Wade's investigation and—"

"Not so. At first, I was surprised when Wade called me in, since he hadn't been very cooperative. Now I know why. Wade's leading me into territory he's chicken to go into all by himself."

She leaned back in her chair. "Explain."

"The Yard has discovered a possible lead on insider trading by Hays and Bolding. Wade called me into his office to let me in on it. It's obvious Wade doesn't want to investigate his boss unless he's damn sure he has a bulletproof case against him. So he's leaving it up to us to follow up."

Arlberg got up and started pacing in front of the window. "Might be interesting, but you know as well as I do, financial matters such as insider trading are out of our jurisdiction."

Dulac looked askance at Arlberg. "Even if it leads to crimes *under* our jurisdiction?"

"You're treading a fine line, Dulac. And at this point that's pure speculation, isn't it? In the meantime, Hays has requested that we, meaning you, confine yourself to a support-only role in the British investigation."

"Hays is in direct violation of Interpol's charter." Dulac sensed some lack of support from Arlberg.

"I know, I know. But you're missing the point."

"Which is?"

"The Britain-Interpol Cooperation Agreement is up for renegotiation next month. I don't have to remind you that Britain is a heavy contributor to our budget. This is not the time to rock the boat."

"You aren't suggesting that—"

"Let me be clear. I don't agree with Hays's position. All I'm asking you is to tread carefully, at least until the agreement is signed."

"I've been known to do that. Sometimes."

Arlberg turned and headed towards the door. "Let's see what Gina and Lescop have to say."

As Dulac and Arlberg reached the conference room, he spotted Daniel Lescop, seated, his bald pate reflecting the rays of the ceiling light. Beside him, bespectacled Gina Marino was immersed in reading a thick document.

They rose in unison as Arlberg and Dulac walked in.

"What do you have, Gina?" Arlberg sat down at the conference table and reached for the glass of water in front of her.

The petite Italian turned and pointed to the large monitor behind her. "I was able to partly reconstruct CD number four and get some—and only some—of the video back." She pressed the enter key on the laptop and the video screen flickered to life.

"Here you see Tariq on the bridge, speaking in his VHF radio. I'll fast-forward to the part that was erased. Here." The video screen flickered, then again showed Assirgan, speaking into a phone.

"He's got a satellite phone," said Dulac. "And from what I'm seeing, it's not mine."

"What do you mean?" said Arlberg.

"Short of it is, we lost it while escaping from below deck."

"As far as I could make out from the timing, Tariq was on his way back from the amphitheater," said Gina. "If you look closely at the picture before—I'll back up a bit. Here. He doesn't seem to have one here. He's not wearing one on his belt or anywhere else."

"So he had to have picked one up somewhere around the amphitheater," said Arlberg.

"What's important," said Dulac, "is that he's communicating with a third-party, presumably on land. Otherwise, he would've used his VHF."

"Could be his Baluchistan Tigers brothers." Lescop squinted at the video.

"Or someone else," said Dulac. "Any way of tracing that call, Gina?"

"Not unless we can pinpoint the make and serial number of the phone and the exact location and timing of the phone call. Even then it's nearly impossible. There are over 100,000 satellite phone calls made per day. Ten thousand from the Atlantic region alone. I can refine the search with Lat-Long algorithms and probably narrow that down to say five hundred or so."

"Sounds a lot better already. Get on it, Gina," said Arlberg.

"Yes ma'am."

"Anything else?"

"No."

"Thanks. That'll be all."

Gina rose to leave, and Arlberg turned to Lescop.

"Your turn."

Lescop opened his laptop.

"I'm still retrieving emails from Binagro's computer. He had some self-erase software which we were able to trace and the software people have helped us resuscitate most of them."

Arlberg looked at her watch. Lescop got the message and pressed the enter button on his laptop. The video screen came to life and a chart with arrows and dollar amounts showed on the screen.

"I was able to retrieve the paths of $15 million in ransom money from the Costa Rica Bank through layers here, then finally through to Bank Eghestad Nivin in Tehran." Lescop pointed at another path of arrows on the chart. "Another $15 million here through Neveran Bank, then through to the Bank Keshanage, also in Tehran."

"Are you sure these amounts are part of the ransom money?" said Arlberg.

"Relatively sure. Binagro's modus operandi was that he usually dealt with one file at a time until he closed it. Speed and untraceability are essential components for these so-called 'investment advisors', read money-launderers like Binagro. All these amounts went through the Swift system of clearance on the same day."

"Why banks in Tehran?" said Arlberg.

"Probably because the Baluchistan Tigers don't trust the Pakistani banks, controlled by Islamabad," said Dulac.

"Exactly," said Lescop. "Plus the Iranian regime is favorable to the Baluchistan rebels, who destabilize the pro-western Pakistanis, which means the Pakistanis are not able to devote more time and money building their war arsenal against Iran."

"And it guarantees the money will never be looked at or seized by any pro-western authority," said Dulac.

Arlberg took another sip of water. "Sounds reasonable. What else? Where did the other $30 million go?"

"This is where it gets interesting." Lescop pressed the forward key on his laptop. "The other $30 million is transferred first through Hana Bank, a South Korean bank, then Binagro orders Hana to send $10 million in two transfers of $5 million each. One to Bank Itex, the other to Bank Julius Baer, both in Zurich."

Arlberg peered at Lescop's computer screen. "And obviously we don't know the account holders," said Arlberg.

"Numbered companies."

"Standard procedure. So what's your point?" Impatience crept into Arlberg's voice. She glanced at her watch again.

"If I can speak for my colleague," said Dulac, "the point is, why would the hijackers not send all the money to Iranian banks, where it is totally protected from potential investigation?"

"You're implying that all of the money did *not* go to the hijackers?" said Arlberg.

"If you're a westerner, you don't want your money sitting in a Tehran bank, for fear of the authorities freezing your account as a reprisal for Western sanctions," said Dulac.

"Interesting theory," said Arlberg. "The hijackers could also be using *prête-noms* in the Swiss accounts."

"It seems odd" said Dulac, "that they would go through all that trouble when they could have just transferred the entire sums to, shall we say, friendlier jurisdictions."

"So you're suggesting that $10 million was transferred to accomplices. Western accomplices?" said Arlberg.

"We can't exclude the possibility," said Lescop.

"The problem is it's going to take forever to access those Swiss accounts, if at all," said Dulac, "and only if we can link the transfers to the crime. By then, the money will be gone."

Arlberg got up to leave. "We'll see about that. Time to give my friend Hans Marti a call."

"The Swiss Minister of justice?" said Dulac.

"The very same. Anything else gentlemen?"

"As a matter of fact, there is," said Dulac. "I'm going to try and access the emails and telcons of the P & W officers, especially Bolding's." Dulac looked at Lescop, then Arlberg. "Just giving everybody a heads-up."

"Good luck," said Arlberg. "You'll need a court order from a UK court, supported by the local police. Whom you've not especially endeared yourself to, as I recall."

"There are other ways."

"What other ways, Dulac?"

Dulac smiled wryly. "You probably don't want to know."

CHAPTER 49

P & W Headquarters, 28 October, 9.15 a.m.

Bolding sat at his desk and read the latest avalanche of cancellation notices from travel agencies. He deposited the papers on his desk and gazed across his office to the far wall at the oil painting of his grandfather, Sir Jeffrey Bolding. The founder of P & W's unsmiling, reproachful glower bored right through Sir Adrian's soul and reminded him of his current disastrous predicament. He picked up the phone and called his secretary. "Any news from Hays?"

"No sir."

Twenty minutes went by and the phone rang. It was his secretary.

"Is it Hays?"

"It's Hugh Walters from the bank, sir."

"Put him through," said Bolding wearily.

A moment later, the monotone voice of the Berkeley's Trust Managing Director of Head Office came online. "We've given you a moratorium Mr. Bolding, but I'm afraid we're running out of time. Unless we receive the funds by noon tomorrow morning, I have instructions to start foreclosure."

"I told you yesterday. I'm awaiting news from Sir Terence."

"You must understand. We cannot jeopardize our privileged creditor status. We—"

"He has to go to Cabinet. Surely, it's not in the bank's interest to destroy my business."

"We've already given you an extension."

Bolding got up, trying not to let despair leak into his voice. "For which I'm grateful. A few more days won't make a great deal of difference to the bank."

"That's what you said last time. I'm sorry, Mr. Bolding. I have strict instructions. Payment before noon tomorrow or we seize the ships."

The line went dead.

"Bastard." Bolding slammed down the receiver. He picked it up again and dialed Hays's personal number. "Terry, Adrian. How did it go at the meeting?"

"I was going to phone you, Adrian. We didn't get around to it on the agenda, but I discussed it informally with members of the exec. They're far from thrilled with the idea of another bailout. I'm afraid—"

"Listen, Terry. I'm going under. Walters has given me till noon tomorrow, otherwise he seizes the ships. But I have another idea."

"Which is?"

"Let me buy you lunch at Giovanni's." Bolding looked at his watch. "Assuming the traffic is still light, I can make it for, shall we say 1 p.m.?"

"Suit yourself."

* * *

Giovanni's restaurant, London, 1.30 p.m.

Humphreys drove the Bentley at 140km an hour and made the trip to London in less than two hours. Bolding spotted Hays at Giovanni's entrance and waved him over.

Hays, preceded by his two bodyguards, smiled briefly at the *maître d'* and walked towards Bolding's table. Bolding felt a slight easing of the numbing pressure on his brain. *At least he'll hear me out.* The bodyguards went to the bar and sat down.

Bolding got up to greet him.

"Afternoon Adrian." Hays usual smile had been replaced by a funereal glower.

"Thanks for coming." Bolding tried to maintain composure.

They sat down and Bolding signaled the waiter, who came over with lunch menus.

"Glenlivet straight up, if I recall?" Bolding eyed Hays.

"I'll have a vodka-tonic, no ice." Hays looked at the waiter, not at Bolding. "Do you have Ultimat?"

"Yes sir, we do."

"Make that two," Bolding said.

The waiter handed them the menus and left with their drink order.

"Afraid I can't stay long." Hays put aside the menu and clasped his hands. "I've a meeting back at the Shop at 2.30."

Bolding felt the thin rays of hope fading quickly. He had to make his move.

"Here's my idea," said Bolding. "Instead of cash, the Government offers Berkeley's an irrevocable letter of credit guaranteeing the 68 million. That way it doesn't have to disburse, and the Bank has a guarantee—"

"We'll get to that in a moment," interrupted Hays. "By the way, I spoke to Geoff Archer at Lloyds. He said he won't budge unless the Swiss reinsurance boys back him up. Otherwise he's willing to go to court on the cross-default."

"Bastards."

Hays shuffled in his chair and Bolding leaned forward expectantly. For a moment, Hays avoided looking at Bolding, letting his gaze wander around the room. Finally he couldn't avoid Bolding's insistent stare any longer.

"There is another problem, Adrian. Jim Finch and Llewellyn Parsons are on the Cunard Board and they've made noises that if we help you, they'll withdraw their contributions to the Party. I don't have to remind you—"

"We're talking of over a thousand jobs at P & W alone, Terry, not to mention the indirect jobs. Come election time, you can be damn sure they won't forget you if they're left high and dry on the street."

The waiter came back with their drinks.

"Thanks." Hays turned and threw a supercilious smile at Bolding. "We've already factored that in. You see, the other problem is your balance sheet, Adrian. We've been told by our people at Avesons' that we'd be throwing good money after bad. I don't have to remind you that when White Star folded, P & W and Cunard were only too eager to pick up the slack."

"That was over forty years ago."

"Still a precedent."

Numbness began overtaking Bolding's brain. "So you won't back me up."

"It's not only up to me, Adrian. I'm but one voice in the choir. The exec has to be—"

Bolding leaned over and looked at Hays, ice shooting from his eyes. "Cut the crap, Terry. You and I know damn well that if you convince the PM on a one-on-one, and the exec will follow suit. I'm not going under alone, Terry. That I swear."

"Meaning?"

"You know very well what I mean, Terry."

Hays looked askance at Bolding. "I don't think I do. Moreover, I don't like the tone of this conversation." Hays started to get up.

"I'm going to call the PM."

"Don't bother. He's been advised not to take your call."

"Really. I'm telling you, Terry. I won't go down alone."

"Do what you will, Adrian. Do what you will."

Hays got up and walked towards the exit, his body-guards closing ranks behind him. Bolding sat dumbstruck, jaw agape. He'd played his last, desperate card and lost. He felt the pangs of failure invading his soul, gripping his every fiber, and squeezing inexorably all the will to fight out of him.

He downed his vodka and signaled the waiter over. He didn't see Hays take his cell phone out of his pocket and dial MI-6's Special Branch number as he walked through the door.

* * *

Bolding exited Giovanni's six vodkas later and nearly fell on the sidewalk. His chauffeur helped him into his Bentley and two and a half hours later, aided by Higgins, Bolding teetered precariously up the entrance stairs of his mansion.

"Vodka on the rocks. I'll take it in the music room." Bolding's speech was slurred. "While you're at it, make it a double."

"Yes, sir." Higgins slipped innocuously into the shadows of the oak paneled hallway.

Bolding went to the library, pulled out an early edition of Hamlet. Book in hand, he entered the music room and sat down at his desk.

Moments later Higgins walked in. "There you are, sir." He deposited the fine linen napkin on the desk and the glass of vodka atop it.

"Will you be having anything else, sir?"

"That'll be all."

"Thank you, sir. Good night, sir."

Bolding got up, walked over to the far side of the room, raised his glass, and looked up at the large oil painting of Sir Jeffrey Bolding. He couldn't help noticing for the umpteenth time the family resemblance between them. Wavy white hair, high forehead, small, stubby nose, fleshy lips with a curl in the upper lip, and a dimple in the middle of the chin. The image of his late father crossed his mind briefly. *Funny how genes sometimes skip a generation.*

"Here's to you, you old fart. Nothing else I could do, is there?" *And no use crying over spilled milk. Tomorrow morning, they'll seize the ships. The Hanover Star will be first. She's an easy mark, right here in Southampton.* Bolding brought the glass to his lips and half-emptied it.

Once the ship was seized, the gunpowder would be lit. Bolding knew that. Tour operators would advise their clients, cancel the rest of his contracts, and hustle to find alternate packages with P & W's all-too-willing competitors. By mid-morning the next day, the press would smell blood, and their news sharks would be marauding at the doors of P & W's offices, waiting for a scoop. Bolding turned, walked over to his desk, deposited his glass and sat down. Elbows on his desk, he clasped his head with both hands and closed his eyes. Tears welled up, and for a brief moment, he fought the urge to let go. An uncontrollable sense of panic started to form at the core of his gut, worked up to his chest and made its way into his head. The room swirled and his shoulders started to convulse. After a while, the convulsions stopped and he regained his composure. Without looking down, he opened the desk drawer. He fumbled briefly to the right and felt the cool metal. His left hand shook slightly as he pulled out the .38 Smith and Wesson. Its polished surface immediately caught the sharp light from the desk lamp. He cocked it and put it carefully down on the desk, next to the empty glass.

CHAPTER 50

Interpol HQ, same day

Dulac sat in his office waiting for Sabine Autissier, Interpol Agent, Financial and Economic Crimes Research Section. He'd been waiting for the past twenty minutes. He looked at his watch, picked up the phone and dialed her number.

"Yes Mr. Dulac."

"You're late."

"I . . . I've been buried in another file. But I do have that info you requested on the P & W officers."

Ten minutes later, a fortyish woman with short cut, dark-brown hair and striking pale blue eyes entered Dulac's office, a thick file under each arm.

"All that?" said Dulac.

"Many of the documents are just legwork to get access to the actual trades." said Autissier. "The London Market Access Rules are very strict, to protect client confidentiality."

"Please," said Dulac, offering her a seat in front of him.

"Thanks." She deposited the files on Dulac's desk and looked at him quickly, avoiding eye contact, before sitting hesitantly. "Anything the matter?" said Dulac.

Autissier cleared her throat. "You realize that technically, we have no authority to investigate internal financial matters of British subjects."

"That's what Arlberg keeps telling me. I disagree. If these transactions are connected to crimes under our jurisdiction, then we have the right to investigate. Unfortunately, we'll only find out once we probe."

"Sort of a chicken and egg situation, I guess."

"We've got to start somewhere. So what is your overall assessment?" Dulac swiveled his chair in the direction of the window, got up and closed the blind.

"There are many small trades in P & W stock by various officers during the past two years. I can't see a pattern here. However, we did some digging on some significant transactions."

"Significant?"

"Transactions where five percent or more of the stock is traded."

Dulac returned to his desk and sat down. "And?"

"A shareholder called Mirolet SA, a Swiss corporation with Head office in Zurich, shorted 6,775,000 Class A shares valued at 9 pounds per share on—"

"What do you mean 'shorted'?"

"Shorting shares is betting the stock of a company will go down. A borrower, in this case Mirolet, borrows a number of the company's shares from a broker and sells them immediately. The broker keeps the money. When the borrower decides that the shares have gone down far enough, he 'covers the short'. He buys an equivalent amount of the shares borrowed and gives them to the broker. The borrower then makes his profit on the difference. To our knowledge, Mirolet has not covered yet."

Dulac scratched the back of his head, then ran a hand through his hair. "So if I understand correctly, the borrower never actually owns the shares borrowed, only their replacement, and only owns them briefly before handing them over to the broker."

"Exactly."

Dulac leaned forward, forearms on his desk. "So why hasn't Mirolet covered the short?"

"They're probably betting the shares will drop even further."

"And if the shares go up in value?"

"They lose. There's no limit to their potential losses."

"Interesting. Very interesting. So when did this shorting of P & W shares happen?"

Autissier looked at the front page of her report. "On 26 September."

"That's about two weeks before the hijack."

"Correct."

"And right about the time Bolding and Hays sold their shares."

"I also noted that coincidence in my report. If Mirolet exercised the short on the shares today, they would make approximately 3 pounds per share, or 20.1 million pounds."

Dulac emitted a loud whistle. "Not exactly chicken feed. Any guesses as to who owns Mirolet?"

"None. It has an answering service and a postal address on Bahnhofstrasse in Zurich."

"Someone has to pay the rent."

"We're looking into it."

"Anything else?"

"Apart from buy-sell transactions in the normal course of business, nothing that stood out."

Dulac leaned back in his swivel chair and pushed himself slightly back, away from his desk. "So we have an absentee Swiss tenant who doesn't want to be disturbed, making a pile of money after the sinking of a ship."

"It could be a coincidence."

"That's what people keep telling me. I don't for one second believe it."

"It's going to take a lot of digging to find out who is behind Mirolet. The Swiss will require proof of a link between a crime and the otherwise perfectly legal stock transaction."

"I think we owe it to ourselves and those dead passengers to do just that. Anything interesting in the emails or other communications of P & W's officers?"

Autissier recoiled slightly, a look of surprise on her face. "Mr. Dulac, you of all people should know that kind of information is strictly off limits without a court order."

"Yes, of course. I just thought you might have had some of it spill over, so to speak. Never mind. Just keep digging on Mirolet. Let me know and thanks, Sabine." He eyed the thick pile of documents. "I'll need only the summary."

Still visibly uncomfortable, Autissier gathered her documents and left.

Dulac knew he'd tested the limits of Autissier's willingness to probe and perhaps gone a bit too far. It was time to try another tack.

* * *

Rue des Forgeron, Lyon

Dulac returned to his two-bedroom flat and made himself a scotch. Glass in hand, he went to the Steinway and sat down on the small wooden bench next to it. He took a sip, swirled it delicately with his tongue and swallowed. He parked the glass on the side table and opened the Chopin Preludes partition at Prelude Number 5. In his youth, he would have played it by heart. Impossible now, without the score. Alcohol, cigarettes and age had wreaked their inexorable havoc on his memory cells. Yet paradoxically, just the right mix of Glenmorangie Single Malt and piano playing would trigger the neurons and synapses and often produced clarity of thought. That's what he needed right now. He started to play, his long fingers flying over the keyboard effortlessly. That is, until the difficult middle section, when his hands began faltering, refusing to follow the commands of his brain. False notes fell one after the other and Dulac winced. I'm getting too old for this. He stopped and took another swig of scotch. Meanwhile the image of Henri Messier crept into his consciousness, then came into full focus.

Dulac hadn't heard about his former Montpelier University classmate. Messier, since the latter had made front page news in *Le Figaro* two years back. Messier had been acquitted of hacking into the security system of the City of Lyon's Department of Pensions and Benefits and trying to steer money into fictitious retirement accounts. In their zeal to catch Messier, the *Sureté* had crossed the line, planted false evidence and been accused of entrapment. Messier had gotten away scot-free.

It was known in the world of cyber-espionage that Henri le Geek as he was called, could do marvelous things with computers. Dulac, along with other constabulary forces in Lyon had used his services more than once. The problem was that some of Messier's methods were sometimes far from legal. Because of his usefulness to the police, they more often than not turned a blind eye to Messier's minor transgressions.

Dulac decided it was time to renew their old acquaintance. He gave Messier a call, recognizing immediately his former classmate's sing-song Marseilles accent.

"Of course I'm open this evening. Can't afford to retire yet," said Messier.

"You're still on *Rue d'Amboise*?"

"Same old place. Same old me. But the cat died last week."

Dulac finished his scotch, went downstairs to the garage, entered his Renault and proceeded to Messier's electronics repair shop, a small place with the neon sign *Microbytes Messier* illuminating its storefront. An assortment of computers and related accessories filled the window display helter-skelter, with no discernible attempt to attract eventual customers.

"If it isn't my good friend and Interpol agent Thierry Dulac." Messier stood behind his counter in a rumpled gray shirt and baggy brown pants. "How are you?"

Dulac couldn't help but notice that Messier had gone almost completely bald, a far cry from the mane of thick brown hair he'd had during his time at the university. "Trying to keep out of trouble. And you?"

"Fine, fine. What brings you to this part of the world, or should I ask?"

"I need a favor, from one of the best computer wizards I know."

"Coming from you, not much of a compliment." Messier smiled, letting show a set of rotten, dark-yellow teeth.

"I have a challenge for you." Dulac well knew Messier's incurable taste for cyber-adventure.

"Official, or unofficial?"

"Just helping an old friend."

"That doesn't put food in the refrigerator."

"Could help bring some criminals to justice."

"Noble thought, but I am rather busy. What's it about, anyway?"

"It's about getting the details of telephone calls and emails of key personnel of a British shipping company, say for the last three months."

"Surely you're joking."

"That difficult?"

"On the contrary. Piece of cake. I thought you said you had a challenge for me."

"I suppose the challenge is keeping this under wraps." Dulac thought he shouldn't remind Messier of his past mis-adventure. "How much?"

Messier rubbed his chin with his right hand. "Well, since this is 'unofficial', say 2,000 euros cash and a laptop."

Dulac emitted a loud whistle. "Not cheap."

"And that's because you're a friend. Market price is double."

"How long?" said Dulac.

"About a day to get an untraceable black-market com-puter, then another couple of days max to do the work."

"I'll need a receipt. Label it 'computer repair'. At Interpol, creativity with one's expense account has its limits." Dulac reached in his pocket and took out a folded piece of paper. "Here's a list of P & W's key personnel. And by the way, we've never had this conversation."

"Of course." Messier winked.

* * *

The following afternoon, Dulac received a call from Messier.

"I have the goods."

"That was quick. I'll be right over."

"Don't forget the 2,000 euros."

"Have it with me."

Dulac put the envelope in his pocket, went downstairs to the garage, jumped into his Renault and drove to *Rue d' Amboise*. He parked in front of Messier's shop. Messier was at the door and showed him in.

Messier went behind the counter, opened a side drawer and reached in. "Voilà," said Messier, handing two USB sticks to Dulac. "One for the emails, the other for the phone calls and numbers."

"That's it?"

"What did you expect? Gift wrapping and sworn affidavits of authenticity?"

Dulac grinned, pulled a white envelope from his coat pocket and handed it to Messier.

Messier folded it and shoved it in his pants pocket.

"Aren't you going to count it?"

Messier smiled at Dulac. "If one can't trust an Interpol agent—"

Dulac looked at the USB sticks. "Anything in particular?"

"I didn't have time to check thoroughly, but one thing piqued my curiosity."

"Which is?"

Messier reached down, took out a dust cloth and wiped the glass countertop. "There are calls made to Switzerland to a company answering service. I tried to get someone on the line, but no one answers. It's Mira something."

"Mirolet?"

Messier stopped dusting and looked at Dulac. "That's it. Mirolet SA."

"Jesus." Dulac's mind reeled, absorbing the impact of the news. "Who called?"

"That's what's strange. The other calls were made either through the company's switchboard or direct dialing, but the calls to Mirolet were made through an encrypted number, so I couldn't trace the calls."

"Very interesting. What does it take to find out?"

"Can't do that without the company log."

"And that means a search warrant."

"Yes, but you might get the number through cross-references with emails."

"Somehow I doubt it."

CHAPTER 51

P & W Headquarters

It took Bolding two days to fully recover from his binge. He stayed at home, half-convincing himself he could better weather the impending storm from the relative quiet of Addington Manor. The morning newspaper had changed that. Now Bolding, his tie loosely tied, his shirt collar open, was sitting in the rear of the Bentley on his way to the office to face the music, feeling his anger mount as he read the Southampton Times' headline article: P & W Faces Bankruptcy. The words screamed at him as he read the article, which cited an anonymous source. *Goddam weasel. I wonder how much he got for that.* He pulled his cell from his pocket and called his secretary.

"Have Mills and Owens meet me in the small conference room."

He pressed the end-call button and shoved the phone back into his jacket pocket. Twenty minutes later the Bentley approached Caravan House, and Bolding could see a bevy of reporters and cameramen waiting in front of the glass doors of the building. When the reporters saw the dark-blue Bentley approach the curb, they turned and rushed down the steps to the street.

"Shall I drive to the rear entrance, sir?" asked the chauffeur.

"No, I'll have to face them at some point. Might as well be now." Bolding opened the rear door, exited the car and was immediately surrounded by a flock of microphones.

"Is it true P & W is bankrupt?" The reporters jockeyed for position, trying to be heard.

"Not so. We're considering all of our options." Bolding hastened his pace towards the entrance.

"Will the passengers be refunded?"

"Our standard cancellation policy applies. First and foremost, we have our clients' interests at heart."

"Will P & W be taken over by Carnival?"

"Not if I can help it."

"Are you insured against the class-action lawsuit brought by the passengers?"

"No comment."

Bolding reached the glass doors. The security guard inside ushered him through and quickly closed the doors in the face of the frustrated throng of reporters. Bolding walked across the reception area, hardly acknowledging the receptionist, and took the waiting elevator. He exited on the second floor, turned right and made his way to the small conference room next to his office. Inside, Mills and Owens were talking excitedly as Bolding entered.

"Anyone know about this?" Bolding waved the *Southampton Times* at them, then pitching the newspaper onto the conference table.

No one spoke.

"So what's happening, people? Talk to me for chrissake. Owens?"

"They've seized the *Hanover Star*."

"And Berkeley's Trust has frozen our accounts and cancelled our line of credit," added Mills.

"Great. Just wonderful" Bolding turned back to Owens. "What about the other ships? Were you able to get them to sea?"

"Yes sir. But we weren't in time for the *Golden Star*. She was seized in New York."

"Damn." Bolding walked nervously back and forth in front of the table.

A woman's voice came from the doorway. "Excuse me, sir, it's—"

Bolding spun around and glared at his secretary. "Now what is it?"

"Sorry sir. I, I have Mr. Toombs on the line. He said it's urgent."

"Put him through. No, on second thought I'll take the call in my office. In the meantime, get Jane and David up here."

Bolding brushed past his secretary, taking off his jacket as he rushed to his office. He slammed the door shut and threw the jacket onto one of the chairs before sitting down at his desk and answering the phone. The nasal voice of his solicitor Andrew Toombs did nothing to calm his temper.

"Hello Sir Adrian. I'm looking at today's papers. How is it at your end?"

"Catastrophic would be putting it mildly. What's up?"

"I just got off the phone with my colleague Arnold Smith at Baker, McKittrich, the lawyers defending the US government in the Bezorban class action. I—"

"Listen Andrew, I'm in a crisis meeting with my people. I don't have time for—"

"Just to let you know that Smith hinted at an offer to join forces against the passenger claimants. Save some legal fees and give P & W the highest possible level of legal representation, is how he put it. Insulting bastard. I nearly hung up in his face, but as your lawyer, I'm duty bound to report this to you."

Bolding settled down a little. "I think I understand what lies beneath their kind offer but tell me anyway."

"That would prevent us taking recourse against the US government. So this started a discussion between members of our firm, and one of our junior lawyers here had an idea. She thinks there may be a way out of your predicament."

Bolding's impatience was mollified by his curiosity, "Really? Tell me more."

"What's your financial situation?"

"We've had our line of credit cancelled and four ships seized. I expect the others to be seized as soon as they reach port. "

"Our plan would take a bit of bluffing to carry you through, but it's absolutely essential that you buy more time."

"How much time are we talking about?"

"At least a week."

"A week? I'll be glad if I survive till tomorrow."

"Whatever. Can you fake a bid for some bridge financing?"

"We can try. What's this plan of yours?"

"It would be better if we met. Perhaps we can come over."

"How fast can you get here?"

"In say, twenty minutes?"

"I'll be waiting." Bolding hung up.

* * *

Bolding went to the small conference room, his spirit slightly buoyed by his conversation with Toombs. He stood at the head of the oval table, facing his key officers. Bolding took a sip from the glass of water beside him. For a moment, he stared down at the table, seemingly gathering his thoughts. All waited expectantly, until finally he looked up and spoke in a grave but steady tone.

"Ladies and gentlemen, over the years we have worked together to make P & W one of the stellar cruise ship fleets of the world. We've all prospered, and I can say without undue boasting that you have found me to be appreciative, including the terms of your remunerations. But now we are at a crossroads. These next few days will be crucial in determining whether we will survive or not." Bolding took another sip of water. "I will need your complete support to carry P & W through these times, but with it I am confident we can pull through. I have just gotten off the phone with our solicitor Andrew Toombs, and he has a plan which might help us avoid the abyss. He'll be over shortly." Bolding took another sip of water.

"But before we proceed, I must be assured of your complete loyalty. I don't want another leak like this piece of crap." He picked up his copy of the *Southampton Times*, waved it menacingly and slapped it back down onto the table. "I want a commitment from each of you that you won't abandon ship."

Bolding eyed Owens. "Dick?"

"I'm in," said Owens.

"Jane?"

"Yes, Sir Adrian." Jane Davies, Director of Personnel and Communications, nodded.

Bolding eyed his Vice-President of Finance. "Allister?"

"I . . . yes, of course."

"David?" Bolding turned to his right and addressed Winston, his Chief Security officer.

"I'm with you."

Bolding eyed Mills again. "Good. Now I want you, Allister, to contact BNP Bank and all the other major banks and send them a request for bridge financing for 30 million pounds, a 6 million pounds line of credit, and—"

"Excuse me, Sir Adrian, but is there something here I don't understand?" Mills looked dumbfounded. "We have no assets to offer that aren't either seized or garnished. We—"

"We must buy time. We must act as if we're going to survive. My grandfather once told me the illusion of financial solidity is as good as the real thing, at least for a while. If my grandfather could pull it off when P & W was on the verge of bankruptcy in 1927, so can we."

"But they will surely ask what guarantees we can offer. What do I tell them?"

"Allister, we just have to start the process. Tell them you have reserves, unencumbered receivables coming in shortly.

Tell them the government is thinking about backing us because if it doesn't, the unions will scream bloody murder. Be creative, Allister." Bolding turned to Winney. "In the meantime, let's go over our communications strategy. Jane, what's your plan?"

* * *

Winney was in the middle of her presentation when Bolding's secretary announced that Toombs and another lawyer had arrived.

"Show them in," said Bolding.

Moments later, Toombs and a tall, beautiful woman with shoulder-length, blonde hair stood at the entrance of the room. All eyes shifted to the woman, her beige two-piece silk suit a proper cut of lawyerly sobriety that still hinted at the curves of her body.

"You're just in time, Andrew," said Bolding.

Toombs turned towards the blonde. "Ladies, gentlemen. Meet Sarah Froome from our litigation department. She has some information we'd like to share with you."

Froome acknowledged them with a curt nod and flashed a quick smile of perfect teeth before she and Toombs settled in at the table.

"Mr. Toombs has briefed me on the present situation at P & W," said Froome. "As part of another file, I've been doing some research on legal actions taken by companies in financial difficulty. I think this research just might apply to P & W's present circumstances."

"And what does that involve?" said Mills.

"We'd be suing the US Government for gross negligence in using an untested, unsafe paralyzing gas, namely Bezorban, and destroying your business in the process. But first, we'd have to secure the services of a large firm such as Phillips and Kent. They're the top international claims lawyers in the country. That would tell everyone we're playing in the big leagues. They'd file suits in London and New York as soon as the claim is drafted."

"Again, I hate to be a naysayer," said Mills, "but if they've read about P & W in the papers, won't they refuse to represent a client who may go under at any time?"

Froome clearly didn't appreciate Mills' question. "With all the publicity they'll get, it shouldn't be hard to convince them to go in on a contingency basis."

Everyone was silent as they waited for Bolding's reaction.

"Assuming they accept, what would be the next steps?" he asked.

"I've prepared a working paper on the heads of action of our claim," said Froome.

"How much is our claim?"

"Four billion pounds."

Another silence in the room. Everyone looked fixedly at Froome, then at Toombs. Finally, Bolding broke the spell.

"What are our chances, Mr. Toombs?"

"Ms. Froome?" said Toombs.

"From what I've seen, fair to good. Of course this will never go to court because the US government will lose, so it will eventually boil down to how much P & W will settle for."

"Surely the Americans will dig in their heels and drag this on forever," said Mills. "They'll delay this until we fold."

"Not necessarily," said Froome. "That's where the bridge financing comes in. Plus we can request a fast-track hearing in the US."

"That's the best news I've heard in months," said Bolding.

"Again, I hate to be the devil's advocate, Miss Froome," said Mills, "but even if what you say is true and all goes according to your plan, what if P & W is forced into bankruptcy before we settle with the US government?"

"That's exactly why P & W is not going to go bankrupt, Mr. Mills." Froome's voice was firm and no-nonsense.

"I think I'm beginning to follow," said Bolding. "You're saying that P & W is worth more, a lot more, as a going concern, even if somewhat a limping one, than its balance sheet shows."

"Exactly, Sir Adrian," said Froome. "My advice is to get as much publicity on the lawsuit as you can as quickly as possible. Berkeley's Trust will wait to see the progression of the lawsuit before pulling the plug. If all goes according to plan, the banks will be at your doorstep, lending a helping hand."

Mills continued to look dubiously at Froome, who saw his hesitation and offered more assurances.

"Mr. Mills a lawsuit, especially when it's large, can be a company's biggest asset."

Bolding felt a wave of relief surge up his spine. He turned to Davies. "Jane, contact the newspapers and coordinate with Froome. Let's get some positive spin out there."

CHAPTER 52

Lyon, Dulac's apartment

Dulac temporarily parked his professional conscience in a faraway place and opened his computer. He began to carefully study the first of the USB sticks Messier had given him. The emails were innocuous, business-related, run-of-the-mill. What he was hoping to find was definitely not there.

He took the stick from his computer and inserted the next one, containing the phone numbers and names of callers. Messier had categorized them by dates:

> *Date — Mills to Bolding*
> *Date — Mills to Bankers Trust*
> *Date — Mills to __ Insurance*
> *Date — Toombs to Mills*
> *Date — Bankers Trust to Mills, etc. . . .*

Dulac scanned through the other calls quickly, until suddenly his curiosity was aroused:

> *Date — Mills to unregistered phone.*
> *Date — Unregistered phone to Mills*

Date — Unregistered phone to Mills
Date — London payphone to Mills

Interesting. This is worth checking out.
Dulac scanned through the other officers' calls:

Date — Owens to Toombs
Date — Owens to NY Port authority
Date — Owens to Southampton Port Authority
Etc. . . . Etc. . . .

The other calls seemed to be in the ordinary course of business. He returned to the beginning of the stick:

Date — Mills to unregistered phone.

Dulac picked up the phone and dialed Messier's number. "Henri, it's me. Nice work on the calls."

"We aim to please."

"Henri, I have a purely hypothetical question. This is a bit dicey, but could you get the name of the owner of the unregistered phone?"

There was a moment of silence.

"Henri?"

"That could be breaking the law."

"I'm not asking you to do so. I was just wondering if it were physically possible."

Dulac heard a guffaw of laughter from Messier. "That will be another 1,000 euros."

Dulac thought hard and quick. If he accepted Messier's price, he was setting himself up as an accomplice to Messier's illegal action. He took a deep breath. He didn't have time to find out what he most likely didn't want to know anyway. "When do I get it?"

"I'll call you."

* * *

Dulac had only just shut his phone when it began ringing again. He recognized Sabine Autissier's encrypted number. "Yes Sabine."

"You asked me to track down the rent payments in relation to Mirolet SA in Zurich."

"Ah yes, our Swiss miscreant."

"We were able to track down through our bank contact at Bank Leu the name of the landlord and—"

"The bottom line, Sabine."

"The bottom line is that Mirolet's rent cheques are signed by an Andrew Toombs, acting for and on behalf of a numbered company. He's a solicitor practicing in Southampton and—"

Dulac let out a loud whistle. "—and is P & W's solicitor. Great work, Sabine."

* * *

Later that afternoon, Dulac went to the bank to get Messier's cash. After returning to his apartment, he gathered the various components of his expeditious dinner on the kitchen table: three slices of turkey, a wedge of brie cheese, a piece of baguette bread and a handful of olives. The TV was on the local channel, and Dulac was busy spreading a layer of Dijon mustard onto the halves of the baguette when something caught his attention on the screen. A group of policemen were closing off the area in the front of a store, and two ambulance attendants were ferrying a covered body on a wheeled stretcher towards the nearby ambulance. The camera focused on the front of the store.

Dulac dropped his knife.

"*Bon Dieu!*" He swore aloud. *Messier's place.* Dulac rushed to the TV and increased the volume. A woman with a microphone stood next to the ambulance."—appears to have been shot twice in the head. No further details will be available on the man's identity until the police notify the next of kin. This is the twelfth homicide this year in the—"

230

Dulac rushed to the living room and grabbed the phone. He dialed Lyon's police headquarters.

"*Centrale*, agent Dutolier," said a voice.

"Thierry Dulac, Interpol. Put me through to the officer in charge."

"One moment."

Dulac waited for a moment and heard the click of his call being transferred.

"*Ici Capitaine Colomer.* Who is this?"

"Thierry Dulac, Interpol. Are you in charge?"

"ID number."

"07 3688-4."

"Just a minute." The phone clicked.

Dulac waited, still watching the TV screen from across the room. There was no more news on the homicide.

Moments later, another click sounded and the voice came back on the line. "You are the inspector from the Chimera case?"

"Yes. Listen, I have to speak to the officer in charge. Are you—?"

"Poitiers is in charge today. I'll put you through."

Another long moment. Another click.

"Poitiers."

"Dulac. You had a homicide on *Rue d'Amboise* today. Who is the victim?"

"What is your business with this?"

Dulac felt his gut tightening. He somehow sensed he didn't want to know the answer to his next question, but he had to ask it. He had no choice. "Is the man's name Henri Messier?"

"I, I am not at liberty to answer. If you have—"

"I'll meet you at the *Préfecture* in twenty minutes." Dulac hung up. *Merde! No such thing as coincidence. Sorry I got you into this, old friend.*

He got dressed, went to his desk and closed his computer. The USB sticks Messier had provided were on the desk, next to the phone. *Better take them with me.* He pocketed them, holstered his .38 Benelli and went downstairs to the garage. He'd entered and started towards his car when he noticed the garage door was open. No car was near the entrance. *Funny. It usually closes automatically.*

That's when the black Mercedes roared down the ramp, tires squealing, and raced through the open garage door. The car kept accelerating, heading straight for him. He lunged desperately between two parked cars, diving onto the floor as the Mercedes whizzed by, shots erupting from its open passenger window. Bullets ripped into the doors and the side windows of the car beside him, showering Dulac with bits of broken glass. Dulac flattened himself behind a concrete pillar just as the Mercedes came to a screeching stop before the garage wall at the end. The driver spun the car around in a cloud of smoking rubber and squealing tires. Dulac unsheathed his Parabellum Benelli .38 from his ankle holster and fired at the Mercedes. From the corner of his eye, he saw one of the apartment's occupants starting to open the metal entrance door of the garage. The Mercedes's gunman shifted his aim and fired at the opening door. It closed quickly. The black sedan roared by Dulac again in a blaze of gunfire, bullets ricocheting off the pillars before the Mercedes exited though the open doorway, bounced up the steep ramp and swerved right onto the street.

Kneeling down behind the column, Dulac felt his hands, his arms, then his whole body start to shake. He took in deep breaths and after a moment, he regained his composure and holstered his gun. He walked over and stood for a moment next to his car. He felt inside his jacket right pocket. The USB sticks were still there. Twenty minutes later, he was standing in front of the *Préfecture Centrale's* reception desk.

"Inspector Poitiers," said Dulac to the female sergeant at the desk.

"Whom shall I announce?"

"Tell him it's Dulac. Thierry Dulac." He could hear the strain in his own voice, an octave lower than usual.

"What is the nature—?"

"Just tell him I'm here."

She turned away and spoke into her headphone.

A moment later a man with brownish, obviously dyed hair and the broken nose of a prizefighter appeared at the desk, looking annoyed. "I'm inspector Pierre Poitiers. As I mentioned earlier—"

"Listen Poitiers, I've just been shot at in my garage and I'm in no mood for any of your secretive, retentive crap. I want you to send a squad to 56 *Rue des Forgerons* and check out the garage. I want to see the man who was murdered this morning on *Rue d'Amboise*."

"What business do you have with—?"

"I don't think I'm getting through." Dulac reached in his pocket and took out his cell. "If I have to call your boss Després in Paris to get answers—"

"Minute, minute. There's no need for that." Poitiers threw up his right hand. "You must understand we get all sorts here. Necrophiles, thrill-seekers, crackpots."

"You've checked my ID. I want to see the body. Now!"

"But why?"

"He was a friend of mine."

Poitiers hesitated, then conceded. "Very well. Follow me."

They walked along the narrow hallway, down a flight of stairs and Poitiers opened the twin doors. The sign above read *Salle du Médecin Légiste*.

"The coroner is working on him now," said Poitiers. "Before being shot, he was tortured."

Dulac bit his lip. They went to the table and joined the man wearing glasses and a green smock. A naked dead body lay on the slab in front of them.

Poitiers made the introductions. "*Docteur* Sançon, Inspector Dulac from Interpol."

Dulac nodded to the coroner and looked at the man on the table. He recognized Messier immediately. He looked down at Messier's left hand and saw that two of his fingers were missing. Dulac's stomach churned. "What was the cause of death?"

"Two 6mm bullets to the left side of the brain." The diminutive doctor pointed at Messier's head with a pencil. "Judging from the wound, I'd say it was a Beretta, but don't hold me to it." Sançon pointed to two red welts on Messier's left forearm. "Cigarette burns."

"They must have wanted something from him pretty badly before they killed him," said Poitiers.

CHAPTER 53

It hadn't taken much more convincing from Froome for Bolding to agree that she should contact the international law firm of Phillips and Kent. They agreed to represent P & W on a contingency basis. Froome would remain lead counsel and review the draft civil actions against the US Government in London's Old Bailey and New York City's Supreme Court before the issuing of the writs.

With this fresh information in hand, Jane Davies immediately went to work, disbursing the information to her all-too-willing press contacts. The morning the story broke, Bolding sat at his desk with Toombs across from him. Both men sipped coffee and admired the results obtained by P & W's Public Relations Officer. Bolding couldn't have asked for better than the *London Financial Time's* morning headline.

P & W CRUISE LINES TO SUE US GOVT.
OVER WRONGFUL USE OF BEZORBAN GAS.

Bolding picked up the phone and dialed a London number he knew only too well, Berkeley's Trust.

"Put me through to Hugh Walters. Tell him it's Sir Adrian Bolding."

After a moment, the familiar voice answered.

"Good morning, Sir Adrian."

"That it is. Did you happen to read today's *Times*?" Bolding knew full well all of London's bankers read the *Times* at breakfast, or on the tube on their way to the office.

"I have. Most interesting."

"I think we should meet." Bolding looked at his watch. "Shall we say 2 p.m. this afternoon at your offices?"

"I, I'll have to check with—"

"Wonderful. I'll see you there."

Bolding hung up and looked at Toombs. "Give me a moment, will you?" He gestured to the door.

Toombs got up and stepped outside Bolding's office, closing the door behind him.

Bolding opened his cell and dialed Sir Terence Hay's encrypted private number. After one ring the automated message came on. "We are sorry, the number you have dialed is no longer in service."

Bolding clicked his phone shut and pressed his secretary's extension. "Get Sir Terence on the line." He looked at his watch. "No, wait. On second thought, I'll call him later." Bolding picked up the *Times*, read the headline quickly again, folded the newspaper and put it his briefcase. He got up and walked to the window. Outside, the clouds had started to dissipate and a ray of sunshine illuminated Temple Square with a solitary beam of light. He went outside his office, where Toombs stood next to the coffee machine.

"Care to join me to see Walters?"

Toombs put down his coffee on the table next to the machine. "If you plan to have a lawyer present, it might be better to have Froome. A junior lawyer will appear less threatening. Besides, she's much better looking than I am."

"Good idea. I'm booked on the 12.05 p.m. train to London."

"I'll have her join you at Southampton Central."

* * *

At 1.55 p.m., Bolding and Froome exited their cab at 48 Notting Hill Gate, and walked into the vast, marble-floored main hall of Berkeley's Trust, its massive white columns and arched ceiling enhancing the impression of permanence, wealth and power. They reached the ramped area bordering the Managing Director's office, where a bespectacled woman with a thin face and wide-set eyes sat behind a desk, typing at her computer. She raised her eyes slowly and put on the perfunctory smile of someone accustomed to being near power and authority.

"Yes?"

"We're here to see Hugh Walters. Sir Adrian Bolding and Sarah Froome," Bolding said.

"I'll tell him you've arrived." She got up and walked to the walnut-paneled door and knocked softly. When a muted reply came from inside, she turned the large bronze door-knob and opened the door slightly to announce the visitors.

She returned to her desk. "Mr. Walters will see you in a moment."

Bolding looked around at the expressionless clerks going about their routines in hushed tones while they waited. After a moment, Bolding looked at his watch, signaled to Froome to follow him. He strode through the gate and past the ramp to the walnut-paneled door.

"Excuse me sir! Sir!" The secretary rushed after them, clearly offended at this breach of decorum. "You can't—"

Bolding gave two abrupt knocks and entered.

Walters looked up from his desk, surprise on his face. To his credit, he recovered quickly and got up.

"Good morning, Sir Adrian." He offered his hand. "And this is . . ."

"Sarah Froome."

"Sorry to rush in, but we have other appointments with your colleagues across town." Bolding fought to keep a straight face.

"I see. Please sit down. Walters gestured to the two chairs in front of his billiard table sized desk. He looked at his secretary, who stood sheepishly in the doorway. "Can we get you something? Tea, coffee?"

"We're fine." Bolding sat down in one of the plush, leather-backed chairs.

The banker sat down and leaned back, arms across his chest. "Now then Sir Adrian, what can I do for you this morning?"

"I'll cut to the chase. Ms. Froome here has something to say." Bolding turned towards the chic blonde barrister.

She cleared her throat. "Mr. Walters, my clients Sir Adrian Bolding and P & W lines have suffered serious prejudice by your bank's unjustified and sudden withdrawal of its line of credit and the seizing of two of its ships. I say unjustified after a lengthy and exhaustive study of the case law, Mr. —"

"Just a second." Walters held his hand up and stopped her. "I wasn't aware you're a solicitor. Perhaps I should call our solicitor and—"

"That shouldn't be necessary," interrupted Bolding. "What Ms. Froome means is that we could take action against the bank without further notice. But that's not going to get anyone anywhere, is it Mr. Walters?

"No, it isn't."

Froome opened her briefcase and took out a document. "I have prepared a claim form, including particulars, against the bank for 658 million pounds in damages. I won't file it or have it served without permission from my client. Also, you are certainly aware that P & W will be suing the US government for 5.1 billion pounds for negligent and wrongful use of the gas Bezorban. We have been forced to react to circumstances beyond our control that threaten the financial security of P & W."

"I was under the impression we were here to discuss business, not lawsuits." Walters looked reproachfully at Bolding.

"We are, Mr. Walters, we are," said Bolding. "No one, least of all I, wants to start lengthy and costly legal proceedings against the bank. I'm just saying that if push comes to shove, we are fully ready to take whatever means necessary, however distasteful." Bolding felt his voice gaining confidence. "I am here to assure you that P & W will ride through this temporary setback, as it has in the past. What we want to know, sir, is whether or not Berkeley's Trust will back us up? Will the bank be our partner in this?"

"What do you have in mind?"

"In practical terms, I want the bank to release my ships and—"

"And what about the mortgage payments in arrears?"

"You can reschedule them. A five-year term would do just fine."

"That's a tall order, Mr. Bolding, coming from the owner of a company on the edge of bankruptcy. What assurance do we have P & W can meet those obligations?"

"None." Froome smiled a Cheshire cat smile.

"I don't follow."

"It's really quite simple. Your other option is to bankrupt the company, end up with a fleet of ships that no one will buy in this already overcrowded and fiercely competitive market, and ensure your investment value sinks to zero. That's not counting the ongoing costs of maintaining the ships in insurable condition, taxes, dockage fees, settlements of garnishments, payment of wages etc. . . . etc. . . . On the other hand if you free the ships, extend the loan and re-establish my client's line of credit, you'll be giving notice to the shipping world that you have faith in P & W's viability. The US government will know that it will have to negotiate, thus securing your investment." Froome paused for effect, just long enough for her statement to sink in. "I'd say that's an easy choice, Mr. Walters."

"So you're saying your lawsuit against the US government is a form of security for the bank?" Walters eyed Froome, then Bolding.

"Exactly," said Bolding. "On top of which, we have asked the British government to guarantee the outstanding loan payments." *That's the truth. Even if they refused.* Bolding had nothing to lose and decided to ennoble the truth. "Sir Terence Hays is bringing the matter up before cabinet as we speak. He assures me he can swing it in our favor."

Walters's look relaxed slightly and Bolding saw the beginning of a ray of hope.

"When will you hear from Hays?" Walters.

"Immediately after the meeting is concluded."

"I see. Perhaps I could take the matter under advisement until then."

"In the meantime, you would do well to free my ships."

"I didn't agree to anything yet, Mr. Bolding. All I can say is that I will discuss the matter with my colleagues."

Bolding decided to go out on a limb. He knew the bank's chairman, a man he disliked thoroughly and with whom he'd had a recent tiff over membership dues at their club. But Walters didn't have to know that part. "Would it help if I called Sir Archibald?"

"That won't be necessary. I'll let you know the bank's decision." Walters got up from his desk. "Good day, Mr. Bolding, Ms. Froome."

CHAPTER 54

Interpol HQ, the following day

Dulac had left the Préfecture Centrale knowing he'd left Poitiers with more questions than answers about Messier's murder, and why he'd been shot at in his garage. He had neither the time nor the inclination to explain the intricacies of a complex case to a local policeman. At least not yet.

The following morning, he went down to the cafeteria and saw Annette Arlberg sipping her usual double espresso and reading a local edition of Le Figaro. As Dulac approached he could see she was absorbed by the headline article of Messier's murder. A pang of guilt overtook him. He pulled up the plastic chair in front of her and sat down.

She glanced up, acknowledging him with a short nod. "Nasty business this." She put down her cup.

"I may have had something to do with it."

"What?" Her eyes locked onto Dulac, and her usually smooth forehead broke into waves of furrows.

"You're not going to like this." Dulac looked around at the employees sitting at the tables around them.

"In my office. Now." She folded her paper and got up.

Dulac followed her.

Once upstairs, Arlberg winced as Dulac explained how he'd had Messier hack into P & W's phone and email logs, then asked Messier to find the unlisted number's owner. He finished with a description of the shooting in the garage the previous evening and his visit to the *Centrale* to identify Messier's body.

"Messier was shot with a 6mm, probably a Beretta. I'll bet my bonus the bullets the police find in my garage came from the same gun."

"So you're saying these people got onto Messier's game, tracked him down, tortured him into telling them the name of his principal, and then went after you?"

"It takes rather sophisticated people and equipment to track a hacker."

"Who do you have in mind?"

"Well, we can safely rule out the FSB and the FBI. They're probably out of range. So that leaves the French *Sureté* and MI-6. And of course us."

"Now really, Dulac. That's pretty wild. Even for you."

"I'm merely pointing out the possibilities.

"So what do you suggest?"

"I was afraid you'd ask that."

Arlberg took in a deep breath. "I know you have something in mind."

"The problem is that MI-6 and the *Sureté* track hundreds of calls daily, but they are recorded in their logs. If we could find out if they tracked any from Messier—"

"You're not suggesting we hack their lines?"

"The thought crossed my mind, but all we really need is a copy of their logs."

"Assuming for a moment you're right, surely the people involved would have eliminated all traces in the logs also," said Arlberg.

"Perhaps, but sometimes the omission is as incriminating as the act itself."

"And who do you have in mind to get copies of those logs?"

Dulac smiled at Arlberg. "Only one person here has that kind of authority level."

"Forget it."

* * *

Karen's apartment, Paris, two days later

Karen had made rapid progress in her recuperation and been discharged from the Centre de Rééducation weeks earlier than originally anticipated. Upon hearing the great news, Dulac had decided he needed a small break from the investigation to clear his thoughts, so had invited her for supper at Chez François. He took the 4.10 p.m. TGV to Paris, and two hours plus a taxi ride later, he stood in front of Karen's apartment on Avenue de Boisbriand. Karen buzzed him in and he went up the stairs, grabbing the handrail to help himself up the last flight. He stood panting at the door for an instant, catching his breath when the door opened.

Karen, dressed in a light blue blouse and cream-colored silk pants, stood at the doorway leaning on a cane. She smiled broadly.

He hadn't forgotten how ravishing she could look.

She leaned forward and kissed him. "Miss me?"

"Very much so."

She took him by the arm. "Come. Let's have an aperitif."

Dulac felt the warmth of the elegantly decorated apartment as soon as he entered. The pastel hues and mixture of classical Louis 16th furniture and pre-Columbian art soothed him. He didn't hesitate to plop himself down onto the plush leather Italian sofa in the center of the salon.

Using her cane, Karen limped slowly towards the bar across the room.

"The usual?"

"Sounds good."

She poured the scotch into two glasses.

"You'll have to come and get them, I'm afraid."

"Of course. How inconsiderate of me. You seem to be doing a lot better."

"Let's say it's very encouraging."

Dulac carried the glasses to the table near the sofa and then turned back to offer a steadying hand. She sat down beside him.

"To you." He lifted his glass and toasted her. "And how are you feeling?"

"Apart from a slight tingling sensation in my left leg, quite well. I have to be careful and remind myself not to lift anything heavy until the stitches are out. Should be early next month."

"You're damn lucky the bullet didn't hit any vital organs."

"Absolutely. But enough about me. What about your investigation?"

Dulac always felt a little uncomfortable when talking shop with Karen. It wasn't that he didn't trust her, but protocol required that you normally didn't confide in your lover about company business. Still, she'd helped him more than once with her insightful outlook on matters criminal. He took a sip from his glass. "Good stuff."

Karen cocked her head and looked inquisitively at Dulac. "And?"

"Ah yes, the investigation. It's either going to blow wide open, or dissolve into a sea of oblivion. Take your pick."

"Care to be a little more specific?"

"For starters, there's Bolding. He sold shares of P & W's stock just two weeks before the hijack. Nothing illegal in that per se, but a bit unethical when one's company is near bankruptcy. Same with Sir Terence Hays, who sits on the board. Then there's this Swiss company shorting P & W's stock, betting the shares will go down."

"Are you suggesting all this could be linked to the hijack?"

"Everybody is saying it's coincidental, but a man is dead, and I've been shot at while trying to find out if there is any connection between these so-called coincidences."

"You've been shot at?"

"Two days ago. A man was trying to get information for me about an unlisted, encrypted number, and paid for that indiscretion with his life. Then a hit man tries to whack me in my garage in Lyon. Someone doesn't want me to get that number's owner."

"Jesus." Karen's eyes widening in amazement. "Can't Interpol get it?"

"Not without a court order." Dulac felt he didn't have to go into the other option.

"So you're saying the hijacking and the unlisted number's owner could somehow be connected?"

"Or the shorting of the shares and the unlisted number, or all three. The problem is that the owner of that number is covering his tracks as we speak."

"So where do you go from here?"

"I've got to keep digging. My instinct tells me Bolding, Hays, Toombs and Mirolet are connected in more ways than appear on the surface. Unless my instincts are dead wrong, and no comment on that thank you very much, they're an integral part of the thread line."

"Leading to?"

"To whoever conspired with the hijackers and caused the death of twenty-seven passengers and the destruction of a ship."

"Speaking of which, we haven't heard anything in the news lately. Surely the Americans aren't going to stand by on the sidelines for very much longer." Karen took a sip of her scotch.

"Based on their track record, I'd have to agree with you."

"Coming back to that attempt on your life, you're convinced that—"

"And by the way, Lescop discovered that before being murdered, Leon Binagro, the hijackers' agent in Costa Rica, made a payment to the Swiss company, most probably from the ransom money. Another coincidence? I think not."

Karen looked probingly at Dulac. "I presume you don't have enough for the Swiss to investigate?"

"Dead on. Besides, anyone owning shares in that Swiss company will have layered his or her ownership through anonymously held, numbered companies."

"An investigator's nightmare."

"Don't rub it in."

At that moment, Dulac's cell rang. Arlberg.

"I've got to take this."

"Sure."

"Mr. Dulac?"

Dulac recognized the voice of Arlberg's secretary.

"Yes Mary."

"Sorry to disturb you sir, but General Secretary Arlberg instructed me to call you. She's just received word from the *Centrale's* Inspector Poitiers in Lyon. She told me to tell you that you've won your bet on your bonus, whatever that means."

CHAPTER 55

Law firm of Andrew Toombs and Associates, Southampton,

His headache throbbing, Toombs was looking at the file of one of his offshore clients when Sarah Froome walked into his office, briefcase in hand.

"So how did it go at Berkeley's?" asked Toombs.

"Quite well, I think."

"You think?"

"Walters is at least going to reconsider, before being stuck with a bunch of rusting ships."

Toombs looked doubtfully at Froome. "Personally, I think you could have put your time to better use."

"I rechecked the law. The jurisprudence is heavily in our favor. Besides, Phillips and---"

"Mark my words. They'll never release the ships, and without that, P & W is a dead duck. They'll never get their day in court."

Froome looked perplexed at Toomb's pessimism.

"I know I might sound negative to you, but I've seen this sort of thing before. I don't want you to waste your time. And mine."

"But I have a meeting with Phillips and Kent this morning, to finalize P & W's claim," said Froome. "They seem to believe in the case."

"All I can say is good luck."

Froome gathered her briefcase and got up to leave.

"Don't say I didn't warn you," said Toombs.

Froome left and Toombs got up, closed his office door and locked it. His headache was getting worse. He went back to his desk, opened the drawer and took out a bottle of Aspirin. He downed two tablets and poured himself a glass of water from the pitcher on his desk. As he waited for the pills to take effect, he went across to the other side of the room, to the cheap reproduction of Monet's water lilies. He removed the picture and placed it on the floor. After a few turns of the dial of the Chubb safe, he twisted the handle and opened it. Inside, next to the 10,000 pounds of cash neatly stacked in 100-pound notes, lay two brown accordion-type file holders. One bore the handwritten name "Miramar SA", the other, "Mirolet SA". He removed the Mirolet file, closed the safe, replaced the picture on the wall and went back to his desk. Apart from Toombs, no one in his office knew of the existence of the files, as they weren't logged in any of the firm's systems.

He opened the file, glanced at one of the numbers handwritten on the inside cover, picked up his phone and dialed. After two rings an automated response kicked in. "We are sorry, the number you have dialed is no longer in service."

He paused for a moment, then dialed Allister Mills's direct line at P & W and left a message. "Allister, it's Andrew, call me concerning the seizure of the ships."

Half an hour later, the phone rang. It was Mills. "What's up?"

"I'll call you back in five minutes." Toombs went downstairs and outside to the red phone booth. He inserted a prepaid card and dialed Mills's direct line.

"It's me. Did you speak to Bolding?"

"No. I haven't seen him this morning."

"We have a problem."

"Oh?"

"Sarah Froome and Bolding just came back from Berkeley's Trust. She thinks Bolding convinced or scared them into extending their credit line and releasing the ships."

"Damn."

"I tried to convince her she was wasting her time. As its lawyers, it's our duty to represent P & W to the fullest extent of its rights and present all the options to the client. She has also convinced Phillips and Kent to take on the lawsuit on a contingency basis. Now I have a serious conflict of interest. And so do you."

"What do you mean?" exclaimed Mills.

"Mirolet. If Berkeley's releases the ships and the word gets out that P & W will survive, even if only briefly, its stock will rise and the short position taken by Mirolet will be worth nothing. It will owe 20 million pounds to the broker. If it doesn't pay, all hell will break loose and I can't guarantee the Swiss won't break their confidentiality rules. Mirolet is also my client, so the conflict is real."

There was a silence. "We'll lose everything," whispered Mills.

"Allister, this is far from a done deal. You know how bankers prevaricate. Chances are—"

"We can't leave 20 million pounds up to chance, Andrew. Have you spoken to the others?"

"I tried but they've deactivated the number."

"We've got to do something. The call on the shares is next Tuesday."

CHAPTER 56

Lyon, Interpol HQ

Dulac received news from Judge Pierre Bellet and scheduled an urgent meeting with Arlberg.

Dulac got to the point as soon as he closed her office door behind him. "After I gave him copies of the USB sticks, he did some investigating on his own."

"The ones with the calls from the encrypted unregistered phone?"

"Yes. I also let him know about the stock sales by Hays and Bolding. It's public information, but I wanted him to put pressure on his sources. Nothing like a bit of political spicing up to ensure interest."

"What was his reaction?"

"Positive. He says his source at *La Sureté* can't precisely identify the owner's name by the phone number but do confirm that the number is part of a series. That series is reserved for members of MI-6 and British government high-level personnel."

Arlberg pushed her bifocals up higher along the bridge of her thin nose. "How reliable is the source?"

"Bellet tells me his man is the French specialist on British intelligence."

"He's a spy?"

"The best in the business, according to Bellet."

She got up and walked to and fro behind her desk, pausing now and then to look over Dulac. "So the French judiciary has more intelligence info than we do on this."

Dulac shrugged his shoulders and arched his eyebrows. "What can I say? It is what it is."

"So if I have this right," continued Arlberg, "according to what's on the sticks, this owner of the mystery phone, either an MI-6 operative or a high-ranking British government official, has called Andrew Toombs how many times?"

"I have twenty-two calls over a three-month period. He also called P & W's offices at their main number fourteen times. We don't know who he contacted there."

Arlberg crossed her arms. She stopped for a moment and eyed Dulac. "And you have reason to believe the owner, either himself or through others, had Messier killed and tried to kill you for attempting to discover his identity. Is that about it?"

"That pretty well sums it up." Dulac scratched the back of his head and ran his hand through his hair.

"All this being purely hypothetical at this point, of course." Arlberg cocked her head slightly from left to right. "So what do you suggest we do?"

"I'll start by what we can't do. We can't go to the Yard on this. At least not yet."

"Why not?"

"Who knows the relationship between members of the Yard and MI-6? One leak and the whole thing gets buried even deeper. Also, we can't very well walk into MI-6 and go on a fishing expedition. What would we say? 'Oh, by the way old chaps, the French *Sureté* knows about your reserved numbers.'"

"Obviously not."

"That really leaves us only one option. And I guarantee you're not going to like it."

"Here we go again. Really, Dulac—"

"We get the French *Sureté* to hack into MI-6. Either they are successful and get the owner's identity, or—"

"Why on earth would they even try?"

"They're into each other's beds already. One more intrusion, what's the difference? If we go that route, they flush the owner out. Either way, he's bound to react. He'll think twice about going after a member of the *Sureté* the way he went after Messier and me."

"That's a pretty tall order."

"Officially impossible. Unofficially, that's another matter."

"Dulac, you realize there can't be a hint of Interpol's involvement in any of this."

"Wouldn't think of it."

"So if, and that's a big if, we eventually find out who this mysterious owner is, how do you go about proving anything else but his or her perfectly legitimate right to having an unregistered phone?"

"That ties in with another idea of mine. We can actually get the content of those calls through the server, through the US government."

"What?"

"There is a strong chance that the NSA has tapped MI-6's lines and certainly the British government's lines. All we have to do is get the number and a contact there. I'll bet my bonus we can get the contents of the calls *and* the identity of the parties."

"So far, I must admit you do rather well when you bet your bonus." Arlberg smirked, "But surely the NSA will be more protective than even MI-6."

"Unless we have something to offer in return."

"Such as?"

"I'll have to come up with something."

"I'm sure you will. Until then, let's get back to the home front."

"I saw Autissier this morning. She's tracking the movement of P & W's shares relative to Mirolet's short position. Since Bolding's going to stand and fight, P &W shares are rising. Not good for an investor with a short position."

"Mirolet. That's the Swiss shareholder of P & W," said Arlberg.

"Correct."

"Anything further on who owns Mirolet?"

"No. I spoke to my Swiss banker contact Gustav Thoeni. All I got from him is that Mirolet's ownership is layered with offshore corporations."

"What about its directors?"

"Under Swiss law, you don't have to be a shareholder to be a director," said Dulac. "They're often front men, paid under the table, who don't know who they're representing."

"Keep me posted if anything develops on Mirolet. I'll want to know when they cover their short. In the meantime, what about Tajar Singh? Any trace of him?"

"Nothing new. I haven't spoken to Lescop, but he has a couple of agents working on it. That guy is probably enjoying some serious protection from someone at P & W."

Arlberg threw another exasperated look at Dulac. "There you go again. Until you give me a shred of evidence—"

"I know, I know, but you've got to admit, these coincidences are starting to mount up to a significant pile of circumstantial shit."

CHAPTER 57

Toombs's offices, Southampton

Toombs phone rang just as he was about to close up shop for the day.

"Hello?"

"It's me." The disembodied voice breathed heavily. "I'm calling from a bus stop."

Toombs didn't like the unusual edge in Mills' voice. "What's up?"

"I just came from a meeting with Bolding. He won't budge. Suddenly all he can see is saving face and his reputation. He sees this civil action against the US government as his salvation. I told him to think about what that would do to the others. I tried, Andrew. I really tried."

"And?"

"He says he doesn't care about crass interests of some shareholders trying to make money on P & W's stock going south. I tried to have him wait, at least until we cover the short, but he says his lawyers told him they must act now. It's a question of credibility, especially for the bankers at Berkeley's."

"So suddenly Bolding has a conscience. Strange coming from a man who didn't hesitate to sell his own shares when the stock started dipping."

"I pointed that out to him. He mentioned it didn't put the company or the jobs of its workers at risk. There's not much I can do if he decides to go ahead. If it weren't for that bitch lawyer of yours . . ."

"Name calling won't do any good, Allister. Besides, Philips and Kent are fully on board."

"What?"

"You heard me. It's out of my control. The file was sent to them."

"Christ!"

For a moment, neither man spoke. Then Toombs broke the silence. "Listen, Allister, I can't do anything more."

"No, but we can."

"What do you mean?"

"The stock is rising. We can't let that happen," said Mills.

"I'm not liking the sound of this. Besides, why call me in the first place?"

"Because if anything goes wrong, you're in it with us. You're not getting off the hook just because you're a solicitor."

Toombs felt sweat forming on his forehead. "So you're tying me in for your protection under client-solicitor privilege. Is that it?"

"Just an added precaution. After all, it's a part of the whole operation. You're a necessary part of that operation."

A solid bar formed in Toombs' stomach. "I only executed the corporate legal wishes of my clients. That's it. End of story. I'm starting to get very negative vibes from this conversation, Allister. Tell me you're not considering doing what I think you're considering."

"The problem is being taken care of."

"Allister, as an officer of the law, I have a duty to report any—"

"We thought of that, Andrew." Mills didn't miss a beat. "Don't even think of it. Look out your window. See anything unusual?"

Toombs went to his window and pulled open the blind. There was a black Land Rover SUV parked across the street in a no parking zone. Its motor was running.

"Listen Allister—"

"No, you listen. Why don't you phone home? You'll find there's a car parked in front. You wouldn't want anything to happen to Sheila and little Patricia, now would you?"

"You bastards. You wouldn't—"

The line went dead.

CHAPTER 58

Addington Manor, Southampton

Bolding left his office in high spirits, in spite of his conversation that afternoon with Mills. Earlier, he'd received an email from Froome confirming that Phillips and Kent had agreed to represent them in their claims against the US Government. He'd set up another meeting with Walters at Berkeley's Trust and Walters had agreed to reconsider the bank's decision about keeping the ships under seizure. At last the dark clouds hanging over his head for the past six months seemed to be dissipating. Somewhat.

"Will that be all, sir?" Higgins deposited the tray containing the glass of scotch on the table next to the brown leather sofa.

"Yes. Good night, Higgins."

"Good night, sir." Higgins withdrew, closing the door to the music room behind him.

Bolding got up and walked over to the medieval armoire across the room. He unlocked its heavy oak doors. Inside, from his vast collection of CDs, he pulled out one of his favorites, Isaac Stern's rendition of Brahms's *Violin Concerto*, and inserted the disc in the CD player.

Instantly, the big Bowers and Wilkins speakers came to life and the soft, warm melody of the first movement filled the ancestral room. He often wondered what life would have been like if he'd listened to his mother and become a violinist. As a student, he'd shown a significant amount of talent, even if his willingness to practice left something to be desired. There was always a soccer game to play, a sailboat to be sailed, or a sports car to be driven. Besides, he knew even then he didn't have that special dose of magic necessary for a concert violinist. Still, with enough dedication and hard work, a position as concertmaster in a world-class orchestra had been within the realm of the achievable.

In the end, his father's admonitions had won the day. "A man's duty comes first," Bolding Senior had said. "Not everyone has the opportunities you were born into. You'd be a bloody fool not to take advantage and make the best of them. When I'm dead, you must run this company, as I did, as your grandfather did. Later, you can fiddle all you want." Torn between his love of music and his father's orders, Bolding reluctantly took the corporate plunge. Upon the untimely death of his father at age 70, Bolding had inherited the full weight of the family legacy.

He returned to the sofa and sat down, engulfing himself in the tempo of the music, occasionally letting his right-hand sway in an enthusiastic imitation of the orchestra conductor.

Immersed in the music as he was, he could never have heard, nor did he in fact hear, the slight rustle of the silk drapes hung over the French windows across the room, behind him.

Nor did he detect the slow, deliberate movement of the man pushing aside the drapes, pulling out a hypodermic needle from its small case, and walking swiftly towards the seated Bolding.

Bolding turned slightly, suddenly aware of a human presence behind him. Too late. He felt a sharp sting in his neck just as he started to get up. He looked at the hooded man in surprise, then fear. Bolding tried to rise, but the man pressed heavily with his left hand on Bolding's right shoulder. He tried to yell, but the sound remained stuck in his throat. After a moment, the black-hooded man released his hand from Bolding's shoulder, pulled out the needle, and put it carefully back in its case. Even through the hood, Bolding could see the man smiling, seemingly satisfied.

Bolding tried to scream for help but could only manage a gurgling sound. He tried to get up but couldn't. His limbs were numb, powerless. He felt a tingling sensation overcome the rest of his body. He was paralyzed.

He sat and watched helplessly as the hooded man, wearing white latex gloves, went to the entrance of the music room and locked the door. He turned back and walked over to Bolding's walnut desk, reached for a pass key in his right pocket and opened the desk drawer. He took out Bolding's Smith & Wesson .38.

My God, how did he know it was there? Bolding struggled to fight back panic. His instincts kicked in. If only he could fall onto the table and knock over the glass, maybe it would smash and Higgins would hear it.

As if he'd read Bolding's thoughts, the assassin went to the armoire. He found the volume control and turned it higher. The orchestra's violins and violas became strident, then the bass and cello section burst into a deafening crescendo.

The man walked over and grabbed a small mauve pillow from the divan opposite them. Bolding watched in horror as the man approached, pillow in one hand, the .38 Smith & Wesson in the other. The man stood beside Bolding and cocked the revolver.

He grabbed Bolding's limp right hand and wrapped it around the gun. With the other hand, the assassin held the pillow to Bolding's right temple, then slowly brought up Bolding's gun-bearing hand.

Bolding never heard the shot.

CHAPTER 59

Lyon, Interpol HQ, the following morning

Dulac was sitting at his desk scanning through the files of P & W's officers and taking notes when the phone rang. It was Arlberg.

"Have you seen the news?"

"What news?"

"Switch on your TV. It's on channel France 2 right now. Sir Adrian Bolding died yesterday. Authorities haven't released the cause of death but they say it might be suicide."

"Good God. I was just making a list of questions for him about his officers." Dulac walked over to the TV monitor across from his desk and turned it on. Images of policemen, police cars with lights flashing and the entrance to Bolding's manor cordoned off with yellow tape, filled the screen. He caught the brunette reporter in mid-sentence. ". . . police are not giving details at this point other than the death occurred last evening."

"I should get myself to Southampton before the Coroner's Inquest," said Dulac.

"Under normal circumstances, I'd tell you to stay the hell out of their business, Dulac."

"Thanks. If the Brits object, I'll tell them you told me that, but I considered these weren't normal circumstances."

"Watch your back, Dulac. Meanwhile, I'll get Lescop to try for a preliminary police report. As a matter of simple courtesy, drop in on Wade before going to Southampton."

"Courtesy was never my strong suit, especially when it's not reciprocated. Besides, it's better to get the information directly from the local—"

"You're not listening, Dulac. See Wade first. Is that clear? You keep forgetting I have to work with these people."

* * *

Apart from the slight delay at departure, the 11.15 a.m. Air France flight to London was uneventful. Upon arrival however, the city's omnipresent fall drizzle did nothing to brighten Dulac's already foul humor. Dulac paid the cabbie, turned up this collar, grabbed his satchel and walked up the four gray granite steps of the Yard's entrance.

As he made his way to the front desk, a text message came in on his cell. It was Lescop.

Preliminary report on Bolding's death. Apparently shot himself with his own .38 Smith & Wesson. Finding door locked, butler and chauffeur broke into the music room, 8.30 a.m. and found Bolding dead. Gunshot wound to the right temple appears to have been caused by .38 Smith & Wesson. Awaiting full ballistic report. Will send more detailed report when available. Lescop.

Dulac closed his cell phone and smiled at the receptionist. "I'm here to see Harry Wade."

"Whom shall I announce?" The petite blonde had a friendly, welcoming smile.

"Dulac. Thierry Dulac."

A few telephone calls later, the receptionist directed Dulac to Wade's office. "Mr. Wade will see you now. Upstairs, sixth floor, then—"

"Thanks. I know my way." Dulac took the elevator. Wade's secretary met him at the elevator door.

"You should've called. He's very busy."

"Who isn't?"

She turned on her heels and walked towards Wade's office.

"Ah, Dulac." Wade sat behind his desk, obviously annoyed to see him. "I can only guess what brings you here."

"The late Adrian Bolding."

"Quite sad, very sad. Please." Wade gestured Dulac towards one of the cheap wooden chairs. "Strange how the mind works some time. It doesn't take much when one is vulnerable, I guess. I'm told he was treated for bouts of depression, though."

"You have access to his medical records?"

Wade looked a little embarrassed. "Well, unofficially of course. Actually, we've been looking at Bolding a little more closely since he sold his company's shares and you tipped us on HOLMES."

"You mean the category 3 finding?"

"That's all irrelevant now, isn't it?" said Wade. "So why exactly are you here?"

"Have you got a report from the local investigating officer?"

"We have a prelim. Clear-cut case of suicide, as far as they're concerned."

"Shouldn't the coroner decide that?"

"Of course. Just a formality in this case I presume."

"Any relatives?"

"His wife died years ago in a car accident. He has a son, and he's requesting the body for cremation. Of course, he'll have to wait for the coroner to decide whether or not he wants an autopsy."

"You mean the investigating officer hasn't ordered one?"

"Again Dulac, it's as clear a case of suicide as we've ever seen. Apparently, the butler served him his usual scotch at 9.30 p.m. Bolding told him good night, and the butler heard

262

Bolding put on music, which he does regularly, and the butler went straight on to bed. When he didn't see Bolding at breakfast the next morning, he searched the house and found the music room locked from the inside, front and back. When he couldn't open it, he called Bolding's chauffeur for help and they forced the door open. They found Bolding lying on the sofa in a pool of blood, with his .38 Smith & Wesson on the carpet by his side. Sure looks like a . . ."

"Just the same, I'm going to take a ride to Southampton."

* * *

Addington Manor

Dulac took a taxi from Southampton Central. Twenty minutes later, Bolding's mansion came into full view about halfway down a graveled road, its simply decorated façade and classical, unadorned lines a typical example of early post-Elizabethan architecture.

The cab came to a stop before the entrance, where a uniformed policeman was walking nonchalantly back and forth, hands clasped behind his back. A dozen yards or so away, a man in plain clothes, obviously another policeman, was busy lighting a cigarette. Dulac paid the cabbie, grabbed his satchel and walked towards the door.

"Sorry sir, no trespassing." The uniformed policeman interposed himself between Dulac and the doorway.

"Interpol. Thierry Dulac." Dulac flashed his credentials. "I need to see the crime scene."

"Nobody gets through this door without Inspector Simeon's say so," said the bobby.

"What if I tell you I have Harry Wade's, from the Yard?"

"Don't know Wade. I need Simeon's ok."

"And where might he be?"

"He's inside."

"Well then, Sergeant, would it be too much to ask for you to go and get him?"

"I'll get him." The plainclothes cop smiled, obviously amused by the exchange.

Moments later, a 60-ish stout man wearing a rumpled, ill-fitting gray suit appeared at the doorway. He looked annoyed.

"Yes?" He threw a baleful glare at Dulac.

"Interpol. Dulac. I'd like to take a look at the crime scene." Dulac flashed his credentials at Simeon, who took out a pair of bifocals from his suit pocket. He studied Dulac's creds carefully, then handed them back to him.

"And what, pray tell, has Interpol got to do with it?"

"It's a long story, but Bolding may have been implicated in the hijacking of the *Caravan Star*."

Simeon's face took on an air of amusement. "Really? Of his own ship? Now that's a new twist. Anyway, he's dead, so it doesn't matter now does it?"

"There may be others involved. Listen, I don't have time to explain all of the ins and outs to you."

"Wouldn't think of asking." Simeon hooked his thumbs inside his bulging belt.

"All I want is a look at your crime scene. If you don't have the authority, I'll—"

"I have full authority. I don't see the point since Bolding shot himself but suit yourself." Simeon stepped aside and let Dulac in.

They entered a vast hall, where paintings of wig-headed noblemen in breastplate armor adorned the walls, looking down scornfully upon anyone entering. Across the hall, above the doorway leading inside, hung a moth-eaten tapestry of uncertain vintage, over which were suspended two crossed halberds, mounted at an angle. Along the walls below the paintings, a series of red high-backed wooden chairs completed the lugubrious décor. Judging from their sorry state of disrepair, Dulac guessed they hadn't seen an occupant for the past few centuries.

Simeon led Dulac through the hall, then along a dark corridor and into a smaller, more intimate room, dominated by two large loudspeakers. To the left stood a desk and a chair. A brown leather sofa was in the middle.

"The music room," said Simeon. "Sir Adrian also used it as his study."

Dulac noticed the light blue chalk mark penciled onto the sofa and part of the floor. He looked casually at the entrance door's lock. The torn-out screws offered mute testimony to the force used in breaking in.

"Deadbolt was in the lock when the butler and chauffeur broke in," said Simeon.

"Any other entrance?"

"The French doors. Over there." Simeon pointed across the room to two floor-to-ceiling window-paned doors. "They were also locked from the inside."

Dulac walked over to the doors and looked out onto a gray marble patio and a gravel courtyard. He checked the locking mechanism of the French doors. It was a simple pivot lock, whereby the lever on one door swung on its axis and fell into a receiving u-shaped latch on the adjoining door. Dulac noted two locks, one at the top, the other at the bottom of the doors.

"Pretty basic stuff." Dulac worked the top lever through its axis. He noticed two sensors at the bottom of each door and bent down to take a closer look.

"Unarmed," said Simeon.

Indeed. Why would anyone arm them if he were going to commit suicide? Dulac looked closely at the doors. A thin gap could be detected between them. "Those latches could easily have been opened from the outside." He didn't bother to look at Simeon.

"Thought of that but an intruder couldn't have locked them back from the outside. The butler and the chauffeur swear both locks were in place when they broke in."

Dulac smiled. "Will you ask for an autopsy?"

"We already have. The pathologist's report is due in a couple days."

"Any fingerprints?"

"My men dusted the room and found some. They're being processed through HOLMES 3 at the Yard."

"But no note."

"None."

Dulac felt a growing sense of disquiet. Seemingly sensing Dulac's uneasiness, Simeon spoke. "Believe me, we've seen many suicide cases without notes."

"You mentioned that the butler gave Bolding a drink, a scotch I believe?"

"Yes, they found the glass empty. We're checking for prints. The results will be in the forensics preliminary report."

"When would that be available?"

"Our people are pretty quick."

"I'd much appreciate a copy."

Clearly impatient, Simeon sucked in a deep breath of air. "We'll see."

At that moment, they heard a disturbance outside the room, the sound of two voices quarrelling heatedly. Simeon walked to the door and swung it open to find the butler in an intense argument with one of the maids.

"I'm not accusing you, Anna," said Higgins. "You simply must have misplaced it."

"Begging your pardon sir, but I didn't. It just wasn't there this morning."

"It couldn't have just disappeared, now could it, Anna?"

"Excuse me." Simeon looked at Higgins. "Mind telling me what this is all about?"

"Oh, it's nothing sir," said Higgins. "Just something missing from Sir Adrian's, I mean the late Sir Adrian's music room."

"And what would that be?"

"A cushion," said Higgins. "There's usually a small mauve cushion on that chair over there. Sir Adrian uses it for the small of his back. We can't seem to locate it. It's a trivial thing but you did ask me to let you know if anything was missing."

Simeon looked at the maid. "Let me know when you find it." He turned to Dulac. "Is there anything else?"

"Not really. At least for the moment."

"Fine. I'll get one of my men to drive you to the station. What time is your train?"

"I'll be sticking around. I've booked a room at the Devonshire Hotel. I've got work to catch up on."

"Suit yourself. I'll have one of my men drop you off."

"Much appreciated." Dulac handed him his card. "Let me know the results of the prelim."

CHAPTER 60

Southampton, the Devonshire Hotel

The following morning, Dulac sat in the hotel's breakfast room and chewed on a cardboard-tasting croissant while sipping a tepid coffee. Hs cell rang. He didn't recognize the number.

"Dulac."

"Simeon here. Wanted to catch you before you left for London."

"Actually I was on my way to P & W."

"Something in the prelim I thought might interest you."

Simeon paused, as though to heighten the dramatic effect.

Dulac took the bait. "And what may that be?"

"The coroner. He found no traces of gunpowder on Bolding's right temple. None whatsoever."

"Interesting."

"But he did find something else."

"Don't tell me. Bits of cloth or duvet."

"Microfibers. How did you know that?"

"Presumably from the missing mauve pillow. Did you find it?"

"Negative. Our men searched the whole house this morning. There's more."

"Always is."

"Our people looked at the glass, the one Bolding was drinking from."

"And?"

"There are no prints on it. Not even Bolding's."

Long pause.

"I'll be right over," said Dulac.

* * *

Dulac entered the hall and went directly to the music room. He smiled at the bobby standing guard at the entrance. Simeon walked to and fro in front of the sofa, hands clasped behind his back. He stopped and faced Dulac. "Seems we might have been a bit hasty on the suicide front."

Dulac smiled and tried not to appear smug.

"Before you ask, we questioned the butler and the chambermaid, and they swear they didn't touch the glass in the music room, never mind wipe it clean."

"Did the butler wear gloves when he served Bolding?"

"Says he did, as usual."

Dulac frowned, then looked at the French doors.

"Listen Dulac, I know you've been thinking this wasn't suicide from the start."

"Never said that."

"But you've been thinking it. That guess about the pillow—"

"Under the circumstances of there being no gun powder residue on Bolding's temple and there being a missing sofa pillow, it's not much of a guess. You have to admit it changes the picture somewhat. Besides, I haven't heard of many cases where the suicidal person takes the precaution of trying to muffle the sound of his gun. Have you?"

Embarrassed, Simeon walked to the far side of the room and stood in front of the French doors. "Still begs the question, though. How the hell could the murderer, if there was one, have gotten back out and locked these doors from the inside?"

"I've been giving that some thought." Dulac turned to the bobby, now standing next to Simeon. "Think you could get me some string, or a piece of wire?"

The bobby looked at Simeon, who nodded his approval.

Moments later, the policeman returned with Higgins, the butler. "I use this to hang pictures," said Higgins, handing a piece of wire to Dulac.

Dulac went to the French doors. He tried inserting the wire between them. "Doesn't fit," said Dulac. "String won't either. The space is too small."

"So much for that theory, said Simeon.

"May I go now, sir?" Higgins asked Simeon.

"Yes, that's all for now, I suppose. Unless Mr. Dulac can think of anything?"

Dulac didn't react, and Higgins started to leave. He was at the doorway when Dulac shouted. "Floss!"

Higgins turned back to Dulac. "I beg your pardon, sir?"

"Get me some dental floss."

Higgins nodded politely. "Yes sir." Moments later, Higgins arrived with a plastic dispenser of dental floss and gave it to Dulac.

Dulac cut two long strands of floss and handed the dispenser back to Higgins. Simeon, the bobby and Higgins looked on.

"Showtime." Dulac walked to the French doors. He stuffed the strands of floss in his pocket and took a credit card out of his wallet. He opened the doors and a gust of fresh morning air invaded the room.

"Close and lock the doors behind me," Dulac instructed. He stepped out onto the patio.

Simeon complied. Dulac took his credit card and inserted it between the doors below the top latch. He struggled at first, wiggling the card upwards, but the latch finally turned. The bottom latch was easier. Dulac opened the doors and entered.

"Step one," he said. "Step two: killer goes to the desk and takes the .38."

"Wait a minute," interrupted Simeon. "How does he know Bolding even has a gun, never mind where he keeps it?"

"He either knows Bolding well enough, or somehow he has access to the gun registry. Even if he doesn't know where Bolding keeps it, where else would you keep a short-nosed .38 and have quick access to it yet have the possession of it remain hidden? There're only two places, his office desk or the bedroom, and the bedroom's more subject to discovery by the maids and other staff. In this case, the killer guessed right. If he hadn't, I'm quite sure he had a plan B."

"All right, so he's in the room. He gets the pillow, then he hides behind say, the curtains over there." Simeon pointed to the drapes. "Then Bolding sits down and—"

"Bolding doesn't have his drink right away," said Dulac. "Instead, he puts the music on, then goes to the sofa."

"Then the killer sneaks up behind him, puts the pillow to Bolding's right temple and fires."

"Something like that, except the killer makes his first mistake. When I was at Bolding's office the other day, I saw him sign documents as I walked in."

"So?"

"He was left-handed."

"Crikey!" Simeon turned to the plain clothes policeman. "And we didn't pick that up?"

The man's face turned crimson with embarrassment.

"The killer then makes his second mistake," said Dulac. "After he shoots Bolding, he sees the glass of scotch, and can't help himself. His mission successfully accomplished, he figures he has time for a quick drink, since Bolding hasn't touched it. So the killer downs the scotch."

"Therefore no prints on the glass, since he's surely wearing gloves," said Simeon.

"Exactly," said Dulac. "Now comes the tricky part. He must get out and preserve the illusion of suicide by locking the doors."

Dulac walked to the French doors, opened the door the levers were attached to, and pulled out the two lengths of dental floss from his pocket. He wound one around the knob of the top lever, then the other around the bottom one, leading the ends of the floss outside along the edge of the open door. Still holding onto the lengths of floss, he went outside, carefully closing the door behind him, the thin floss fitting between the closed doors.

He started lifting the top length of floss on the top latch upwards. The latch rose, then with a quick snap, Dulac lifted it all the way. The latch completed a semicircular arc around its pivot and fell into its u-shaped receptacle on the adjoining door.

"*Voilà!*" Dulac repeated the procedure on the bottom latch, then pulled the floss clear.

After Simeon unlocked the doors, Dulac walked in, not bothering to hide his air of triumph.

"Incredibly simple," said Simeon.

"And effective."

Simeon turned to the bobby and the plainclothesman. "We'll be keeping a lid on this for the moment, do I make myself clear? And as for you, Mr. Higgins, I'd appreciate your cooperation with keeping this little discovery strictly between the people in this room. The longer the assassin thinks he got away with this, the better."

All three men nodded.

"Shall I call the forensics people to have another look around the grounds, sir?" the plainclothesman asked Simeon.

"Call Morehouse. Tell him to bring Jenkins. I want this place gone over with a goddam microscope." Simeon turned to Dulac. "Any ideas on the killer's motive?"

"Nothing firm, no," said Dulac.

"Care to share your thoughts?"

"Not yet."

CHAPTER 61

The Devonshire Hotel

Dulac was on his way up to his hotel room when his cell rang. Dulac recognized the number. It was Wade.

"Simeon filled me in. Nice work. I have a bit of news myself. We picked up Singh. He was trying to board the Dover ferry. Thought you might be interested."

"I'm on my way."

Dulac packed his bag, paid the bill and grabbed a taxi to Southampton Central. Moments later, ticket in hand, he was waiting on Platform 3B for the London — Waterloo Station express to arrive. He grabbed his cell and dialed Lescop's number.

"Lescop."

"It's me. Wade's men have picked up Singh. I'm on my way to the Yard right now. Any news on Mirolet?"

"Not much. We've only been able to break through the first layer. Five owners, all numbered companies, all incorporated in Zurich. Beyond that, we can't pierce the corporate veil, so to speak, without furnishing proof of a major crime to the Swiss."

"Great. Just pissing great. Anything on the ownership of the unregistered phone?"

"I spoke to Gina and our guys downstairs last night. They don't dare try any harder to break through MI-6's firewall. They say it's too risky. Might show up on their screens. If it does, we'll have a major diplomatic row."

"Damn. On another subject, remind me again. The cross-default clause on P & W's ships' insurance policy was triggered by the non-payment of which policy?"

"The building policy."

"And the payment was withheld on Bolding's instructions?"

"The cheque had been issued by accounting, but was actually stopped by Mills, the CFO. If you recall, he and Bolding said there was a cash-flow problem. We have no evidence that Mills acted under Bolding's instructions."

"Makes sense."

"What?"

"Never mind. My train just arrived. Talk to you later."

* * *

Two hours and ten minutes later, Dulac stood in front of Wade's closed office door. He knocked.

"Come in," said Wade.

Wade was sitting at his desk, busily typing on his computer when Dulac walked in. Wade rose slightly and extended a moist right hand across his desk. Dulac shook it reluctantly.

"Where is Singh?" said Dulac.

"He's in a holding cell downstairs," said Wade. "Claims he left P & W two weeks ago because he was having a nervous breakdown. He's been seeing a Doctor Dagmar Dokkar. A few days ago, this doctor conveniently recommended Singh take a vacation. Apparently, that's when he decided to leave for France."

"Yes, very convenient."

"Under the Antiterrorist Act, we can only hold him for one more hour. He's called his barrister."

"Let me take a crack at him," said Dulac.

"Be my guest."

They took the elevator down. Accompanied by two constables, Wade led Dulac along a narrow corridor, lined on both sides with the heavy metal doors of the holding cells. Near the end, they stopped and a constable unlocked the door of Cell 15.

Dulac entered the small room, where a tall, middle-aged, bearded man wearing a white turban walked back and forth nervously behind a small table. A wooden chair was set in front of the table. The man stopped and looked at Dulac with suspicion.

"Interpol. My name is Dulac. Mind if I sit down?"

"I want my solicitor. You have no grounds to keep me here." Singh thrust his chin forward in defiance.

"We'll see about that. So you were sick?"

"I have a medical certificate to prove it." Singh started pacing to and fro again.

"Supposedly. You must admit it's a hell of a coincidence that you fall sick just as the people you hired happen to hijack the *Caravan Star*. While your solicitor's on the way, let's chat about P & W, shall we? You're aware that Sir Adrian Bolding was murdered?"

Singh stopped pacing and looked at Dulac. "Murdered? The TV said it was suicide."

"That's what the assassin wants us to think. Obviously, Bolding wasn't playing ball, as the Americans say."

"Don't know what you're talking about."

"I'm sure you don't. Does the name Leon Binagro mean anything to you?"

Singh shrugged his shoulders and resumed his walking.

"How about Henri Messier? His name ring a bell?"

"Never heard those names before."

"Well, it doesn't matter. Except they're both dead now too. Murdered." Singh stopped, and Dulac noticed a small twitch in the right corner of Singh's mouth. "When was the last time you saw Allister Mills?"

"I suppose before I left P & W. Two weeks ago."

"About the same time Mirolet was incorporated?"

"Don't know what you're talking about."

"Sure you don't. Probably don't know Andrew Toombs either."

"I'm not talking until I see my solicitor." Singh stopped pacing. He crossed his arms against his chest and leaned against the wall, facing Dulac.

"Of course. Let me do the talking for now." Dulac dropped his fists down onto the table and rose. He leaned across and locked his stare onto Singh. "Let me tell you a story, a story of what I think happened. You are, or were, a security officer at P & W, but you are also a member of the Baluchistan Tigers, with whom you have a dormant relationship."

"Nonsense."

"You, the Tigers and their accomplices have been planning the hijack for some time, carefully replacing the *Caravan Star's* security officers. That would have been key to the operation to control the passengers. You had to do this gradually, lest you attract unnecessary attention and someone started to get suspicious. Your plan was just about complete when Allister Mills mentions that the company is in trouble during a corporate meeting you were attending with your fellow officers. In fact, P & W's been edging closer and closer to bankruptcy. This threw a wrench in your hijacker friends' plans. When you told them this, they realized they had to act before P & W did in fact go bankrupt and you lost your privileged position at P & W. Out of a job, you'd have been useless to the Tigers and their accomplices. Besides, in the event of foreclosure, there'd be a strong chance the ships would be seized. You couldn't afford to wait. The hijacking had to go forward."

"I have no idea what you're talking about."

"Oh really? Then tell me how it happened that at the time of the hijacking, all the security officers aboard the *Star* were Baluchistan Tigers? You were responsible for hiring them, weren't you?"

"I didn't check what province in Pakistan they were from. There are many other Pakistanis aboard P & W ships fulfilling many other functions. I don't choose personnel based on race or nationality. That would be against the law."

"And you wouldn't do anything illegal, of course. So to continue, your accomplices still needed some vital info to control the ship, such as the ship's detailed schematics, and only a few senior officers such as Mills and Owens, the VP Ops, had that info. But you happened to know that Mills has an extravagant lifestyle. When I reviewed his file recently, his credit rating was triple C. Not good for a VP Finance. I found that he applied to P & W for a loan, presumably to cover his debts. But now that the company is in financial difficulty, you and he knew there was no way the Board of Directors would approve that loan. So you saw a potential ally in Mills, because desperate men do desperate things. Plus, if P & W went bankrupt, Mills would be out of a job, too, with no chance to pay back his debts. Some of his creditors wouldn't have taken too kindly to his defaulting. But Mills knew there was one way to make money on P & W's demise, by selling some of its stock short. But Mills is a drowning man, he hasn't got enough money to make that option work, either. That's when you decide to throw him a lifejacket, but first you have to talk to the others."

"This is going from the ridiculous to the sublime."

"Is it? So humor me a bit longer. You need that info, and time is pressing. You talk to your accomplices and they decide having Mills share in the ransom isn't a big deal. There's plenty of money to go around. They tell you to get him on board. But you see where you could make a nice pile of money instead of just being a good soldier for the Baluchistan cause. You tell Mills you and he could partake in the ransom directly. So Mills authorizes Toombs, P & W's solicitor, to form a nice, discreet, hermetic Swiss corporation, in which Mills and you and possibly others will have shares. You contact Tariq and the Tigers and they agree that in exchange for the info they desperately need, Swissco, alias

Mirolet, will get part of the ransom money, funneled through Leon Binagro. Still with me, Tajar?"

"You have a vivid imagination."

"But for the plan to succeed, especially with P & W being strapped for cash, you and Mills need a guarantor, or at least a strong chance that someone else would pay the ransom. Mills knew that Bolding fraternized with Hays. We happen to know that Mills, as CFO, signed Bolding's expense accounts, which included many dinners with Hays. But here's where it gets tricky. We know Toombs had numerous telephone calls with someone at the Home Office but—"

Suddenly, the door opened, and a tall, dark-haired man with graying temples wearing a three-piece suit entered, briefcase in hand. He tossed it ceremoniously onto the small table.

"Giles Blount. I'm Mr. Singh's barrister. On what grounds are you holding my client?"

Dulac turned. "Oh, I don't know. Try conspiracy to acts of terrorism, conspiracy to hijack a ship, accessory to murder of twenty-seven passengers aboard the *Caravan Star*. Evasion of justice. Accessory to Bolding's murder. I'll think of a few more while I draft Interpol's red flag warrant for your client's arrest."

Blount stared at Dulac. "Unless you charge my client now, we're leaving."

Dulac looked at his watch. "Under the Antiterrorist Act we can still hold him for another half hour. Just a moment." Dulac got up and opened the door. Wade stood at the doorway and Dulac took him aside. "How fast can you get some wire taps on P & W's and Mills's phones?" whispered Dulac.

"It would take a couple of hours to prepare the papers and go before a magistrate. And there's no guarantee it'd be allowed." Wade looked doubtful.

Dulac scratched his scalp. "Singh is starting to get nervous. I've got him thinking that he just might be next on their hit list now that he's been caught. We've got to offer him a deal."

"That's way out of my jurisdiction," said Wade. "Besides we only have your theory to go on. We have no hard evidence."

"Once Singh leaves, he's bound to warn the others and we can't stop him. I'm going to make him an offer he can't refuse."

"You can't—"

"Just watch me."

Dulac re-entered the room and closed the door behind him. He eyed first Blount, then Singh.

"Here's the deal. I've spoken to Wade and what I'm about to offer you is the best deal you'll ever get. Right now, you're facing two conspiracy counts of two murders, conspiracy to hijacking a ship, aiding in the concealment of weapons to be used in a crime, multiple violations of the British Antiterrorist Act and willful disregard of human life. Since your 'friends' seem to be rather trigger-happy, there's a strong chance they're going to get rid of you as well. Especially now that you're a potential witness against them."

"Mr. Singh has not said or done anything incriminating," said Blount.

"Possibly. But do his friends know that for sure? Are you willing to put Mr. Singh's life at risk?"

"Mr. Dulac, you're an Interpol agent. You have no authority to offer any deal here," said Blount.

"You're right. That's why my offer is conditional to what Mr. Wade accepts."

"Then why doesn't Wade make the offer?"

"So you're saying you'll consider the offer."

"I didn't say that."

Dulac looked at Singh's face. His expression shouted of quiet desperation.

"I think your client thinks otherwise," said Dulac.

Blount turned to Singh, then back to Dulac. "I want to confer with my client outside."

"By all means."

* * *

Blount paused on the steps of the main entrance under the suspicious gaze of two policemen. He took out a cigarette, lit it and looked at Sing. "How much of Dulac's info is correct?"

"I don't know how he got it. It's scary."

"Doesn't matter." Blount took in another deep drag from his cigarette. "He still has no hard evidence. They've got a long way to go before they can even think of getting a conviction in court. In the meantime, whatever you do, don't contact anybody except me. I'm sure they're going to wiretap your phone if they haven't already. Don't speak to anyone without going through me first, is that clear?"

"How bad is it?"

"They're going to offer you reduced charges in exchange for your testimony against the others. Are you prepared to do that?"

"So if I shut up and I'm convicted, I spend the best part of my life in jail. If I talk, I get a bullet."

"We'll make witness protection part of the deal."

Silence.

"I'll have to think about it," Singh said finally, resignation on his face.

"It's a hard choice, but it's my duty to tell you that your friends may not be so sure you haven't talked already. Is there anything else I should know?"

Singh hesitated. "No, not really."

"Are you sure?"

"Yes. So what should I do?"

"Let's hear what they have to offer. It won't hurt to listen."

While Blount and Singh conferred, Dulac convinced Wade to drop the conspiracy to murder Bolding charge and offer a reduced, criminal negligence charge related to the dead passengers in exchange for Singh's eventual testimony against Mills and the naming of his accomplices. Dulac and Wade sat and waited in the interrogation room for Singh and Blount to return. Dulac's cell phone rang.

"Dulac."

"It's me, Gina. I'm with Director Arlberg. Can you talk?"

"You sound nervous."

"We were able to break through MI-6's firewalls and trace the owner of the unregistered phone."

"Fantastic."

"Are you sitting down?"

"I am. Why?"

"It's Sir Terence Hays."

"Jesus Christ!"

"Arlberg wants to speak to you."

Dulac got up, gesturing to Wade that he needed to take the call in private. He opened the door and exited the room.

"Where are you?" said Arlberg.

"Scotland Yard. They have Singh, but he's not singing yet."

"No points. Dulac, promise me you won't do anything rash until we see the implication of this."

"You mean I can't go to the press?"

"Very funny. Until we see where this goes, keep this strictly to yourself."

"I wasn't thinking of sharing it with Wade, if that's what you mean."

* * *

Singh and Blount returned, walked past Dulac, and Wade directed them into the interrogation room again. "I've got to go. Call you later," said Dulac. He ended the call and entered the room.

"What's your offer?" Blount looked at Wade.

Dulac made a timeout gesture. "Wade, can I see you for a moment?"

The two left the room and closed the door.

"Something's come up," said Dulac.

"Yes?"

"I can't tell you what."

"I thought we agreed to share all info." Wade looked royally annoyed.

"Believe me, if what I just heard is true, ignorance is bliss."

"What about Singh?"

"Let him go. Keep him on a tight leash. Tap his phone, get a tail on him and hold his passport. He's bound to contact the others. Meanwhile I'll pay a visit to Mills, P & W's new president. If I'm not mistaken, he already knows Singh is here."

"What about the offer to Singh?"

"It can wait."

CHAPTER 62

P & W's headquarters, Southampton,

Allister Mills, acting president of P & W, was sitting in his new office smiling as he looked at the latest dramatic drop of the company's shares when the phone rang. It was Toombs.

"I've had a phone call from Singh's barrister, Giles Blount," said Toombs.

"Singh's barrister? What's happening? What do you mean?" Mills's smile evaporated as he looked up from the London Stock Market Report.

"You heard me. They picked up Singh for questioning."

"They, who?"

"Scotland Yard. And Dulac."

"Christ! That's all we need."

"Listen, Dulac's putting the pieces together. Singh told Blount that Dulac apparently knows about Mirolet. He also mentioned that you stopped payment on the insurance policy."

Mills felt the blood rush to his temples. "We were trying to save the company. It was a cash-flow issue."

"Sure, sure. Save your breath for the policemen, Allister."

"I'm looking at the share price. It's down to 2.6 pounds. We have to cover the short tomorrow morning."

"Are you out of your mind?" said Toombs. "I tell you they have Singh. He's scared shitless that what happened to Messier, Binagro and Bolding will happen to him. He's about to blab to the cops and you're talking about covering the short on the stock? They're going to eventually take a closer look at Mirolet and put two and two together."

"Aren't you the one who said no one can touch Mirolet?" said Mills. "To quote your very words, it's an 'impregnable fortress in an unreachable legal galaxy'. I believe that was your expression."

"What I meant was with the numbered companies, no one can find out about the ownership of Mirolet. But if Singh blows the whistle on it as a shareholder, the Swiss will have to investigate."

Mills thought fast. "Can't we close the short, then dissolve Mirolet?"

"The shareholders can do what they want, but personally, I'd rather play Russian roulette."

"We lose over 20 million pounds if we don't close," said Mills.

"Do what you want. But remember Allister, I'm not a party to any of your physical stuff," said Toombs. "I've drafted an affidavit to that effect. If something happens to me, the whole world gets to know everything, and I mean everything down to the last detail. Tell that to your friends so they don't get any funny ideas. And tell those fucking goons in the Land Rovers to get off my case."

The line clicked dead.

Mills put down the receiver just as he spotted Bolding's secretary walking hurriedly towards his office. "Excuse me sir, it's Inspector Dulac."

"Again? Tell him I'm busy."

"I tried, sir, but he—"

Dulac brushed by the brunette and burst into Mills's office.

"What the hell is the meaning of this?"

"Just a few questions."

"I don't have time. Unless you have—"

"I can wait." Dulac settled into one of the chairs.

Mills looked at his watch. "I have a meeting downtown in 10 minutes."

"It can wait."

"What is so damn urgent that you can't take an appointment, like everybody else?"

"Let's start with Tajar Singh. Of course you know we've arrested and questioned him." Dulac looked intently at Mills for a reaction.

Mills was expressionless. "No. I didn't. Where is he?"

"Scotland Yard. He's going to talk to us about Mirolet."

"I'm sorry, you've lost me. What is Mirolet?"

Dulac couldn't help but appreciate Mill's performance. "All right, I'll play along and make believe you don't know about the Swiss corporation Andrew Toombs incorporated two weeks before the hijacking of the *Caravan Star*, the one that benefited from part of the ransom money."

Mills stood up. "I don't know what you're talking about, Mr. Dulac. Now if you'll excuse me, I must go."

Dulac stood before the doorway, blocking Mills's exit. "Why did you stop the payment of the insurance policy, Mr. Mills, thereby triggering the cross-default clause?"

"I've mentioned it before and I'll say it again. We had a cash-flow problem and I had to manage various debts in order of precedence. Besides, I fail to see how that's any of your business. What exactly are you doing here, Mr. Dulac?"

"I'm piecing together a puzzle. A puzzle involving the deaths of twenty-seven people aboard the *Caravan Star* and the murders of Sir Adrian Bolding, Leon Binagro and Henri Messier."

"Sir Adrian committed suicide. Now if you don't mind, I have a meeting to attend." Mills moved until he stood directly in front of Dulac.

"Actually it was murder."

"Really? And why would anyone want to murder Sir Adrian?"

"Try greed for one, and possibly—"

"I don't follow."

"I think you do."

"I don't like the tone of this conversation, Mr. Dulac." Mills crossed his arms on his chest.

"I didn't think you would."

Mills went back behind his desk and picked up the phone. "I'm calling my solicitor."

"Andrew Toombs, presumably."

* * *

Twenty minutes later, with his tie askew and his forehead sweaty, Andrew Toombs entered Bolding's office. Toombs glared at Dulac. "You realize you have no authority here except as support to a British investigator. I don't see one here at the moment."

"You disappoint me, Mr. Toombs," said Dulac. "As a lawyer, I thought you'd be aware of Section 23 of the Britain-Interpol Cooperation Agreement, which gives me the right to arrest and hold any criminal or criminals suspected of a cross-border crime."

"And what has this to do with my client Mr. Mills?" said Toombs.

"Let me draw you the picture, Mr. Toombs. We've learned that a portion of the ransom money was transferred to a Swiss corporation named Mirolet SA, the corporation you yourself incorporated two weeks before the hijacking of the *Caravan Star*. We have a copy of the incorporating documents."

"So what? Lawyers around the globe incorporate Swiss corporations every day. They can't be held responsible for what the clients do afterwards. What I'm curious about is how can you be sure that part of the ransom was received by Mirolet?"

"Leon Binagro's CD transfer files. The Costa Rican police obtained possession of them before his killer was able to."

"Interesting. As I said, my involvement stopped after the incorporation."

"Yet Mirolet's PO box rental payments were traced back to you."

"That's done automatically for all my clients with off-shore accounts."

"So we tried to take a peek at who's behind Mirolet and of course we hit the proverbial Swiss brick wall. They need proof of a major crime before they'll investigate. So we say "Hello? Hijacking is not a major crime?" To which they answer we must prove to them that those particular payments were linked to the hijacking, as they received funds from Binagro on a regular basis, quite a few that day. So we asked them to at least look at the amounts to see if they correspond to the amounts of the ransom. They said they'd take the issue under consideration."

"So what has any of this got to do with my client?" said Toombs.

"Mirolet has taken a short position on P & W shares, betting they will go down."

"That's done thousands of times a day all over the world by sophisticated investors who want to protect their portfolio," said Mills.

"Against unexpected, unforeseen negative events, Mr. Mills," said Dulac. "Otherwise you're doing insider trading, a criminal act. But let's leave that aside for the moment. So we continued to dig and we found that Mr. Toombs here has been receiving a lot of calls from Bolding and—"

"Of course. He's P & W's lawyer," said Mills.

"And from a mysterious caller whose phone is encrypted and unregistered. So when we tried to find out who that mysterious caller was, Henri Messier gets killed and I get shot at in my garage. All within 24 hours. As a lawyer Mr. Toombs, wouldn't you say that's a few too many coincidences? You wouldn't care to tell me who the owner of that phone is either, would you, Mr. Toombs?"

Toombs coughed and cleared his throat. "Even if I knew, I would be breaking my oath of confidentiality if I told anyone."

"Of course you would. Just testing. Anyway it doesn't matter. We already know who that person is. But let's continue, shall we? So we identified the owner and were just about to call on him and ask him questions when Bolding got murdered in his home, just after P & W announces that it's about to sue the US government for 5.1 billion dollars. The stock reacts first positively, then starts to dive upon the news of Bolding's death, thereby validating Mirolet's short position. Still with me gentlemen?"

"Very entertaining, Mr. Dulac, and entirely speculative," said Toombs. "You still haven't told me what this has to do with my client, so if you have nothing further to say, I suggest—"

"Unless of course he's a shareholder of Mirolet."

Mills shot up from his seat. "I take offence to what you're implying. The record shows that I haven't spared any effort in trying to keep P & W afloat, notwithstanding these hard times. I helped secure the loan with Berkeley's Trust. Mr. Hugh Walters will attest to that. I have always done my utmost to—"

"Do you deny being a shareholder of Mirolet, directly or indirectly through corporations that you own or control?" asked Dulac.

Toombs stepped up between Dulac and Mill's desk. "You don't have to answer that, Allister."

"I absolutely and unequivocally deny it," said Mills. "I have nothing to hide."

"Good. Then you have nothing to worry about you, do you?" said Dulac. "Well, maybe there's still that nasty bit about insider trading of course." Dulac's cell rang.

"Dulac."

"I was expecting you back in Lyon." Arlberg's tone was adamant. "Where are you?"

Dulac put a hand to the mouthpiece of the telephone. "Excuse me. Got to take this." He rose and went to the doorway. "I'm at P & W's offices with Toombs and Mills."

"Surely you haven't mentioned what we discussed."

"No. Not specifically."

"Don't. Dulac, this is way bigger than we thought."

"What do you mean?"

"In case you haven't noticed, I'm calling you from a public payphone. Gina has reason to believe our lines at HQ have been hacked. Her team is reconstructing firewalls as we speak. In the meantime MI-6 knows that we know about Hays's phone. Is Wade with you?"

"No. We agreed he would apply for wiretaps on P & W while I shake up Mills a little."

"From what I can see, you've done more than enough of that. By the way, do you trust Wade?"

"Don't know yet. So far, no reason not to."

"You'd best get back here. I'm worried you've worked yourself into a hornets' nest."

"I can take care of myself. So what's all the fuss about?"

"I've had a call from Sir Terence Hays. He's going to shut you down."

"Really? On what grounds?"

"On the grounds that you're going on a fishing expedition and interfering with the Yard's investigation of Bolding's murder. He instructed Wade to have nothing to do with you. You're persona non-grata. He's given Wade instructions to have you physically removed if you don't leave England voluntarily by tomorrow morning."

"And what did you say?"

"Listen, Dulac, I may not agree with him, but I have no say in the matter. After all, he is the Home Secretary."

"Bastard. So he's feeling the heat. Just when I've gotten the ball rolling with Toombs and Mills."

"Dulac, we're talking about the Home Secretary, the top justice officer in England. I can't stop him on his own turf. He owns the damn turf. There's nothing more we can do."

"For the moment."

CHAPTER 63

The Devonshire Hotel, Southampton

After leaving P & W's offices and a quick meal of fish and chips at The Empress restaurant, Dulac returned to his hotel, phoned Karen and levelled his usual litany of complaints. "Bloody politics again. Sticks to me like scrap metal to a junkyard magnet."

"I can't believe Arlberg is forcing you to back off just because Hays tells her to."

"To be fair, she's caught between a rock and another rock. Without Hay's approval, we have absolutely no jurisdiction in England."

"And Hays is protecting his own interests big time."

"All I need is that little bit of tangible evidence."

"Which you don't have."

"I'm so close to it I can smell it, dammit."

"So close, yet so far."

"Don't rub it in."

"So what now?"

"I'll take the morning train to London. I've booked the 11.30 Lufthansa to Lyon."

"So when will I see you?"

"First I've got to have it out with Arlberg."

* * *

The next morning, Dulac was jostling amongst the passengers on Platform 3B and looking for the second-class coaches of the London train when his cell rang.

"Dulac."

"Wade here. Where are you?"

"Listen, I got the message. I'm at the Southampton train station. I'm on my way to Heathrow and I'll soon be out of your hair. Good enough for you?"

"Glad I caught you. I think we should meet."

"What?"

"I said I think we should meet."

"I don't understand."

"Trust me. You will."

"All right. Where? At the Yard?"

"Not at the Yard. I'll meet you at your hotel. The Devonshire if I'm not mistaken. Or better still at the—"

"But I'm about to board the train."

"Cancel it. I guarantee it'll be worth your while. There's a pub called *The Lantern* on Sedgwick Street about 10 minutes by cab from Southampton Central Station. Give us about an hour and a half, say."

"But—"

The line went dead.

Mystified, Dulac cancelled his flight, took a cab back to the hotel and went to the reservations clerk. "Do you have a room in case I have to book this evening?"

"Yes, no problem, sir. I can book it now and you can cancel later if you wish."

"Fine. Thierry Dulac. You have my information."

"Yes, Mr. Dulac."

Dulac went across the lobby and plopped himself in one of the leather chairs. He opened his laptop and checked his emails. Lescop had written him at 7.10 a.m. *Tariq Assirgan died this morning from complications at the Santo Espirito Hospital.*

Damn. That route just evaporated.

Dulac waited in the lobby for 20 minutes, then took a cab to *The Lantern* pub. As he entered the low-ceilinged room, wooden cross beams seemed to reach down, trying to connect with his head. The place reeked of musty, worn leather, sweat and stale beer. He went to the bar and ordered a coffee. Half an hour later, as promised, Wade walked in, accompanied by a policeman in uniform. Dulac didn't attempt to hide his surprise and got up from his stool.

"Inspector Dulac, meet Sergeant Cummings, from Homicide."

Dulac put up his hands in surrender. "I didn't do it. I swear."

"Very funny," said Wade. "You're probably puzzled as to why I called you."

"To put it mildly."

"Singh has come in from the cold," said Wade, watching Dulac carefully for his reaction.

"Well, well."

"He's agreed to testify in exchange for reduced charges."

"Great, but I'm still curious. Why call me? Hays wants me out of the country."

Wade reached into his breast pocket and took out an envelope. "You'll understand when you read this." He unfolded two sheets of paper and thrust them in front of Dulac on the bar.

Dulac glanced at the photocopy of the typewritten script. He looked at the second sheet of paper, focusing on the bottom of the page. Below a scrawled signature and the date, the name "Tajar Singh" had been typed in. He returned to the first page and started to read:

I, Tajar Singh, the undersigned, residing at 47 Lumney Place, London, make the following statements of my own free will, without any coercion, menace, threat, or offer of any gain, advantage or profit whatsoever, but in the sole interest of furthering the cause of British justice:

1) During my employ at P & W Cruise Lines, as VP Security, I came into contact with a certain Tariq Assirgan, through mutual friends in the Pakistani community. I met him socially a few times, but on one occasion, about three months ago, he asked me to meet him privately to discuss a certain business matter he was involved in. I agreed to meet him over supper at the Natraj Balti restaurant, and that is when he told me he was from Baluchistan, as I was. He asked me to hire him and four friends of his as security officers aboard the Caravan Star. I told him that was impossible, as P & W was not hiring at the moment, and that in any case it took experience and references.

2) That is when he said that he wasn't asking, he was ordering. He said he was a member of the Baluchistan Tigers and that if I didn't hire them and if I didn't give him access to certain information concerning the Caravan Star, my family in Baluchistan, namely my sister Raja, my brother Humel and my mother Rania, would be executed. As proof of seriousness of his threat, he handed me a jeweled locket I had given my mother as a birthday present. I was shocked. I can only dread as to how he got it. He said if I cooperated, I would be rewarded appropriately. He added that if I went to the police, I would receive the severed head of my mother by DHL.

3) Knowing the history and reputation of the Baluchistan Tigers, I knew I had no choice. I proceeded to the hiring over a period of two months, then gave Tariq information concerning the maintenance of the Caravan Star's lifeboats, details of the ship's internal deck layouts, fire drill instructions and other information he needed.

4) About two weeks later, Allister Mills called me to his office and asked me why I had shifted certain security officers to other ships and added five security officers to the list of the Caravan Star's already complete list of personnel. He also mentioned that he was aware of my taking copies of the company's detailed layouts of the Caravan Star and asked me why. I broke down and told him the whole story. To my great surprise, Mills said he would take this matter under advisement and in the meantime instructed me to keep this matter confidential.

5) A week later, Mills called me to his office again and told me that P & W was in financial difficulty. He said that he had poured all of his life into the company and he was going to make sure that he would come out on top.

6) On 6 June, I received a package containing incorporation documents of a Swiss numbered company, of which I was the sole shareholder. I also received stock certificates issued by a company called Mirolet SA, by which the numbered company was the owner of 10,000 class B shares in Mirolet. There was no accompanying letter.

7) Later, Mills called me again to his office, and said that I should take a leave of absence, as things might get sticky. As chief security officer, it would be best for me to lie low, he said. Although I was getting quite worried as to what Tariq and Mills might be up to, I had no idea the Caravan Star was going to be hijacked. I followed Mills's advice and went to stay with my nephew, pretexting I'd had a fight with my wife and was under considerable stress.

8) Upon learning of the hijack, I initially decided to turn myself in, but after consulting with a solicitor, and since I had not known about the

hijacking, I decided to follow his advice and to wait. I saw my name all over the newspapers and that I was wanted for questioning by the police. I left my nephew's house and went to a cheap hotel in the East End. After two weeks, unable to sleep, feeling constantly nauseous and getting palpitations, I went to see my doctor. He said I needed a less stressful environment and so I decided to visit my cousin Naguib in France. After the police stopped me at Dover and took me in for questioning at Scotland Yard, I learned about the murder of Sir Adrian Bolding and others mentioned by Inspector Dulac, so I decided to make the above statements to clear my name and to help justice take its course.

Signed in London, this 6th day of November.
Tajar Singh

Dulac emitted a loud whistle. "Now we're getting somewhere."

"Indeed," said Wade.

"I like this bit where he affirms he had nothing to do with the hijack. It's as if he wants to believe it even though no one else does."

"Typical self-affirmation of the unrepentant. We had to go along with Singh and promise him reduced charges and witness protection. He's agreed to testify against Mills."

Dulac tried to get the bartender's attention. "So when will you arrest Mills?"

"According to Arlberg, we have a bigger problem," said Wade.

Dulac swallowed hard. By speaking to Wade first, Arlberg had deliberately blindsided him, and there was no way of knowing what she'd told Wade.

"Such as?"

"So you haven't spoken to her?"

"Not since yesterday."

"I see."

There was a silence, as Wade looked away from Dulac's hard stare.

The silence grew more and more uncomfortable. Dulac turned on the barstool and looked at Cummins. "Sergeant, would you mind if Inspector Wade and I had a private chat?"

"Not at all."

Dulac got up, spotted an empty table across the room. "After you." He motioned Wade towards the table.

They walked over and sat down. Dulac turned to Wade. "Since you're not talking, I'll start. Say you arrest Mills and this goes to trial. During the trial, the ownership of Mirolet is bound to surface. Let's say for argument's sake that your boss Hays, the Home Secretary and the head of Scotland Yard, holds shares in Mirolet. What then?"

Wade's face went red, but he remained silent. They both knew that if Wade arrested Mills, there was absolutely no way to evaluate, much less control, the inevitable collateral damage.

"That's why I asked you to come," Wade finally admitted.

"To give you moral support or to have a fall guy if all hell breaks loose and this investigation goes belly-up?"

"Both."

"Thought so. My orders are to get back to Lyon." Dulac smiled.

"And mine are to have nothing to do with you." Wade smiled back.

"So let me ask. With the amount of evidence you now have against Mills, is there any legal reason why you, and by that I mean we, wouldn't arrest him?"

"None. That's why we're here."

CHAPTER 64

P & W's offices, 15 minutes later

"What the hell is the meaning of this?" Mills bolted up from his desk as Wade, Cummins and Dulac burst into his office.

"Mr. Mills, you might want to contact your solicitor," said Wade.

"Why? What's this about?"

Wade looked at Dulac quickly, then back at Mills. "It is my duty to arrest you and charge you with conspiracy to hijack the *Caravan Star*, charge you with the manslaughter of twenty-seven passengers aboard, the names of whom are on this document." Wade handed him the list and continued. "As well as conspiracy to commit acts of terrorism aboard the *Caravan Star*, including the destruction of the ship and criminal negligence in the willful disregard of human life. You are also charged with conspiracy to murder Sir Adrian Bolding. Other charges will follow. You have the right to free legal advice should you so request. You do not have to say anything, but it may harm your defense if you do not mention when questioned, something which you later rely on in court. Anything you do say may be given in evidence."

The blood drained from Mills's face. He sat down, his lips trembling. "This is a terrible mix-up. You have no proof. I did nothing wrong . . . I—"

"That's not what Tajar Singh is saying," said Wade. "I must ask you to come with us. I suggest you call your solicitor. He can join us at the Yard."

His mouth slack, his eyes hollow, Mills looked as if he'd been told he had terminal cancer. He picked up the phone and dialed Toombs's number. "It's me, Allister. I'm being arrested. They're taking me to London, to Scotland Yard." He propped himself up from the chair with this left hand and put the phone down slowly with his right.

* * *

London, Scotland Yard, mid-afternoon

An hour and a half after leaving Southampton, the police car containing Wade, Mills, Cummins and Dulac reached the Yard's headquarters on Broadway Street. Handcuffed, Mills was escorted by two constables to one of the detention cells on the third floor.

Wade signaled Dulac to follow him to his office. They were about to enter when Wade's secretary intercepted them.

"Excuse me sir, but you have four urgent messages from Sir Terence Hays. You're to call him immediately."

Wade looked at Dulac. "The shit has hit the fan. I believe that's the American expression."

"If Toombs called Hays, this is going to get way messier," said Dulac.

The secretary continued. "Also a Mr. Jennings has been waiting for the last half-hour. He has something important to give you."

"Jennings the barrister?"

"I believe so."

"Did he say what?"

"No. He says he had to see you in person. He's over in the small conference room. Shall I get him?"

"Send him in." Wade and Dulac entered Wade's office.

"Well, the deed is done," said Wade.

"I have a feeling things are about to get worse," said Dulac, as a tall man carrying a brown leather briefcase approached Wade's office.

The man opened his briefcase and took out a folded document. "Inspector Harry Wade?" He looked first at Dulac, then at Wade.

"I'm Harry Wade. This is Inspector Thierry Dulac from Interpol."

"David Jennings, barrister acting for Mr. Allister Mills. Mr. Toombs sent me to serve you with this writ of Habeas Corpus for the release of our client. I've scheduled a bail hearing before Judge Pamela Ogilvy at 5.45 this afternoon at the Old Bailey. See you there, gentlemen." Jennings smiled, turned and walked out.

"Great, just pissing great," said Dulac.

"To be expected," said Wade, reading the document of Habeas Corpus.

"Toombs didn't waste any time."

"Neither did Jennings. I've seen him in action before. He's one of London's best. With an ego and a price tag to boot."

At that moment, Dulac's cell rang. It was Arlberg. Dulac inhaled deeply.

"Yes."

"Where are you?"

"Sitting in Wade's office."

Dulac could feel Arlberg seething. "I thought I gave you strict orders to get back to Lyon."

"Something important came up."

"I have Hays phoning me saying that he has reason to believe you're still interfering with Wade's investigation. Tell me Hays is wrong."

"Absolutely. Wade showed me a signed confession from Tajar Singh saying Mills was in on the hijacking. We've just arrested Mills."

"I see. But how does that justify your presence there?"

"I'm curious. Why aren't you concerned that Hays is the one interfering with this investigation?"

There was a short pause before Arlberg spoke. "Dulac, I have full confidence in Scotland Yard's ability to deal with this. You said yourself you had no reason not to trust Wade."

"Actually, he's asked for my support."

"What?"

"I'll fill you in later on the details. Right now, I've got to go." Dulac clicked his phone shut. "Wade, let's get a bite to eat before she calls back. My treat."

CHAPTER 65

The Bistro 51 restaurant, 4.15 p.m.

Dulac and Wade sat down at a table in the far corner of the room. After perusing the menu, they gave their order to the short, burly waiter with a ruddy complexion. Moments later, the waiter returned with two wine glasses and a carafe of house red.

"As my American uncle used to say. It's shootout time at the OK Corral." Dulac lifted his glass and toasted Wade.

"Yes, but between whom?" said Wade.

"It's beginning to look as if we're on our own. Frankly, I'm worried."

"About Hays?" asked Wade.

"About Arlberg. She's not one to usually back down from a fight."

"What are you suggesting?"

"I'm not suggesting anything, but her quietly abiding by Hays's orders to remove me is definitely uncharacteristic of her."

"You're worried. I don't know if I still have a job," said Wade.

"Join the club. In the meantime, let's go over what we have."

"Now that Assirgan is dead, apart from Singh's confession tying Mills to the hijacking, we have nothing but conjecture about why Bolding was murdered, or who was behind it."

"The only motive I can think of is that Bolding was in on the deal somehow and it went sour," said Dulac.

"By selling the stock?"

"He probably did it twice. Seeing the company was well down the road to bankruptcy and wanting to protect his investment, he sells the stock openly, which he must as an officer of P & W. Then he gets greedy and shorts it under the cover of Mirolet."

Wade took a sip of his wine. "The latter remains unproven."

"In any case, it's immaterial now. The question is, did Bolding have anything to do with the hijack? At first, I thought so, but now I'm not so sure."

"What do you mean?" said Wade.

"If he was going to hire the Tigers to hijack his ship to collect the insurance in order to bolster his ailing company's finances, the first thing he would have done is make damn sure the insurance was in place and the premiums were fully paid. He wouldn't have trusted Mills or anybody else with that. There was too much at stake. After the *Caravan Star* gets hijacked and the US Navy gasses the passengers and crew with Bezorban, Bolding sees an opportunity. There's a possibility of saving his company by taking a multibillion-dollar lawsuit against the US government."

"So he changes his mind?"

"He's in a quandary. If the company's stock goes south, he'll make money on the Mirolet short, but lose his reputation and be forever known as the heir of the Bolding Empire who screwed up and bankrupted the company. He hesitates, but the opportunity of the lawsuit against the US Government is irresistible. Even if P & W never goes to court, he can leverage negotiations with the Americans into enough cash to save the company and then some. It seems providential. He finally chooses the path of righteousness and decides to try and save the company and his reputation. Only there's a problem."

"If the stock goes up, the shareholders of Mirolet lose their investment," said Wade. "One person in particular can't afford to lose. Allister Mills."

"Exactly. Another is the owner of the unregistered phone," said Dulac.

"And we don't know who that is."

Dulac took in a deep breath. Did he trust Wade enough to give him the news? He decided that now was the time to drop the bomb.

"We have a preliminary on who that is. And you're not going to believe me."

Wade stared at Dulac, his expression deadpan. "Try me."

Dulac stared back, ready to gauge Wade's reaction. "Sir Terence Hays."

"*What?*" Wade's face went white. "*Jesus bloody Christ!* Are you sure? I mean, how did you get that information, or do I want to know?"

"Suffice it to say we have very efficient information-gathering resources at Interpol."

"You mean you hacked the British Government Personnel lines?"

Dulac arched his eyebrows slightly and cracked a wry smile from the corner of his mouth.

"Even if it were Hays, that doesn't tie him in automatically to the hijacking," said Wade.

"Maybe, but there is the disturbing fact of those repeated calls to Toombs and to P & W with that phone. If Hays wanted to speak to Bolding or anyone else at P & W for that matter, why not use an ordinary phone? But let's leave him out of it for the moment and continue. The most certain way to make sure the stock goes back down is to get rid of Bolding, the major shareholder and controlling mind of the company. Sure enough, immediately after the news of his death, the stock plummets."

"Surely, you're not suggesting Hays was behind Bolding's murder? They were good friends."

"So were Caesar and Brutus," said Dulac.

"Point taken. But how do Messier's murder and the attempt against you fit in? Surely, you're not suggesting that's Hays' doing also."

"I'm having trouble believing it but right now, he's a prime candidate."

"That really is pushing the envelope," said Wade.

"Another possibility is someone at MI-6. They're the most likely people capable of detecting any attempt to hack into the British government's telephone lines."

"And Interpol," said Wade.

"Granted."

"So where does that leave us?"

"With a few loose ends. There is something else that bothers me," said Dulac.

"Which is?"

"What if someone else used Hays' phone? How tight are the security checks and logs on the use of government personnel's unregistered phones?"

"I can find out. I would need the phone's ID number."

Dulac clicked his cell open and dialed Gina's encrypted number.

"It's me. Do you have the unregistered phone's ID number?"

"I can get it if you have a moment," said Gina.

"I'll wait." Dulac took a sip of his wine, then took out a pen from his breast pocket. A moment later, Gina was back online.

"It's RTF 5679-39401."

Dulac wrote down the number on a napkin and handed it to Wade.

Wade took a sip of wine and wiped his mouth with his napkin. "There's nothing more we can do about Mills until the outcome of the bail hearing this afternoon. I'm sure Jennings has told Mills to keep his mouth shut. In the meantime, I'll have our people check this phone ID number."

"Let me know. While we're waiting, I'll get a room somewhere. Any hotel you would recommend?"

"The Bristol is nearby. It's not too expensive, in terms of—"

"I know it. Stayed there before."

"Great. Meet you at the Old Bailey at 5.30." Wade signaled the waiter over to pay the bill.

* * *

Dulac went outside and hailed a cab. Fifteen minutes later, he phoned Arlberg from his sparsely decorated but comfortable art deco room at the Bristol.

"How nice of you to call," she said. "Are you still working for Interpol? I have a mind to cut off your expense account and credit card as of right now."

"Mills's bail hearing is set for this afternoon. If the judge refuses bail, I'll interrogate the hell out of Mills. Maybe get a confession. Wade is also checking the usage record of the unregistered phone."

"Fine. Let him. Let him proceed with the investigation. It's their business. They have all the information they need. They—"

"Why do I get the feeling there's something you're not telling me?"

"Dulac, I find that comment highly offensive."

"Sorry. It didn't quite come out as I intended. Listen, if I get a confession from Mills I can go to Switzerland. The Swiss can't hide behind their bloody Omerta with two confessions. They'll have to open their books on—"

"You listen, Dulac. They'll never open Mirolet. They have the British government's interests to protect. This is out of our jurisdiction, Dulac."

"I don't follow."

"I've heard that Mirolet has British National Security written all over it. I can't be more explicit than that. It's not in the Swiss or British national interests."

"Did you get that from Hays?"

"As a matter of fact, I didn't."

"And what about the interest of twenty-seven dead passengers' families, including Governor Dickinson? Don't you think they have the right to know the truth?"

"Of course, but—"

"Look, all I ask for is another day."

"Dulac, I really can't be seen to be dragging my feet any longer."

"Twenty-four hours."

"Damn you, Dulac." Arlberg hung up.

CHAPTER 66

Central Station, Southampton, 8.45 p.m.

David Jennings had argued convincingly before Judge Pamela Ogilvy that his client Allister Mills had no criminal record, was an outstanding member of the community, and that Singh's confession was worthless, having been obtained in exchange for reduced charges. Notwithstanding Jennings's arguments, Judge Ogilvy had ordered bail at 50,000 pounds, and Mills had had to deposit his passport at Scotland Yard.

Jennings had arranged for a bail bond and upon his release, Mills had left for Waterloo Station and bought a ticket to Southampton, arriving at his destination two hours later. He went to a phone booth and dialed the unregistered, encrypted number.

"It's me. Allister."

"How did it go?"

"The judge set a preliminary hearing date for next week. Wade refuses to drop the charges and they've set my meeting for questioning at the Yard with Wade and Dulac tomorrow afternoon. This is getting pretty rough. I'm warning you, I'm not going down alone. I won't be the fall guy."

"Where are you, Allister?"

"I'm at Southampton Central Station. They have Singh's confession and—"

"I'm told it's worthless. That's the reason you got out so easily. You've got to get a hold of yourself, Allister. I'm not a lawyer but I'm told they don't have a case without that confession. In the meantime stick to your guns. You must be seen as cooperating with justice."

"Easy for you to say. It's my neck out there under the guillotine. If that damn Dulac gets wind of—"

"Allister, I'm afraid I can't be of further help. I've done all I can. Do not contact me again."

"What?"

The line went dead.

"Bastard!" Mills shouted out loud as he banged down the receiver. *Leaving the sinking ship, is he?* He walked out to the street and hailed a cab, directing the cabbie to Hingham's Pub. He didn't notice the two men who entered the cab behind his, the same two men who had taken the train, the same two men who had followed him since he'd left the Old Bailey.

* * *

Bristol Hotel, London, 11.15 p.m.

Arlberg's warning kept prodding Dulac awake. That and the signs of an impending headache. Unable to sleep, Dulac dressed, went to the bathroom, took two Aspirins and downed them with a glass of water. Throwing a cursory look at the mirror, he surveyed the havoc the previous week had wrought on his face. The furrows at the corner of his mouth had become more pronounced and his eyes had sunk deeper into their sockets. He patted the loose flab under his chin quickly and looked away, feeling suddenly much older than his forty-nine years. He went back to the bedroom, grabbed his pack of Gitanes, donned his overcoat and headed down to the lobby. He nodded to the tall bespectacled night clerk and exited through the revolving door. Outside, the air was damp. He turned up his collar and lit a cigarette. The first lungful felt ever so good and tasted even better. In front of him on Sloane Street, a steady flow of cars moved by. In the distance, the bluish lights of London's Shard skyscraper pierced the busy horizon. Heavy traffic for this time of night.

He turned and headed eastward, needing to clear his thoughts. As he walked, the idea that had germinated during his conversation with Wade took hold. At least two persons had an immediate, greater interest than the "British National Security", as Arlberg called it, in finding out who might be behind the hijacking. One was Captain Goran Peterson's widow. The other was Governor George Dickinson. Dulac recalled his conversation with Arlberg when she'd assigned the case to him. *'Director Nancy Lombardi at Homeland Security is in charge in the US.'* It was worth a try.

He took out his cell and dialed Gina's home number.

"It's the middle of the night and you want me to get whose number?"

"Nancy Lombardi's office number. She's the Director of Homeland Security. While you're at it, get me her home phone number too."

"Mr. Dulac, I'm not sure I can access those databanks from here."

"I wouldn't call you unless it was damn urgent."

* * *

Half an hour later, Dulac's phone rang. He recognized Gina's number.

"I could only get her office number. I doubt you'll get through, though."

"Thanks, Gina."

Dulac looked at his watch. 11.25 p.m. . . . There was a six-hour time difference and with any luck, Lombardi could still be in her office. He punched in Lombardi's number and heard the typical North American ring tone. After four rings, a female voice came on the line, "Director

Lombardi's-office-how-may-I-help-you?" she shot out in one volley.

"My name is Thierry Dulac. I'm with Interpol. Is the Director in?"

"Is she expecting your call?"

"No, but I'm sure she'll speak to me."

"I'm sorry, but the Director is quite busy at the moment. Who did you say was calling?"

"Dulac. Thierry Dulac. Tell her it's about the hijacking of the *Caravan Star*. Tell her it's about Governor Dickinson's wife's murder."

Moments later, a voice came online. "Lombardi."

"I'm inspector Thierry Dulac. I'm with Interpol."

"I remember the name. You were on the *Caravan Star* when she was hijacked. You tried to save the ship."

"Well, E for effort doesn't count."

"How may I help you, Mr. Dulac?"

"I'll get straight to the point. I'm phoning you about getting access to telephone conversations of a high-ranking British official."

"What?"

"I'm thinking these telephone conversations could help us find who was behind the hijacking."

"Listen, I have no way of checking you're who you say you are. Besides, your request is pretty damn unusual. You're asking me—"

"Director, this is urgent. There are reasons why I can't use, say, the usual channels. What I'm about to ask you is strictly off the record. If you want to check me out, my Interpol ID number is 07 3688-4. Have your people run a scan and they'll confirm it. I'm staying at the Bristol Hotel in London and they can check that also. If you want, I can go to the lobby and have the manager sit with me and you can take a look for yourself on my cellphone. You can check out my picture with what you have on file on me at Homeland. Besides, there is no reason why I would call you at this time of night other than the one I'm giving you."

There was a pregnant silence before she spoke. "All right. Assuming your identity checks out, what are you asking me to do?"

"I'm asking you to contact the head of the NSA and get transcripts of calls for the last three months for the following phone. Do you have a pen?"

"Yes, but I—"

"Here's the reference: British Government service. Serial no. RTF 5679-39401."

"And what has this got to do with the hijacking?"

"That's what we're about to find out."

CHAPTER 67

Scotland Yard, 8.00 a.m. the next morning

Dulac arrived early. His time was running out. He knew he'd pushed Arlberg way beyond her tolerance level for his "digressions", as she called them. He flashed his creds to the receptionist. "Inspector Harry Wade is expecting me." He didn't wait for her approval and made his way to the elevator. He was walking towards Wade's office when Wade's secretary intercepted him.

"Mr. Dulac." She looked surprised. "I wasn't—"

"I'm early, I know, but I must see the inspector now."

"You just missed him. He was called down to the morgue to identify a body."

"Anybody I know?"

"He didn't say."

Dulac took out his cell and punched in Wade's number. "Wade."

"Dulac. I'm at your office."

"I didn't get a chance to phone you. It's Allister Mills. I had his body sent overnight when I heard the news from Southampton Station 2. We're—"

"His body?"

312

"He was badly beaten up, almost unrecognizable. They fractured his skull. The police officers found a business card in his coat pocket. I'm having the coroner confirm his identity."

"Jesus! Binagro, Bolding, Messier, now Mills. They're falling like flies. Any witnesses?"

"According to the officers who checked in the vicinity of the crime scene, Mills was last seen leaving Hingham's Pub at around 12.15 last night. The bartender said Mills was pretty drunk."

"An easy mark. That's all we need. With Mills dead, Singh is our only suspect."

"Don't worry, I've doubled the guard on him 24/7."

"See you at the morgue."

* * *

Twenty minutes later, Dulac stared down at the remains of Allister Mills, his face disfigured by a bloodied, broken nose and swollen eyelids.

"His skull was fractured in three places," said Wade. "The coroner said the imprint on the nose and skull matches a flat object, possibly a cricket bat. He said he'll know more when the skin is checked for traces of the murder weapon."

"Any signs of a struggle?" said Dulac.

"None. He was probably hit from behind first, then they bashed his face in for good measure. They also stole the money from Mills's wallet and left the wallet and credit cards next to the body."

"An obvious ploy."

"Perhaps."

"Our key suspect gets himself murdered just before he's about to go to trial. You call that a coincidence?"

"I suppose not." Wade sighed. "So I'm back to square one."

"*You're* back to square one? You mean *we*—"

Wade looked embarrassed. "Dulac, I don't know quite how to put this, and believe me I had nothing to do with it,

313

but I . . . I have strict instructions to escort you personally to the five p.m. Lufthansa plane to Lyon."

"Really? Who made the reservation?"

"We did. I had no choice. You're officially *persona non grata*."

"Let me guess. Hays."

"Is it relevant?"

"It is to me."

Wade's expression hardened. "Sorry. My hands are tied."

"So that's it?"

Wade nodded.

Dulac's frustration fought with relief. This was the end of the road. There was nothing more he could do. He'd run out of options. He was out. He breathed a sigh of disappointment. "Well inspector, I can't say it was pleasure. Anyways, good luck."

Dulac didn't bother shaking Wade's proffered hand. He turned and walked out.

* * *

During his cab ride back to the hotel, hundreds of questions rushed to the fore of his brain. Who had ordered his departure? Wade on Hay's orders? Had Wade collapsed under pressure to save his own neck? He probably didn't have enough to go on to investigate Hays. Was Arlberg folding under political pressure? She'd given him twenty-four hours. Had she decided to shorten his stay and called Wade's boss?

So many loose ends, and Wade isn't going to tie them up all by himself. But I can't do anything about it.

Dulac exited the cab, went to the front desk and checked with the clerk. "Any messages for room 367?"

"No, sir. No messages."

He looked at his watch. 12.10 p.m. He hadn't eaten yet. A good meal might help digest all of this and ease his brutal, precipitous removal from the case. Dulac started walking towards the dining room. Suddenly he became aware of

314

someone following slightly behind him. Dulac half-turned and saw a short man in the process of donning a tweed sports jacket. The man was matching his pace.

"Don't turn around. Just keep walking." The voice was firm, but not threatening.

"You're being followed by two men in the lobby."

"Who the hell are you?" said Dulac.

"The Director sends her regards. Meet me in the men's room in 15 minutes."

The man walked away, leaving Dulac perplexed, curious and cautious as he made his way towards the entrance of the dining room.

"For one, sir?" The *maître d'* cocked his head obsequiously to one side.

"Yes." Dulac followed him to a table at the far end of the dining room.

"Your waiter will be with you shortly."

Dulac nodded. Moments later, the waiter handed Dulac a menu, from which he ordered a steak, medium rare, and a glass of house red. While he waited, Dulac scrutinized the patrons of the dining room. Apart from two Chinese men in black business suits, the others were dressed casually, probably tourists. The man who had approached him was nowhere in sight. Dulac leaned nonchalantly towards the table. With his right hand, he reached down, under the tablecloth, raised his right pant leg slightly and unstrapped the holster of his Benelli .38 Parabellum. He stood and walked across the room to the *maître d'*.

"Where is the men's room?"

"To the right of the elevators." The *maître d'* pointed towards the lobby.

Dulac walked past the elevators to the men's room and stopped. He looked around, assuring himself he was alone. He reached down, took the Benelli from its holster, removed the safety catch and put the snub-nosed pistol in his jacket pocket. With his other hand, Dulac opened the men's room door. The place was empty, except for the man with the tweed sports jacket standing at one of the urinals. He looked at Dulac and nodded. Throwing a quick glance at the bottoms of the toilet stalls, Dulac walked over to the adjacent urinal.

"Already checked. There's no one." The man reached into his jacket pocket and pulled out a small, square envelope. "Sam Nunn. NSA." He handed Dulac a transparent plastic envelope containing a USB flash drive. "With Director Lombardi's compliments."

"Thanks. Who are the guys following me?"

"No idea."

"Are you sure they didn't see you approach me in the lobby?"

"Pretty sure but watch your ass." The man turned, walked briskly towards the door and out of the men's room.

Dulac put the envelope inside his jacket pocket and returned to his table. His steak was on the plate, getting cold. He ate quickly, gulped down his wine and gestured to the waiter for the bill.

Back at his hotel room, Dulac took the envelope from his pocket, removed the USB flash drive and put it on the small desk beside his bed. He took off his jacket, sat down and opened his laptop.

Dulac froze.

The blue backdrop was adorned with the picture of a white skull. Underneath, an inscription read YOU'RE NEXT.

Dulac took the Benelli from his pocket. He stood, gun held at the ready, and walked carefully to the bedroom. Clear. He opened the bathroom door. No one. He walked over to the front door, turned the lock, flipped the safety catch into place. Feeling perspiration form on his forehead and upper lip, he walked back to the window and peered carefully outside onto the street. Below, a few pedestrians were hurrying to get out of the downpour.

He went back to his desk and deposited the Benelli next to the computer. He inserted the USB stick into his computer

316

and started reading the text transcripts of various telephone conversations had been sorted out by date.

1) Date _____ Encrypted Unregistered Phone serial no._____ (EUP) and phone _____, owner Sarah Bowen, call girl working out of El Paso Bar.

Male voice (MV): Hello sweets. Are you free this afternoon?

Female voice (FV): Hello Terry Darling, I've got a busy schedule this afternoon. Can you make it tonight?

MV: Impossible. Pamela is giving some stupid dinner party for the head of the local Children's Aid society. Got to attend.

FV: Let's see. I guess I could squeeze you in between 3 and 4 this afternoon. (Giggling sound)

MV: I'd love that. See you then sweets.

End of call.

Dulac read through the next four pages. Hays's dalliances with Bowen were getting more explicit, kinkier. He scanned through the pages quickly.

9) Date _____ Transcript of call between encrypted unregistered phone (EUP) and no. _____ phone belonging to P & W lines, Southampton.

MV1: Hello Gillian, can you pass me to Sir Adrian?

FV: Yes, Sir Terence. Just a moment.

Pause.

MV2: Hello Terry.

MV1: Adrian, I'm calling you about Mirolet. Since you weren't at the board meeting last night, I'm letting you know we decided to short P & W's shares.

MV2: Really?

MV1: We see no upside; only downside for the moment at least. We can make a killing if they seize your ships and . . .

MV2: I know it looks bad, but I have a plan. I saw Toombs yesterday and he thinks we can sue the hell out of the Americans. They've destroyed P & W with their damn Bezorban. In the meantime, I've secured a bridge loan and—

MV1: Adrian, I wouldn't do that if I were you.

MV2: Oh, and why not?

MV1: Adrian, the decision was unanimous. The only way to make money is to cover the short. You have no guarantee that you won't go under before the Americans come to the table. Time is on their side. They'll string you along until you cave in. Trust me, Adrian. Forget the lawsuit.

MV2: Like hell I will. I'll do everything I can to save my company. I have 2,000 employees and their families who depend on the survival of P & W. They've supported me all these years and if I have to go down—

MV2: Adrian, don't do it.

Call interrupted and ended.

Dulac kept reading, scanning through reams of conversations between various members of cabinet, the Prime Minister and Hays. It was bewildering. The NSA was eavesdropping on all of the British Ministers' conversations with total impunity. Suddenly, a paragraph caught his attention. It had been highlighted and underlined.

34) Date _____ call between EUP and Tariq Assirgan, Nepiltan, Pakistan

MV1: *Salaam Aleikum.* All is Ok. They have agreed to form Mirolet. It will be a subsidiary of Miramar. With what I know about Miramar and the moneys transferred to it by the ministers, there is no risk. The Government will pay us when we hijack the ship."

MV2: Good. That is very good. *Aleikum Salaam*, Zabin.

Call ended

37) Date _____, call between EUP and Tariq Assirgan, Turbat, Pakistan.

MV1: *Salaam aleikum* Tariq. "

MV2: *Aleikum* Salaam.

MV2: Singh has hired the last of the security officers."

MV1: Any problems?

MV2: None. Mills is in. For his share in Mirolet, Mills agrees to turn a blind eye.

MV1: What about the equipment?

MV2: Saquil says it's on board.

MV1: Good. We must move fast. Mills says the company is in trouble. If it goes under, they'll seize the ships.

MV two: I'll contact the others.

Call ended

38) Date—— Call between EUP and —— Tariq Assirgan Nepiltan, Pakistan

MV1: *Salaam Aleikum*. What's happening?

MV2: *Aleikum salaam*, Tariq. All the Mirolet shares have been issued, including yours and Sing's. The packages are being sent today.

MV1: Good.

Call ended

Dulac perused the remaining transcripts. The last one caught his attention. It was dated 3 days ago.

56) Date—— call between EUP and another UP.

MV1: The problem is getting worse. He's onto Mirolet and he's trying to go upstream. If he finds out about Miramar—

MV2: He won't get far. The Swiss will block any attempt to—

MV1: You're not listening. With Singh's confession and now Mills, he—

MV2: If you hadn't botched the job in Lyon, there wouldn't be a problem, would there?

MV1: He got lucky. This time, we won't miss. Call ended.

Jesus. They're playing for keeps. Just as I thought, someone else must be using Hays's phone. Are they in this together? I've got to call Gina. He picked up the phone and punched in her encrypted number.

"Gina Marino."

"It's me."

"Yes Mr. Dulac."

"Are you sure that unregistered phone belongs to Sir Terence Hays?"

"Absolutely. We checked with the French *Sûreté.* They confirmed it. Why do you ask?"

"Apart from Hays, someone else has been using that phone. Someone named Zabin. He's involved in the hijacking."

"We can't trace that without the original recording," said Gina.

"I have a strong inkling that same person hacked into my computer. He may have had access to data. That person wants me dead. Can you track this hacker?"

"We can try. In the meantime, don't use your computer until we've scrubbed it clean from here. I'll phone you when it's safe."

"Great. I'm—"

Dulac heard the distinctive ping of another call coming in. He looked at the number. Arlberg. Not now. "Gotta go, Gina."

Dulac had just clicked his cell phone shut when the hotel room telephone rang. Surely it was Arlberg again. He

320

let it ring until it stopped. She probably had gotten wind of his request for transcripts. He remembered what she'd said. *"This is bigger than both of us."* What did she mean? What was she not telling him? His doubts about her willingness to pursue the investigation were becoming more concrete by the moment. For the second time in less than a day, he thought the unthinkable. *Is she in on it?*

He picked up the hotel phone and listened to Arlberg's message "Arlberg. Call me back."

He went to the minibar, grabbed a Perrier, then returned to the desk and sat down.

Dulac thought hard. There was only one person he could talk to about the transcripts and the use of Hay's encrypted phone. One person who was on the outside looking in. One person who could follow up after Dulac left England. He dialed Wade's number.

"Wade."

"Dulac. Can we meet at the bar of the hotel, say in half an hour?"

"Aren't you on your way to the airport?"

"Christ. It's only 1.30. Are you in that much of a hurry to get rid of me?"

"Well, no, but—"

"It's in your best interest, Wade."

"What about?"

"As you told me recently, I guarantee it'll be worth your while."

CHAPTER 68

Dulac took the Benelli from the desk and slid it back into his leg holster. He walked to the window and peered outside. The rain had stopped. He took out the USB stick from his computer, slipped it back into the envelope and tucked it into the breast pocket of his jacket. Grabbing his passkey, he exited the room, walked down the corridor and turned right towards the elevators.

* * *

Dulac saw the man's swinging arm and cricket bat just before it connected with his head. For a millisecond, the lights on the wall danced crazily as he felt his knees buckle. Then everything went black.

* * *

The jolt of something hard against his left shoulder made him come to. He didn't know how long he'd been out. His head was throbbing and it was dark. His knees were tucked up against his chest and the air was stale. He heard the rumble of a motor. Another jolt and he hit the side of his head.

The pain seared through his skull, and he felt his body being tossed from side to side. *I'm in the trunk of a car.*

Dulac reached over to his left leg. The holster was empty. He braced himself with his arms so as to avoid hitting his head against the lid of the trunk. He needed air. He felt for the safety latch, and felt a wire attached to it. He pulled the wire and nothing happened. The car swung to the left and he was compressed onto the right side of the trunk. *Think, Dulac! They must want me alive, or they'd have killed me already.* He tried to concentrate on breathing as little as possible, taking short breaths.

After what felt like an eternity, the car slowed and came to a stop. Dulac heard doors open and two men's voices. The trunk opened. A man wearing a khaki vest pointed a pistol at Dulac's face.

"Get out." The man motioned with his pistol.

Squinting in the sunlight, Dulac pulled himself over the lid of the trunk and swung his numb legs onto the ground. Another man, tall and wiry, a scraggly beard adorning his gaunt face, grabbed Dulac's left arm and the three of them started towards what looked like a large hangar. To the left, Dulac could see containers, stacked in high rows.

We're at the London docks. As they approached the hangar, the bearded man let go of Dulac's arm, opened the metal door and the three of them entered.

Rays of sunlight were streaking in from windows high up near the roof and lighting the inside of the hangar, half-full of crated cardboard boxes of varying sizes, stacked in sections. The gunman pointed his pistol to an area at the far end of the hangar. "Over there." He closed the door behind him.

The bearded man grabbed Dulac's arm again and the threesome walked over to the far side of the hangar, where pieces of wood, coils of metal strapping and flattened cardboard boxes lay haphazardly about. To the right, next to a workbench was a wooden chair.

The gunman shoved Dulac down onto the chair, while the bearded man picked up a roll of gray duct tape from the workbench. He taped Dulac's wrists to the back of the chair.

"Couldn't keep your nose out of our business, could you?" The gunman stood over Dulac and waved his pistol.

"What business would that be? Hijacking, extortion and murder?"

The gunman drew his arm back and swung at Dulac's face. The blow sent Dulac reeling, the chair almost tipping over backwards.

"Can't say we didn't warn you."

"Just like you warned Bolding, Messier and Mills, I guess."

The man pistol-whipped Dulac across the face again. "A bit of respect, Inspector Dulac. You've been nothing but a source of grief from day one of this operation. You've gotten the wrong people really pissed off. Especially when you went digging into Mirolet, and now Miramar."

"Out of curiosity, who the hell are you?"

"None of your bloody business."

"What do you want? Or does it matter?"

"I'll make a deal with you, Dulac." The man took out the envelope holding the USB stick from his pocket and waved it at Dulac. "Tell me who else knows about these transcripts and we'll do you a favor. No pain. One bullet, with your own gun. Isn't that considerate of us?"

"Fuck you."

The man whacked Dulac with the pistol again. Dulac could feel the blood dripping from his nose.

"Suit yourself. You see Dulac, you're going to give us the information sooner or later. My friend here can be very persuasive. Then you are going to commit suicide." The man waived the pistol in Dulac's face.

"Just like Bolding did," said Dulac.

"He didn't cooperate either. Now you're going to tell us who knows about the transcripts."

"You mean apart from the NSA, the CIA and by now, Scotland Yard?"

"Do not make fun of us, Dulac. In Pakistan, we have ways of making people talk which are infallible. Believe me, Mr. Dulac, you'll be begging for that bullet, I guarantee you."

He nodded to the bearded man, who leaned over the workbench and grabbed a pair of wire cutters.

"Crude but very effective," said the gunman.

Suddenly the hangar door swung open. "Drop your gun, Mehta. You're surrounded."

Dulac recognized Wade's voice and looked towards the door. He caught sight of Wade and another policeman as they separated and went for cover. The gunman turned and fired, then ran behind one of the stacks of crates. The bearded man did the same. The policemen fired back, taking cover behind two large crates. Dulac heard the pinging of bullets bouncing off the steel pillar next to him. He swung his weight sideways and the chair tipped over. He was out of the line of fire. For now. Bullets flew as the gunman and his accomplice slowly backed their way towards a metal staircase at the side of the hangar.

Wade and his fellow officer worked their way closer to Dulac, alternating hiding behind crates, then firing.

"Are you all right?" shouted Wade.

"I'm okay!" Dulac tried to inch his way towards the open wire cutters that the bearded man had dropped. He couldn't get close enough.

"Mehta, give up," shouted Wade. "You don't stand a chance."

The bearded man leaned out and fired at Wade, then ducked back behind the crates. The policeman fired back at the crates. A scream, then the bearded man teetered out from behind the crates and collapsed forward.

"Cover me," Wade shouted to his backup.

The policeman fired in the direction of the other gunman while Wade crept his way next to Dulac. He freed Dulac's bound wrists.

"Thanks," said Dulac. "Give me a gun."

Wade didn't answer. He shouted at Mehta again. "Your friend is dead, Mehta. Last chance."

Mehta fired back from the base of the staircase. "Why don't you go after the real criminals Wade, or have they bought you also?" he shouted.

"Bugger you. We know about your extortion racket on Hays and the other ministers," said Wade.

"That money they're funneling offshore through Miramar is our money, Wade! The taxpayer's money. Yours and mine."

"Last chance, Mehta, or—"

"Come and get me, Wade."

Dulac looked up. The staircase led to a long metal passageway, which spanned the entire width of the hangar.

"I need a gun," Dulac repeated.

"I don't have—"

In a flash, Dulac was up and running to where the bearded man had fallen.

"Hey!" shouted Wade.

Shots erupted and Dulac hit the dirt, next to the bearded man's immobile body. Wade fired into the crates, covering Dulac, who grabbed the dead man's gun and aimed at Mehta, who was starting up the staircase.

Dulac pulled the trigger and nothing happened. Damn. He fumbled in the dead man's pockets, found another clip and reloaded. Mehta reached the top of the staircase and ran along the passageway, towards an open skylight at the far end. Dulac steadied his hands, aimed, giving himself a lead on Mehta. He gently squeezed the trigger. The man fell forward onto the passageway, his gun falling on the metal grating. Dulac waited, but the man didn't move. After a moment Dulac went to the bottom of the staircase, then climbed carefully up the staircase and along the passageway. Mehta lay on his side, breathing with effort. When he saw Dulac, he tried to speak. Dulac leaned over, felt in the man's pockets, took out the envelope with the USB stick and shoved it in his jacket pocket. Mehta, his eyes half glazed over and moist, tried to speak, but the words didn't come out. Blood poured from his mouth. Dulac leaned close to his face.

"You ha— you have the wrong man," whispered Mehta.

"Like hell I do," said Dulac.

"It's—"

"Who?"

"It's—"

Mehta exhaled slightly and lay still.

* * *

"Are you okay?" Wade and the other officer joined Dulac in the passageway.

"Fine." Dulac looked at Mehta's inert body. "Who are these guys?"

"He's Zabin Mehta," said Wade. "Officially MI-6 counter-espionage section. The other one I don't know." He picked up Mehta's gun from the grating, then searched through the man's pockets. "Mehta's a mole we've been tracking for two months. He works in the cryptology section. He's the missing link in the hijacking."

"He must be the guy using Hay's unregistered phone."

His face expressionless, Wade looked at Dulac.

"That's what I was calling you about," said Dulac. "Someone else involved in the hijacking was using Hays's phone."

"He didn't have to. He's been developing a new algorithm at MI-6 labs. Ever heard of cyber-transposition?"

"No."

"With this algorithm, a person can attribute telephone conversations to any other telephone he or she wants, so to someone listening and tracing the call, it appears to have been made by that other telephone. Latest weapon in misinformation techniques of MI-6. Very sophisticated stuff." Wade shot a side glance at Dulac. "So you have Hay's transcripts?"

"By the way, how did you know where to find me?" said Dulac.

"When you didn't show up at the hotel bar, we checked your hotel room and you and the transcripts weren't there. We put two and two together and figured Mehta might have gotten hold of you. We activated a GPS emitter we'd planted in his car and that led us to the hangar."

Something Wade said bothered Dulac, but he couldn't put it in focus. His head ached terribly.

"So you knew they were coming after me?"

"We weren't absolutely sure."

"Great. Just pissing great. And all the while I thought I was playing you."

"I know," said Wade, a sly grin hanging from his ruddy cheeks.

"So why didn't you pick Mehta up earlier?"

"We had to catch him committing a crime."

"Like killing me."

"Let's go." Wade motioned to his fellow officer.

"Aren't you calling the morgue?" said Dulac.

"Plenty of time for that." Wade looked at the bodies. "They're not going anywhere."

"Guess not."

They walked out of the hangar and towards the black car parked diagonally across the entrance to the hangar.

"So where are the rest of your men?" said Dulac.

"Actually we were bluffing a little. We had to keep this low key."

They got in the car, Wade's fellow officer in the driver's seat and Wade sitting next to him. Dulac sat in the rear.

The car pulled away along the docks, slowly gathering speed.

"I thought the Yard was north of here," said Dulac.

"Too much traffic. This way is faster," said the driver.

The road seemed to narrow. Dulac felt dizzy. His nose and skull were hurting. To add to his misery, that issue about what Wade said kept coming back, not quite in focus.

Then it hit him. Wade had said that when he saw the empty hotel room, they'd searched for Hays's transcripts. Dulac was sure he hadn't mentioned the transcripts. *Jesus. Wade knew about them already.*

Dulac looked outside to the right. The Thames was a shimmering glow of silver, a few barges cleaving ever-widening wakes in their paths. Dulac put his hand discreetly to the inside of his jacket. The envelope was still there, next to the gun he'd taken from the bearded man.

"So how does Hays fit into this?" asked Dulac. "Was he in on the hijack?"

"Negative." Wade kept looking straight ahead.

Dulac felt perspiration trickle down his armpits and his pulse quicken. "That's not what I heard on the USB stick."

Wade turned towards Dulac. "So you took the transcripts from Mehta?"

"Funny, isn't it?"

"What's funny?"

"I don't recall mentioning the transcripts were about Hays, or the other ministers, or anybody else. As a matter of fact, I didn't mention the transcripts at all."

"Well, I . . . I think you must have." Wade turned to Dulac. "In any case, they'll be safer with me."

"I don't think so."

In one swift movement, Wade drew his gun and pointed it at Dulac's face. "I insist."

Dulac felt a cold tingle creep up his spine.

"Woah! Take it easy." Dulac put up his hands in protest. "So that's it. You knew about them also. Probably hacking Mehta's info as he did mine. But of course you couldn't arrest Mehta on extortion because that would have brought up the whole issue of the ministers and Miramar, including Hays. Now you need a patsy, and I'm it."

Wade's face hardened as he looked down the barrel of his gun, trained on Dulac. "Congratulations, Dulac. You're beginning to figure it out."

"So when Mehta beat you to the punch for the transcripts, you followed him."

"You don't seem to realize that those transcripts can't be seen by anyone, much less the general public."

"You mean that bit about the ministers transferring money to Miramar? I suppose that might prove a little embarrassing." Dulac felt his tension level rise by a few thousand volts.

"It's a matter of National Security, Dulac. You went one step too far. Arlberg told you so and you chose not to listen," said Wade. "Now hand them over."

"What about the NSA, and the CIA? Surely, they have an interest in—"

Wade shook his head. "I can't believe how naïve you are, Dulac. Think for a second. Do you really think they can publicly admit making those transcripts? Eavesdropping into the very core of the British Government? It's political dynamite. For them those transcripts don't exist. Besides, the money transfers and Hays's dalliances are the least of their worries."

"What about Dickinson? Surely, he knows about them."

"As far as Dickinson is concerned, his only interest is getting the man who's responsible for his wife's death. That's Zabin Mehta and he's dead. We'll send Mehta's DNA and pictures of his body to the NSA, copy to Dickinson. End of story. Case closed."

"Neat. So you get rid of Mehta and his accomplice without out a messy trial, MI-6 doesn't have the embarrassment of admitting having a mole, Tajar Singh's confession is probably worthless without Mills's corroboration so the Crown will not prosecute, and everything is how they say, hunky dory."

"Exactly," said Wade, his gun still trained on Dulac's face.

"So what now?"

Wade glanced quickly at his watch. "When you hand over those transcripts, we get you on your flight merrily back home, and you confirm what we're about to tell Arlberg. The case is closed."

"Except for one small detail. Hays gets away with murder."

"I don't have time to argue, Dulac. Hand over the transcripts."

"And if I don't? Going to shoot me with your own gun, Wade?"

"You haven't been paying attention, Dulac." Wade grinned, the pistol in his hand still steady, still pointing at

Dulac. "This is not my gun. It's Mehta's gun. If I'm forced, I'll use it, trust me. Later, when they find your body at the hangar, I'll regretfully confirm that there was a shootout and you were shot in the line of duty. So it's your choice. The transcripts, or else."

"Very clever. And of course without the transcripts, I have no evidence and no one would believe me. And no witnesses. That's why you had no support."

"You're beginning to see the light, Dulac. Now hand over the transcripts. Slowly. Don't even think about reaching for your gun."

Dulac let out a sigh of resignation. "Why not?" Dulac reached into his jacket pocket.

"Easy. No sudden moves."

Dulac took out the envelope and handed it to Wade.

For a split second, Wade looked at the envelope instead of at Dulac.

Dulac went for Wade's gun with both hands and swung it towards the driver. The gun went off, and blood and brains splattered on the side window. The car suddenly shot forward as Dulac and Wade struggled for the gun. The car accelerated wildly, narrowly missing a fire hydrant. Dulac clamped both his hands on Wade's trying desperately to keep the gun away. Another shot rang out.

"Jesus!" Dulac yelled as the car hit the curb. It flipped onto its side, slid and crashed into the hangar's brick wall with its roof.

Smoke erupted from the bent, twisted hood of the car. Dulac was jammed against the front seat, pinning Wade forward and upward onto the car's roof. Only the driver's airbag had deployed and it was covered in blood. Wade's head was wedged in an impossible position between the roof and the right door's side pillar, his neck seemingly broken, his mouth agape. He was barely breathing. The USB envelope had fallen between the seat and Wade's left hip. Dulac looked up. The right rear door was partway open. He reached down in front with his left hand, picked up the envelope and shoved it into his jacket pocket. He pushed with his feet and opened the door a bit further, then crawled out. He stood up slowly on wobbly knees.

Dulac looked up and down the road, which surprisingly was still deserted. He pulled out his cell and called 999 for an ambulance.

CHAPTER 69

Dulac walked away from the overturned car, down the narrow road, turned right onto a main artery and joined the flow of bustling pedestrians. Two corners later he took a cab for the Bristol Hotel. Upon arrival, he went up to his room, and gathered his things. He looked at his watch. 3.55 p.m. With the late afternoon traffic, he knew it would be tight. His head hurt and he felt so, so tired. It would be so easy to lay down on the bed, which looked so inviting . . .

He thought of Wade and his driver and the inevitable complications of going to the Yard. No, he had to leave. He extracted four pills from the bottle of Aspirin on the dresser, gulped them down with a glass of water, went downstairs and left the hotel.

* * *

An hour and ten minutes later, Dulac had missed the 305 Lufthansa flight, but was in line to book a ticket on the 6 p.m. Air France flight to Paris when his cell rang. Arlberg.

"I'm at Heathrow. My plane leaves in twenty minutes," said Dulac.

"I want a full report by 10 a.m. tomorrow. Meet me in my office at 2 p.m."

The line went dead.

CHAPTER 70

Interpol HQ, the next day

The next afternoon, Interpol's General Counsel Ian Carruthers and Dulac sat next to each other in Arlberg's office, waiting for her to finish reading Dulac's report. Finally, she took her bifocals off and deposited them on her desk.

"Interesting stuff. You've been quite busy." She looked Dulac up and down, assessing his condition. She turned to Carruthers. "Anything to add?"

The lawyer cleared his throat. "We have a problem with the transcripts. In Britain, communications illegally obtained can't be used in a criminal trial. Section 17 of the Regulation of Investigatory Powers 2000 Act of the UK, to be precise."

"What about in the US?" said Arlberg.

"The law in the US is even stricter. It prohibits the use of all evidence obtained illegally."

Arlberg grabbed a pencil off her desk and started to twiddle with it between her fingers. "So you're telling me that with even this," she pointed with her pencil at the USB stick, "that bastard Hays can't be prosecuted?"

"Not necessarily," said Carruthers. "The British Financial Services Authority doesn't have the same restrictions. They can use illegally obtained evidence to open an investigation. Evidence obtained by them could eventually be used by the British Crown prosecutors. The problem is Interpol doesn't have jurisdiction. And as I was telling Dulac this morning, the contents of our file are logged, and will be locked away, and we really can't help. Besides—"

"Fine, I get the picture," said Arlberg.

"Sorry not to be more positive," said Carruthers.

"Thanks anyway," said Arlberg. "Well, I guess that's it then." She crossed her arms on her chest and reclined back in the chair.

Carruthers and Dulac got up to leave.

"Oh, Dulac, stay a minute, will you?" Arlberg called Dulac back as Carruthers turned and left.

Arlberg waited, making sure Carruthers was no longer within earshot.

"I believe I owe you an apology."

Dulac looked suspiciously at Arlberg. She was not in the habit of handing out apologies.

"What for?"

"I was rather rough on you these past weeks. Now I know you were right on staying the course."

"Just doing my job."

She looked conspiratorially at Dulac. "Just between you and me, I don't . . . I don't suppose you kept a personal copy of that stick, per chance?"

Dulac took in a deep breath, arched his eyebrows and smiled broadly.

"Thought you'd never ask."

CHAPTER 71

Dulles International Airport, Washington DC, 15 December 2017

Dulac had left the preliminary briefing meeting at Langley with CIA agent Jim Crothers on the Ellipse case an hour before, and the taxi had stopped abreast of the Arrivals section's main entrance. He paid the cabbie, entered and made his way through the heavy crowd to the Arrivals notice board. He glanced upward. Air France Flight 256 from Paris was on schedule. He looked at his watch. 10.45 a.m. If he hurried, he still had time to intercept Karen before she exited the airport.

He checked again for the small card tucked between the ribbon and the box of chocolates, making sure it hadn't slipped out, and hurried towards the Arrivals section.

Moments later, he saw Karen, wearing a dark beige outfit, her shoulder-length, thick auburn hair partially wrapped in a blue scarf. Dulac noticed a very slight limp in her otherwise determined gait. He waved.

She recognized him and waved back. All smiles, she walked over, hugged him and gave him a long, sensuous kiss.

"I missed you," she said.

"And I you," said Dulac, his right hand still behind his back. "How was your flight?"

"Fine. What's the surprise?" She tried to peek.

Dulac brought his hand in front and offered her the box of chocolates.

"Godivas, my favorite! You remembered." She squeezed him.

"For medicinal purposes only." Dulac grabbed her overnight bag. "Come, let's get a cab to the hotel."

Twenty minutes later, they were sitting in the lounge of the Jefferson Hotel, sipping on their glasses of *Pouilly-Fuissé* white wine.

"The last I heard, you were about to take a flight to Lyon." Karen deposited the high-stemmed glass on the table. "Where is it all at?"

"Officially, the investigation is closed. To make a long story short, Singh is charged with conspiracy to hijack, the other conspirators Assirgan and Mehta are dead and Hays—"

"The Home Secretary?" Karen looked bewildered.

Dulac leaned over, kissed her left ear and whispered, "None other. Hays is in deep-doodoo with the Financial Services Authority on insider trading, possibly money laundering. I wouldn't be surprised if he resigned. I've heard that even if the file is officially closed, Bolding's murder is still being investigated and—"

"Murder? I thought the press said it was suicide?"

"I know different."

"Why hasn't that been released?"

"Because that would lead to motive, which in turn might lead to questioning some pretty high-profile people, including Hays."

"Wow!" Karen leaned back in her chair, hands on her lap. "But why can't you—?"

"Interpol doesn't have jurisdiction anymore. Mills' and Bolding's murders were attributed to a Zabin Mehta, a Baluchistan Mole working for MI-6. Trouble is he's also dead so we can't know for sure if he had accomplices." Dulac looked at his watch and got up. "We'd better hurry. You might want to freshen up before we head to The White

House. Secretary of State Nancy Lombardi has invited us for lunch. She mentioned our friend Hank Porter will be there too."

"Thierry, you're changing the subject again. I get the distinct impression we're talking cover-up here."

Dulac gave her a comforting kiss and whispered. "Don't worry, darling. Not for long."

EPILOGUE

16 December 2017, The Washington Post, page 3

"Interpol Inspector Thierry Dulac and retired army officer Henry Porter were among the four recipients to be honored by the President yesterday, who awarded them the Presidential Medal of Freedom, the US's highest award for bravery. The medal was awarded to Dulac and Porter for their roles in the rescue of the ill-fated cruise ship Caravan Star from hijackers off the Azores. Disregarding personal safety and under gunfire from the hijackers, Dulac and Porter helped save many lives by their courageous actions. Governor George Dickinson, who was aboard the ship when she was hijacked, was among the dignitaries present at the ceremony. Also present were recently appointed Secretary of State Nancy Lombardi and CIA Director Don Peters."

27 December 2017, The Daily Sun, London

"Following the explosive revelations of an anonymous source in what is being dubbed by the British press as "Downingate", and the resignation of Home Secretary Sir Terence Hays three days ago, the Sun has learned of possible wire transfers of sums of money from Hays to Switzerland to a corporation named Miramar SA headquartered in Berne. The source also disclosed that Mirolet SA, a wholly owned subsidiary of Miramar, may have been used by Hays to short-sell shares of the now defunct P & W Cruise Lines. The UK's Financial Services Authority is also looking into possible allegations of insider trading. When contacted, Swiss authorities failed to comment. Rumours are to the effect that other British ministers could also be involved. In parallel, Scotland Yard is investigating a possible link between the death of the late Sir Adrian Bolding and the transfer of sums to Mirolet and Miramar."

10 March 2018 The New York Times, page 7

"The US Government has reached a settlement with the victims and heirs of the dead passengers of the Caravan Star, the cruise ship hijacked off the Azores on 15 October 2017. The total amount of the settlement was not disclosed. The claimants had sued the US Navy for 5.1 billion dollars, claiming it used an unsafe, untested nerve gas called Bezorban in an attempt to subdue the hijackers, resulting in the death of twenty-seven passengers and injuries to 158 passengers and crew, many of whom still suffer debilitating effects from the gas.

Bezorban is similar to the gas used by the Russian government in 2002 in their rescue attempt of hostages in a Moscow theater, where 130 people died."

20 July 2018, The Daily Telegraph, Page 1

"HAYS NOT GUILTY

After deliberating for nearly a week in the sensational trial of Sir Terence Hays for the murder of Sir Adrian Bolding, a jury of 8 men and 4 women returned a verdict of not guilty as to the charge of first-degree murder. When interviewed, Hays's barrister John Falk says he always believed in the innocence of his client and that justice had been served. Crown prosecutors James Waddell and Judy Dill declined to say whether or not they will appeal the verdict. They say they are investigating allegations of jury tampering and may ask for a retrial. Hays, who has pleaded guilty to charges of insider trading, also faces charges of conspiracy in the hijacking of the cruise ship *Caravan Star*. The date of that trial has not yet been set."

THE END

ACKNOWLEDGEMENTS

I wish to express my gratitude to the many people who contributed to the making of this book. In no special order, they include the readers of my early manuscripts Denise Faille, Harold Wilson, Jennifer Neri, Patricia Vollstaed, Karen Skinner and others, whose ideas and insights kept me on track.

I would be remiss if I didn't mention my wife Louise, who after all these years still supports me through the many ups and downs of the fiction writer's world. Above all, she has taught me perseverance and patience.

ALSO BY ANDRÉ K. BABY

THIERRY DULAC THRILLERS
Book 1: DEAD BISHOPS DON'T LIE
Book 2: THE CHIMERA SANCTION
Book 3: JAWS OF THE TIGER

Thank you for reading this book.

If you enjoyed it please leave feedback on Amazon or Goodreads, and if there is anything we missed or you have a question about, then please get in touch. We appreciate you choosing our book.

Founded in 2014 in Shoreditch, London, we at Joffe Books pride ourselves on our history of innovative publishing. We were thrilled to be shortlisted for Independent Publisher of the Year at the British Book Awards.

www.joffebooks.com

We're very grateful to eagle-eyed readers who take the time to contact us. Please send any errors you find to corrections@joffebooks.com. We'll get them fixed ASAP.

www.ingramcontent.com/pod-product-compliance
Lightning Source LLC
Chambersburg PA
CBHW030555180626
46816CB00005B/1550